W9-BZT-854

Praise for the novels of

KAREN HAMILTON

"The Ex-Husband by Karen Hamilton is the perfect slow-burn thriller... Tense, twisty, and absolutely gripping, it's impossible to put down."

–SAMANTHA M. BAILEY, *USA TODAY* **and #1 nationally bestselling author of** *Woman on the Edge*

"In *The Ex-Husband*, Karen Hamilton shows us the deliciously dark side of paradise...[that] no matter how far out you sail, you'll never escape your past."

–TARA LASKOWSKI, author of *One Night Gone* **and** *The Mother Next Door*

"In *The Ex-Husband*, Karen Hamilton takes her readers on a wild ride, all the way from Cornwall's sandy beaches to a sun-kissed Caribbean cruise... Fast-moving and twisted...[this is] sure to be another smash-hit."

–HANNAH MARY McKINNON, internationally bestselling author of *You Will Remember Me*

"Don't let the idyllic setting fool you–*The Ex-Husband* takes its readers on one dark and twisted ride. With secrets, lies, and rapidly escalating tension, this story will hold you captive until the searing final pages. Karen Hamilton is masterful at crafting a simmering, transportive, edge-of-your-seat thriller. Escape into this luxurious, deceptive world where you won't know who to trust until it's too late."

–LAURIE ELIZABETH FLYNN, bestselling author of *The Girls Are All So Nice Here*

"[A] gripping thriller... Everybody has a nasty side, but that's just one of the pleasures of this cunning whodunit. A devious plot is another. Hamilton knows how to keep the pages turning."

–PUBLISHERS WEEKLY on *The Last Wife*

"*The Last Wife* is a deliciously dark and gripping psychological thriller with a fascinating central character that will keep you hooked until the last page."

–OLIVIA KIERNAN, author of *Too Close to Breathe*

"A twisted page-turner that should appeal to fans of *You*."

–EntertainmentWeekly.com on *The Perfect Girlfriend*

Also by
KAREN HAMILTON

The Perfect Girlfriend
The Last Wife

THE EX-HUSBAND

KAREN HAMILTON

GRAYDON
HOUSE

If you purchased this book without a cover you should be aware
that this book is stolen property. It was reported as "unsold and
destroyed" to the publisher, and neither the author nor the
publisher has received any payment for this "stripped book."

GRAYDON
HOUSE®

Recycling programs
for this product may
not exist in your area.

ISBN-13: 978-1-525-81160-9

The Ex-Husband

First published in the UK in 2021 by Wildfire. This edition published in 2022.
Copyright © 2021 by Karen Hamilton

All rights reserved. No part of this book may be used or reproduced in any manner
whatsoever without written permission except in the case of brief quotations embodied
in critical articles and reviews.

This is a work of fiction. Names, characters, places and incidents are either the product
of the author's imagination or are used fictitiously. Any resemblance to actual persons,
living or dead, businesses, companies, events or locales is entirely coincidental.

This edition published by arrangement with Harlequin Books S.A.

Graydon House
22 Adelaide St. West, 41st Floor
Toronto, Ontario M5H 4E3, Canada
www.GraydonHouseBooks.com
www.BookClubbish.com

Printed in U.S.A.

For my family and friends.

THE EX-HUSBAND

1

A TIP-OFF. THAT COULD BE THE ONLY EXPLANATION.

Dreaded realization filtered through the rows of passengers and crew in the cruise terminal via mutters about delays intermingled with curiosity and general resignation at the inevitable holdup. Sickening dread roiled deep in my gut. Surreptitiously, I glanced back at the queue snaking behind me. Still no sign of Sam. Where was he?

The person in front of me took a step forward, pushing his backpack with a foot. Reluctantly, I followed.

Sam had only darted back to the ship to pick up his watch, carelessly left beside the basin in his cabin. It should have taken him fifteen minutes—twenty max. He had insisted that I save our place in the line to save time. Our flight to freedom was less than four hours away.

I messaged him.

Where the hell are you? Hurry up! I am nearly at the front of the line.

Well, not quite, but it was true enough.

No reply.

Indecision kept me rooted to the spot. Sam would be annoyed if I lost our place. It would break one of our rules about blending in. Then again, neither of us was thinking straight. Our nerves were frayed. We were both tense after a wakeful night dissecting what had gone wrong, each of us blaming the other. But he left me with no choice. We always disembarked together. We had each other's backs. Rule number one.

I tried to calm my fears. The upheaval wasn't necessarily anything to do with us. I was too quick to jump to worst-case scenarios, usually after my conscience had given me a good poke. Sam and I excelled at slipping beneath the radar, despite his popularity.

In the corner of the vast, high-ceilinged building, portable air-conditioning units blasted out woefully inadequate cool air. My heart pounded so hard it almost hurt. Sweat slid down my spine. I stepped out of line and walked back in the direction of the ship. James, head of the ship's security team, was standing by the exit. Relief. He would know where Sam was.

Strangely, James didn't acknowledge or return my greeting. His manner was uncharacteristically off. No, he said. I couldn't go back on board.

"But Sam should have been back by now," I said. "He only went for something he'd forgotten."

James shrugged.

"Just wait for him in line. He'll show up. There's nowhere else for him to go. This is the only exit."

"What's going on?" I said, trying to cajole James into thawing his attitude.

I opted for a friendly, neutral tone. And why not? We were colleagues, after all. Friends, companions. Equals, really.

"There are searches, from time to time."

"Not that I've ever seen," I said. "I hope it doesn't hold us up. What is it? Drugs? Weapons?"

I smiled, safe in the knowledge that I was carrying neither.

"Get back in the line," said James. "Wait for Sam there."

I had no choice. As I turned, I saw Sam up ahead. He must have joined a different line. His bag was already being searched. How the hell had we missed each other? Why hadn't he called me? Why did he go through without me?

There was nothing I could do but rejoin the queue and watch. I couldn't read the expression of the person searching his bag, but the body language appeared at ease. Jolly, even. Everything felt off, badly wrong. Fragments of our heated conversation last night started piecing together. *Just wait until I get hold of Sam*, I thought. I would kill him for breaking our rules and putting me through all this extra stress.

I watched as Sam exited into the outside world. I could imagine the sun brushing his face as he inhaled the warmth of the Caribbean air. I distracted myself by dissecting the type of people they *were* pulling over. Lone travelers. Fresh, bubbling red rage at Sam rose. I called him. Straight to voice mail.

I was now among the stragglers, recognizing some of the faces. God, this was torture. I fought the urge to push to the front, explain about Sam and ask to be whisked through so that I could catch up with him, find out what the hell he was playing at. *Breathe, breathe, breathe*, I repeated over and over in my mind. *I can do this. It's all about playing the game.*

A calmness descended over me as I was beckoned forward. One step after another, a neutral expression on my face. I could see the sun through the glass doors. No sign of Sam in the crowds beyond. I focused on the large brandy or whiskey I was going to order on the flight. I thought about the type of

movie I would watch, a comedy or something light and easy
to absorb. Or maybe I wouldn't bother with any distractions
at all. I could use the time to *think*.

Half a yard, then another. The man in front was pulled over
to my right, with a brusque wave. A harmless-looking elderly
couple was also summoned. Not me. Not yet. I was so nearly
there. *Please, God. I know I've made mistakes. I know I've made
bad choices, but just let me keep walking and I will make amends.*

"Miss?"

Shit.

"Yes?"

"Can you come over this way, please, and place your bags
on the table?"

I smiled. "Yes, of course."

Everything turned numb, as though this was happening to
someone else. Invincibility was Sam's superpower, not mine.

Victimless. That is what Sam and I had always said about
the people we befriended. *Relax*, I told myself. *They won't find
anything.* I'd triple-checked, hadn't I?

My bag felt unusually heavy as I lifted it up. It was still covered in hotel, airline and cruise stickers. Funny, the inconsequential things I focused on. Sam often told me to scrape
them off. *"Bland and anonymous is always best. The smallest of
details can offer up rich clues to the wrong people."* He would know.

"Open your bags, please."

"Sure."

My mouth was dry. I rotated the combination on my lock:
one, *eight*, *eight*, my birth date and month, a small act of rebel-
lion when it came to Sam's insistence never to do the obvious.
It clicked open. Yet I couldn't bring myself to lift the lid, to
display my personal belongings ready for public inspection.
It was humiliating.

The officer lost patience and did it for me. Time slowed as he unzipped the bag. Nestling on top of my favorite red blouse was something that, although familiar, didn't belong to me.

Blind panic.

"That's not mine." I reached to grab it, to remove the emerald necklace from its nest among my possessions. Someone had put it there.

"Stand back, please."

I felt the fresh horror rise inside me as two other customs officers walked over and peered at the necklace.

"I said it's not mine. Someone has been in my bag."

Stony faces, bland expressions, dismissive words.

I tried again.

"You need to go through the CCTV, check who entered our cabin. Someone planted this."

I looked from face to face.

Still nothing.

I should've kept quiet. They'd already decided that I was guilty. A thief. Someone without rights.

Anger replaced fear as my privacy was violated. My swimwear, toiletries, underwear, shoes, travel guides, my Spanish-language course books, my costume jewelry, my every-bloody-thing was removed and examined by careless rubber-gloved hands.

A glimmer of hope ignited when their search concluded. All they had found was something that was such an obvious plant. The necklace rested on the side of the counter, taunting me. Not for the first time either. Magpie-like, the moment I had first spotted the emerald-and-diamond choker with a tear-drop pendant, I longed to own it. Green was most definitely the color of envy.

"Come with us, please."

I was shown to an interview room. I could hear a baby

crying outside. Alone, without my belongings, I had time to piece things together. Grim reality, like a blast of icy water. I had been sacrificed, thrown under the bus. Sam *knew*. He'd been tipped off. Instead of saving the two of us, he'd chosen to save himself. *"For better, for worse"* clearly no longer applied. It was a final act of cruelty. A brutal end, regardless of how rocky our marriage had been. All that mattered was himself.

Time spooled and distorted. I sat, trying to appear nonchalant, yet as outraged as an innocent could be, robbed of her freedom. I felt watched. The heat stifled me. I wanted to plunge into a cold pool, swim below the surface, somehow wash away the dirty feelings that threatened to swallow me whole.

Anger took over as I sat there. I wasn't taking the rap—no way. As two police officers walked into the room, I was prepared to embrace my inner canary. Whatever it took. But it became clear I wouldn't need to sing that day.

I was free to go. It had all been a terrible mistake. Huge apologies. Strange, but true. My belongings—even the necklace— were returned.

Outside, despite the heat of the midday sun, I wanted to run. I had got away with it. I was free. Except... I wasn't.

I didn't like the person I had become—hadn't for a long time. Something needed to change. Sam's customary reassurances that "all would be well" had been my elixir. It smoothed away fears and doubts, the ones my conscience tried in vain to shove to the forefront of my mind during the darkest hours. The sudden and horrible unraveling of our gilded situation was the result of arrogance. His *and* mine.

But for now, I had to put myself first. I walked toward the shade and sat on a bench beneath a palm tree. I had less than two hours to catch my flight, but I could still make it. I sent Sam a message.

Call me. ASAP.

Nothing.

I hailed a cab to take me from the cruise terminal to the airport, deciding to make one detour to a friend's house en route. I wanted to hide my pot of gold somewhere safe.

As we drew into the airport, fear took hold again. What if I was making a mistake? In a daze, I checked in. The airline staff wouldn't tell me if Sam had checked in too. I called him again even though I knew, deep down, that there wouldn't be an answer. As I placed my bag down to go through the X-ray machine, I heard my phone beep. I had to wait more painful minutes while my bag passed through the checks before I could snatch up my phone and read it. Sam!

One word.

Sorry.

What the hell was he doing?

Sam's empty plane seat taunted me all the way to London as I planned the things I was going to say and do when I next saw him. Because I *would* see him again. He wasn't the only piece of unfinished business, because there was someone else I needed to track down too. The real owner of the necklace and the catalyst behind our downfall and the death of our marriage.

2

I know what you both did.

I DROP MY PHONE AND IT CLATTERS ONTO THE PAVE-ment, narrowly escaping a puddle. I pick it up and wipe off the rain with my coat sleeve to clear the screen. Smudges distort the original message, so it reads:

...what you...did.

I cry out loud as someone grabs my hair before I realize that I'm part of an accident. Just a totally unnecessarily large blue-and-white-striped golfing umbrella. For God's sake! Why do people carry those? The person responsible doesn't even offer the briefest of apologies and continues on their oblivious-to-other-pedestrians way.

I am on my way to work, while most people are on their way home. I envy them. I take a deep, calming breath and compose myself. Business is slow. My event- and travel-planning business is still in its infancy—six months. I specialize in genuinely tailoring requirements to my clients' needs. *Tailoring* is not a meaningless "sell" word to me but a vital necessity so that clients can trust me. My specialty of late—not through choice— has been European destinations or seaside-town bachelorette parties. I hate them. Too much naive hope in the myth of wedded bliss. I recently updated my website to make it more alluring. I placed more focus on the type of work I wish to attract: bespoke holidays, in the UK or abroad; murder-mystery events in atmospheric castles; or race-car driving. Reinvention is an essential skill.

Enough daydreaming for now; I need to be switched on, pleasant. Still. My first instinct, however perversely, is an overwhelming desire to speak to Sam. The drizzle eases. Evening sun breaks through the clouds. I remove my jacket hood but I can't stop shivering. I cross the road and walk, leaving Windsor Castle and the town center behind me, putting one foot in front of the other. I stop in the middle of the sloping bridge that leads to Eton. I lean against the rail and stare into the water. I realize I am scared. I need to think things through. Recent downpours have filled the Thames, the tide rushing below. I find it as mesmerizing as flames.

Something is missing from my straight-and-narrow life, however much I fill it with different men, the gym, friends, or whatever else I can to distract my mind from the mundanity of my new world. I used to live to work. Now it is the total opposite.

The problem is I tasted the forbidden. I took great big greedy bites and it was delicious. Knowledge doesn't fade, sadly. Sam and I will be forever intertwined.

For worse, obviously. Not better.

I just *know* that whoever is behind the threat is in the *revenge is a dish best served cold* camp. In this case, eighteen months of chilled silence, an intangible Sword of Damocles hanging above my new life. I like to think it is because I have been super discreet online and tried not to use obvious identifying features. Yet I suspect the truth is that my tormentor wants me to suffer to the maximum. I already have a suspect. I knew her well. I have tried time after time to contact Alexandra Armstrong, but she lives behind a shield of staff and I am persona non grata.

The first time I saw her, she stood out. The cruise waiting lounge was crowded, but she strode through the room as though she owned it.

She wanted to be noticed, dressed in an elegant, cobalt blue pantsuit and clutching a vanity case that gently swung as she walked. Behind her, a porter pushed a large trolley bursting with a steamer trunk, hatboxes and matching suitcases.

Staff hovered around her. I wanted to age like her. To be wealthy enough not to care, to travel the world alone, do as I saw fit.

A call comes in. Flora Miles, my client. Crap. I'm late.

"Where are you?" she says. "I'm at the party boat but there's no sign of you."

"Almost there," I say. True enough.

Weird as this sounds, I sometimes imagine the words *truthfully* or *untruthfully* being automatically placed at the end of my sentences, like a comic strip. True or Untrue. No middle ground.

I mute my phone notifications, determined to focus on work for the next few hours. I retrace my steps, then stop. I hesitate. I don't need to look out for security cameras or CCTV. I'm not doing anything wrong. It's a hard habit to break, but I hate the thought of being watched, regardless. I take a deep breath. Damn Sam. Damn Alexandra. At times, I have been able to kid myself that I am protected in my new, safe, quiet life. My dreams are of financial security, maybe even another great love affair, an all-encompassing one that will make what I had with Sam fade into nothingness. I walk to the river's edge.

"The Host," as I think of Flora, is standing near the boat, talking to one of the staff. I feel a pang of guilt at my lack of professionalism. She looks anxious and uncomfortable in her smart two-piece skirt suit with high stilettos. This evening is a big deal for her. A local business owner, she wants to impress and thank her most loyal customers.

"Charlotte, I am so pleased to see you," she says, turning as I approach. "There's a problem with one of the fridges. The champagne isn't chilled."

"Don't worry, I'll take care of it. Sorry I'm a little late. I got held up by another client." Untrue, obviously. "Go and take a seat on board," I say. "Relax. There's loads of time."

She doesn't take my advice, but hovers, alternating between tapping on her phone and looking past me to see if there are any early party arrivals.

I introduce myself to one of the waiting staff. I know most of the other crew and get confirmation of the warm champagne. I call a nearby pub—I'm friends with the manager—and arrange for emergency buckets of ice to be delivered. The Host looks impressed. I'm pleased. Wish fulfillment is my talent.

Once all the guests have arrived, we pull away from the small dock, heading for Royal Windsor Racecourse. I feel instantly at home on the water. Sam felt the same. It was to our advantage. The cruise guests we befriended weren't on their home turf, so it added a layer of vulnerability, which Sam was all too happy to exploit. Everyone is happily sipping chilled champagne and nibbling on quail's egg and smoked salmon canapés. Ed Sheeran is playing in the background. Swans glide nearby as if they own the river. I detest them. Their outward grace is pure illusion. I hate the way that they watch me with their predatory eyes whenever I pass by the river's edge.

I focus on the guests again so that I am not tempted to look at my phone. I am surrounded by the various interpretations of "smart casual": ripped jeans, jumpsuits, shirts and ties, long and short dresses. I am wearing my typical work uniform, which is a black skirt and top that I dress up or down, depending on requirements. Bland, yet real, pearls adorn my right wrist. If anyone were to study me closely, they may see the slight circular ridge of an anklet, with a slim silver mermaid dangling, barely visible through the stocking on my left leg. I wear it as a physical reminder of a trap—just in case I'm tempted to respond to Sam's pleas for my help. He ghosted me on and off for over a year while lying low in Mexico (allegedly) and now he's bombarding me with calls. He can wait until I'm ready. A gust of wind brushes my arm and I shiver.

Thinking about it, in Sam's last message, he sounded agitated. *"I'm being threatened, Lola. It's serious."* It was infuriating that he still used his nickname for me. He had no right. Just as he had no right to contact me because he was supposedly in trouble. But now that I've received a threatening message, too, it has muddied the waters. *"Two heads are better than one,"* his message said. *"I've got a plan. It could save us both."* Perhaps I should stop reacting out of pique. Yet it's hard because, as much as I don't trust Sam—for all I know, the message could be one of his scams to stop me from demanding my share of our money back—I need other things from him too. A divorce, for one. Sam still holds all the cards.

"Enjoying the trip so far?" I say, approaching a huddle of guests standing near me.

"Yes, wonderful."

"Super."

Satisfied that all seems well—for now—I focus on the Thames. Every now and then, I take a small sip of white wine. I would rather have a Coke—I need to stay fully alert—but it is all about blending in. Soft drinks sometimes make other people feel uncomfortable, suspicious that I am listening in on their alcohol-fueled conversations. Once upon a time, they would have been right.

Tonight, though, I'm not interested in mining their chitchat for gold. My mind is in overdrive. My problems—past miscalculations—just won't die. That message on my phone.

I know what you both did.

I used to have the Midas touch, so it's disconcerting, this sense of not being in control. Goose bumps prick my arms; I wish I had worn long sleeves. My sixth sense has me on high alert, feeling shivery with anxious anticipation because the threat has heightened my ever-present fear of exposure, my past actions held up for public dissection. Greed was my vice. Still is. I work hard to suppress it. *Avarice.* Now, there is a nicer word. I take a large sip of wine, grateful for it, after all.

We dock at the island, a short amble from the racecourse. I hear the sound of the crowds in the near distance. As we disembark onto the private jetty, I hand out betting guides to those who want them and the enclosure passes.

"You're welcome," I reply to all the polite thank-yous.

Everyone follows me toward the hospitality entrance. Once inside, it has a great view of the track and the winning post on the figure-eight course. Regardless of my viewpoint, I can never watch, anyway. I worry too much about the horses' welfare. Sam took me to the races a few times, but I hated seeing the horses whipped and pushed beyond their limits.

The guests huddle near the bar and I order several bottles of champagne, as instructed by Flora.

Those who don't want to bet online hand me cash to place bets on their behalf so they don't have to queue. As I stand with hundreds of pounds in my hand, temptation pulls as I think of my increasing credit-card and new business debts. I have borrowed too much after some creative accounting and using my sister as a reluctant guarantor. I am a changed woman, I remind myself. Don't give in. It's hard, though, because what is small change to some are riches to others. Me.

Excitement builds as the ground thunders like an earthquake. Guests, buoyed up with champagne and the thrill of a win, lean forward and yell.

"Come on, Star!"

"Move, Luna! I think she's going to make it!"

"Yes!"

"Come on, Magic/Duke/Misty/Stormy…"

A man behind me in line passes on some tips. The temptation is building. I could place my own bets with all the cash. As long as I don't lose it all, no one will check. The guests are not proper gamblers; they're out on a free trip. If I bet on the favorite to win, I'm probably doing everyone a favor. At least four of them picked horses simply because they liked their names; Sam would say they don't deserve to win. My heart rate picks up, and the dormant, yet bittersweet and addictive taste of danger returns. I get to the front of the line.

I mustn't do it. It's a slippery slope. I swore to myself that I was going to change, that I wasn't going to be weak. The man behind the counter at the bookmakers is staring at me. Heat rises in my cheeks.

I distract myself, looking down at the list of requests on my phone and working my way through them with a curious mix of relief, pride and frustration.

"Each way on Gold Charm, please."

"Midnight to win."

Job done. I need a drink.

As I stand at the champagne bar, I get another strong sense of being watched. Yesterday, I thought I saw Sam in the cereal aisle of a supermarket. Doppelgängers, in my opinion, are reminders of unfinished business. I look around, and although nearly everyone is facing the track, I don't like the sense of the many hidden eyes behind their binoculars. It feels eerie. Paranoia is just the worst feeling. My mind, lighthouse-like, seeks to unmask Whoever It Is so that I can turn them into an unthreatening person. Alexandra would hire someone to do her dirty work, wouldn't she? Sam, on the other hand, would not.

I take out my phone again and reread the message.

I know what you both did. You must return what you stole, plus blood money. I won't stay silent.

The demand makes it sound as though Sam and I were *gangsters*, for God's sake. Blood money! I'm not a murderer. Whoever It Is doesn't have a clue what they're talking about or they would be more specific. I put my phone back in my bag. Directly in front of me is a couple with their arms wrapped around each other, indifferent to the racing. The woman is wearing a distinctive pale pink Versace dress and heels. She looks happy and carefree and I am briefly envious. As if she senses me staring at her, she looks around. We exchange brief smiles. To my right is a man with a copy of the *Racing Post*, oblivious. To my left, a cluster of female friends. They show zero interest in me.

I feel sick at the thought of everything I have worked so hard to rebuild from the ashes of my wrongs being snatched away. I can't let that happen—not on the back of a text message. I have played over and over in my mind the memories of the day it all unraveled. Now I often obsess about what it would feel like to be arrested in a crowded place. I have practiced my expressions in the mirror. I would appear astonished, yet dignified. I would be politely cooperative and plant the necessary seeds of doubt. I'll never give in to fear again. I message Sam.

I'll call you later tonight.

I can't resist typing *Charlotte* at the end to make the point that I am no longer Lola.

If he's lying, if he's making these threats up to scare me into forgetting what he did, or if he's spinning some elaborate yarn as to why I may never see my money again, he's in for a fight. It's time for us to meet face-to-face. I can't ignore him anymore. Sam's messages said that he's no longer in Mexico, he's now in Wales. Let's see if he's telling the truth.

I keep checking but he doesn't respond.

The penultimate race of seven is announced. People move forward. Someone bumps into me, knocking my glass of champagne to the ground. Flora kindly offers to find me another, but I decline. It's not her job to look after me.

Despite the group's haphazard approach to betting, there are surprisingly more gains than losses. I collect their winnings, commiserate with those who lost, all the while feeling huge relief that I didn't give in to my old ways.

On the return boat trip, lights reflect and shimmer on the water. Planes, prevalent throughout the day, are noticeably absent when Heathrow quiets for the night. Most of the guests are merry or high on the excitement of their evening's winnings.

"Beginner's luck," says someone in response to another's success.

I take out my phone. Seven missed calls since I last checked, back at the racetrack. What the hell? I scroll. Sam. No voice mails. I find a quiet corner to the rear of the boat and call him back. No reply. I don't leave a message. I then check through his old messages to see if I missed anything.

Keep safe. Bon voyage.

I obviously didn't read the last one properly. I want to throw up over the side of the boat. *Bon voyage* was our code word: the shit hit the fan. Sam is truly in danger. I start to type back.

Where are you? Answer me! Now!

Nothing. I wait, shivering in the early-autumn evening chill. After several minutes, my phone is still silent. As I slide it back into my bag, I feel something hard, sharp and metallic wrapped in fine paper. I almost slide it out but I realize from the shape that, oh my God, it's a knife! Bloody hell. I look around as though someone on board can tell. They are all drinking and singing, dissecting their evening. I push the blade to one side and feel around the bottom of my bag gingerly. There is nothing else. As I discreetly remove the paper from around the blade, I see it has a typed note on the other side: *Watch Your Back!* Then I realize that it is not a knife but a multi-tool, the type Sam favored. Concealed inside its handle is a memory stick.

I look over the edge of the boat and back at the receding lights of the racecourse grounds. But I know that it's fruitless. There is no one there. More disturbingly, Sam would never have relinquished control of his secrets to me unless he absolutely had to.

3

THE STRANGER BESIDE ME POINTED AT THE NECKLACE.

"It would suit you."

"I beg your pardon?"

I'd wanted to window-shop in peace. I was half embarrassed at being caught out in a daydream of obvious longing, half annoyed at being interrupted by a salesperson. My glance had been caught by a pendant, a silver mermaid, elegantly displayed on black velvet surrounded by shells and petals.

I turned to walk away. The stranger followed and fell into step alongside me. So, not a salesperson after all. I hesitated near the edge of the waterfront in the welcome shade of an almond tree, unsure in which direction to turn in order to shake him off. It was my first visit to Bequia, a small, absolute hidden gem of an island.

"I'm sorry, that came out totally wrong. Feel free to give me a slap." He grinned. "The truth is that I noticed you on board the *Wanderlust* last night, and in my mind, I felt as if I already knew you."

I looked up at the man to ask him to leave me alone, but it

was only then that I properly took note of him. He was clean-shaven and had a wide, friendly smile that showed off his perfect white teeth and dark, kind eyes that crinkled slightly as he smiled. His pale green T-shirt was immaculate, not a single crease. He looked as if he'd just stepped off a photo shoot.

"What do you mean?"

"Let me start again." He held out a hand. "Hi, I'm Sam."

"Charlotte." We shook.

"Apologies if this sounds a bit...stalkerish, but I also noticed that you were traveling with friends."

My traveling companions on the ten-day cruise stopping at Aruba, Saint Lucia and Barbados were not exactly my cup of tea. Then again, I am sure I wasn't theirs. There was Alistair, who hated it if people shortened his name to Al (fair enough), Felicity, Graham; then there was Jayne "with a *y.*" We were all travel consultants for various companies and that was pretty much where the similarities ended.

"Kind of," I said.

Despite Sam's clumsy introduction, I was intrigued by him. I had a whole day to fill on my own. The others had gone snorkeling but I had opted for solitude on the truly beautiful island. According to my guidebook, Bequia translated to "island of the clouds."

"Who are you on holiday with?" I asked.

"I'm not. I work in the casino. You should come along tonight. Win a fortune," he said with *that* smile again. "Bring your kind-of friends."

Gambling wasn't my thing, but I didn't say that.

"Perhaps. Thanks." I smiled back. "They're travel industry colleagues. We all work for various holiday companies, and they're nice enough, but..."

"I understand. I feel the same about a lot of my work colleagues." He broke off. "It makes sense to me now. You didn't look as if you were having the time of your life. Listen. There's a wonderful place nearby that serves a lobster salad and a rum punch to die for," Sam said. "If you're interested?"

I wasn't sure if he was offering an invitation for me to join him or if he was suggesting I should go alone. I looked around to buy time, as if mulling his suggestion over. Port Elizabeth was a small waterfront town, with views over the bay. In the distance our vast cruise ship dominated the scene. The sky was pretty much cloudless and the sea glistened. I was in paradise. With this man who, although forward and overly confident, came across as...lonely. Something I understood.

I hadn't been looking to meet anyone on *that* cruise. Long term, I would have liked a relationship, sure—but the demographic of the cruise's passengers meant that romance had never crossed my mind. I lacked the patience to fall for a much older man. I ate too quickly, walked too fast. I'd stop and smell the roses when I'd finally made it—whatever "it" was.

"I've never been here before," I said. "I'm happy for you to show me all the best places to recommend to future passengers and tourists."

Damn. I sounded tense.

"Excellent," he said. He pointed toward the seafront. "It's a little along the way to the right. I know the owners..."

I fell naturally into step beside him. We passed a market selling brightly colored fruits and vegetables—plantains, yams, okra, mangoes, grapefruit, guavas. Alone among the fresh produce stalls was one selling models of sailboats. It took time to get to the restaurant because Sam seemed to know so many people. We were greeted with *hello*s and *long time no see*s and knowing looks were surreptitiously cast in my direction. The strange thing is I didn't mind.

I don't remember much about the restaurant because I barely ate, despite Sam being right about the lobster salad. I was too mesmerized by the stories of his travels, his freedom.

"What about you?" he asked after a while. "You haven't told me much."

"There's nothing much to tell." True.

So far, I had dabbled at life: waitressing, bar work, cleaning, housekeeping, receptionist, customer service agent, retail assistant, au pair; now a travel agent. None of these jobs paid well enough, but they'd given me an insight into human nature, both good and bad.

"I'm an old black-and-white movie fan."

"Which are your favorite ones?" Sam asked.

Easy. "*A Streetcar Named Desire, Casablanca, Sunset Boulevard,* to name a few."

"Excellent choices. I like your style. Why do you prefer them to contemporary movies?"

I mulled it over.

"Escapism, I think. The past feels like a safer place, full of glamour and places to hide."

"Places to hide?"

I blushed. "That came out wrong! I meant, anonymity. No work emails, no phones, no internet, no social media. The past feels like it was cloaked in anonymity, the ability to reinvent oneself. I love the desperately sad, yet passionate, love stories and secret affairs."

I stopped, feeling self-conscious at my revelation. I'd never told anyone before how, when I was absorbed in a movie—especially when I was a teenager—I felt safe. It blocked out the sadness, gave me hope for a future where I, too, would lead a life full of burning passion and enchantment.

"I love that! It's so true. Tell me more," he said.

"Like what?"

"Like…where did you grow up?"

His eyes didn't dart downward to his phone, he didn't look past me, he ignored the sounds of excited children coming from the beach and the small band playing guitars in the corner of the open-air café. Encouraged by his genuine interest, I continued.

"My father died when I was nine." Out of nowhere, a lump formed in my throat. I took a large sip of my rum punch and quickly skimmed through the rest of the details. I edited them as I spoke, trying not to make it sound too sad. "A heart attack. Stress induced. Not the official diagnosis but the one my entire family believed to be true. My mom, and then later my older sister, worked multiple jobs to keep the money coming in. My mom passed away when I was nineteen."

He reached over and took my hand. I could have gone on, but no one tells the absolute truth about their history when they are trying to impress someone. Because that's definitely what I wanted to do: impress him.

My openness seemed to touch him because he told me a bit more about his background.

"My mother died when I was six. So, I do understand what it feels like. My dad did his best but I know he struggled. I would have loved a sibling."

I felt a pang of guilt. My sister, Louise, and I were not the best of friends.

Sam and I gently squeezed hands over the table. I had never felt so seen, so understood, so full of desire and so sure that our meeting was *meant to be*. Maybe my myriad of jobs and situations were all part of some great unseen plan to lead me to this point. There was a shift in energy as if we both wanted to banish past sadness and root ourselves in the wonder of now.

"I adore the sea," he said. "It's the only place I feel at home."

"Same," I said, marveling at how much we had in common. "I love inhaling the salty tang in the air, the vastness when looking out at the horizon, the sound of the waves. It's soothing."

We walked back to the ship together. We passed by an assortment of wooden signs nailed to a tree: *New York 1788 miles. London 3323 miles. Toronto 2104 miles. Berlin 5579 miles. Happiness is right here.* So true. By the time we arrived back on board the *Wanderlust*, I'd agreed to go to the casino after dinner that evening.

Sam was working at the blackjack table. He didn't notice me enter, so for a while I was able to discreetly observe him at work. The first thing I noticed was that passengers were drawn to his table. The other tables weren't nearly as busy. Sam's smile was infectious. I saw people tilt back their heads and laugh, even when they had been on a losing streak. Eventually, he spotted me standing by the slot machines and beckoned me over.

Someone stood up to offer me his place at the table.

"I'm done," the man said. "Let's hope you have better luck."

I could feel everyone's eyes upon me as I placed my chips down. It was as if they sensed that Sam had picked me out as someone special, which then elevated me in their eyes too. It was exhilarating. I felt alive.

Sam dealt me my cards. A queen and a three. My next card was a nine, which tipped me over.

I won, I lost. I lost, I won. I won. Time really did appear to stand still as I focused on assessing how much to gamble, whether to accept another card or stand. I could barely breathe. The tantalizing hope of winning was intoxicating. Not just the

winning, which felt like free money, but the thrill of anticipation. The encouragement from the people crowded around
me, congratulating me when I won and commiserating when
I lost, was electrifying. Sam's smile encouraged me further. I
was center stage even when I eventually had to make way for
other players. Turned out gambling was my thing after all.

Under Sam's guidance, I was introduced to poker, to roulette, to the dream of winning. My mind ran away with me,
imagining placing higher bets, winning a fortune, buying a
house, paying off my car loan, money for five-star holidays…
and then I lost. And lost again. They weren't large amounts—
of course not, I couldn't afford it—but it was still deflating.
Caught up in the moment, I'd so believed I was in with a
chance of winning big.

Sam was in demand. A woman with a large bag of chips
was holding him captive at the roulette table. I slipped away,
out onto the deck. The short time I had spent with him had
opened my eyes to what was lacking in my life. I realized I
wanted to stay out at sea, experience new adventures.

I joined my colleagues in the palm-tree bar and drank
cocktails named "coconut clouds" and "dark and stormy."
We played drinking games and ordered late-night burgers
and fries to soak up the alcohol. As we all said good-night by
the elevators, I felt empty. But back in my cabin, along with
the chocolate on my pillow, there was also an envelope on my
bed, propped up against a towel-art bear.

At first, I assumed it would be a receipt for my day's over-
spending. But the package bulged slightly. I ripped it and inside was something wrapped in powder blue tissue paper. I
unwrapped it. Nestling in the cloud of paper was the silver
mermaid pendant and a note.

Your winnings.

4

NOW

ALL AROUND ME IS *NORMALITY.* GUESTS DISEMBARK from the boat, thank me and their host, then head in the direction of the train station. I feel dizzy, seasick, even. My mind is a maelstrom of thoughts and fears.

"You are a natural at making people feel at ease," Flora says as we both walk up the slope leading away from the river.

She gives me an awkward drunken hug by way of a goodbye, along with a generous cash tip. I am pleased. (For the tip, not the hug.)

I give a modest smile. "Thank you. It's my job." True. "I pride myself on repeat business and referrals, rather than puffed-up advertising."

Untrue. I do whatever it takes and work best in the circumstances.

One more hug from The Host and I am released. I am free. For now. Because the event is local to me, a luxurious rarity, I can walk home. One of my closest old school friends, Lewis, lets me use his spare room until I can decide where I want to put down more permanent roots. Thing is, I shouldn't walk home alone, not after what's happened. And yet... sometimes, in a perverse, twisted kind of a way, I half like placing myself in danger. I see it as giving the universe (or whoever, whatever) a chance to strike me down. If I was caught off guard, it could potentially be one bash over the head with my tormentor's weapon of choice. One stab, maybe. Then the game would be over. Mini punishments such as these (like also not allowing myself to smoke at the moment) are to give karma a helping hand so it doesn't need to concern itself with conjuring up some terrible fate from its own imagination. All of this seemed to work.

Until today.

I hesitate before I cross the road and walk up the hill, keeping Windsor Castle to my left, because there is an alternative route. It would take me along the river, then beneath a small underpass. But tonight, I have managed to stay safe, despite Sam getting close enough to plant a cryptic note and a memory stick on me. I shouldn't tempt fate any more than I already have. It's surreal to think that I didn't sense him, or even smell his favorite aftershave. He was ghostlike while using his pickpocketing skills in reverse.

I focus on the rhythmic echo of my heels on the paving stones. I like the sound, but it draws too much attention to my lone walking. I stop, lean against a wall, unzip my bag and change into flat boots. No one else walks by. I am alone.

I pass an antique shop, then the theater, and keep making my way up the hill. All is quiet, which is usual for a weeknight. The windows in the outer castle brick walls are mostly unlit. The arrow slits always give me the creeps, even in daylight. As I walk past my favorite Thai restaurant, the entrance door opens and two couples emerge, laughing before they walk down the hill, away from me. Yet I'm aware of a single set of footsteps close behind me that pierce my arrogance. I stiffen, shove my right hand deep into my bag and grip the handle of Sam's gift.

The spear point blade is sharp enough to use as a weapon.

The footsteps stop. I watch as a gentle breeze nudges a chocolate wrapper, lifting it off the pavement, then discarding it. Trying not to make it too obvious, I up my pace. My own steps echo in time to *blood money, blood money, blood money.*

The footsteps get closer. I swing round.

"Sam?"

I call out just as the short, slight physique of someone wearing a woolly hat pulled down low speeds past, almost as if he or she had been debating how to overtake me without causing alarm, yet still messed up. Sam was considerate. If he saw anyone walking alone in a deserted spot at night, he would cross the road so as not to scare them. Or so he said.

The mound of a homeless person in the navy thermal sleeping bag I bought him gives me comfort. He is not in his usual doorway. I wonder why? I pause beside him. It is reassuring to see someone familiar.

"Grant?" I say. Loud enough to wake, but not so much as to frighten.

He doesn't reply.

As I lean over to ensure that he is all right, the sound of his gentle snoring reassures me. On second thought, I leave him be. He has had a pretty shitty life; sleep hopefully brings him brief, yet blessed, respite.

I walk past the tourist shops, their windows filled with the faces of the monarchy, soldiers in their distinctive uniforms, the castle and other related images on tea towels, posters, magnets and masks. Turning right, I run through a familiar short alleyway that leads away from the main shopping area and onto Lewis's road. It starts to rain.

His house is a two-bedroom end-of-terrace. We didn't plan to become housemates, didn't want to risk our friendship. But a week before I arrived back in England, his renter moved out. So we fell into it. Sam had all but emptied our joint bank account after our abrupt breakup, and although we own a joint property—what was supposed to be our dream home near a Devon beach—my hands have been tied by Sam's absence. Practically speaking, I am in limbo, unable to sell the place and move on. Until recently, Sam got away with a lot.

Any potential new boyfriends are suspicious of what's going on between Lewis and me. Women ask him the same questions. Have we ever…you know…nudge, nudge…? But the truthful answer is no. Lewis and I have been friends since the first week of secondary school when we couldn't find our first-ever French class in time for the lesson. Neither of us wanted to make an entrance, or have to apologize in front of our classmates. We hid in an empty art-and-textiles room until it was over. We bonded, surrounded by pictures of landscapes, fruit and the faceless dummies used for fashion design. By the time we emerged, we were friends.

There is a Victorian-style lamppost on the pavement outside his house that reminds me of Narnia. I love it, even if cost-cutting measures mean it's switched off during the loneliest hours of the night. Now, as the Narnia lamp comes into view, casting a pool of light across the pavement, my heart rate picks up at the sight of a lone figure standing beneath it, rain drizzling over them.

"Sam?"

I run toward the figure, but when he turns around, it's

Lewis. Wishful thinking. The buildup of anger I feel toward Sam is ready to burst.

"I've been looking out for you," he says. "I was worried. Why aren't you answering your phone?"

I take it out and see two missed calls from Lewis. They must've got lost among the many from Sam.

"Sorry. Busy evening. I was distracted. What's up? Why are you waiting out here for me?"

I can't tell him about Sam and the mystery gift. Lewis believes that Sam led me astray. He doesn't know even a quarter of what went on and I love his faith and loyalty in me.

"I'll tell you inside."

This doesn't sound good.

As soon as he shuts the front door behind him, I turn to him. "Just spit it out. You're scaring me."

I've had enough bad surprises for one day.

"This came in the mail." He hands me a newspaper clipping. I unfold the sheet of paper. It is a black-and-white photograph of Sam and me, on our wedding day. I am wearing a new long indigo dress and strappy heels. I had worn a bracelet dotted with dainty sapphire seashells he had given me as an engagement gift. Sam had a thing about discretion when it came to certain gifts, which I appreciated. The bracelet was my something blue, earrings my something old. They were given to me by my mother, one of the last few items she was never forced to sell. The earrings had been passed down to her by my grandmother, who had received them from my grandfather for their golden wedding anniversary. I'd kept the bracelet in my clutch bag, and after the formalities I draped it around my wrist. I could no longer resist showing it off. I loved it.

I didn't think I was doing anything wrong.

Yet Sam went white when he noticed the bracelet as our wedding photographs were taken. He whispered angry words in my ear.

"What happened to discretion? I thought we'd agreed not to flaunt our wealth? It invites trouble. You know that."

I didn't know that the couple who were the guests of honor at our wedding were quite so well-known locally. It certainly wasn't obvious. They were kind and humble, despite their great wealth. They offered, no, *insisted* on paying for our wedding. How was I to know that there was a newspaper photographer and journalists there among the many guests? I wrongly assumed that the day was about me, the bride. I didn't fully understand why one bracelet mattered so much.

Of course, I do now.

I wish that I hadn't worn the bracelet. It ruined what should have been a perfect day. Sam bought me orchids to apologize for his anger, but a bunch of flowers, however beautiful, couldn't undo what had been done. That tiny error of judgment is still haunting me because my wrist is now highlighted in the photo, with a red halo of marker pen. Beside it, these words are scrawled:

Dear Mr. Mason [seems strange to think of Lewis as Mr. Mason],
We feel it is our duty to warn you that you are harboring a thief.
    With best and kind-intentioned regards,
A victim and those who care about them.

"Bloody hell," I say, looking up at Lewis.

"What's this all about?"

I hesitate, hardly knowing how to explain. "It was Sam's ex's bracelet," I begin. "I thought he had bought it for me at the time. But he should never have given it to me, because it wasn't his to give. It then went missing after I'd worn it, and I have no idea where it is now. I don't appreciate being called a thief." True.

Lewis had been right about Sam, all along. I hate admitting that, even now. He gently warned me to hold back a bit. The truth is that *no one who truly knows Sam likes him*. The only people who love him don't know the real him.

"So it's Sam this person really needs to be in touch with." Lewis shrugs. "If his ex-girlfriend ever returns."

Thank God. He still has my back.

"Seems odd, though, after all this time. You and Sam…" He hesitates, before pointing out the obvious. "You guys weren't married for long."

I shrug, pretending that I'm not rattled. But I am. I dread to think what other photos Whoever It Is will manage to unearth. Sam and I were careful, but it's impossible to hide completely.

When Lewis goes to bed, I lock myself in my room. Sam's memory stick is password protected, but it is one of the passwords we used jointly, which means he wanted me to gain access. Still, around a quarter of his files are encrypted. It will take time to get myself into Sam's head and figure out exactly what is hidden here. I make copies of all the encrypted files. This is Sam all over. He trusts me, yet he doesn't. He needs me, but also resents the fact that he does. I browse through the few files I *can* access. It's all the usual mundane life admin, like the paperwork from buying our house in Devon, along with title deeds to an apartment in Cardiff I didn't know anything about. Mortgage applications, buildings and contents insurance, bills he's paid. Résumés. A pension I'm surprised he paid into. Bills he hasn't. There are loan applications from his student days.

Exhaustion takes hold. Since receiving the threat, I have lived on adrenaline. I have been kidding myself, thinking that I could turn over the proverbial new leaf without fully exorcising the past. The truth is that once the shock of potentially getting caught wore off, I was able to rewrite the story, bury the shame and the guilt. But I'm pulled constantly, craving a better life, yet tugged back to the past.

When I stood in that customs line, abandoned by Sam, terrified, I made a silent bargain with God, the universe, anyone or anything that could protect me. I promised that I would be a good person for the rest of my life, if only I was saved. I had seen the error of my ways, seen how I had been too trusting, too selfish. I was going to do better, help others, be a valuable member of society.

Upon my return, I was so grateful not to be imprisoned that I would have been almost happy to live anywhere, work anywhere. But shock wears off. Complacency weaves back in. The desire for the nicer things in life took hold. Nonetheless, I stayed true to my own code of conduct. I have resisted any desire to revert to my old ways. Having said all that, life is expensive. I had forgotten the value of money, had no clue how to budget anymore. Sam knew what I wanted, and like magic, it often appeared.

Staring at that photo again, I realize I have decisions to make. Tough ones.

I remove my contact lenses but then put on my glasses while I try to call Sam one last time. I don't get it. One minute he is frantically calling me, the next his phone is switched off. It doesn't go to voice mail. I can't even begin to guess what game he's playing at now. I climb into bed and lie awake, listening for unfamiliar sounds.

The note rests beneath my pillow, along with Sam's dark secrets.

5

THEN

The Caribbean

SOMETIMES I IMAGINE THAT IF MY LIFE WEREN'T real, if I were a character in a film…when should I have walked away? Would the moment be highlighted for the audience with dramatic music or a blatant clue? Did I miss something obvious? Or did I turn a blind eye? Did I focus too hard on the positives, sift away the negatives? It is hard to be objective.

The day after I met Sam, I was out walking on the upper deck, wearing the mermaid pendant. I loved being out at sea. I took hundreds of photos of the turquoise water as I watched the sun reflect off the waves. Everything looked brighter and shinier than usual. I had treated myself to some expensive sun cream from one of the gift shops and my skin smelled of papaya, coconut and shea. Apart from other cruise ships and yachts, there was ocean as far as I could see. I was cut off from the rest of the world; the rules didn't apply. It was invigorating. I realized I didn't want to return to real life. I wanted to stay here, in the fantasy one, with endless buffets and entertainment, where credit-card bills, housework and work commutes didn't exist.

I spotted Sam standing against the railings. Leo in *Titanic* sprang to mind—minus the tragedy. The fluttering sensation in my stomach was something I hadn't experienced in a long while. I had forgotten its thrill. I was summoning up the confidence to go over and say hello, when a woman with long dark hair approached him. I recognized her from the casino the previous evening. She'd wanted the dealers—Sam, especially—to know that she was in for a fun time. She took risks and seemed to revel in the high energy of the casino crowds. I had dismissed her as an attention seeker.

I stayed where I was and watched. Clearly, she was enthralled by Sam. She dropped something—a piece of paper—and as it blew across the deck, Sam caught it. His attention returned to the woman. She opened her bag and handed him something small, rectangular and gift wrapped. He leaned forward and said something in her ear. She laughed, touched his arm as she replied, then walked away, past me.

Sam slid whatever it was he had been given into his pocket and leaned over the railings again, staring out to sea. He was being polite. That had to be all it was. She was merely an appreciative guest. With me, things were different—I felt sure. I gathered myself and walked over to stand alongside him, fixing my own gaze on the horizon. Waiting. For a moment, neither of us spoke. Then Sam broke the silence.

"You were watching me."

I felt my cheeks flame at having been so obvious. Still, I wasn't above asking the question that was plaguing me. "What did she give you?"

He leaned back and laughed. "You did not just ask me that!"

I couldn't help laughing too. "I can't help it. I really want to know!"

He looked at me, then smiled that smile again. It felt as

though I'd known him for much longer than twenty-four hours. He slid his forefinger and thumb along the chain he had given me the previous night until he reached the silver mermaid that rested in the middle of my chest. Nestling its smooth beauty in his palm, he smiled in admiration before letting go.

"It's perfect on you."

"It was a lovely surprise, thank you. But are you trying to distract me?"

I was surprised to hear that my voice sounded normal because, for me, the rest of the world had faded away. Nothing felt normal at all. Sam had taken center stage in my world.

He laughed. "Yes, and no. Truth is, I can't think straight. You have that effect on me."

"I'd still like to know."

As though it was any of my business! But jealousy made me push for an answer. Although, I already knew that it was almost too late, that I was falling for him; he was unlike any other man I had ever met.

Whenever I repaint a picture in my mind, it is important to remind myself that I wasn't a total pushover.

"Some people like to reward good service individually," he said. "It means fewer tips, but I don't like hurting feelings. It doesn't happen all that often, so I figure, sometimes…what's the harm? Like everything in life, it's about balance."

"Fair enough. I shouldn't have asked."

He didn't disagree.

Our next stop would be Aruba. Our last chance. I was due to disembark in Barbados a few days later and catch a flight to London. I didn't want the trip to end.

"We could go out in port," I blurted out. "If you have time off? If it's allowed?"

I paused, feeling clumsy and stupid.

He answered quickly, saving my feelings. "Sure. I'd love to. Rules are just guidelines," he said. "It's up to me what I'm *allowed* to do."

"It's all about interpretation."

He grinned. "Exactly. There's this stunning beach—Eagle Beach. Miles of white sand."

I opened my mouth to say that I knew, that I had been on a previous work trip, but I stopped myself. He looked so excited, so full of energy. Why burst his bubble? Was that my first mistake? To let him think that he was the first one to introduce me to the beautiful things in life?

But I'd seen it before.

I'd worked in Val d'Isère one ski season. A friend of a friend had recommended me as a chalet girl. It had opened my eyes to the disparity between my life and those of others. Sometimes, I used to play at living the Fairy Tale. When the guests were out, I would pretend that the chalet was mine.

In between guests, I'd invite other chalet staff over and we would use the hot tub, pool and sauna, all taking turns to cook and clean up. Happy days. Once, we went out clubbing and I met a man who assumed that the place was mine. I didn't correct him. All fairly innocent, fun stuff, even though it created a yearning deep within me.

There was one guest, Harry, who took it upon himself to teach me how to ski. Afterward, we'd hang out together in the chalet while his friends were still on the slopes. As I made dinner for them all in the evenings, he and I would share knowing looks. After a few days, we gave up on the skiing. I'd stay in his room every night and during the day we would swim, have lunch together in bed and share our dreams.

I'd assumed that it was only a matter of time before he'd

tell his friends or they caught on. I imagined packing my bags at the end of the season and making a go of our relationship in England.

On the group's last evening, they decided that they were going to eat out at the best restaurant in town. I imagined that this was the perfect opportunity, that Harry would suggest that I join them too. But as the time for them to leave approached, it dawned on me that that was not how things would be.

"Be a sweetheart and make sure the nightcaps are ready when we return," said the girlfriend of one of his friends.

Harry gave me an apologetic shrug, leaving me alone, like Cinderella. I was done then. Immediately, I packed my bags and ordered a cab. I left the dishwasher unloaded, their bedsheets not turned down, the fire unlit, the cushions un-plumped.

Lesson painfully learned.

So, no, Sam. You weren't the first person to share these things with me.

Still, the two of us visited Eagle Beach. We took pictures of each other leaning against the contorted bark of one of the widely photographed Fofoti trees that leaned toward the green-and-blue sea. Sam arranged loungers for us where I lay and watched snorkelers, jet-skiers and swimmers dotting the clear water. We took a quick dip to cool off before we sipped a cold beer beneath the shade of gently swaying palm leaves. Even so, we were there for less than two hours before we gave up on any pretense that we wanted to do anything other than simply be together. We sneaked back to my cabin, all the more thrilling because it was very much "against the rules."

"I wish I wasn't leaving tomorrow," I said, as we lay on my bed.

Sam pulled me close to him.

"Come back to the Caribbean," he said. "I know someone who works for a specialist recruitment agency. You could get a job on a cruise ship. I'll put in a good word."

A fluttering in my stomach.

"What would I do?"

"There are loads of jobs. Just see what is available and apply for one. Florist, wardrobe supervisor, makeup artist, steward, PA, sales… The possibilities are endless."

I laughed. "I am most definitely not a florist! Or a makeup artist, even."

"Fake it until you make it. Don't you have friends who could vouch for you? Provide a reference? Loads of people learn on the job. It's all about confidence." He stopped and gazed at me. "I believe in you. You can do anything you put your mind to."

I laughed again. "I'll do my very best."

"Do. I want to see you again. And I know you love it out at sea as much as I do. It gets in your blood."

Sam had a shift at the casino and had to leave then. As I saw him out, Alistair emerged from his cabin. His expression was disapproving as the two of us watched Sam walk down the corridor.

"I thought he had a girlfriend," he said.

"No, he doesn't," I replied quickly. "He's been single for six months since his last girlfriend left him to go and work in the States on some billionaire's private yacht."

Sam told me how heartbroken he'd been.

I saw him hesitate. "Okay. Maybe I'm mistaken. I thought I saw him with someone. But…maybe I was wrong."

"Maybe so," I said, shutting my door.

6

NOW

IT'S HARD NOT TO LOOK BACK ON *THAT* DAY, DESPER-
ately scanning for the precise moment to freeze it, ready for
dissection. I want to know when the overriding desire and
greed enveloped me, forcing me to make a fatal decision. I
want to rewrite history.

I sit at the kitchen table with a coffee and stare at the newspaper clipping to try to match the person I was in that image
with the person I am now. It is like night and day. I want to
go back in time and give past me a good shake and a warning.

Don't mess it up.

Since then, I have been humbled. Humiliated. I want to go
back and do it all differently. Some things, though, I wouldn't
change. Certain people deserved all they got.

But recent events have awoken a new restlessness. I hate
that Whoever It Is has this hold over me. The power to upend
my peace of mind.

I check my phone.

Nothing.

The mailbox rattles, making me jump. Nothing out of the

ordinary lies on the mat. Lewis has already left for work at his garage—the one he's built from scratch ever since leaving school.

I scroll half-heartedly through work emails and sales offers.

The host from last night, Flora, has sent a thank-you message. I must have hidden my distraction well. I add her message to my website testimonials.

Highly recommended!

Wouldn't trust anyone else.

A true professional.

When I read comments like these, despite a small sense of pride, I find it hard to relate. Maybe I am being too hard on myself. Times have been stressful.

I open more work requests. Someone wants me to organize her sister's bachelorette party—tastefully. Whatever that means. Another woman is looking to celebrate her sixtieth. There is one from a personal assistant with an address for the meeting we have at midday regarding an important event in November. It is hard to feel 100 percent enthusiastic, given my current state of mind, yet I need all the clients I can get. The fees they're prepared to pay for this job should be worthwhile because it involves some travel, according to their initial inquiry. From a quick online search, I see that the house has a tennis court, two ponds with fountains in the center, an indoor pool, seven bedrooms, a home theater and so on. My interest picks up.

I reply enthusiastically to everyone. I need to earn a living while I figure out my next move. Move out of Lewis's flat. Change my number. Start again. These things aren't impossible. I check out jobs, both here and abroad. I make another coffee.

Our hideaway in Devon was meant to be the first of our

forever homes. A cliff-side cottage with seaside views. It meant
that we never had to leave the sea behind. Landscapers had
transformed the garden into a mini reminder of our Caribbean adventures, with palm trees and exotic flowers. The plan
was that we were going to buy another one in Spain, one on
the Côte d'Azur, another in Bermuda. A long list of ambitious dreams and plans. Both of us were determined to live
our lives to the utmost. So, even now, it feels freshly frustrating that one bad decision has led to such utter destruction. I
check out how much notice our long-term tenants in Devon
require to move out. Three months.

I reach for my phone and call Sam. His number is still disconnected. I plug in the USB again, make a fresh attempt at
going through his files. My coffee grows cold and my back
aches as I stare at the screen. It doesn't amount to anything. I
glance at the time: 10:47 a.m. Crap. I don't have much time
to make myself presentable for the meeting.

A rushed shower, and then I choose from my wardrobe.
This will do—a pale blue designer dress. Professional, bland,
safe. Constant moving about has not been conducive to a larger
wardrobe, so I "borrow" items as often as I can. I pull it on
carefully over my head and tuck away the label. I wear borrowed items only once before I return them. I'm very strict
with myself when it comes to that rule. Wearing an item more
than once would make it feel like a proper theft. This makes
sense. If shops are going to charge a fortune for what is, es-
sentially, a piece of material, then I choose not to feel guilty
about my recycling habit.

I slide my jewelry box out from a dressing-table drawer. At
times, it feels odd keeping valuable items in such an obvious
place, but I have learned that it's the best way to hide things.
All my valuable jewels were repurposed and disguised as cos-

tume jewelry. Sam wasn't the only person to make useful contacts; I did too. Every job Sam and I did, I kept a memento. My inner magpie would seek out the latest, whispering in my ear, *"It would look better on you."*

Today, I choose a pendant, a ruby heart to complement the dress. A calmness descends as I do up the clasp behind my neck. It's perfect. It was a brooch in its former life but it looks so much more attractive as a necklace. Feeling like *me* again, I slip on some heels. I study myself in the full-length mirror. My mermaid anklet doesn't go with the overall outfit, but I will continue to wear it to remind me of my independence. Sam is history.

I smile at myself in the mirror, a habit Sam got me into.

"It sets a positive scene in your brain," he used to say when I noticed him doing it before we left our cabins.

Some of the habits he taught me I should make more of an effort to break free from, but this one is harmless enough. I don't fancy public transport after yesterday, so I message Lewis.

Can I borrow your car? Running late!

Yes. Keys in my bedside drawer. Drive SAFELY.

Lewis owns a red Porsche. His family situation is sad and complicated, albeit different from mine, because mine started out idyllic and fairy-tale-like before badness and sadness changed things. Lewis always said that as soon as he could, he would buy a car like this. He achieved his goal by the time he was twenty-five (a combination of hard work and loans) and I never give him a hard time because I appreciate how much the dream of owning one is what kept him going through some bleak times.

He would never have let me borrow it when it was new, but he's now got his eye on a Nissan GT-R. I have no clue what type of car that is. It could be a monster truck, for all I know. At least I can picture what someone is talking about when they mention a Porsche, Ferrari or Lamborghini. Lewis's diminishing pride in his car highlights the fact that we all want what we think we want until we get it, but—sooner or later—it loses its shine. Nothing can fill the void for long enough. That's how it all began for me, really. I developed a taste for the finer things in life, and I liked, then craved, how it made me feel, and from then on, there was no unknowing or undesiring.

I tap in the destination postcode for the estate where I'm to meet Thomas, this personal assistant who contacted me about the event in November. It's a forty-minute drive away.

After I've set off, I check my mirror several times, especially when stopped at traffic lights. At first, I suspect a black van is following me, particularly once I'm on the freeway and it passes every time I do, but then it exits at the first off-ramp. Still, I speed up, it seems a shame not to, given the luxury of the car I'm driving, and change lanes several times before feeling satisfied that I am not being followed.

I drive down a small, narrow lane, snaking past a village green and a pretty pub with lots of hanging baskets overflowing with creeping Jenny and petunias. Once I arrive, the house itself has a long gravel drive but it's not quite as grandiose as I had imagined.

I do a final check of my appearance, smoothing down the stiffness of the dress as I get out. I shut the door quietly and walk over to the front door. After pressing the bell, I step back, standing between two potted olive trees. I feel watched by a camera I can't locate. I stand, with just a hint of a smile, oozing an air of patience and professionalism.

Nothing.

A plane flies overhead. I hear footsteps and see a mailman approaching. I put out my hand to take the letters he is holding. He hesitates, but the front door opens, so he hands them to me.

The letter on top is addressed to a Mr. H. Jacobs. But the name of the person interviewing me is Thomas George. The PA.

"Hello," I say to the man framing the door. "I'm Charlotte." I hand him the mail. "I just met your mailman."

"Thomas," he replies, accepting the letters. "Sorry to keep you waiting. Please, come in."

He is younger than me by a good five years or so. Tall, wearing a maroon sweater, black jeans and designer sneakers.

I step inside. Thomas places the mail down on a table in the hall. I look around. Opulence. A sweeping staircase, designer vases, the pictures on the wall expertly framed. The decor is not to my taste. I would modernize; some of the furniture appears to be family heirlooms. Despite this, briefly, it feels like coming home. Situations such as these always make me forget how much I have to force myself to like the ordinary, when, really, my tastes always veer toward luxury.

"This way, please," says Thomas, leading me into a kitchen. He indicates a bar stool.

I perch on it. "Nice place."

"May I offer you a tea or a coffee? Or an iced water, perhaps?"

"Iced water sounds good. Thank you."

After putting my phone on silent, I place it in my bag. Sam and I had rules about giving people our full attention. Any hint of disinterest or boredom can make the smallest difference when it comes to building trust. Thomas may be the assistant, but I know that, despite his lack of warmth, he will undoubtedly be a hard worker and he is the trusted gatekeeper to whoever wants me to hold an event here. As such, Thomas deserves my respect. It is what I desired wherever I worked and was often in very limited supply. I always swore that if I ever "made it"—no, *when* I made it—I would never look down on anyone in the way that I have been.

I sip the water Thomas hands me, garnished with a slice of lime. I like that he has done that. I despise it when people make me an instant coffee, especially when I know they have a sparkling, shiny, expensive coffee maker that they would use if I was someone more important.

A rush of rage toward Sam comes from nowhere. This is not how things were supposed to turn out. I don't want to be sitting in a stranger's kitchen, wondering if Whoever It Is will pounce again or if they just wanted to rattle my cage. I want Sam to tell me useful things, not sneak up on me and plant cryptic items in my bag without my consent or knowledge.

"Before we begin," says Thomas, "I would like to tell you a bit about the type of person we are looking for. Someone unflappable. Someone who can—and I know this is an over-used phrase, so please forgive me—but someone who can think outside the box. The person we'll choose will be prepared to put their all into it."

"Naturally. I never give anything less than one hundred percent." True. "How did you hear of me?"

"You came recommended. I checked out your website, too, and as well as having relevant experience for a unique role, it states that you travel for work."

"Yes, Europe, mainly. But the work is varied. I've even ar-ranged a small wedding at a safari lodge in Kenya." Untrue, but

Sam's voice is in my head, reminding me that everyone flowers up their work history. "May I ask who recommended me?"

"A friend of my employer's." He mentions one of the first parties I ever arranged, a thirtieth in a historic building near Windsor. "We usually use an agency, but their fees no longer seem worth paying for. There is another PA who usually travels with us, but sadly, she's been involved in a cycling accident and in all likelihood won't be well enough in time to travel. I have visas to arrange, travel to book."

"Sorry to hear that. I'd really like to know a bit more about what type of event you need assistance for and any other details. Where would I potentially be traveling to? Those are the type of things that are good for me to know."

"It's more important that I get an overall feel for how you would work with me first. I'm looking for the *personality*. I could hire any freelance assistant, which I appreciate you are not. However, given the nature of the upcoming event, we would value your event-planning skills. Our fee will naturally reflect the qualifications and experience of the person we hire."

He stops.

"Sounds intriguing," I say.

If there is a large budget, it will extend to my fee. Selling my jewelry will always be a very last or desperate resort. Plus, it's fair enough that he would like to know a bit more about me. I imagine it's harder recruiting for an employer than it is for oneself. It's not as if I don't know how to say what people want to hear. I'm feeling energized because it taps into my dormant skills: looking for the right clues and signs.

Thomas asks several questions before focusing more on me.

"Tell me about your background," he says. "I'd like to hear

it in your own words. You don't have much of a social media presence."

"I'm camera shy. Always have been since I was younger and wore glasses that didn't suit me. I felt self-conscious."

I did hate my glasses and I'm not particularly fond of photos of myself, but social media is the enemy. I hate all the reminders, all the *"This time two/three/four/a hundred years ago you were with blah, doing blah."* No, thank you. I want to be forgotten, not remembered. I tell Thomas what he wants to hear. About my cruise-ship background, then my well-rehearsed lie about missing life on land, wanting to set up my own business. So much easier than telling the truth. *"Flower it up,"* Sam's voice whispers in my ear.

"Interesting. The events I'm arranging will take place on board a private superyacht sailing from the Bahamas, mid-November. My employer wants to host an engagement party for some close friends plus a seventieth-birthday celebration for her mother. Your cruise-ship experience may come in useful, especially as you obviously don't suffer from seasickness." He pauses to smile.

I smile too. "No, definitely not."

"However," he continues, "most important, I need someone who can assist me without question—within reason, of course. I need a person I can trust but who also doesn't feel as if it's beneath them to follow orders. It's important to understand the amount of work involved in planning these events."

"I understand."

"Did you come across many famous people on your travels?"

Aha. That's what all this is mainly about. Confidentiality and privacy.

I put on my most prim voice.

"I wouldn't say even if I had. I value privacy."

"Excellent. Good to know."

"I read somewhere that the pleasure of sharing gossip only lasts a few seconds, but the shame, guilt and fear of breaking a confidence lasts so much longer. It's not worth it."

Shut up! I tell myself.

"Fascinating." He smiles. "Any questions for me?"

Thomas has an oddly formal manner about him, as though he is fifty years older than he actually is.

"What is the itinerary, please?"

"The plan is Nassau, Turks and Caicos, San Juan, Antigua, Saint Lucia, Barbados, Trinidad and Tobago. This is not an exhaustive list, however, and is subject to change, even once we've set sail."

"What other staff would there be?"

"The yacht crew are permanent. As well as you and me, there will be a beautician, security staff and specialized villa staff who will also be free to assist with the events or any other jobs that crop up. When we arrive in Barbados, they will disembark to go ahead and make things comfortable for my employer and her guests at her property there."

"Are you able to tell me a bit about your employer and the other guests?"

Mr. H. Jacobs, for one.

"Not at this stage, although I most certainly can be more transparent once I've made a decision. I have two more people to see today. I'll think things through this evening."

I turn against Thomas, despite the lime garnish.

"When can I expect to hear? My diary is already fairly full for November. Precise dates would be good."

Even as I say this, I know I've made a big mistake. Never show overeagerness.

"You'll hear from me by the end of the week. Thank you so much for coming."

I am dismissed. It irks.

When I get back to Lewis's place, there's a police car outside the house, parked beneath the Narnia lamp. The urge to run almost takes over, but I hold my nerve, take out my house keys from my bag and unlock the front door. I hear a car door shut, then footsteps behind me. I turn around. Two police officers.

"Are you Charlotte Wilson?"

My heart pounds.

"Yes?"

"We're very sorry to tell you that your husband, Sam, has gone missing."

I can barely hear the rest of their words, it's all a blur, but what is clear is that they don't think he's alive.

Sam is missing, presumed dead.

And with that news, I feel my whole life crumbling. New leaf or no new leaf.

7

SAM WAS WRONG. WHEN I SPOKE TO THE RECRUIT-
ment agencies, they doubted I'd find a position on board a
ship so quickly.

But I didn't have time to spare. I had to be with him. We
spoke every day and exchanged hundreds of messages.

"I promise I'll do whatever it takes," I said during one of
our chats.

He had been unable to hide the disappointment in his voice
when I told him that it was taking time.

"I'm relying on you to make sure we're together as soon as
possible," he said.

"There was one position for a couple…" I said. "But it was
in the Mediterranean and it was for a chef and a chief steward
on board a smaller ship."

"I am a croupier," said Sam. "It's what I excel at. Desperate
as I am for us to be together, I'm afraid I can't give that up."

I got it. His job was who he was.

"How did you get into that line of work, anyway?"

"I always wanted to be a croupier, as soon as I was old

enough to know that such a job existed. My father would have friends around on a Sunday evening and they would play poker into the early hours. Initially, I would sneak downstairs and listen in, but when I was older, I was allowed to stay up later. I watched and learned."

"Sounds almost idyllic."

"It was. It was like a scene out of a movie. Dad and his mates, surrounded by smoke, the smell of whiskey and beer. The excitement, the fear when someone was losing, the fake bravado, the camaraderie. I learned to read people and I got really good at guessing who was bluffing and who wasn't."

I loved hearing the passion in his voice. I almost envied him being so sure of what he wanted to do in life. I had wanted to be a vet. But we could barely afford a pet dog, let alone expect my mom to find enough money for me to study veterinary medicine.

I encouraged Sam to continue, to tell me more.

"It was a big event in our house," he said. "Every Friday, Dad would take the kitty money and spend it on supplies for the Sunday evening—the drink, the cigarettes, the snacks. If there was any money left over, I would be allowed to buy something for myself. I used to buy sweets, fizzy drinks, all the usual, until I realized that if I saved up a little, I could buy something better. But all I really wanted was playing cards. The first-ever pack of cards I bought myself stands out as one of the best days of my life. The newness, their shiny, pristine condition, the sheer possibility that lived among those cards. It's hard to describe my joy."

"You're doing a good job," I said. "I love hearing this."

"What did you want to be?" he said.

"I love animals," I said. I explained about my desire to be a vet. "But," I continued, "I had to start earning as soon as I could. Money was tight after my father passed away, and my sister, Louise, who is five years older than me, started work when she was sixteen." I paused, wondering how to word the next part without sounding ungrateful, but then I thought, *So what?* Sam and I were baring our souls; there was no reason not to be truthful. "Louise and I have a complicated relationship. She partly brought me up when our mother first fell ill, but we're not close. She rarely gets in touch unless it's to ask to borrow money. Or if she wants to moan about Drew, her partner, and my first-ever proper boyfriend, whom she stole from me."

"Wow. Sounds pretty unforgivable."

"I tried to forgive her because she's my only family, and I would have been successful had Drew not become a permanent fixture and father to her four children. I find it hard to listen to anything he says, so I try to visit only when he is out—which is frequently, from what I gather—or at work, which I suspect is infrequently."

One thing we both agreed on—neither of us wanted children. I loved all my nieces and nephews in different ways but that was as far as it went. Sam and I agreed we were too self-absorbed. I liked that about us, that we could so openly admit to our faults.

In the meantime, the two of us being together was our number one priority. And that meant a job. A couple of vacancies on board Sam's latest ship came up, one being a florist and the other being a wardrobe supervisor. Neither of which I was qualified for.

"Does it matter?" Sam said when we spoke. "Just fill in the application form, so that we can be together. That's the most important thing. How hard can it be to arrange a few flowers or keep some stage costumes tidy?"

"I don't want to lie," I said.

"Then it will take longer." He sounded crushed. "It's not lying, anyway. Everyone is creative when it comes to résumés."

"I guess."

After that, doubt haunted me. I applied for jobs in sales and excursions, on the front desk and even as a childcare assistant. I took a silver-service course and other online courses that promised they would be able to fast-track me to the job of my dreams.

After four long months with no firm job offer in sight, Sam spoke to a friend—and I was offered a retail position in one of the boutiques on the same ship as him.

I landed in Nassau, expecting Sam to be waiting for me, partly like the famous scene in *An Officer and a Gentleman* but at the port instead, obviously. The reality was different. I didn't see Sam for nearly forty-eight hours after boarding the cruise ship because our shifts clashed. It was immediately clear that I was there to work, not play. I expected that, I wasn't naive and was grateful for the job, but it was still a rude awakening to have zero time to recover from my jet lag and to find my feet with the new job.

The job was an eye-opener. Passengers would spend thousands of dollars on handbags, shoes, accessories or jewelry and designer gifts without even asking the price. I spent a lot of time back and forth in the stockroom, fetching, carrying, tidying and cleaning.

Our eventual reunion was rushed, as we only had an hour before Sam's cabinmate was due to come off his shift. Sam and I rarely saw each other. We had separate cabins. He shared with two other men and I shared with a woman named Ingrid, who worked in the art gallery. Ingrid didn't appear to like me. At first, I didn't know why until she snapped one evening.

"My friend should have had your job. It's all right for you, having someone put in a good word. It's not fair."

After that, we avoided each other as much as possible, which was hard, given the close proximity of our living arrangements. I told Sam about Ingrid and that I felt bad that he had spoken to a friend to secure me the position.

"Don't worry about Ingrid," he said. "Or anything that anyone else ever says. We're together, that's what matters."

"Except we're not."

Our time alone was brief and stolen, always listening out for the return of Ingrid or his bunkmates. I was lonely. Horribly lonely, surrounded by strangers all day, alone in my cabin pretending to read when Ingrid was there, too, or walking around the ship aimlessly. At first, the ship felt massive—colossal—but after a while, familiarity made it shrink. I felt claustrophobic. There was no natural light below the waterline, no porthole, certainly no balcony, no fresh air. The cabin was barely big enough for one, let alone for two people who didn't get along. I had to walk along dimly lit corridors with visible pipework. It was like living in the dungeons. Alone, if I let my mind wander—which it frequently did—I could conjure up all sorts of terrible fates down there where no one could hear my screams above the noise and vibrations. It most certainly wasn't what I'd envisaged and I told Sam so.

Sam promised it would get better.

"Trust me," he said.

He listened when I told stories about some of the customers. There was this one woman who expected me to force her feet into shoes a size too small.

"As I knelt down on the ground, I told her I couldn't do it. That it wasn't a good idea. She told me to try harder! Honestly, her feet smelled of talcum powder and Lord knows what else, and it started making me feel sick. I looked up at her cross face and all I could see was a brooch the color of blood and these too-chunky gold rings squashed onto her fingers and it made me mad. Like—how come someone like her gets to treat someone like me as if I'm her personal assistant? She bought the too-small shoes and handed me her old ones, which were brand-new. To discard."

I paused for breath. Sam looked distracted. I was turning into a misery. It wasn't the real me, so I made more of an effort to look for the positive in my days. The pleasant customers, the ones who bought me little gifts and thanked me for helping them choose items. Still, I couldn't help longing for more. Sam and I would lie together in the darkness whenever it was possible for us to be alone, usually by Sam bribing or begging his cabinmates, and make plans for our future: better jobs, fewer hours, more time off on beautiful islands. Sam promised me that it wouldn't be like this for much longer.

"I love you, Lola," he said. "I was just drifting along in life before I met you."

I knew that his ex-girlfriends had all moved on, to other ships, to different countries, to a life on land. No one could stand the lifestyle as long as he. I was different. I wasn't going to abandon him because things weren't yet perfect.

"I love being away at sea. I couldn't bear the thought of being stuck in one place. That's why I'm so glad you feel the same."

I did feel the same. I didn't want to be one of the people who settled for just anything.

One evening, Sam announced that he had a surprise planned when we had rare time off together. We'd been looking forward to it for weeks—nearly a whole day in Falmouth, Jamaica.

The ship docked early morning. I imagined us finding a

secluded beach where we would be hidden away—God, I wanted a break from crowds—but what he had planned was even better.

In the garden of a luxury hotel, he ordered me a Buck's fizz and asked me to wait for him. As I sipped, my neck and back stopped aching, the side effects of all the physical work, and I listened to the birds. I noticed—properly noticed—the colors of the flowers, the rich green of the grass and the beach with the sand freshly raked. My eyes closed as it suddenly all felt worth it.

"Lola," said Sam, gently. I looked up. "Come with me."

He took me by the hand and led me along the grass. The sun was baking hot even though the day had barely begun. We walked around the side of the hotel, behind a hedge and leafy green plants toward a secluded private plunge pool and a small patio area with two loungers and a table. Glass doors stood open, organza curtains floating gently in the breeze.

Inside, a single stem of rich pink orchids rested on the bed, beside towel art in the shape of a heart. A silver ice bucket containing a frosted bottle of champagne rested on a small table in the center of the room. Opera—I think it was *Madame Butterfly*—played in the background.

"Oh. My. God," I said. "This is amazing."

"We have to take our moments where we can," Sam said. "I promise, you'll have the best life with me."

I believed him.

I walked around the suite, brushing my fingers along the sofas, picking up ornaments. This was real. Space, light, luxury. All because of Sam. The misgivings I'd had about my job, our lack of time together, dissolved.

He poured us two chilled glasses of champagne.

"Let's go to the pool," he said, handing mine over.

"I didn't bring a bikini."

"You don't need one," said Sam. "The pool is for sole use of the guests occupying this suite."

I stepped into the pool behind Sam, quickly, self-consciously, breathing in as I adjusted to the cold water. I glanced around nervously, but we were hidden beneath a canopy of plants. It really was just us, finally.

"Cheers." We clinked glasses. "To us."

As the bubbles dissolved on my tongue and the alcohol hit my empty stomach, all my inhibitions lifted. This was the life.

"Just remember, Lola," Sam said afterward as we were lying on our backs, drying out on the sun loungers. "We could live like this, all the time, if we want it badly enough. This is just a taste."

He sat up, leaned over and reached into his backpack, took out a small jewelry box and handed it to me. I sat up, too, facing him.

"A keepsake," he announced. "Open it."

Inside, a ruby brooch. A flower, its circular dark red center surrounded with delicate diamond petals. A brooch was not something I had ever thought I wanted, but receiving it as a gift from Sam, touching the smoothness of the stone and marveling at the perfection in its colors, I changed my mind.

"It's vintage designer," he said. "I'm so pleased you like it."

"I love it." I looked up into his face. "Where did you get it? You've already spent a fortune on today."

"I have friends who can get good deals," he said. "But be discreet about wearing it. There are a lot of green-eyed monsters on board." I remembered the woman who'd handed him a package. "I don't want to draw attention."

I went and sat beside him. He placed a hand in my damp hair and pulled me into him. We kissed. His skin was smooth and fresh, tinged with chlorine. His breath tasted of champagne. Sun burned on my back, but I was barely aware. The rest of the world didn't exist. Even then, I think I somehow sensed that time would never be on our side, that we would always have to make the good moments burn brightly.

Afterward, we lay entwined, dozing, happy. Beside us, the empty bottle and glasses rested on the ground among our discarded clothes. I could've stayed there, happily, forever, but there was a knock on the main door. Sam leaped up from his lounger.

"Get dressed!" he said, throwing a towel over me.

I quickly pulled on my underwear, scrambled into my crumpled dress and did up the strap on my sandals. I ran my fingers through my hair and picked up my bag, dropping the brooch inside. Sam was already in his shorts and T-shirt, wearing one of his favorite navy caps.

"Put on your sunglasses," he said, taking my hand.

"What's going on?"

"Trust me," he said. "Walk casually."

He snaked his arm around my waist and kissed me. Then we walked out the same way we came in, past the hedge and toward the hotel entrance. A security guard was speaking into a walkie-talkie.

"On second thought, walk a little faster," said Sam.

He guided me out into the street, where he hailed a cab and named a beach several miles away. As we sank into the back seat, my heart was pounding.

We retreated to a beach café, ordering crab and mussels. I also ordered a large gin and tonic. As we ate, I asked him a question I didn't really want the answer to.

"You never paid for that suite, did you?"

He looked amused. "Did you enjoy yourself?"

I couldn't help grinning. "You know I did."

"Well, then…" He shrugged as he scooped a mussel out of its shell and swallowed it greedily. He wiped his mouth with a linen napkin. "Some guests check out early. Shame to waste an opportunity. The hotel cleaning staff had no qualms about letting me into 'our' room when I explained that we had already checked out but had forgotten something. I did an impressive spruce up, I think you'll agree?"

He looked at me, gauging my reaction. I sensed that I was being tested.

"Have you done it before?" I asked.

"No. But I've been planning it for days in my head. I wanted us to be alone. I wanted to make you happy. What we had this morning was magical."

It was intoxicating. That's the thing. I always felt confused and conflicted when it came to Sam and his schemes. Yet there was also no denying that I had crossed a line. I was both secretly thrilled and appalled.

"The orchid stem? The champagne?" I asked, already knowing the answer.

"Taken from a vase in reception. Then, the minibar."

"Someone else will get charged for that," I said.

He shrugged again. "They'll dispute it. No harm will be done."

I mulled this over. I felt conflicted, but I didn't want to burst the happy bubble.

"And this?" I said, taking the brooch out of my bag, now realizing that I had seen it before.

"A gift in lieu of a tip."

"And you regifted it to me? The shoe lady is a gambler?"

"Was. She disembarked this morning. She has a flight back to California."

"I don't know what to say."

True. I felt disappointed that he hadn't bought the flower brooch, and yet…there was something undeniably alluring about the fact that he had truly listened while I was complaining about the very job that he had pulled strings to get me. He tried to choose a gift that I would like, and with thousands of guests on board the ship, it couldn't have been easy to identify the shoe lady. I love presents. After the disappointment of rarely getting what I wanted for Christmas as a child, to meet someone as giving as Sam was thrilling.

Sam took the brooch from me, leaned forward and pinned it to my dress.

"How do you feel?" he said.

"Like a million dollars." True.

"I can teach you more about the value of particular types of jewelry, if you would like me to. What's worth investing in, what isn't. Over the years, I've picked up a few tips."

Life in that moment felt like ours for the taking.

The day got better. My cabin was finally free of Ingrid and her belongings. She had jumped ship, rumor had it. Boyfriend troubles.

Sam and I had a space to call our own, at least temporarily. We didn't waste any time making the most of it—Sam pretended to be too ill to work his shift that first night.

My life was falling into place.

"This is starting to feel a bit more like it," I said.

"I told you the bad times wouldn't last," said Sam. "I have a lot of plans for the two of us. Trust me."

I did. He had opened my eyes, brought me to life, and it was hard to look back. Although, I did try. I feel it's important to note that.

8

NOW

I AM SITTING ON THE SOFA IN LEWIS'S LIVING ROOM,
opposite two police officers. Lewis sits beside me and intermittently pats or strokes my hand, awkwardly. I can't believe that
Sam is missing, presumed dead. That isn't how it is worded
but I am certain it is how it's meant to be interpreted.

"But I only heard from him a few days ago," I say.

One of the officers seems particularly interested because he
leans forward slightly.

"When was that exactly?"

Damn.

My cheeks feel hot at the thought of the memory stick beneath my pillow. I need to get a grip.

"He called me, several times," I say. "I tried calling him
back, but his phone appeared to be disconnected."

According to the officer sitting directly opposite me, Sam
was reported missing by Penny, his girlfriend. She went to
meet him at his house and there was no sign of him. His
phone, laptop and wallet were also nowhere to be found.

"He carried his backpack containing his valuables everywhere," I say. "Where has he gone missing?" I add.

A horrible thought suddenly crosses my mind. If Sam isn't found, it could take up to seven years by law for him to be declared dead. I push away those thoughts, hoping that guilt doesn't show on my face. My mind conjures up the South of France, Spain or an unnamed exotic island, sapphire-like, glinting seas, palm trees, treasure chests, sharks circling...

"Devon."

He names a village. Oh. My. God. My world tilts. Like seasickness. It is the place where Sam and I bought our "forever" home. It is remote, the cliffs are steep (as cliffs are). In darkness, in bad weather, even just in the winter months, it is perilous.

"Do you think he might really be dead?" I ask.

"There's no sign of a body, but Sam hasn't used his phone or bank cards, nor been seen anywhere, for a couple of days. According to his girlfriend, his distinctive Dolce & Gabbana jacket was found nearby snagged on a rock jutting out of the sea."

I bought that for him the first time we visited England and Sam forgot to bring anything warm enough.

"Where were they staying?" I ask.

"At your address in Devon."

"But we have tenants," I say.

"According to his girlfriend, they were away and had given Mr. Young permission to use the property in their absence."

Like hell they did. Sam has been up to his old tricks.

I hate the thought of strangers trudging through my haven. Although, if Sam is actually dead, the property now belongs solely to me. I'll be much better off than when he was alive. But under these circumstances, that isn't necessarily a good thing.

The voices continue. "So, you haven't seen him recently?"

"To be honest, I thought he was in Mexico," I say. There is no harm in admitting that. "I was curious as to why he was suddenly getting in touch. We are estranged, obviously."

I want to distance myself from Sam as much as possible.

Lewis lets go of my hand and I'm aware of him shifting slightly next to me. "What about that newspaper clipping?" he asks.

"I don't think it's related," I say quickly.

But, of course, the police aren't going to let me get away with that. I am forced to retrieve it and hand the picture of the sapphire seashell bracelet over for inspection.

"You don't know what this was about?"

I tell them the same thing that I told Lewis.

"It was an ex-girlfriend of Sam's bracelet. There was a misunderstanding. The bracelet went missing the day after that photo was taken, so I'm pretty sure she took it. She wasn't happy about our marriage. She gate-crashed our wedding day, made all sorts of accusations. None of which were true."

"And her name was…?"

"Ingrid," I say, reluctantly.

I didn't put two and two together at the right time. No wonder Ingrid hated me. And the sheer arrogance of Sam knowing he would get away with it makes me feel murderous. I dread to think what he told Ingrid about me to keep her quiet. Or what he threatened her with.

I must look pale or shaky because I am asked if I need water. I shake my head. I am trying to digest everything. I stick to the story: I don't know why anyone would want to harm Sam.

Untrue.

"Do you have Ingrid's details?"

"No," I say.

I am asked when I last saw him, if he had suffered from depression or had been distressed over our breakup.

I resist the urge to say, "Do you really want to know what that bastard did to me? The last time I saw him, he was leaving me behind in Barbados. He most definitely was not distressed over our breakup. Quite the opposite."

Instead, I press for more details of what happened to Sam. His girlfriend said the property was unlocked but empty. No sign of Sam. The kettle wasn't warm, the heating hadn't been on. There was nothing in the fridge. No car. She waited and waited until she raised the alarm earlier today. I shiver. The sea is deep and rocky and treacherous in that area. It's easy to get disoriented, especially in the dark. Especially if Sam was trying to hide from someone.

"Did Sam seem depressed from his most recent messages?"

"I wouldn't know. What about his girlfriend? Wouldn't she know better than me? Sam and I have been split up for a while."

"Yet not divorced?"

Unfortunately not.

"Like I said, he was in Mexico. It made things more complicated." I pause. "How is his girlfriend?" I'm trying to shine the attention back on her.

"She is being reassured and looked after by her family."

"Did they have an argument?" I persist. "I'm wondering if she is a suspect?"

"She is a witness."

It doesn't answer my question but I don't want them spending too much time on me.

"Sam had a temper," says Lewis.

I wish he wasn't here. He isn't helping.

"I should offer you some tea or coffee," I say, hoping that Lewis will take the hint and make it for them.

"No, thanks," both officers say simultaneously.

I hope it means that they won't be here much longer.

"Was he ever violent toward you?"

"No," I lie.

Silence.

"It doesn't make any sense," I say. True. "Sam wasn't stupid." Also true. "He was experienced in sea life. He wouldn't have gone near a cliff edge in the dark and the rain."

I stop. Had it rained recently? Yes. I remember seeing the drops beneath the Narnia lamp.

"He was a croupier," I add, as though that explains something.

The police officers look at me. I can't remember what they said their names were. Their impassive expressions suggest that they are mentally studying me to see if I give anything away. Good luck to them. I spent years walking through customs not attracting suspicion. Sam helped me to perfect my poker face.

Yet I can't help picturing the scene. I know from man-overboard drills that if Sam did go over a cliff into the sea, the odds are against survival, however much I used to try to reassure passengers that the crew would do everything they could, should the worst happen. *"Just don't try to climb the railings,"* I would always advise. *"Especially after a cocktail or two."* *Ha ha* type of thing.

The reality was that unless someone saw a person fall in (preferably in daylight, of course), it would be nearly impossible for rescuers to locate the right spot—even with a floating dummy.

"I'm really sorry that I can't be of more help," I say now. "If I could think of something useful to add, I would." Untrue.

I know a lot that I can never tell.

After the police leave, with a promise to keep me informed that feels more like a threat than a goodbye line, I feel…numb.

The truth is I never wished Sam any harm. I just wanted him to go away. Wanted him to pay me what he owed and to find gradual disillusionment with someone else. Someone who was a match for him, someone who would keep him in line. I wanted him to be someone else's problem. We made a big mistake. We tried to tame each other. It was never going to work.

I accept the glass of vodka that Lewis hands me and down it, the burning sensation in my throat giving way to the warmth of numbness. He drinks his quickly, too, and pours us another.

"Oh my God," says Lewis. "That was unreal. I am sorry about Sam, though. How are you feeling? It must all be a real shock."

I wish I could tell Lewis the truth, what I'm truly afraid of. But I can't for fear of seeing the shock in his eyes. Of losing my oldest friend.

He stays up late with me, dissecting the news. Sam has hundreds of online friends. His posts were always fake. Still, I click on the comments.

Mate, get in touch. Let us know you are safe.

Thoughts and prayers.

Anyone up for setting up an independent search party?

I find his girlfriend, Penny. She has posted a picture of a broken heart and has been inundated with comments of love and support. She kind of looks like Ingrid, but Sam…he never had a type.

No one mentions me, which is good. Sometimes, I wonder how many people even knew Sam had a wife. I search for Ingrid but cannot find any matching profiles. I do another search for Alexandra while I'm at it. Again, nothing new.

Lewis offers words of comfort and advice, unaware that there is nothing he can say or do to help me. He has no idea that I do not want the police digging into Sam's past. The very thought fills me with terror.

I pretend to be fine. Lying to Lewis does not make me feel good about myself.

Although he may not know everything about me, he does understand the pain of disadvantage. He gets what it must have felt like not to be able to see properly as a child whenever my glasses broke, or were deliberately broken. I don't need to explain the agony of picking up bent metal frames from the playground, knowing that I would have to deal with the vulnerability of semiblindness. Okay, maybe that's a bit dramatic, but that's what it felt like at the time—until they were mended or on the rare occasion I got a new pair. I didn't want to cause my mother any stress. I wasn't sure what it was, but I knew that stress was bad.

Lewis's thing was soggy socks when the holes in his shoes grew so large that the cardboard patches leaked.

The sheer joy of being able to buy new items will never leave me.

At midnight, I try calling Sam again. I don't believe for a second that he is dead. I don't believe he went over the side of a cliff. I believe he did it on purpose to hide from Whoever It Is, to throw them off the scent. Or, even worse, to send them my way. If I'm gone, there are no witnesses to what we did. No one who can spill the beans about Sam's true nature.

My thoughts scatter in an explosion of catastrophic scenarios: prison, death, a life on the run. Maybe I left it too late for any intended new leaf.

Sam is out there, somewhere, reinventing himself. I'm sure of it. If it has got that bad, then he will want me to take sole blame. But he has made an error. I am not the woman he married.

Utterly exhausted, I finally give in to sleep.

When I come around, it is to the familiar early-morning traffic noises, which, on the whole, are pretty universal unless I'm out at sea. A pang of homesickness permeates my consciousness. The sounds of being on land are a constant reminder of all I have lost.

There's no hiding from the truth. I have been in constant denial as I have tried to readjust, lying to myself and telling myself that this life is fine. Every time I have to change my own bedding, put out the trash, go to a supermarket, travel to work, decide what to wear, clean, do admin, deal with the mundane necessities to make my life merely livable—then I realize how perfect I had it. Even the bad bits. Being at sea meant not having to deal with anything. I need a better plan because my values ebb and flow according to the level of danger I am in.

Unwelcome memories from yesterday flood back. My phone rings. Unknown number.

"Hello?"

Silence.

Just as I'm about to hang up, I hear a deep voice.

"You haven't responded to my request."

"Who is this? What are you talking about?"

"Blood money," says a robotic, distorted voice. "Haven't you ever heard of retributive justice?"

Icy fear forms in the pit of my stomach.

"Wrong number," I say as I disconnect, but not before I hear the voice say: "An eye for an eye."

I don't like the sound of retributive justice, which is clearly the point. It conjures up all sorts of horrible, violent images.

The call disconnects. Hands shaking, I call Sam again. No ringtone, nothing. It is as if he truly has disappeared, leaving me to fend for myself.

My phone rings again. My hands are still shaking as I pick it up to tell Whoever It Is to leave me alone, but it is my sister, Louise. Relief.

I tell her about my visit from the police as a distraction. Louise never met Sam but said that he sounded like a snake. She would know. Upon my return, I was cagey about why we had split up, but she said that it had all sounded like a true case of "Marry in haste, repent at leisure." Again, she would know. She is stuck with Deceitful Drew.

"There was a plant left here for you," she says. "On my doorstep."

"A plant?"

"Yes. There's a card addressed to you. Shall I open it?"

"Okay," I say, even though I have a bad feeling about it.

"'No place to hide,'" Louise reads out. "Strange. It doesn't say who it's from. It's an expensive-looking potted plant, though," she adds. "I'll send you a picture. Wait…"

I open the photo. My screen fills with the magenta and pale pinks of an orchid. The exact type Sam used to buy me as an apology when he had done something wrong or had something to hide.

9

SAM PULLED MORE STRINGS BY USING HIS ANONY-
mous contacts and we transferred to a different ship, one that
was less than two years old. My position was still in retail, this
time in the largest gift shop. Nearly five thousand passengers
were on board by the time we left Southampton for the Caribbean. The decor gleamed. Slate and silver dominated, but
it didn't feel dark or oppressive. The furniture still smelled
newish and fresh. All the staff seemed to take extra pride. We
had our own cabin—a rarity, and a relative luxury, despite the
bunk beds. Sam knew some of the staff, and he'd arranged for
us to accidentally sneak into unoccupied suites. Strictly forbidden, a fireable offence—utterly addictive.

The penthouse suite, with its split-level living space and
floor-to-ceiling windows with endless ocean views, was my
favorite. We would swing in the hammock chairs on the balcony, sunbathing or drinking coffee at sunrise. Sam and I also
loved sitting in the Jacuzzi, drinking fine reds or port while
planning our future. We would dream of owning our own

yacht, hiring our own staff, the world really, truly, being our oyster.

Although it wasn't ideal, not yet, we had each other. But even then, I should have known that it wouldn't be enough for Sam. Nothing ever was. So when he took his petty schemes to the next level, I shouldn't have been surprised. But somehow, I still was. That's the thing I don't always take into account when I look back: Sam's timing was impeccable. He always knew exactly when to push us to the next stage. Actually, that's not entirely true. He knew exactly when to push *me*.

"There's this woman…" he said, late one night.

At first, I wasn't sure if I had heard him correctly above the noise of the water jets.

I couldn't see the horizon. It was dark, but we had the patio doors open, so I could still sense the vastness. Sometimes, lying with my eyes closed, warm water bubbling around me, alcohol relaxing my mind, I would imagine the ocean below us. I would picture the world unfolding in my mind—the different types of fish, coral, dancing green and blue seaweed, sharks seeking prey, crabs skittering across the seabed.

Sam's words crashed into my dreams.

"Her name is Betty," Sam continued. "Her husband, Jim, he seems like a nice man. He was in a car accident several years back and has trouble walking off the beaten track, so to speak. We were all chatting in the casino last night and I offered to take Betty sightseeing in Aruba tomorrow. She loved the idea. You're down to work all morning, but how about you offer to take Jim to the game room and play cards with him in the afternoon?"

"Why don't I join you and Betty?"

A flicker of annoyance crossed his expression before he smiled at me.

"Because she feels bad about leaving Jim. She's fed up with en-masse guided tours on her own. I thought I could take her. She's keen on the donkey sanctuary and the butterfly farm."

"Is she, now?"

"Don't be like that," he said. "They are loaded—the real deal. We'll be helping them out and they'll be appreciative when it comes to cash tips at the end of their cruise. Think of the money. Think of our future."

"I just have a bad feeling about it," I said. Sam took my champagne glass from me, placed it on the side. Then he kissed me.

"Trust me," he said. "I'm doing this for us. We have talked about this. There's no way we can earn enough between us to set up on our own unless we have the odd harmless sideline or two. We're not hurting anyone. We're not doing anything wrong. Jim is a nice man, seems really interesting. What's the harm in keeping him company over a game of canasta?"

"What? Just me and him? I get little enough downtime as it is."

Sam always had one of two strategies. He either embellished details or oversimplified them. There was rarely a middle ground.

I broke away from him, stepped out of the Jacuzzi and began to towel myself dry. We always brought our own towels from our cabin. We had got into a routine. Sam's friends would be understandably annoyed if the rooms were left anything other than pristine. He had an agreement with them (among the many agreements and arrangements Sam made with people): he usually brought a small towel to wipe down the Jacuzzi or any marks we had left on any surfaces; we would wash up the glasses, put them away and take away our own bottles of fizz or wine, or whatever we had brought. Sam's secret skill was towel art—he would often remodel the ones on the bed or by the side of the bathtub. No one else ever knew we'd been there.

After Sam had dried himself and dressed, he took out his phone and began tapping while I cleared up. I hated it. I hated having to wipe away all evidence of my existence.

After sneaking out, back to our own cabin, discontent took hold. It felt like a comedown with nothing tangible to immediately look forward to. Our cabin, despite our best efforts, was dark and poky, but at least we had his-and-hers bathrobes, a memento Sam had taken from the hotel in Jamaica. They took up too much of our limited space, but it was the little touches in our cabin that made things bearable. Sam would bring flowers or place chocolates on my pillow, replace the toiletries in our bathroom with the more luxurious guest ones. It made our lives feel less about work and more holiday-like. Until then.

It turned out Sam was right. Jim was at least interesting. We met in the game room. I nearly didn't turn up but I felt guilty at the thought of just abandoning him while his wife was off seeing the sights. Jim had traveled widely. We shared stories of our favorite places. Mine was Italy; his was Japan. I mentally added Tokyo to my ever-growing wish list as we played gin rummy. He wasn't the best card player, and although I let him win occasionally, it was nice to not always lose. My mind kept drifting to Sam and what he was up to. I could picture him making Betty laugh.

Sam always played to win, was aggressive and merciless. Once, when I was getting close to winning, he pretended to lose interest in the game. He had pushed the cards off our bunk, so that they mixed up on the floor, all under the pretense that he desired me so greatly, that he couldn't wait a moment longer to undress me. I went along with it, that time. I accepted his inability to lose as a character quirk. Maybe I let too many of the little things slide in the beginning. Perhaps that was my mistake.

"He seems like a nice young man, Sam," said Jim, as if he had sensed my distraction. "Very persuasive. Do you often spend your free time with guests?"

"It depends," I said, unsure how to respond.

I glanced at my phone. Still no messages from Sam.

"They're late," Jim said after checking his own phone. "Why don't you come back to our suite for afternoon tea? I'll order it for four. By the time the tea arrives, they'll be back."

"I can't accept, I'm afraid," I said. "We're not supposed to visit guest cabins."

Jim looked surprised.

"But Sam came in for a tipple of cognac last night."

News to me. I stayed silent. I hated being put in this position.

Jim, sensing my discomfort, didn't push the issue.

"I'll walk back to the suite with you," I said. "But then I must head off."

I wanted to get off the ship, stretch my legs on land. And phone Sam.

I walked slowly along the corridor with Jim. As he reached into his pocket for his key card, the door opened and Sam stepped out.

"Hello!" he said. "I was just on my way to find you both."

But it was Betty, framed in the doorway, who caught my attention. Her expression was pure cat that got the shagging cream. A sickness that I hadn't experienced since Deceitful Drew cheated on me with my own sister knotted my insides.

I couldn't look Jim in the eye. I quickly said goodbye and walked away as fast as I could, back to our cabin.

Sam followed.

"What's up?" he said.

"You must think I was born yesterday," I shouted as he shut the door behind him.

"Don't you want the best for us?" he said.

"Naturally," I replied. "But I don't see how other women are best for us!"

He put his arms out to calm me, but I lashed out, my nails scratching him.

"You've got totally the wrong idea," he said. "I'm not Drew."

A low blow.

"I know what I saw."

"No, you don't."

Sam denied, denied, denied, so much so that I began to doubt myself. Still, that evening, I slept on the top bunk, and he stayed on the bottom.

Over the next days and weeks, we both worked hard on different shift patterns. The slinking off to unoccupied suites ground to a halt, as did the gifts of chocolates and flowers.

Betty was a smoker. Sam and I enjoyed the occasional one, too, and I found an engraved silver lighter *To Darling Betty* in his beside drawer. Another gift. I could just imagine what she'd said to Sam when he'd borrowed it—*"Keep it, I have loads. Something to remember me by."* I resisted the urge to hurl it into the ocean, but instead hid it away. There wasn't anything Sam could say to accuse me, after all. It should never have been in our cabin.

But then things changed again. One evening, I came back

to our cabin to discover a bouquet of orchids on my pillow, along with a small neatly wrapped gift. I untied the ribbon. Inside was a pair of dainty diamond earrings. I recognized them; they had been bought in the gift shop only a few days ago by a woman with long red hair. I remember because she appeared to value my opinion on which pair she'd selected.

"Joanne is a friend of mine," Sam said when I asked him about them. It turned out that she'd been the mystery shopper—the woman with the long red hair. "I asked her to help me choose something you'd love. I want this unpleasantness between us to end."

"And Betty?"

"Long gone. They disembarked in the Dominican Republic. I wish you would believe me and trust me a bit more. That was a mistake. I'll never go to anyone's cabin alone again."

He helped place the earrings in my ears. I felt a sharp stab as they dug into my lobes because I hadn't worn earrings in a long while. I looked in the mirror and liked what I saw. I loved how they made me feel. There was something transformative about jewelry, something so delightfully decadent about wearing things that cost so much.

"You're beautiful," Sam said, kissing my throat. "Wear them tonight. I'm taking you for dinner."

We docked in Haiti that day. He'd booked us a table at a hotel restaurant. It was all white tablecloths, flickering candles and roses. We ate from a charcuterie board: cheese, meat, pomegranates, melons, grapes. Our wine was an expensive pinot noir.

"Let's make plans," he said. "Ones you are happy with. How would you feel about teaching yoga one-on-one, say, on the beaches when we dock? Or reading tarot cards? You could befriend passengers, too, offer to take guests to the various markets to ensure they don't get ripped off. I could teach people the tricks of the gambling trade." He took my hands. "There's loads we can do if we're discreet, bold and imaginative enough."

"My yoga knowledge is fairly basic," I said. "And I've never even had a tarot reading, let alone given one."

That was the thing with Sam—his enthusiasm was infectious no matter how outlandish his ideas were. I got caught up in them without stopping to *think*.

"You can learn." He squeezed my hands. "I have every faith in you."

I laughed. The wine had gone to my head, and I began to recite an imaginary tarot-card reading. "You will meet a tall, dark, handsome stranger," I intoned, dreamy-eyed. "You will win the lottery."

"That's the spirit." Sam laughed too. "But I would go more along the lines of, 'You will donate more of your time and money to charitable works, you will benefit greatly from helping those less fortunate.'"

"Seriously, though." I had to admit, I was curious. "How would it all work?"

I had visions of some of the crew having a thing or two to say if they caught wind of our scams.

Scams. The subtle shift in my terminology was maybe the beginning of my acceptance, the understanding of what I was agreeing to, of what I was becoming. This probably would have been a good point to challenge Sam's ideas more. Hindsight isn't very helpful, in my opinion, because there's no going back. That's what frustrates me now, that I can't change who I was, what I did. What I wouldn't give sometimes never to have met Sam.

"We befriend the right people—people like Betty and

Jim—and take it from there. We find out what they want and offer it to them in a way they can't turn down. We make them feel special, that they are not simply guests for us to serve and keep happy for our paychecks. We make them believe that we genuinely like them. To be fair, I do like some of them."

I pushed thoughts of Betty from my mind. I didn't want to ruin the evening. I shouldn't have. I should have stayed rightfully angry. Things would have been very different.

That was when we came up with the idea. And so the stories began. We made some of them up over dessert and coffee, feeling creative and fun. It was a bit like Sam did with his customs declarations. Our jobs meant that we met so many people with different backgrounds and situations. We decided that we would mix and match the tales we'd heard from various crew and passengers (careful to protect identities, of course) because truth really was stranger than fiction.

After dinner, we walked hand in hand around the lit hotel gardens, beneath the palms and past pink, red and orange hibiscus as we made up our stories. When we caught a cab back to the ship, I had to admit to being just a little disappointed that Sam hadn't arranged any surprise suites or unexpected detours. Something was missing from our evening; I had got used to his unpredictability. I wasn't yet brave enough or creative enough to think of anything I could do myself to match Sam's flights of fancy. Instead, to comfort myself, I focused on our stories.

Story Number One:

Sam and I grew up in a religious commune. When we were older, we fell in love. Our birth families disapproved and separated us, putting us to work in different sections of the community. The other members, our friends, our extended family, all the people we had grown up among, were tasked with spying on us, in order to ensure that we stayed apart. We tried, but we couldn't. We truly believed that we were meant to be. However, it all went wrong when we were caught together, forcing us to flee in the early hours, on a dark winter's morning, with practically no belongings or money to call our own.

Passengers would always ask where this commune was. We changed its location depending on our mood.

An American desert somewhere. On the outskirts of a jungle. A rural area in Australia.

"It sounds like a cult, not a commune," they would say, just as they were meant to.

"Do you know what? You're right," we would reply. "It's funny you should say that..." And then we'd move seamlessly on to the second part of our story.

When we realized that we'd grown up in a cult, that we had been brainwashed (a gradual, but shocking revelation), we began learning how to live our lives anew. This was with the help of a kind couple who befriended us at a church / religious place / community support group. We owe them everything. We're trying to earn as much money as we can to send back to help others who have been in a similar situation as us. We also want to help our families escape, but sadly they would have to want to. We have had to live a life on the run to stop them forcing us back. Hence, our choice of jobs and nomadic lives. "It's hard to capture people who are always on the move."

I discovered that I was good at telling stories when Sam and I were reeling people in. I would study our audience's reactions, tailoring the beginning, middle and end to what they wanted or needed to hear. I thrived on entertaining them, giving them their money's worth. It seemed a fair exchange. They got something in return for any inconvenience.

This is the short version, naturally. What Sam taught me is that you can't make people believe what they don't actually want to believe. If you tell the story right, they want to give you money. They want to help. Genuinely. And help us they did. Sam was creative with the funds—part cash, part paid directly into an account "for the benefit of others." We didn't tell total lies—we did donate some of the money. In fact, it was pretty easy to convince myself that not only were we not doing any wrong, but we were doing good. We never coerced anyone. We had rules and codes of conduct. One of them was perfectly simple to follow—that people only ever gave of their own accord.

"I have learned that people generally trust a man in a tailored suit." Sam grinned. "I can say or do almost anything I like."

Arrogant, but true nonetheless.

I can't think of a better way to describe Sam than handsome. And when he was dressed for work, when he turned on the charm, men and women alike would be drawn to whichever table he was at. In the casino, he always received generous tips. Passengers would ask if they could have their photo taken with him. There must be hundreds of happy photos of Sam out there in the world, showing him sandwiched between happy guests.

Our mutual endeavors soon injected a new lease on life into our relationship. At the end of our contracts, we arranged a flight to London. Sam wanted me to meet his father and I wanted him to meet Lewis.

Sam insisted on forking out for business class because he claimed he was too tall to travel in economy. We were immediately upgraded to first class. At first, I didn't understand how he'd managed it. Upgrades simply didn't happen to people like me. All I know is that I spotted Sam having a discreet word with one of the cabin crew. But once we were up in the air, it all became clear.

After a lunch of crabmeat, roast chicken and half a bottle

of a white Bordeaux, I was about to settle down to a movie, when Sam removed my headphones.

"There's something I want to ask you," he said. Before I knew what was happening, he got down on one knee and presented me with a distinctive red-and-gold box. He opened it to reveal a stunning diamond engagement ring.

"Lola, Charlotte…will you marry me?"

"What a…surprise!"

It genuinely was. Sam and I had discussed marriage, but I'd imagined that it was a long way off, at least until we'd made our fortune. I loved him, of that there was no doubt. We were planning a great future together and I loved the idea that getting married would play a role in our amazing journey together.

Behind him, the crew clapped and took photos, poured champagne. The other passengers stopped whatever they were doing to offer their congratulations. A steward handed me a bouquet of red roses. The captain appeared with a map, highlighting in red marker the exact spot where we had just passed. He signed it with his name—*Captain Roy Downes*—and sketched a heart around a plane.

Among all the attention and congratulations, I realized that I'd never actually said yes. But then again, it never crossed my mind to say no either.

10

NOW

THESE DAYS, ORCHIDS GIVE ME THE CREEPS. MAYBE the person threatening me is not Alexandra or anyone similar. Maybe it was Sam all along. The orchids my sister received could be some kind of hint as to his whereabouts. Or then again, not. My mind goes back and forth, trying to figure it all out. Maybe Sam is dead. Maybe someone wants me to think that he is alive. But the orchids? No one else would know the significance. Sam and I were careful what we posted online. We were bland and safe, deliberately dull.

I phone Sam's father, George. There is no reply. I leave a guarded message on his answering machine—I only have his landline number. It's difficult to phrase the message; I don't want to give false hope or have him think that I know for a fact that Sam is alive, or where he is. Then again, for all I know, he could be lying low because he knows exactly where Sam is. Maybe Sam is hiding in a garden shed or a loft? Any number of possibilities scroll through my mind. Perhaps George has absolutely no intention of speaking to me.

It makes me wonder. Where would I hide if I had to? Our

house in Devon, tenants aside, feels violated and no longer seems like an option. I feel fresh anger that Sam led the police and Lord knows who else to X marks the bloody spot. There is nothing incriminating because Sam and I barely lived there; we merely furnished it. But, still, it feels violating. Hidden away in boxes in the roof of the double garage are mementos—the ones I bought to remind myself of good times. His-and-hers aprons decorated with dainty orange crabs, their pincers curled benignly inward (Seattle, Megs and Jake). A sailboat inside a small bottle (Guadeloupe, Maggie and Colin). A glass vase, with pressed red, yellow and orange flowers in its base (Grenada, Natalia and Stan). A type of snow globe, with gold glitter for sand and sunlight on a brilliant blue beach (Martinique, Nico and Jenny).

An eye for an eye.

In an attempt to drive the words from my mind, to give myself space to *think*, I make the half-hour walk to Louise's house. I ring the bell. Ryan, her eldest son and my favorite nephew, clomps down the stairs behind his mother. He is tall and broad, with a huge smile. Louise had him in her early twenties. In fact, she was already pregnant with Ryan when I caught her and Drew entwined in his car in our street late one night. He'd told me that he was bowling with friends. (He hated bowling. It should have clicked there and then that something untoward was up.)

"Hey, Ryan," I say. "Too old for a hug from your favorite aunt?"

He makes a mock pretense of looking around and checking that none of his mates are in the street before he allows me to scoop him up in my arms. It's a ritual Ryan and I have repeated since he was about ten. Ryan is one of the people I care most about in the world; he is the child I will never have.

I opened a bank account in his name (he doesn't know) into which I paid large sums whenever I could. It will hopefully ensure that he has freedom of choice when it comes to university, future travel, anything at all that gets him away from here. There will, of course, hopefully be money for all my nieces and nephews in the not-too-distant future. I want to save them from what could have been my fate.

"Help yourself to coffee and make me a large one while you're at it," says Louise, leading the way into the kitchen.

I follow.

"Only one sugar, mind," she continues. "I'm cutting down."

It's wrong to judge, especially as I am not exactly a housekeeper extraordinaire myself, but I just can't help it. The place is a total state. The trash needs taking out, the fridge needs a good scrub. I used to send Louise money regularly and I suggested getting someone in to help clean, but she just laughed and said that was the difference between her and me and why we will never truly understand each other.

I hand Ryan a fifty-pound note. "Go to the shop. Buy trash bags, milk and lots of fruit. Then you can keep the rest for yourself, if you swear not to spend it on booze or drugs." I pull a funny face to show I'm joking.

"Booze and drugs." He laughs, too, tucking the money into his back pocket. "Get you being up with the latest words. But thanks. And don't worry, I'll spend it on sweets." He winks.

The whole exchange reminds me that I currently feel much older than my thirty-odd years. As I wait for the kettle to boil, I clean up in the kitchen while Louise takes my youngest niece through to the living area.

After a few moments, I walk into her living room carrying two cups of coffee. And, although I'm expecting it, although it isn't a surprise, seeing the orchid sitting innocently on Louise's dinner table unsettles me. The card is propped up against the plant pot. *No place to hide.* My legs feel weak.

I sit down.

I stare at the orchid as though it will yield clues if I look at it for long enough. But it's just an orchid. It will be dead within days. Louise kills plants. It's a family trait.

I'm still not feeling myself by the time I leave, after warning Louise to be careful. "Just in case."

"Just in case of what?"

"Just in case Sam's disappearance wasn't an accident."

Louise frowns and I notice her clutch my niece's hand just a little tighter.

"Well, what's that got to do with you? Or us?"

"Probably nothing. Humor me."

I would never forgive myself if anything happened to any of them as the result of my past mistakes.

I still can't get the words out of my head and I hate myself for feeling unsafe. I go back home and reply to work emails—nothing from Thomas—then google houses to rent in various parts of the country and jobs abroad. My tenants have left a disgruntled message. Sorry as they are to hear about Sam, they are not happy about the fact that he entered their home unlawfully while they were on holiday. I don't blame them for being annoyed. I send them an apology with assurances that it won't happen again.

Someone has written a horrible anonymous comment online about my "lack of communication and enthusiasm," saying that they wouldn't recommend my services. My fingers type: *Fuck off, you liar,* but I resist the urge to post and, instead, delete and ignore.

Then there's a new sound as an email pings through from an anonymous sender.

My stomach drops. Sam used to send emails from anonymous accounts. As soon as I see the subject, however, it plummets further.

Subject: Blood money

The phrase alone makes me feel sick; I don't want to read it but I have to.

Arrange payment of one million pounds. Click on the link to transfer the funds anonymously. Failure to pay ASAP will result in it being taken from you by force. Your choice.

It is impossible for many reasons. One, it's double what Sam and I earned in our last six months and, besides, I still don't have access to our money. Sam, the true thief, does. He withdrew our funds. He has left me to deal with all the shit alone. After pointlessly trying his phone again, I go online to his dormant social media pages. The chatter and speculation about his whereabouts are dying down.

Cold reality well and truly hits. My past isn't going to quietly fade away while I work hard at building up a legitimate business. It isn't going to wait until I can make amends. Someone is determined to force the issue, to try to steal from me, unless I stop them. I am freshly angry with myself for being drawn in by Sam—for believing him, trusting him. While he is God knows where, I have to carry on with my working days as normal, outwardly acting as if all is fine, while inside I am a mess. It bugs me, immensely so, that Whoever It Is—and others—believes in retribution or teaching others a lesson as if, somehow, it will fix everything. It is my belief that people are capable of teaching themselves their own lessons.

They will learn what they will learn, regardless, but in their own time and, even then, only if and when they are ready.

I'm relieved when Lewis gets home earlier than expected from work.

"You're early," I say.

He goes to the fridge and takes out a beer. "Want one?"

I nod. He takes out another and hands it to me.

"I arranged a second date with someone, but she's ghosted me. I couldn't concentrate on work properly."

I feel fleeting pleasure at this news; I don't want to spend the evening alone.

"What happened?"

"I don't know. We got on well enough. She even came back here for a drink and a bite to eat while you were working one evening, and now…" He shrugs. "Nothing. I think the fact that I was living with a woman got to her. She asked a lot about you, but no matter how many times I explained that we were just friends, the conversation came back to you again and again."

A chill grips me.

"I'm sorry," I say, trying to keep my tone neutral. "Show me her dating profile. I'll see if I can decipher anything amiss."

"She doesn't have one. I met her in real life. She got her car serviced at my garage."

"What's her name? What kind of things did she ask?"

"Samantha. She asked if we had ever slept together, if you had a boyfriend. I told her you were getting divorced. Maybe I shouldn't have done."

"What did she look like?"

"Pretty. Blonde. Does it matter?"

"Guess not. She doesn't deserve you."

True. Lewis doesn't deserve to be dragged into my sorry

mess. He is one of the nicest, kindest men I have ever known. He wants a happily-ever-after with the woman of his dreams, lots of children, a trampoline in the yard and nice cars.

"Never mind. It obviously wasn't meant to be. What are you up to this evening?" asks Lewis.

As well as feeling guilty, I also feel rage at the person who has done this to him.

"Not much. Making plans." I pause. "I'm thinking of moving out," I say. "It's time. I love living with you, but it was never meant to be long-term."

I expect him to protest, to say that I can stay as long as I like, but all I see is barely disguised relief.

"Any news on Sam?"

"No," I say.

I can't tell him about the threats, not without admitting that they are based on truth, so I make something up about feeling bad for imposing for so long. I add that the weird newspaper clipping showing the photo of my wedding day was the final straw, plus the police visit. *Blood money. Justice.* I don't want Lewis to be caught in the cross fire.

We clink our beer glasses to our friendship. My phone rings. I ignore it.

"Aren't you going to answer it?"

"No."

"It might be something to do with Sam."

"I doubt it."

There is a voice mail. I listen to the message. Thomas. He asks me to call him back this evening to discuss things further.

I tell Lewis.

"Call him back."

"There's no point if I'm moving on."

"I didn't realize you were planning to move out this minute. Anyway, I assumed you would stay local? What's the point in throwing away your business and all that hard work for nothing?"

Curiosity takes hold. I phone Thomas back. He has thought things over and decided that I am the best candidate for the role.

"Congratulations!" he says. "I look forward to us working together."

His assumption that I will accept on the spot makes me dig my heels in.

"Wonderful, thank you. Please can you send over all the details, including the name of your employer," I say. "I need much more information if I'm to consider it."

"Naturally. I will mail all the requirements and paperwork over to you now. There is a lot of admin, but I'm sure you'll be familiar with most of it."

I push it.

"My fees will be slightly higher than I originally quoted," I say, "as I'll have to put my other work on hold if I accept. I'll let you know when I've read everything through."

Sam believed that people valued things more if they were more expensive and harder to attain. Thomas is silent. I almost regret my attempt but after a few seconds he agrees.

"One thing I do need are some more recent testimonials," he says. "Do you have any clients who would be prepared to give me a few moments of their time?"

"I'll get on to that," I say. "I'll send you the details when I've checked with them."

Easy enough. I have many satisfied customers—Flora Miles, the host from the Windsor racecourse party, being one.

We end the call. I feel conflicted. I need air. I go outside to stand beneath the Narnia lamp, lighting a cigarette with Betty's lighter. I feel a combination of pleasure and self-loathing at break-ing my self-imposed smoking ban. I inhale, exhale. Sam. In one of his last messages, he said he had a plan. What if he has some-how arranged this to get us both out of the way from the per-son threatening us? Away from someone like Alexandra. Can I still trust Sam? No. But we have too much unfinished business and I'm not the infatuated, compliant person he remembers. I am stronger and filled with rage. I take a deep, welcoming drag, then exhale, watching the smoke dissipate. The lamp's welcom-ing glow is temporarily soothing even though I keep an eye out, half expecting someone to jump out of the shadows. It's hard to believe that such a short time ago I sometimes tempted danger by walking home alone. It's easy to be flippant about danger and death until it feels horribly imminent.

I check my phone. Thomas's email has appeared in my inbox as promised.

His employer's name is Josephine Fox-Smith. She is hold-ing the engagement party for her friend Gina Williams. Both Josephine's parents will be attending, Alicia and Charles, and Gina's mother, Norma. There will also be a celebration for Alicia's birthday while on board and several other old school friends of theirs will be joining in (names to be confirmed). I wonder if one of the guests is the Mr. H. Jacobs I saw on the letter I took from the mailman. I stub out my cigarette on the pavement and get googling.

Thomas doesn't have much of a social media presence, ei-ther, which I note after his comment about my own lack of one. Neither does Josephine. But her friend Gina used to be a reality TV star. There is loads of information on her. Tu-multuous relationships, good and bad decisions. I get drawn into her world instantly. She has put her past behind her now and lives a quiet life. Like me, then.

I follow her on social media under one of my old fake accounts, posing as an adventurous traveler.

Nothing out of the ordinary leaps out, no obvious links to Sam, or anyone he knows, but then there wouldn't be, would there? I mull it over. They haven't found a body. There's no reason for me to believe Sam is dead. I've been checking every day on news updates. Naturally, I've also searched *People swept out to sea / missing at sea / how long does it take for a body to be found / faking your own death*. There are endless stories of faking death to get sucked into, but something that became very clear to me was that, with enough determination, desperation and, in Sam's case, contacts, it's not impossible to disappear.

I allow myself a slight sense of hope and optimism—I've been itching for a reason to return to Barbados. The scene of the crime, so to speak. I go back inside to tell Lewis the good news. It will be good to get away and I could even apply for a permanent superyacht job while I'm out there. The police don't consider me a suspect. I am free to go and I'd better leave soon in case they change their minds. If they dig into our past, they will find a lot more reasons why I should hate Sam.

"A change is as good as a rest," Lewis says. "Let's open a bottle of champagne to celebrate."

We high-five.

The more I drink, the more I realize that there are many ways to turn over a new leaf. I don't necessarily have to suffer while doing so.

I email Thomas back, accepting the work. He sends a response by return, with a confidentiality contract and a note to say that travel details will follow in due course. He agrees to my fees with some provisos, which I quickly scan—nothing that raises any red flags.

Lewis is happy for me. He and I are on the same team.

That's where Sam went so horribly wrong. He didn't appreciate that one, very simple thing. He stopped consulting me,
did as he saw fit. And look where that got him.

11

LEWIS AND SAM DID NOT HIT IT OFF.

On landing in London, we cleared immigration and customs with no issues, then we hired a convertible. Lewis had offered to put us up, but Sam didn't like staying with strangers, so I'd booked us an Airbnb overlooking the castle.

The three of us had a meal in Lewis's and my favorite restaurant. I kept my left hand hidden because I wanted to tell Lewis all about the proposal. I also wanted Lewis and Sam to love each other as much as I loved them. I had it all pictured in my mind—a happy meal with lots of laughter and natural banter.

Instead, after a stilted start, Sam went to the restroom, and Lewis leaned over the table to take my hands.

"He's charming, for sure," he said. "A fling, perhaps. But not for life."

When Sam came back and raised the subject of our early wedding ideas—barefoot on a Caribbean island, no guests, minimal fuss, maximum champagne—the moment was ruined.

Lewis did an excellent job of saying all the right things.

Congratulations. I hope you'll both be very happy. But the damage had been done.

After that, I changed my mind about introducing Sam to my sister. I wanted to get away—far away. Earlier than planned, Sam and I went to Cardiff, Sam's home city, taking turns driving. As we crossed the Severn Bridge, and the sun gleamed, bright and golden, it dawned on me how much more I preferred being a visitor rather than living in the UK full-time. I had resisted, up until then, some of Sam's more outlandish suggestions of how I could make more money on the side. But the trip and my experience with Lewis were a reminder that I had changed. My tastes had changed. It was time for me not just to test the water but to dive right in and embrace opportunity.

I no longer wanted to settle for cabin bunk beds and desperately long hours, only catching the merest glimpses of a paradise meant for cruise passengers and hotel guests. I now understood why Sam strove for more. I wanted some of the power and confidence that he had.

The moment I met Sam's father, so many things about Sam clicked into place. His laissez-faire attitude, his disdain for "non-go-getters." George was proud of the fact that although he'd left school young, he'd worked hard to give him and Sam a good life. "Only had three days off sick in my life." He was welcoming and gave a good show of being genuinely interested in me.

After lunch (which Sam ordered in from a local Italian restaurant), George announced that he needed help with something in the backyard and asked Sam to go outside with him.

I sat alone in the living room, surrounded by old copies of the *Racing Post*. The few photos of Sam were of when he was a much younger child, say five or six. I studied them, his cheeky grin, trying to marry him up with the man I knew now. Sam and George were gone fifteen, maybe even twenty minutes. When they returned, they both smelled of bonfire smoke.

"What was all that about?" I whispered to Sam.

"Just some old paperwork he needed help getting rid of," he said, before announcing to George that we had to leave early because we had a four-hour drive ahead of us. News to me.

"I think he was disappointed we left early," I said to Sam as we pulled away from the street.

I twisted around and looked out the back window. George stood there waving until we could no longer see him.

"I know, and I feel bad, but I don't like staying there for too long," said Sam. "I start to feel restless. It was right what he said—he did his best and we had a good life, but I wanted more, you know?"

I did know, only too well. It's not ingratitude, it's a desire to fit in, to have the same kind of holidays abroad or birthday parties as the other children at school, or to be able to return their invitations.

"I get it," I said, leaning over and putting my hand on his thigh.

He squeezed my hand. "Besides, I'm excited about the surprise we've got ahead."

Excitement built within me, too, as we passed Bristol, then Exeter. By late afternoon, after navigating precariously narrow lanes with hedgerows towering over the car, we found ourselves turning up a gravel driveway, past a wooden For Sale sign, leading to a mansion. It had a large veranda that reminded me of a house I had seen in Australia on one of my first-ever trips as a travel consultant. This place had a huge garden, with at least seven palm trees and just as many rosebushes.

I opened the car door and stepped out, stretching. We were

close to the cliffs, with the most breathtaking view of the sea as far as I could look. I felt a sudden yearning to be on a boat.

"What is this place?" I asked.

"It could be ours," Sam said with a grin. "Our base. Our first-ever home of many. Our safe house."

"Can we go in?"

Another missed opportunity I chose to ignore in my excitement. Why didn't I question why he used the term *safe house* to describe what was supposed to become our dream home? Sam knew by then that I was never going to say no to anything. My belief in Sam's vision for us was all-encompassing.

A car pulled up behind ours and a man in a suit stepped out, clutching sheaves of paper and an iPad. A real-estate agent. He let us in and showed us around. It was way too big for two. Five bedrooms, an indoor and outdoor pool, Jacuzzi, BBQ area, a study, a large, light kitchen. We could throw parties, invite friends to stay. Sam and I could be ourselves here, without fear of slipping out of character. I hardly dared believe it was a possibility, though. But I desperately wanted to. Already, no other house I could imagine would measure up to this one.

The house was furnished, but the real-estate agent assured Sam that the current owners could move everything out at fairly short notice.

"It's a divorce situation," he said, pulling a sad face. "They both want out and to divide the money as soon as possible."

After the viewing, once the agent's car had pulled away from the driveway, Sam didn't put our car into Reverse. Instead, he got out and lifted our bags from the trunk. I walked behind him as we made our way to the back door. It was open.

"You did not…?" I said, laughing, as he switched off the burglar alarm too.

"I did. I memorized the code and unlocked the back door.

There was a spare key in the kitchen drawer. It seems a shame to spend money on a hotel when this place is going to be ours, anyway."

We stood in the living room with the magnificent view of the sea in the distance, admiring the house once again.

"What if he comes back? Has more viewings?"

"I overheard him on the phone saying that we were his last viewing of the day. Now, what should we do first now that we have this place all to ourselves?" he said with that smile of his I loved. "Which room should we start in?"

"Right here," I said, as I undid the zip on his jeans.

I had never desired Sam more than in that moment. I do wonder about that, sometimes. Was it Sam I fell in love with, or was it what he offered me? I think it was both.

We walked to the village shop, along a path at the edge of the cliff. Below, waves crashed against the rocks. Sam and I walked arm in arm, and I felt safe and happy, like I had made all the right decisions. We ate dinner at a seafood restaurant to get a feel for the place, then bought wine and beer to take back to the house, which we drank by candlelight.

"No point in pushing it by switching on lights," Sam said. "Let's not draw attention to ourselves."

The house did already feel like ours. I wanted it. I wanted it badly. Sam asked me about any savings I had (not much), but we agreed to pool our resources (90/10). I was not in his league but we reckoned we could afford to buy the place outright.

"It's better than having the money sitting in the bank."

The fact that he casually had over a million pounds just sitting in his bank account was eye-opening.

"We'll have to rent it out to start off with," said Sam. "It's all about knowing what to spend and what to save."

I already didn't like the thought of strangers in our home,

polluting it with their taste, their friends and family, swimming in our pool, having sex in our bedroom.

"Not for long, though," I said.

Sitting in the dark that night, drunk, mesmerized by flickering candles and filled with hope and possibility, sparked the idea for Story Number Two.

Sam's best friend since school days struggled with drug addiction. A typical story about the wrong crowd and shady figures who would hang out at the local basketball and tennis courts, tempting teenagers away from sports. Sam's friend—we named him Gus—spiraled into the darkness of addiction. He progressed into crime, burglary, petty theft, and ended up in prison. It was the wake-up call he needed and Sam thought he had turned over a new leaf, but the drugs were stronger than him. We would encourage people to share their own sad experiences with drugs to show that we were united by a shared experience. We would then reveal that Gus had sadly passed away before his twenty-fifth birthday.

"I tried many times to save him," Sam would need to say here, sorrowfully, "but I couldn't."

This would then link up nicely to drop in details of the charity Sam had set up to help people like his friend.

Once back at work on our third ship together, it was surprising—or maybe not—how many people just didn't check that ours was a registered charity before handing their money over. Some of them would even share their bank details so that Sam could help them navigate the deliberately complicated site.

Sam told me about a friend of his who believed that people were greedy and that was the way to get money out of them. "Offer them a 'get rich even faster' scheme and they'll be hooked," he'd suggested to Sam. But Sam believed that it was better to offer people a way to be good.

After I started learning from Sam, it was like magic. Passengers would tip me generously, tapping the side of their nose for me to keep it quiet. I always did. If money wasn't forthcoming, there were other ways. I still worked long hours in the gift shop but offered to go above and beyond for some guests to make their holiday even better. Sam was right. People wanted to do good—to atone for past selfishness and mistakes. That's where we stepped into the picture. We offered spiritual guidance, of a fashion. We gave people something they had been subconsciously seeking—self-forgiveness.

We developed a system. First, we'd ascertain who had cash to splash. This was done in various ways: by how much they spent in the casino (not foolproof, Sam had to keep an eye out for those with uncontrollable gambling habits), through striking up casual conversations, by befriending them or by noticing the little clues, like jewelry, clothes, length of cruise, previous holiday choices. Some passengers were suspicious of everyone. They didn't want to make new friends, kept their handbags, wallets and sea passes close, their private lives vague, their room keys hidden from view. They were the smart ones.

Our wedding, however, was one of our best fundraising ideas of all. Sam and I had befriended a couple who had been married for thirty years with never a cross word between them. Basil pulled out Madelaine's chair at every meal, they told positive stories about each other, they held hands, never left the penthouse suite without each other. But those weren't the details we focused on. They were rich and generous, so much so that we couldn't find fault with them, couldn't find a reason to spin one of our usual tales, despite the temptation. Neither of them had anything they needed to forgive themselves for.

"I hope we're still in love in thirty years," I said to Sam, as we were mulling things over.

"That's it!" said Sam, kissing me. "You genius. I'll tell them about our wedding. Ask them for advice on how to choose the right life partner."

"I don't get it."

"You will, trust me. You will just *love* my idea."

"I want to know now."

"It will ruin the surprise," he said, kissing me again, knowing that was enough to make me stop asking questions.

Two mornings later, emerging from the shower, I couldn't find my engagement ring on the basin. I got down on my hands and knees and searched the bathroom floor, stripped the bunks. Nothing. I could remember taking it off and placing it on the side next to my body lotion. So where was it now? Sam was already in the casino. I messaged him.

My ring's gone. I'm freaking out! Have you seen it?

I could see that he had read my message, yet he didn't reply.

Later that afternoon, after my shift, there was a handwritten note that had been slid under our cabin door.

An invitation...

Dear Samuel [Sam was a Sam, not a Samuel, but no matter]
and Charlotte,
Basil and Madelaine request the pleasure of your company in their suite at sunset.
Dress code: Something special.
P.S. We've okayed it with your manager.

Wow. That was unexpected.

There was a separate note on my pillow from Sam saying to meet him there.

I had an inkling—of course I did—but even so, I was blown away. The penthouse had been decorated in roses and curls of ribbon. Balloons bobbed against the ceiling. There were ornate seashells, gold baubles, diamond-encrusted tea-light holders. Christmas wasn't far off and I felt the sort of excitement I hadn't felt since I was about five years old.

Sam, dressed in his most expensive suit, got down on bended knee at sunset on Basil and Madelaine's vast balcony and presented me with my lost engagement ring as if it were the first time.

I looked into his eyes, mutual delight passing between the two of us, and this time...I said "Yes!"

Madelaine and Basil clapped and said "Congratulations!"

If I'm being fair to myself, it was so easy to feel special, to think that we had been "chosen" and that we were immune from the mundanity of life. It felt like we had the golden touch.

The champagne the four of us toasted with was Dom Pérignon vintage. Afterward, Madelaine took me to one side and told me that she hoped I would be as lucky as she had been.

"He's besotted," she said about Sam. "That man would move heaven and earth for you."

"I didn't have much luck with men before Sam," I confided. "He's my first proper relationship."

I told her about Deceitful Drew, Harry in Val d'Isère and a man I had met while au-pairing in Italy. He was the son of a neighbor. My employers were furious when they discovered my—not his—indiscretion. I was asked to pack my bags with only one day's notice and a week's pay. It wasn't all bad, though, because my time in Italy really ignited my love of travel.

Of course, Basil and Madelaine offered, no, *insisted* on paying for our hotel beach wedding in Barbados the following month when Sam and I both had a week off between contracts. Basil and Madelaine were guests of honor.

A good friend of Sam's, JJ, who once worked as a chef on the same ship as Sam, was the best man. His full name was

Jason, but Sam had a few friends with the same name, and two called Jay, so Jason became JJ and it stuck. Sam introduced us the night before the wedding. JJ's girlfriend, Jilly, offered to be my bridesmaid.

"I won't be offended if you say no," she said. "I realize that all your good friends are in England, so the offer is there if you'd like it."

"Thank you," I said, touched.

Sam warned me not to get too friendly with her because she wouldn't necessarily be around next time we visited Barbados. JJ didn't have long-lasting relationships, apparently.

Jilly was clearly very much in love with JJ. I could see why. He was nice, had good manners, was interested in others and had matinee-idol looks. She lent me a silver clip for my hair, which I wore up.

After the formalities, during the photos, I saw Ingrid, my first-ever cabinmate, among the guests, staring at me. Sam turned on me. He whispered angry words in my ear for wearing my bracelet, then dragged me by the wrist outside and asked what the hell I was playing at.

JJ appeared and took Sam to one side to calm him down. Jilly led me to the ladies' room to help fix my eye makeup, which had smudged when I couldn't hold back the tears. Afterward, I saw Sam taking Ingrid to one side, speaking close to her ear, angrily.

Basil spoke to the hotel security and Ingrid was escorted from the premises. Rumor went around that she had threatened Sam in the past, was an ex who hadn't taken their breakup well. Long story short, it meant that I got married wearing something old, something new, something borrowed and something stolen. And not just stolen—it wasn't that that bothered me the most. It was the fact that Sam had kept his previous relationship with Ingrid a secret, that there had been an overlap, that I had worn a bracelet that Sam had first given to another woman, who now hated me. Superstitious or not, it felt like a bad omen. It was the first time I properly questioned myself and what I was getting into. What if, I thought, behind the glitz wasn't more glamour but something darker? For the rest of the evening, throughout the dancing, I couldn't help feeling that I had made a big mistake.

"Why didn't you tell me you and Ingrid had had a fling?" I asked as we walked along the hotel corridor to the honeymoon suite (all legitimately paid for by Basil and Madelaine). "I hate that I was in the dark. I thought she just didn't like me."

"It was a brief, meaningless fling. Please don't let her ruin our special day."

I should have said more but it was our wedding night and I wanted to salvage what was left of it.

But it was already too late. Our wedding night was the first time in a fancy hotel room that we didn't have sex. Not only that, I couldn't enjoy, or appreciate, the luxury. I hadn't earned it. It seemed that without the danger and the threat of being caught there was no joy to be found in life's pleasures. And even though I didn't admit it to myself then—not that night, anyway—I already knew that I craved a bigger high, and that I would probably risk more to experience it. Feeling flat, feeling betrayed, lied to and conned were all feelings I was going to numb and bury—for now.

12

NOW

I AM IN MIAMI AIRPORT, ABOUT TO BOARD A PRIVATE jet to Nassau, the capital of the Bahamas. I had dreams of this type of thing happening to me one day, of course. I'd pictured myself in dark glasses, like some sort of movie star, jetting off to one of my many private mansions. I'd had many grand ambitions but I hadn't ever visualized my own plane. I hadn't aimed high enough. Perhaps that's where I'd gone wrong.

I am personally escorted to the aircraft. There is no hassle, no fear that any airport staff will sniff out my guilt and search me. It is disappointing that the flight to Nassau will take only a mere hour, unlike my never-ending flight in economy from London yesterday. I spent the night alone, in a hotel with views of the cruise port. Nostalgia hit hard. I had forgotten just how majestic, how colossal, how enticing cruise ships were. I could feel the pull of life at sea enticing me back.

Although I swore that I would never again get caught up in any of Sam's schemes, this is different. This is self-preservation. The only way to be free of Sam is to confront the past, which I cannot do while living half a life at Lewis's house, looking over my shoulder. People say: "Don't do the crime if you can't do the time," but what I did didn't *feel* like a crime—that's the thing that's hard to explain. This trip is my opportunity to escape.

As I'd waited to check out of the hotel, I couldn't help but overhear a couple directly in front of me; their snippets were conversational gold. *"Fifth cruise"* would have translated to Sam and me that they had money to spend. *"Need to buy myself some new dresses."* Money to splash on board. Her diamond earrings glittered with authenticity, a good few thousand pounds. Her shoes—designer and barely worn.

Old, dormant me is back, but without Sam dangling his many carrots, I can hold back and keep myself in check. One thing is for sure—I don't wish to go back to rebuilding a life at home.

"Hello, Ms. Wilson."

The crew welcome me on board as if they genuinely mean it. Then again, I would, too, if this was my working environment. There is no stress, no queuing, no getting whacked by someone else's bags, no mess. In the lounge area, fresh roses burst from fixed silver vases. Small ceramic bowls are filled with nuts and chocolates. Cocktail sticks rest neatly beside green and black olives. Slices of pineapple and watermelon fan out across a silver platter.

It appears that I am the first person to board. The dozen or so luxurious leather seats are empty. A magazine rack holds a wide selection, covers displaying the type of lifestyles I dream of. I sit down and shut my eyes, allowing myself to feel a strong sense of sheer blissful relief at leaving fear and blandness behind. The only message I have received today so far is an *"I'm so jealous"* one from Lewis. If Whoever It Is is watching his place, they're going to be disappointed.

There's a sound of voices and I open my eyes. Five people

board: a woman and two couples in their sixties or early seventies. I look again at the final passenger list that Thomas mailed to me this morning. Mr. H. Jacobs is Josephine's partner.

Josephine Fox-Smith and Harrison Jacobs

Their parents (Alicia and Charles, Sebastian and Arabella)

Gina Williams

Gina's mother, Norma

Mariella Green

Garth Ford

Thomas—along with the other guests, staff and crew—is already on board the superyacht, the *Cleobella*. The little I know about Josephine Fox-Smith from my online digging is that she runs a successful chain of fashion boutiques. She has won awards, raised thousands for various charities, is a captain of industry. There is little on her personal life, other than a very old picture in *Tatler* many years ago. I do know that she inherited when she was eighteen from a wealthy grandfather. Whichever way I look at it, chartering a private yacht means serious money.

Just before the doors are closed, another two women and a man board. They look a similar age to me. They're followed swiftly by another two men. The first three appear to all know one another; the latter two sit directly behind me. I go through my mental list again to marry up names with real-life faces.

The aircraft doors close. There are a few brief smiles of acknowledgment, but after that, no one pays any attention to me. There is much opening and closing of cabinet doors, removing and hanging of outerwear, last-minute phone conversations, a discussion about snacks and one or two requests for drinks.

We begin to taxi. I love that there is no safety demo. No one orders me to put on my seat belt (although, of course I do), we just…take off. The movements on a small plane are accentuated; my stomach drops as we lift up, rock sideways and judder slightly before we break through the clouds and into the clearest of blue skies. I have never appreciated the view more.

Whoever It Is is now a good thirty thousand feet or so below me and four and a half thousand miles away. My mind clears for the first time in days and my body relaxes into the leather seat. Everything is going to be all right. Despite Sam, despite the threats, despite all the mistakes I have made. I feel as if I belong here. As I gaze out at the horizon, it strikes me that it is the reverse of looking at it from a cruise ship. The white clouds are below, the blue sky is above. I'm used to looking out at the ocean, as far as I can see, the skyline above.

I stand up to go and explore the plane at the same time as the man behind gets up. We smile at each other, but he doesn't look as though he relishes the thought of chitchat. We end up walking along a small corridor together, where there are two bathrooms, complete with showers and basins with gold taps. The scent of luxury soap wafts as I dry my hands on soft white towels.

When the man emerges, he sits at the bar and is offered a drink. I do the same, only I order a Bloody Mary instead of an espresso.

I introduce myself.

"Charlotte."

"Daniel," he says, glancing at his watch.

Daniel is not on my list.

"How do you know Josephine?" I ask.

"I don't."

"Oh."

"New to this?"

"Kind of."

"I'm a freelance security guard. You?"

"Assistant PA." I lower my voice. "What about everyone else on board?"

"The guy next to me, Steve, is one of the chefs," he says. "The others are all family and friends. They won't be interested in chatting to us."

"How long have you been doing this?"

"Too long. Every job I promise my wife I'll quit, but the money is good. Your turn."

"Long story," I say, taking a sip of my drink. The vodka tastes strong. "Do you know any of the friends and family? Have you worked for them before?"

He gives me a look as if I've said something wrong.

"They pay us to be discreet," he points out. "We aren't paid this type of money out of the kindness of their hearts. It is out of 'Shut the fuck up.' See no evil, hear no evil, speak no evil. Don't forget that. It will make the difference between being told to pack your bags in the middle of the night and being shipped off into the darkness and dumped onshore to make your own way home, your tail between your legs...or not."

"You sound very sure of this."

"I've seen it happen many times," he says, but doesn't elaborate.

"I know how to be discreet."

"The best advice I can give you is to remember that no one is your friend, however chummy they seem. Do your work, sleep when you can. Work hard and save the playing hard until you have been paid and are far away."

We begin our descent into Nassau. We finish our drinks and return to our seats. I press my face against the window and peer down. The turquoise water that I've missed so desperately makes me smile. The islands come into closer view: strips of lush green and windswept white beaches. As we continue to descend and the land comes into sharper focus, some of my earlier shine, bravado and optimism wear off. I wonder just how involved the job is actually going to be. It's hard not to wonder—what exactly am I getting myself into?

13

THE LIBRARY BECAME MY HUNTING GROUND; THE casino, naturally, was Sam's. Despite this, our next targets were not chosen while reading or gambling but found as they accepted celebratory martinis from a head butler. It was during sail-away cocktails in the VIP section on board the *Wanderer*. Sam and I were focusing on the wealthier end of the market. This was our fifth working cruise together, and our first time on an Alaska-bound, cold-weather one.

Our latest guests of interest were another couple. The man's dark hair was neatly combed, his cologne slightly too strong. I detected hints of Oud. His shoes were bespoke, his patterned shirt was flattering and clearly made-to-measure. The woman was slender, slightly taller than him. Long strawberry blond hair frizzed slightly at the ends. Gold earrings matched the lettering on her Cartier handbag and matching high-heeled sandals.

Her martini was quick to disappear, and I witnessed the man impatiently beckoning for service by waving his right hand. I overheard her asking for "champagne this time, as long as it's deliciously cold." She smiled, as if to dilute the sting of her insinuation that they'd ever dare serve her anything less than perfect. Her jacket sleeve rode up slightly as she reached for the champagne flute offered to her from a silver tray and I spied more gold in the form of a chunky bracelet coiled around her left wrist. *Left-handed*, I noted. No sign of a watch.

I was so intent on my people-watching that I almost cried out when Sam appeared at my side and snaked his arm around my waist. He pulled me out of sight, behind the sauna and steam room, and kissed me. The feeling of his black-tie jacket against my too-thin sleeves was alien. Our normal contact was skin to skin.

"We shouldn't…" I said. "We're at work. Someone will see."

He pulled me closer, squeezed tighter, bending to kiss my throat. Lust still kept our relationship afloat. That and gifts. Sam had exquisite taste. Since our wedding day, however, and my stolen bracelet, I had begun to feel the struggle between the wanting and the not wanting. It was a deep, dark truth that I could barely admit to myself: the pleasure of what we were doing was no longer driven solely by Sam. I was torn between wanting to experiment myself, and yet wanting to impress him with how far I had come. Shame and guilt simmered around the edges of avarice and ambition. We made new rules. We would pick only unworthy people or ones who needed humbling. It was easier to justify. We had one rule that we agreed we'd never break—we never took from anyone who couldn't afford it.

I suppressed a shiver. It was noticeably different to breathe in air tinged with early autumnal chill, to view coffee-table-book perfect snowcapped mountains instead of beaches. The Caribbean hadn't lost its shine, but it was time for a change. I looked over Sam's shoulder and focused on our new surroundings, a seaplane landing in the distance. Tiny in comparison. Sixty-plus meters above the waterline, cocooned in the exclusive zone, known on board as the Cove, I felt alive, invincible. We would shortly be leaving Seattle. Eight days of decadence.

"What are you thinking?" Sam said.

"That I don't like the look of them, he looks smug—which means they're perfect," I replied.

This was always a crucial stage. If we befriended the wrong people now, it could be hard to shake them off and refocus our attention on others more deserving.

"Facts, not feelings" had become an important rule.

I went through the facts now. "A recent windfall," I surmised. "Maybe a lottery win. There's too much gold, almost everything is designer."

Real wealth was discreet, rightfully fearful that human magpies would swoop.

"I don't know," said Sam. "I'm not so sure. He looks as if he's been used to the finer things in life for longer than a few years."

I loved this part of our game. The raised hairs on my arms, the thrill at the start of a chase. Nothing had ever beaten that feeling. I feared that nothing ever would. I buried those thoughts back then and I still choose to ignore them even now, because if those fleeting moments were truly the ultimate high, then, as with any addiction, it's not wise to dwell on potential alternatives to fill the inevitable comedown and void.

"Let's get to work," I said.

Sam kissed me one more time before we emerged. The Jacuzzi and the heated pool were behind us, steam wafting above the aquamarine surface. We emerged from the double sun loungers and pods, the baskets of pristine, neatly folded, fresh white towels upon which rested stems of pale pink and purple-tinged orchids. Ornate potted palms dotted the area. The pianist was playing a safe, classical tune discreetly in the background as we approached the couple who had caught my eye.

"Hi, I'm Charlotte," I said, offering my hand. "And this is Sam."

They initially looked startled at our sudden introduction, but then beamed. The woman stood a little straighter. The man, I was sure, sucked in his stomach a little. Sam had that effect on people.

The couple, Megs and Jake, reciprocated with their own introductions. They were from London, it was their first cruise and they were still learning the ropes.

"There's twenty-four-hour service," Jake marveled. "I intend to make the most of everything there is to offer."

"I'm sure you will," I said. "You'll never want to travel any other way again. Trust me."

I offered to fetch more champagne and left them in Sam's capable hands. After all, it was his turn to choose, which meant that he should have the final say. I waited longer than necessary before returning. *Slowly and softly.* Rule number two.

I could hear Megs speaking as I approached.

"It was my birthday in the summer and Jake said we should push the boat out. So, we have—almost literally!" she laughed.

"A big-number birthday," Jake stage-whispered.

Sam smiled politely, as did I, even though doubt hit. If this was a once-in-a-lifetime treat for them, then they were no use to us. Sam and I had so far stuck to our codes of conduct and standards.

"Got to splash the cash somehow," Jake added, lifting up his arm and pointing at his Cartier watch.

Although, we had an exception: boastfulness.

It turned out that Jake had made his fortune in the construction industry. Although I knew it was irrational and nothing to do with Jake, it made me dislike him even more. By that time, I had begun to find reasons for choosing our particular targets. My parents had once been ripped off by someone pretending to be a qualified builder. This, I decided, would become the reason on this occasion.

I insisted that we never coerced too much from anyone, that we always left them with more than enough. Sam agreed but it was mainly because there was less chance of being caught or people bothering to report us once they suspected that they had gifted to a perhaps-not-quite-so-worthy cause. Plus, sometimes a little humility was no bad thing. It all evened out in the end. Money comes; money goes.

I dug deeper with Megs under the guise of discussing excursions. I needed to learn how much of their particular boat they had already pushed out. I tended to discover a lot from how people chose to spend their leisure time and money. I had, by now, secured a position in wish fulfillment—in other words, VIP sales and excursions, a nice change from retail. Less temptation too. Although, it did hold a mirror up to how far Sam and I were from our goals. Being constantly surrounded by pampered guests cocooned in luxury wasn't necessarily helpful either.

I listened as she reeled off "whale watching, bears, eagles, exploring Juneau, Ketchikan, Skagway…" (she had clearly read a guidebook). "And the glaciers are meant to be breathtaking. Simply out of this world."

Glacier Bay National Park is likened to real-life jewels, according to some of the guides and online descriptions: shades of dazzling blues among the mountains and sea.

"There is a lot more you can do," I said. "Some more offbeat options." I paused, waiting for her to bite.

"What do you mean?"

"Hiking, for one. You two look fit. The views from the mountain are to die for. Not literally, obviously."

Megs smiled. "What do you think, honey?" she asked Jake. "Charlotte here reckons that we have options, that we should be more adventurous and exclusive."

Sam and I exchanged a discreet look.

"I could put together an itinerary for you?" I offered.

"Sure. Sounds good."

Megs and I chatted like new best friends. She had always *known*, deep down, that she was destined for bigger and better things somehow.

"Jake just had it, you know. He was ambitious and I knew he would do well."

There was no mention of children. Although, they had a nephew they loved to spoil. Same as me, really. I told her so. It was good to home in on these little connections. People liked it. But that's where the similarity ended. Over the years, Megs's mother had often mentioned "nest eggs" and "rainy days." It turned out after her death three years previously that people had different ideas about savings. Several millions in difference. It irked me slightly that they were already wealthy before they'd inherited even more. I was getting fed up with being ordered around by people who had no idea how fortunate they were.

"I like the sound of exclusive," said Jake. "I hate being shoved in with the masses. That's why we opted for the Cove. Think of all those poor people way below us, crammed together."

Indeed.

"It's going to be a fantastic trip," said Sam.

"A fantastic trip" was our code that meant that he agreed

that this couple could be suitable. Sometimes, it took three or four attempts and we would be forced to cast our net wider, be more eagle-eyed, dig deeper beneath the social surfaces and outward appearances. It occurred to me that Sam and I were becoming stronger as a working team.

"I agree," I said, with a smile.

As Sam asked Megs about their previous holidays, I focused on Jake.

"Are you a gambling man?"

"I like to dabble," he said, tapping the side of his nose, looking around for someone to fill up his champagne flute.

I could have offered, but I didn't.

"What will it be this evening? Poker? Roulette? Blackjack?"

"I'm a poker man, myself," replied Jake.

"Then," I said, "you will be in safe hands with Sam." There I went, dangling an illusionary carrot of nonexistent insider tips. "He's an expert."

Some people think their gambling habits are a skill until they have a run of inevitable bad luck.

As Jake began to discuss restaurants and fine dining, I steered the conversation toward the Cove's award-winning signature spa treatment. A friend of mine, Lucy, was also on board; I had met her on my second working cruise. She was a top therapist and genuinely interested in people, naturally bubbly, and I knew she would unwittingly fill me in on any gaps in Jake's history if need be. He briefly touched my arm once or twice when emphasizing a point, and smiled as though we had a connection. All the while, I was planning what memento I was going to acquire after this particular trip. I quite fancied a new watch...

Hours later, however, while I was stuck in my bunk bed situated well below the waterline, reality hit. The weather had turned rough once we were out at sea. Sam had a late-night stint in the casino. I was on an early-morning shift. I worked on Jake and Megs's exclusive excursion itinerary with the help of my new guidebook. I bought them for most new places we visited because nothing online could beat the joy of reading about adventure by experienced travelers. It began with a hike along a quiet, yet stunning mountain path claiming incredible views of alpine meadows. The timings had to be perfect because, depending on our limited time off work, either Sam or I would accompany them.

High above me, people like Jake and Megs lay in king-size-bedded luxury with their own hot tub and ocean view, along with the ability to summon people who were paid very little to fulfill almost any of their desires. It didn't matter how rude, how unrealistic their demands, how entitled they were, we had to smile and appease. Sam rarely arranged for us to visit empty suites anymore, and the one time I had tried, the crew member I had attempted to coerce to turn a blind eye after they had cleaned it looked at me as though I was suggesting a crime of the century. It made me feel ashamed, but I hadn't done anything wrong.

It was time to up the ante, to take bigger risks. Nothing else made sense. Otherwise, I had to put up with crap living conditions.

I stayed up too late, plotting. We needed a fresh story, one specifically tailored to Jake and Megs's more charitable urges. Sam and I had observed that when people come into money unexpectedly, they feel the need to share some of their good fortune to ward off the evil eye. The trick was to tap into that fear. I would suggest to Megs that her mother sounded like a generous, kind woman who would want her to "do good" with her inheritance. It was all about risk calculation, and I figured, back then, that I was already an expert in the subject. I hated (and still do) any sense of superiority. Our targets always had one main thing in common: they assumed they were better than us.

It is perhaps strangely fitting that my past arrogance is now my biggest regret. The rules were there to protect Sam and me. We should never have broken them. The fractures were irreparable.

14

NOW

GLINTS OF WHITE AND GOLD SPARKLE OFF THE SEA
and reflect off the vast assortment of yachts and sailboats in the
marina. I stand on the jetty, enjoying the heat seeping through
my bones after the plane's air-conditioning. Surrounded by
luxury and decadence, I inhale warmth and feel a great weight
lift. There is nothing like it, the feeling of being let off the
hook and the sweetness it offers, along with a fresh apprecia-
tion of my present surroundings and precious freedom.

I look around. A crane in the distance mars my perfect view.
A slight wind blows the fronds on the palm trees and an ice-
cream wrapper skitters along the ground near my feet. These
small intrusions tug at my mind and remind me of Whoever
It Is. I bite the bullet and check my phone. Blessed nothing
outside the usual sales emails and requests for feedback on various products. It is satisfying to press the Trash icon. I glance
down at my anklet. *Look after number one*, I silently remind
myself. Just like Sam.

Daniel is ignoring me, despite us sharing a cab that I ended
up paying for.

"Keep the receipt," he said, before sitting on a wall, putting in headphones and facing the ocean.

Two cars with blacked-out windows park nearby. The rear doors are opened by the driver and members of the party emerge. Every single one of them is wearing sunglasses. Alicia reminds me of Lucille Ball and Charles of Gene Kelly. Arabella is much younger than Sebastian. She is wearing a lemon linen dress that has creased since I first saw her on the plane.

Despite the sunglasses, I recognize them as Gina Williams; Gina's mother, Norma; Mariella Green—she looks vaguely familiar—and Garth Ford.

I recheck my email from Thomas to see if I missed anything.

> A small boat will take you to the main yacht, the *Cleobella*, where I will already be on board to give you up-to-date instructions.

There are no specific timings. Feeling like the new girl at school, I decide to take control. I will ignore Daniel's advice and try to win them over.

"Hello," I say, as the group are ushered by the driver in my direction. I smile. "I'm Charlotte. Thomas asked me to make myself known. I'm his assistant for this trip. I am making my way on board the *Cleobella* with you."

I receive polite, tight smiles, "hellos" and "nice to meet yous" in response, along with subtle appraisals, which I sense coming from behind their dark sunglasses.

"Hello," says Mariella. She removes her straw hat, tilts her head back and gives her long dark hair a gentle shake. "That's better. This *heat!*"

I do recognize her. She was at the Windsor racecourse. Not as one of Flora Miles's guests, yet she stood out from the crowd because of her distinctive Versace dress and the fact that she looked so happy. It makes me think that the man she was with was not her husband. She looks at me now as though she can't quite place me. Something passes over her face and the look she gives me next implores, *Please. Keep quiet.* Or to use Daniel's phraseology, *STFU.* It throws me slightly, pulls me right back into remembering Daniel's warning.

"It is hot," I agree, blandly.

I mentally reassess my approach as I follow the group to the tender. I feel like a stalker until I think about how Sam would approach the situation. He wouldn't act like an outsider and he definitely wouldn't give off any vibes of feeling out of sorts.

I hand my bags to the driver, so he is forced to pass my bags on to the tender crew, along with all the baggage. Two porters appear beside the jetty with luggage carts.

Once the elder members have boarded, I step on board the tender—nicer and more luxurious than many dinghies I have been on in the past. The white leather seats are all under cover. I study the others discreetly. Garth holds out his hand to assist Mariella, then Gina. None of them sit beside me, and I don't know if I imagine it, but I'm pretty sure that I spot Gina nudge Garth in his side. I feel freshly annoyed that Thomas didn't provide more detail on these people. I smile over at Daniel, who gives me a short nod in response.

I take out my phone as if concentrating on work. The boat rocks gently side to side before we pull away, pick up speed and cut through the turquoise water. I give up my pretense of working and gaze out at the horizon. I have returned to paradise, yet again. The hardships I have endured, the bleak gray and drizzly days, the terror of exposure, Sam's disappearance— all thousands of miles behind me now. I can temporarily push my fears to one side, bury them in my full-to-bursting mental compartment of *Don't Go There.*

I study Mariella. She has a white cashmere cardigan draped over her shoulders, the arms knotted across her chest. She looks contemplative. Charles clutches a walking stick, even while sitting down. Arabella takes out a packet of chewing gum, offers it around. Daniel looks as if he is taking stock of the surroundings. Gina takes photos and posts them on Instagram. "Twenty-three likes already!" She fancies herself a photographer. To be fair, her images online are stunning. I was impressed when I came across them during my online digging into her background. Gina favors sunrises so is clearly a morning person, and countryside views on her morning jog. Garth plugs in headphones, acting as if this is all day-to-day stuff for him.

As the *Cleobella* comes into sight, I almost gasp. Although Sam and I once went on board a superyacht in Monaco for lunch with a friend of his, that one pales in comparison. *Sleek* is the word that immediately springs to my mind. *Beautiful* is the second. All glistening white and silver, clean and smooth. It has four decks, spoiled only by the sight of a large red-and-yellow slide attached to one side. I'm not a fan of waterslides. I hate the way the water stings my nose and dislike the moments plunging beneath the water before I can rise to the surface. I see Jet Skis crisscrossing each other near the back of the yacht.

The thundering of an approaching helicopter in the distance slices into my daydreams.

"That'll be Josephine," says Alicia, twisting around to look. "Such a horrible, noisy way to arrive. It's so much more pleasant traveling this way."

"It depends," says Mariella, raising her voice to be heard

above the noise. "I think I would quite like making an entrance."

Our boat holds back, circling from a distance, as the helicopter's downwash makes violent ripples in the sea as it hovers and lowers, before touching down on the helipad. Our boat rocks and sways.

"For goodness' sake, what bad timing," says Charles.

By the time we alight, I am feeling nauseated. I need to regain my sea legs.

Thomas is waiting to greet us. He is full of smiles, looking as relaxed and chilled as someone who has just been on a fortnight's holiday. He is wearing shorts, a navy striped top and a cap, the wrong way around. His feet are bare.

"How was your flight?" he asks, as The Party—my new name for them—disembark.

I'm last.

Thomas looks pleased to see me. "Charlotte, hello! Glad you made it all right."

"Thank you."

The yacht crew direct The Party up some stairs to our right. Thomas and I hold back.

"So, you've met most of the party," he says, "which is great stuff. However…" He lowers his voice as though he is about to let me in on a fascinating secret. "I'll formally introduce you to Josephine. She's the one you need to impress. She trusts my judgment, so I very much hope you won't let me down."

He smiles as if I should be grateful for his insights.

"It was lovely to meet everyone," I say, sounding as pleasant as I can. "I would appreciate some more background information, though. I'd also like to know where my cabin is so that I can get my bearings. An itinerary for the rest of the day would be good too."

"Of course," he says.

I watch as the crew off-load my bags among all the others. I feel stuck in the middle—neither guest nor crew.

"Follow me," says Thomas as he leads the way up some steps. "You'll be sharing a cabin with one other person," he says over his shoulder, "but I'm sure you'll love her and get along like the proverbial house on fire. She's a great laugh."

Crap. I knew I would probably have to share living quarters; in fact, it was inevitable, given that space on boats, regardless of size, is at a premium, but still… I am not keen on the sound of someone who is a great laugh. It could mean anything.

We reach the top deck, where everyone is standing at a safe distance from the black helicopter, hugging and exchanging greetings with one another. I scan the small crowd and pick out Josephine.

She is not exactly how she looks in her pictures; they don't do her justice. She is stunning, with long red hair and pale skin. Her eyes are hidden by sunglasses, but I know that they are green. She has a presence that is about more than just money. Sam and I would have referred to her as confidently wealthy. We used to categorize people, number them in order of interest. Josephine would have made number one. On her wrist is a silver-and-ruby bracelet. I can't make out her earrings from where I am standing but they appear to be a matching set with the bracelet. Envy jolts. I want to be her.

"Step inside, please," a yacht member is asking us all. "The helicopter is going to depart."

We all do as we are told. The lounge area, decorated in cream and burgundy, feels gloomy now that we are out of the sunshine. Most of us remove our sunglasses, blinking as our eyes adjust.

Outside, the roar of the helicopter's engine shudders the

glass as it drowns out any chance of conversation before it lifts off and heads back toward shore. I watch it go. The tender has gone back to shore too. I wonder who else it will pick up.

"Charlotte," says Thomas.

I turn away from the window, somewhat reluctantly. I feel oddly homesick.

Josephine is at his side.

"This is Charlotte," says Thomas. "My godsend. And this is Josephine Fox-Smith."

"Nice to meet you."

Her voice is calm and measured. She is a Josephine, not a Jo, not a Josie. It's important. I get it. I am a Charlotte. Not a Lottie, not a Char (heaven forbid) or any other such variation that people try to impose on me. The only exception was when Sam called me Lola.

"Nice to meet you, too," I say, reaching to shake her hand. "I am thrilled to be here."

"As am I. I'm so glad you're going to help run things smoothly. It's so important, don't you think, to make the most of everything?" She doesn't wait for a response before continuing. "Thomas is a workaholic, but even he needs to sleep."

Polite laughs all around as Josephine turns.

"Harrison! Come and say hello."

A man appears at her side; a jolt of recognition hits because it's a face I've seen before.

"Hello," he says.

"Hello," I reply.

I am unsure what else to say. The last time I met this man, he was in Val d'Isère and he went by the name of Harry.

15

MY THIRD FAVORITE STORY WAS THIS:

My parents were conned out of their life savings by a rogue builder and plunged into a previously unknown world of debt. [True.] *The consequences were devastating; my father had a stress-induced heart attack and died.*

"Did they ever find the cowboy?" asked Jake. "There are rules and regulations, ways of checking these things out."

I hoped he wasn't trying to *blame* my father.

"This was a pre-online world," I replied.

I think Megs detected the ice in my voice because she quickly stepped in. "So awful. So cruel and tragic for you and your family."

We had arranged to go hiking in Alaska, just the three of us—me, Jake and Megs. I was legitimately allowed to go because Megs personally requested my assistance. She told me this as though she had done me some sort of huge favor and I should fall on my knees in gratitude.

I didn't.

Prior to the trip, I visited the spa to see if either Jake or

Megs had taken me up on my suggestion of indulging in some treatments. Megs had booked in for facials and a hot stone massage, Jake had used the hydrotherapy pool and the gym.

"Why do you need to know?" Lucy asked.

"I'm arranging a hike for them. I want to know how fit they are. The trails can be challenging."

"Sounds wise," she said. "You don't want to end up in a tricky situation." Lucy logged in to the system and talked me through their health and fitness questionnaires. It was certainly illuminating.

On the back of it, I arranged a five-mile trek, with promised views of meadows, dams, glaciers and ice caves with warnings of danger and not to visit without an experienced guide. I didn't share that last detail. We passed the organized tour group fairly early on with a sense of satisfaction.

"You were right," said Megs. "It would have held us back and we wouldn't have seen nearly as much."

We stopped for lunch at a bench beneath a canopy of spruce and pine. The cold seeped through our wet-weather gear as we feasted on prawns, crayfish and beef sandwiches made in the ship's galley early that morning, all packed into a neat picnic basket.

As we ate, Megs probed into my life, and I fed her the answers she wanted to hear.

"Sam and I loved our work, but we were keen to start a family, put down roots." Untrue. It naturally led to a story about another family…

Sam's nonidentical twin brother had gone missing while hiking in Scotland / India / the Grand Canyon [we changed the destination simply for variety]. *Devastatingly, the search had been scaled down or had trickled to a halt. Sam's parents were distraught—obviously—and Sam and I were trying to raise funds to continue the search. We had a fundraising page set up especially, as it happened. So nice of Megs to ask…*

Megs opened up too. They were not childless through choice. I said that I hoped Sam and I weren't leaving it too late. Even I really believed my lie at the time. The words felt so true.

Jake went over to examine a fallen log, as we continued to chat.

"It was Jake who didn't want children," Megs blurted out. "I always do what he wants. It makes for an easier life. He has a son as the result of an affair very early on in our relationship. He's a nice young man and I do love him, but…" She bites her lip, before looking up at me, eyes brimming. "It hurt, you know?"

"You are a saint," I tell her, placing a hand over hers.

The sadness in Megs's eyes touched something in me. Sam's flirting hurt too.

I was used to sharing confidences—up to a point—with other crew. Lucy and I sometimes drank together in the crew bar. We shared stories of past boyfriend disasters. It would have been good to off-load some of my ever-increasing secrets, yet I knew silence was everything. One drunken slipup and I would risk too much.

I had never had a guest open up to me quite like Megs before. Usually there was a natural *us and them* barrier, regardless of how friendly and full of bonhomie it was on the surface.

Jake chivied us along the moment we had finished eating. As the trail became steeper, his breathing became more labored. According to his medical questionnaire, he had suffered a foot fracture only last year and had multiple back-pain issues. I felt simmering rage at his treatment of Megs, despite not knowing her long.

As we stood at yet another view, for more pictures, a seed of badness flittered into my mind. How easy it would be to set up a fall, an accident.

"Shall I take a photo of the two of you?" I offered.

The backdrop of the clouds skimming the tops of the mountains in the distance against the luxuriant greenery was perfect. Below, a river snaked through the gorge.

Jake put his arm around Megs as they posed, smiling. They looked happy.

The urge to give Jake a shove swiftly darted away. Yes, I had crossed dubious lines, but it didn't mean I needed to cross them all. I wasn't a bad person.

We took the descent down the mountain trail slowly and I didn't try to speed Jake up.

There was nothing else I needed to do. Megs had already guaranteed me success. Before they'd left the ship, she had not only donated to Sam's charity but given me the biggest cash tip I had ever received.

"Keep it secret," she said. "Even from Sam. You just never know."

I didn't have time to ask her why. I did feel a twinge of guilt at how nice she was being. I felt hollow. I did what she suggested; I kept the money secret. Just as well, considering what happened later.

I thought that would be that. We didn't keep in touch with people, regardless of how friendly we had become, how generous they were, how much we genuinely liked them. That was another rule. A clean break was best, although we had to be careful not to do it too abruptly. Our ghosting was always slow and gentle. Busy lives, erratic schedules—all very plausible. Not every holiday friendship lasts; people understand that. Some may have suspected that they had had their heartstrings played, or maybe (and I really hope this was the case with re-gard to Betty) they eventually accepted that Sam's Casanova act had been just that—an act—but they either felt foolish for falling for it or accepted it as the price to pay for the fantasy. That, or shame. Shame is a great silencer; I should know.

Megs, however, proved to be persistent. She wrote several times. I took my time replying, but when I did, I would al-ways keep it light, mentioning the places we had last visited, the views, the shopping, the sightseeing. Until her last email.

> Dearest Charlotte,
>
> I hope you and Sam are well.
>
> I haven't been in touch for a while because we have been living a nightmare. Jake's identity has been stolen and his primary bank account hacked. We've both been struggling with the stress of it all. I'm only mentioning it because I feel certain that it happened while we were on our travels. I would hate the same kind of thing to happen to such a nice person as you. Could you spread the word, please, to help ensure that this horrible, invasive crime doesn't happen to anyone else? Tell people to be on their guard.
>
> Much love, Megs and Jake

I wrote back soothing words of sympathy, then directed any future mails from her to Junk. The only way I could deal with it was not to think about it. The words *crime* and *strug-gling* jarred. Crime was murder and violence. Crime was bla-tant theft, like burglary or mugging. People who can afford to go on cruises do not struggle. If I had—still have—one trigger, it is wealthy people who casually suggest that they are *struggling* while mentioning substantial pensions, wealth portfolios, shares, favorable interest rates, rising school fees, the difficulties their offspring (or they) are experiencing in hiring decent nannies for the grandchildren and so bloody forth, all in the same breath. It is rare, in my experience, to hear them discuss real problems: war, hunger, cold, poverty, severe disadvantages. Crime was lots of horrible things—it was not what Sam and I did.

But still, something niggled.

"Megs has been in touch," I said into the darkness of our cabin one night.

"Who?"

"Megs. You know, Megs and Jake."

"Oh, them. Yeah."

"Jake's identity was stolen, a bank account hacked."

Sam went silent.

"It's not anything to do with us, though, is it? It's a coincidence."

I so wanted it to be the case.

"Not directly," he said.

I went cold.

"There's money to be made in selling information," he said.

He pulled me close to him and stroked my hair away from my face. I stiffened. It wasn't romantic sharing a single bunk any longer. It was claustrophobic and uncomfortable.

"You didn't discuss it with me," I said.

"There was no need. I thought you'd be grateful. What you don't know, you can't ever be held accountable for. I wouldn't worry about it. Insurance companies exist for this very reason."

"So, you were doing me a favor?"

"Yes, actually."

"I liked Megs," I said.

"And therein lies the problem," said Sam, sitting up.

He switched on his lamp; the light felt blinding.

"What do you mean?"

I sat up too.

"You like the fact that I'm the bad guy and that you're the good guy," he said. "It suits your narrative."

"That's not quite true. I have my limits. You, on the other hand…"

I didn't finish my reply.

Sam got up and pulled a T-shirt over his head.

"And yet you're happy enough to spend the money on shit," he said. "Whatever shiny thing takes your fancy, you just have to have it. If we saved more than we spent, we could get out of this quicker. But you and your expensive tastes are stopping that."

He left the cabin and didn't return until the early hours, smelling of chlorine and spa soap or shower gel, none of which were able to disguise the smell of cigarettes and brandy on his breath. He ignored me when I reached for him and pretended to go straight to sleep.

It was then that I realized that we had never discussed an end plan. We were drifting. Sam was right that we needed to save more. Otherwise, there was every chance we would become trapped in this life. With only each other. That was the first time it hit me: we needed an endgame.

16

NOW

EITHER HARRISON IS A GOOD ACTOR, OR HE GENU-
inely doesn't recognize me. Either way, it speaks volumes. I
remember everything about him (even though I didn't put two
and two together when it came to his initial and surname),
despite the fact that the last time I saw him he was definitely
not in shorts and a T-shirt but dressed for the snow.

"Champagne?"

A steward offers us glasses of champagne on a silver tray.
Josephine and Harrison both accept a flute.

"Gosh, I need this," she says. "Traveling is exhausting."

There is an awkward silence until Thomas offers to show
me around the yacht.

I glance back and notice Harry/Harrison watching my departure. As our eyes lock, he looks away, quickly. Telling.

We walk past an elevator. "I wouldn't bother with it,"
Thomas says. "It takes all bloody day to move one deck. Best
bet is to use the stairs."

On the next deck, the marble floor is spotless. Framed
pictures—which I will study much closer later out of curi-

osity because they are no doubt valuable—adorn the walls. A sculpture of a man stands in a corner. His face looks toward a rectangular porthole, like a sailor staring out to sea. His expression is forlorn rather than hopeful, and I wonder why someone would choose this above any other piece of art.

"On this deck is the business center, a conference room." Thomas opens doors and points as though he is showing me around his own home. "This is one of the three lounges."

"Impressive," I say. True.

I spot a piano in the corner and what looks like a well-stocked bar. Sam would love it here. He'd feel right at home. I feel a fresh pang at his disappearing act.

An aquarium fills the space adjacent to the elevator. Bursts of colorful fish dart between the greenery. I follow Thomas down a curved staircase that leads to the outdoor decks. I glance around to take in a pool, two Jacuzzis, three bar areas, an outdoor pizza oven, a teppanyaki bar, a sauna, a gym. The list is impressive.

Back inside is a beauty salon, shelves lined with expensive brands. On one side, there is a massage table, and on the other a hairdresser's chair. I catch sight of myself in the mirror. My face is tinged with red, my bangs need a good cut. I could do with a few hours in there.

The grand tour continues past the intimate cinema room. There are eight large red velvet seats with spaces for drinks. I could see myself sitting here watching black-and-white movies to my heart's content as the sea rocks me into a chilled, blissful state. Thomas interrupts my fantasies.

"And this," he says, opening a door farther along the short corridor, "is your cabin. Ta-daaaa!"

He hovers at the door while I look around. It is spacious enough, with twin beds and an en suite bathroom. Luxury, of a sort. I can't help wondering what Josephine and Harrison's cabin is like. I imagine it has a balcony, for sure. My bags have been opened by someone. My dresses are hanging up in the wardrobe, all neat and color coordinated. In the bathroom, my makeup and toiletries are neatly arranged on a narrow shelf. I'm not sure how I feel about people going through my belongings. Even though my valuables are safely in my handbag, it makes me feel exposed.

"Where is my roommate?"

Thomas checks his watch.

"Lucy is due to board any moment," he says. "What do you think, so far?"

I feel a sudden surge of affection for Thomas. He genuinely appears to care that I like the space.

"It's lovely, thank you. It's way more spacious than any crew accommodation I've experienced in the past."

"It's actually a guest room," he explains.

"Of course."

"Well, I'll leave you to get settled." He hands me a file. "I've emailed these to you, but these are backup copies of the itinerary for the rest of today. I will do the same thing every morning, first thing. I've learned not to totally rely on Wi-Fi out at sea."

"Wise," I say, taking the folder and removing the first page, skimming the instructions.

"No need to read them now," he says. "We can meet tomorrow morning in the conference room. You can ask any questions then. I'll expect to see you on the main deck at six o'clock for cocktail hour and sail-away drinks. You can get to meet everyone properly then. Professional mingling."

I resist the urge to make a face.

"Sure."

Thomas disappears, leaving the door open. I wait a few minutes, then shut it gently behind him. Finally alone, I take a deep breath. I check my phone for messages. I promised myself that I wouldn't do this, that once I was away, I wouldn't give Whoever It Is any more power over me. Easier said than done because I also need reassurance. I send Sam a message.

Important things to tell you.

Curiosity is a good hook. Now that I'm here, it's time for him to reveal his latest scheme. Despite all the badness, all the dark stuff, he was a big part of my life—he was my husband. Nothing changes that, no matter what. I keep checking for a reply. No response. I poke again.

I'm on board.

Still, nothing. Doubt slithers, worming into my thoughts.

I sit on the bed closest to the porthole and study the cabin again. On the desk is a fruit basket bursting with bananas, mangoes, grapes and apples. Beautifully arranged on a china plate: olives, crisps, celery, carrots, dips, caviar and salmon canapés. I go to open a small fridge in the cabin. Champagne and bottles of still water. Clearly, these are considered the two essential drinks for the next ten days. I smell the pale pink roses in a small crystal vase. Heaven.

I sit back on my bed. I have already decided that it is mine because it's closest to the porthole. First come, first served and all that. I slip off my shoes and lie down, accidentally squashing the perfection of the towel art—a swan. Sam had a thing about towel art. He used to compliment the staff who created it, so much so that it became a game, almost, to see who could create the best, most elaborate pieces for him. It made Sam feel guilty about unraveling the towels after his showers. I used to tease him about it.

"Ooh, look, you've just pulled the trunk off an elephant or the wings off a poor swan."

He would flick me with the towel and I would dodge him, laughing.

I wish Sam had been who I thought he was.

Outside, I can hear the screams and laughter of those braving the waterslide.

I close my eyes and feel myself drifting off. Just ten minutes... In the background I hear laughter, and a door slams. I familiarize myself with the feel of the yacht. I used to familiarize myself with the sights, sounds and smells of each new ship. The rocking movement is barely perceptible; ditto with the slight creaks and groans. The dominant smells are of flowers, fresh linen and the sweetness of ripe fruit. The stress of the past few years dissipates. All is well.

The door opens. I open my eyes and leap up. I don't want to be caught snoozing.

"Charlotte! Oh. My. God! You're my cabinmate?"

"Lucy?"

What a joy to see a familiar face.

I haven't seen Lucy for over two years, not since the Alaskan cruise, but we have liked and commented on our respective social media posts from time to time. She looks exactly the same. Tanned, makeup done to perfection, long eyelashes and bloodred false nails. Her curly dark hair is shorter, but that's the only difference.

We hug.

"What on earth are you doing here?" she asks.

"Assistant PA," I say. "You?"

"Beauty therapist. I'm also their hairdresser, which I'm really nervous about, as I'm rusty. Well, that's putting it politely. I'm actually pretty bloody useless. I trained when I was seventeen but never really pursued it beyond that. But you say what you have to to get these kind of jobs, don't you? I was so fed up of having to do a hard product sell after every spa treatment on board the ships I last worked on. I worked in a clinic where they specialized in cosmetic procedures like Botox for a while but I missed being at sea."

I remember her mentioning it on Facebook a while back.

This kind of thing used to happen all the time, even on larger ships. It is a very small world in this industry, but given that this yacht, although magnificent, is on a much smaller scale than the cruise liners, it never crossed my mind that I would see a friendly face. Mind you, that can backfire too. Sometimes it was hard to shake off the people I didn't like.

"Is Sam here too?"

I hesitate.

"We split up."

"Oh. Sorry to hear that. You guys were so cool together. I did hear that he'd stopped working in the casinos, but I just assumed that you two were together doing some kind of shore-based work."

I wonder what else Lucy had heard about us. Even though I'd been reassured by ex-colleagues that the anonymous tip-off that a staff member was a smuggler—which had resulted in the thorough customs search—had been hushed up, there's no way snippets of speculation wouldn't have filtered through the vast crew gossip system. Everyone knew I had been stopped and briefly detained.

"Sam wasn't the man I thought I married. He was..." I stop. "I don't even know where he is at the moment." True.

"Well, onward and upward, as they say, and anyway—this is amazing!" She glances around the cabin. "We are going to have such a blast."

Lucy unzips one of her many bags and starts unpacking. I check my phone. Nothing. I get a sudden urge to unburden myself of at least one secret.

"You won't believe this, but I know one of the main guests. As in...*really know*."

I don't know what makes me blurt this out. I am usually a lot more guarded, but it's so nice to have someone to confide in, especially after the shock of seeing Harry. Lucy always loved gossip.

Her eyes widen.

"Who?"

"Harrison. Only I knew him as Harry."

"Tell me more. Was he the reason you and Sam split up?"

"No, Harrison was pre-Sam, a while ago when I worked in a ski chalet. I was his secret, though. I don't think he wanted his posh friends to know."

"So, I'm guessing he won't want his girlfriend to know, either," she says. "But don't worry about it. If he's horrible or disrespectful in any way, I will make it my personal mission to ensure that he is one of the first in my chair. He can be my experiment to see quite how rusty my skills with the scissors or clippers are."

We both laugh. It feels good. I have missed the quick familiarity and the picking-up-where-we-left-off of working friendships out at sea.

"Seriously, though," Lucy continues, "I'm hoping that they all just want their hair in an updo, or curled or straightened. Simple stuff. My great plan is to wow them so much with my beauty talents that they won't worry too much about their hair."

"Excellent strategy."

I had forgotten how much Lucy loved to talk. I glance at my watch.

"I should get ready for the sail-away drinks," I say. "I don't think Thomas will be impressed if I'm late." I pull a face.

"Oh, do you not like him?" Lucy says. "I think he seems like a darling."

"He's okay," I say. "A little intense."

I shower, get dressed and reapply my makeup. By the time I'm ready to leave, Lucy is still getting ready.

"I'll join you up there shortly," she says.

I pick up my handbag. It will not leave my sight. It's not that I don't trust Lucy, it's that I don't trust anyone. People trusted me in the past when they shouldn't have.

"Sure. See you later," I say to Lucy, closing the door to our cabin behind me.

I decide to try out the elevator. It can't be as bad as Thomas suggests. I press the call button. There are a few moments' wait, then the doors judder open. I am about to change my mind; I don't fancy being stuck inside. But Harry—Harrison—steps out. There is an awkward pause when we both hesitate before I step into the tiny elevator. He follows me back inside. We're immediately too close together. The doors shut. There is a slight jolt as we begin to move.

I pause. "Hello, Harry."

"Charlotte, nice to see you. Listen, let's keep quiet about having met before," he says. "There's no point in complicating things. Can I trust that you will let sleeping dogs lie?"

It sounds as if he has been rehearsing those sentences from the moment he saw me.

He looks pale. He should. I remember lots of things about him. Things I know he wouldn't want me to share with Josephine.

I put him out of his misery.

"My lips are sealed," I say.

The elevator stops. The doors judder open.

"But," I say, unable to resist, "it would be nice to catch up properly at some point."

"Of course," he says, without smiling. "Thank you, Charlotte. I'm glad you understand."

Thing is, I don't understand. Not yet. Why would Josephine care about a fling years before the two of them met? I intend to find out.

"A pleasure," I say, stepping out of the elevator.

A man who is polishing one of the tables looks at me as I emerge. I smile at him and he reciprocates. I note him clock Harrison exiting the elevator behind me. Up high, on a shelf behind a vase, I'm pretty certain that I catch the slight shine of a hidden camera lens.

It is a good reminder that not much will go unseen while on board.

17

SAM BEGAN TO WITHDRAW. IT WAS SUBTLE. SURFACE-wise, we were the same. We were Charlotte and Sam, newly-weds, with dreams of our future. I knew that over time love became less intense, but I missed the old Sam. I wanted him back.

It began with lies. Silly ones. For example, Sam would tell me that he had a shift in the casino when he didn't, or he would say that he had been in our cabin when he hadn't. At first, I shrugged it off. Maybe I had misunderstood, hadn't heard properly. But that wasn't the case.

We gave up on cold weather and returned to the Caribbean. Sam perked up, seemed happier, but for me, paradise had begun to look the same: sun, blue skies, rare storms, beaches we weren't allowed to visit because they were for cruise guests only. Luxury suites with private pools that weren't for us. Tailoring dreams for other people. The unhappier I became, the more money I spent, until one day I concluded that we needed to spice things up a little. New stories, new experiences, a date for our endgame. Proper, concrete plans to stop us drifting.

Sam grinned. "I like the sound of spicing things up."

It fired up hope in me. All was not lost, it had just been temporarily buried. We had a fortnight off. We flew to England to check on our house, then to the South of France and Monaco for two days on a superyacht that belonged to a friend of Sam's, and he promised me that one day we would own our own as we sat out on deck, sipping cocktails at sunrise. Sam's friend, Owen, was dull and liked the sound of his own voice, but he was "a busy person" and spent most of his time taking calls from "Russia, Malaysia, Cyprus, New York," as if each country itself was a real person.

"Where did you meet him?" I whispered to Sam.

"In my first-ever casino job I worked with him," he said. "He was patient with me. He was brought up by someone whose primary belief was that the world helps those who help themselves. He had started out with small, low-level cons. *The usual*," Sam added, as if I would automatically know what that meant.

I knew about the common tourist traps: the friendship bracelets wound tightly around wrists and aggressively sold, the tourist asking you to take a photo of them with their phone, then dropping it as you hand it back, then demanding payment to get it fixed. These types of things had always just seemed annoying to me, rather than blatant theft.

"And look where he is now," said Sam, watching him on the phone.

If I could have waved a magic wand and given Sam everything his old friend had, I would've done it in a heartbeat. He appeared to idolize his friend, spent hours talking to him while I sunbathed or shopped alone. Sam insisted on taking him out to dinner "to say thank you," and I felt a mixture of pride and pain as Sam paid the extortionate bill even though we were less well-off than Owen. His wealth had shown me that we still had a long way to go.

Sam liked us both to wear designer clothes, real jewels, and sample the best of everything. I did too. We lived two lives: the one where we lived in cramped conditions, worked long hours for relatively little pay, and *the Other Life*, as I referred to it in my head.

On the flight back to Barbados we both felt a restlessness and a discontent that, although they had been brewing for a while, felt significant. We stayed with JJ (same nice girlfriend, Jilly—Sam had been wrong) and had barbecues on the beach, swam in the sea every day. I did normal things like collecting seashells, shopping at the local markets, sleeping late every morning. Maybe we didn't need more money. Maybe we just needed more time.

Sam disagreed.

"I'm bored," he said. "I want to get back to work. I'm looking forward to spicing things up."

On our last night, I got up to get a glass of water long after midnight. JJ was sitting alone outside on the porch. I joined him for a beer.

"How long have you known Sam?" I asked.

"Years and years."

"What was he like?"

JJ gave it pause for thought.

"Restless," he finally said. "I wasn't surprised that he married you, though."

"Oh?"

"He was always looking for an anchor."

"I'm not sure I appreciate that analogy," I laughed.

"Sorry, that came out wrong."

"And you, why did you give up ship life?"

"I like my own bed," he said.

I swung gently on the hammock chair.

"I know what you're both up to," he said.

"Excuse me?"

"I'm here, if you ever need me," he said. "That's all I want to say. I know how persuasive Sam can be. Just remember, he will always save himself first. I am his friend, but I like you too."

I felt disloyal and uncomfortable. Back in bed, I tried to wake Sam up but he was too drunk, and come morning, it felt like a dream. JJ acted as if the conversation had never happened either. I filed it away and tried to forget about it.

I wanted Sam and me to work. I loved him. I believed in what we were doing. That's what's so hard to remember now, that I really loved him. Now that I hate what he did, it seems easier to look back and wonder at my own choices. Without the lens of love, things look different. I get that now. If there was a magic pill that made people fall out of love with the wrong people, the world would be a different place. It's easy to look back and think that you would have done this, that or the other, but you have to remember how you *felt*. That's what I tell myself when I have been too hard on myself. Remember how I *felt*.

Our sixth ship started off as a disaster. We were in separate cabins, both of us sharing with other people. I hated my position in sales and excursions. It was one thing persuading people to donate money to Sam and me, another for a giant corporation. All the fun and inspiration had been sucked out of us.

Then we met Maggie and Colin. The lottery winners.

Colin and his friends loved to confuse and humiliate the serving staff, as if it were a sport. They treated them as if they had no one else to serve but them. They created drama or made complaints where none were needed or when a simple, polite request to tweak a meal or have something changed would have sufficed. It aggrieved me further because I knew that one of the waiters they were belittling hadn't seen his family for months and had a lot of people who were relying on him financially. I saw red. Something snapped.

It was the smirk on Colin's face that got me. That and the fact he most certainly did not deserve his lottery win. Why him, of all the people on the planet?

I followed him out to the smoking zone where he had his predinner cigar every night.

"Mr. Williams," I said, "I have some good news for you. As one of the ship's most valued guests, you have won your own seat in the exclusive casino tonight."

His eyes lit up. He believed me. He actually believed there was such a thing.

"I have been sent to personally escort you to the casino," I explained.

As soon as he had finished his cigar (the smell made me feel sick), I walked along the deck with him. He was drunk, more so than I had originally realized. I got him a glass of water from one of the bars before I guided him into the elevator and up to the VIP section. One of the Japanese restaurants had a private dining area and I had convinced the manager that Colin had asked me to make a reservation on his behalf.

As Colin walked along the stepping-stones, past the fish-pond, he wobbled. After steadying himself, he made it to the other side and he smiled at the view. Past the bamboo plants and the indoor waterfalls, a table had been laid with an array of sushi, sashimi, tempura and small bowls of miso soup. No expense had been spared because it was all going on Colin's account. I took his cruise card to the till to process it myself.

His guests joined him, all thanking him for his generosity, to which he smiled and nodded, then winked at me as though we shared a secret.

Sam made an appearance after the meal with his best playing cards for a special, exclusive, cash-only game. Colin had this thing about carrying a wallet full of cash, so he couldn't argue. I sat at one end of the table where an array of knives not yet cleared away from dinner were laid out in front of me; one was especially long for slicing tuna. Once the game was underway without complaint and Colin had resigned himself to losing, I returned them to the kitchen before the chefs reported them missing. I sliced my finger on one in the process and had to wash the knife and my blood away in the sink.

As I watched Sam from behind a mesh screen, decorated in pale pinks with blossom, irises and wisteria, I fell in love with him all over again. There was something about watching him doing what he did best. His passion brought him to full, Technicolor life.

Colin's friends called it a night before he did; he was stubborn, determined to win back his money. Sam let him think he was in with a chance for a game or two, then, just as swiftly, disillusioned him.

Colin became belligerent and aggressive, demanded to speak to the manager. With the main restaurant in darkness, apart from the glow of the fish tanks, Sam escorted an indignant Colin along the stepping-stones. I watched. For a moment, I thought that Sam was going to push Colin into the pond, but he didn't; he ushered him to the fire exit that led outside.

I followed them.

"You're a bloody crook, that's what you are!"

"Keep your voice down, Colin."

I could tell by Sam's tone that Colin was getting to him.

"I'm going to report you to the management. I know your game. You and that butter-wouldn't-melt missus of yours."

Sam shoved Colin up against the wall. I held my breath. As I stepped forward to intervene, to calm Sam down, he let go, and Colin started walking down the stairs. Sam stood at the top as if watching him. I slipped away and returned to the restaurant.

I waited in the semidarkness, sipping a sake, again paid for by Colin. Ten minutes passed, then fifteen. I drank another. Finally, the door opened and the dark silhouette of Sam slipped in.

"What took you so long?"

"He had an accident," Sam said. "Bloody nightmare. He fell down the stairs. Had to get the medics to take a look at his ankle and he was a bit concussed. I explained that he was drunk, that he'd been aggressive and accused us of all sorts."

I only half listened because, finally, Sam and I had space to ourselves, and it was the spark we needed. Sam held me tighter than usual; he didn't seem to want to let go. The fun had eased back in at the right time. I felt a great sense of achievement. As with every game, sameness and familiarity got dull, needed reshuffling. We needed to cast our net wider, be braver, more creative. I felt invincible. We drank more sake; Sam kept topping up my glass and then a whole bottle of a fine red—"Cheers, Colin." We kept raising our glasses to him.

But then Sam's mood shifted. It wasn't like him to get maudlin when drunk, but something seemed to be bothering him.

"I have to go and fill in a report tomorrow because of Colin's accident," he said.

"That's normal, though."

There were always forms to fill in.

"He hit his head on the steps on the way down."

"But it was an accident," I said.

"Yeah," he said. "That's right. An accident. You saw it, didn't you?"

I didn't. A slight chill went through me, but I dismissed it. I was happy drunk. I think deep down I knew that it was best to stay that way.

"I love you, Lola," said Sam into the semidarkness.

"I love you too."

It was the last time I remember either of us ever saying it.

In the morning, there was a pounding on my cabin door. My cabinmate opened it, muttering about her sleep being interrupted. Sam, unshaven and red-eyed from his obvious hangover, beckoned me out. I followed him along the corridor and out on deck, my head throbbing, my throat dry. I could barely remember getting back to my cabin the previous evening.

Our game had gone too far. No, *Sam* had gone too far.

Colin had died in the night.

18

NOW

I AM ALONE ON DECK, TOO UNFASHIONABLY EARLY for sail-away drinks. I am glad, though. It's peaceful.

I watch as the tender approaches. Crew meet and greet the boat and begin unloading more crates and boxes. I have noticed that the crew wear darker colors, like black and navy. Although my knee-length skirt is black, I am wearing a pale pink top. I have tied my hair up into a knot and put a string of understated pearls around my neck, to add a touch of old-style glamour. It has been such a long time since I've been able to do this. Just wearing the pearls makes me feel a bit like my old self. Surrounded by so much wealth, I blend in.

A breeze brushes my collarbone. I inhale sea air, tinged with—paraffin? Seaweed? I gaze out to the horizon. *Where are you, Sam?* I silently will him to just let me know that all's well. It's not entirely unselfish. If Sam is all right, chances are I will be too. I jump as someone stands alongside me, bringing with him the scent of one of Sam's favorite aftershaves.

"Harry!"

He is now wearing a fresh salmon pink T-shirt and white

jeans. His eyes are hidden behind sunglasses, despite the setting sun.

"It's Harrison," he says. "If you don't mind. I just want to
say that I appreciate your discretion. Sorry if I came across as
a bit intense earlier. It was...a surprise, seeing you."

"I'm sure," I say.

It was a surprise for me too.

I glance behind us. A few staff are milling by the bar, but
other than that, we are alone. It is a mistake to think that the
crew won't pick up on anything, though. Then again, it's not
as if I am the one trying to hide my past.

"You treated me disrespectfully," I say.

"I'm sorry." He holds his hands up. "What can I say?"

I shrug. "How long have you and Josephine been together?"

"A while."

"Are you happy?"

Not that it matters but I'm curious.

"Of course," he says. "Hence the request for silence and
discretion."

"But we happened years ago."

"Josephine and I were on a break at the time. There's no
point in muddying the waters."

"If you say so," I say. "I'm not really in a position to disagree."

"Thank you."

"You're welcome," I say.

"Can I get you a cocktail?"

"Yes, please. You choose."

As he turns around, I see Lucy approaching. She winks at
me at the sight of Harrison. I pretend not to notice, already
regretting my indiscretion.

She comes up to me.

"Sorry, did I interrupt anything?"

"No, not at all."

"I have a confession," she says. "I was being nosy after our conversation about Sam, so I checked out his Facebook."

I am not sure how to respond. There is great power in silence.

"I'm sorry," she stumbles on. "I wasn't sure whether to mention it or not. I saw some stuff on Facebook. Is it true?"

"Is what true?"

She looks awkward.

"Does it upset you, talking about it?"

"Yes and no. But I'm fine with you asking questions, so go ahead."

I want to know what she has to say.

She speaks quietly. "It looks like he's dead. That he was depressed."

"No," I say. "That's totally wrong. He's keeping a low profile. Some people, including his own father, believe he is dead. But, apparently, he went missing in bad weather near a cliff edge. The police are looking into it still and are keeping me updated."

I take a breath. Lucy's words have hit me hard. I hate that people think that Sam is dead.

"How awful," says Lucy. "What do you think could have happened? Where could he be?"

"Time will tell."

"Yes, but you look so calm, Charlotte."

"I need to work. Sam and I were well and truly over, but I would never wish him any harm. I couldn't do anything back at home and Sam has my number."

"Of course," says Lucy, "I'm sure you're right and I'm sorry,

I didn't mean to make it sound like a judgment. It feels odd. Sam was so…vibrant. It's shocking."

"He still is vibrant, for all we know," I say.

I can't face the pity in Lucy's eyes any longer, so I look over her shoulder. I see Josephine, followed by Mariella and Gina.

A server approaches with a tray of champagne and a green cocktail that looks more like a smoothie.

"From Harrison," she says, handing the cocktail to me.

"Thanks."

Lucy winks again as she helps herself to a champagne flute. I take a large sip.

"Cheers!" says Lucy. "Come on, Charlotte, drink up. How often do you get to be served? I'm sure you're right and that Sam is fine. From what I recall, he was able to look after himself well enough."

She's right, but it feels odd, being in this limbo. Neither guest nor crew. Being with people who knew Sam, too, is also freshly unsettling. It wouldn't feel out of place if he were to suddenly appear on deck, glass in hand, full of bonhomie. Instead, I spot Garth and Thomas joining the others.

Thomas heads over in our direction. "Hi, all," he says. "Enjoying yourselves?"

"Is that a trick question?" I say, with a smile to let him know that I only half mean it.

"Ha ha," he replies. "Don't get drunk, by the way. It's not a good look. Come, I'll reintroduce you to everyone."

Lucy and I follow Thomas over. We join in at the tail end of a conversation about the difficulties of raising teenagers in the age of the internet.

Mariella smiles a lot and makes the most effort to draw Thomas and me into the conversation. Harrison avoids eye contact with me.

"I was thinking, Charlotte," says Mariella, "that it would be fun to have a quiz in the reading room one night. A spill-the-beans on the bride- and groom-to-be. One of those necessary-evil type of things. What do you think? Thomas thought it was something you'd be ideal to help with."

I think she's being super friendly to buy my silence over her mystery man.

"It's entirely up to you," I say. "I am happy to arrange whatever you, or Thomas, would like me to."

I take a sip of my cocktail. I smile at a man behind the bar to indicate that I need another. Mariella's words come back into focus.

"We will make Gina's evening as tasteful and as untacky as possible," says Mariella. "Like it or not, it's a tradition within our friendship circle. Gina will go mad and protest like crazy, but she'll love it, really. She insists that she's not going to be a bridezilla." She lowers her voice a notch. "Her mother is on her own, recently widowed. This is all for her, really."

Gina and Garth are a most unlikely couple. I would not have put them together. I discreetly observe them. They are standing side by side, laughing at something, but I'm pretty certain it's the first time that I've seen them together.

The crowd on deck swells.

Daniel is introduced as "Daniel, our resident James Bond."

He smiles the smile of someone who has heard that too many times before and knows they will endure it a great many more times too. The captain makes a "welcome on board" announcement. The anchor is raised, and suddenly we are on the move. Slowly, but enough to create a welcome breeze. The buoyant mood and energy on board tangibly heightens. The anticipation at the beginning of a trip is always magical, but this time, even more so. Even I feel special.

Mariella insists on a group *Titanic*-style photo (as I think of them).

I watch as Mariella charms everyone into small huddles against the railings and gets them to "Smile!" while raising their arms.

Sam posed like that with many passengers. When it all got too demanding at times, he would invent a fear of heights. Doubt slithers. Perhaps I am in denial. Perhaps it is wishful thinking that Sam is alive, hiding on a deserted island somewhere, living some sort of high life. It's too hard to think of someone as alive and spirited as Sam dying young. It's scary, the thought that I may have to face the consequences of our actions alone. I had a warped faith in my husband.

I sit down on a stool. Gina comes over to place her drink on the bar counter.

"Enjoying yourself?" she asks.

I quickly gather myself. "It's an incredible experience. I can't wait to build your itineraries along with Thomas. I am going to send you all a message asking about your absolute top musts to make sure you all at least do the one thing you are dying to do."

"Here's two already—Garth is at his calmest underwater, so diving is always good for him. I'm a thrill seeker."

"Excellent," I say. "Thank you. I'll make a note of that."

"Wonderful," she says, accepting another glass of champagne. "Maybe I should take a water, too," she says. "With lots of ice."

"I'll bring it over straightaway," says the man behind the bar.

"Great."

Gina turns to me.

"Nice pearls, by the way."

My gut tightens.

"Thanks. They were a gift."

"My mother loves pearls. She says they are a timeless elegance. My father gave her pearls on their last anniversary before he died. She was burgled a few months after his funeral and, of course, the lowlife seized them. It was devastating. When you lose someone you love, these things increase in importance."

"Of course. And I'm sorry to hear that." True.

I relax again. That's the problem when you cross a line—you can no longer take casual comments at face value. It robs life of uninhibited relationships.

I feel annoyed at Gina for ruining my enjoyment of wearing my pearls, though. They are rightfully mine. I earned them; I didn't steal them. I am not a lowlife.

Darkness has fallen and I cannot see any lights from the shore. We are out at sea, leaving behind all my problems on the shore for the time being. I surreptitiously glance over at The Party. As I do so, I see Gina watching me. Harrison too. A tingle of unease forms, which I try to bat away. I haven't felt like this since I last had something to hide. I must not give in to paranoia. I have done nothing wrong.

I want a crystal ball. Sometimes, I also want the old me back. Not because of regret, but because I want to warn myself of what dangers lie ahead.

Like the one I find resting on my pillow when I return to my cabin. A note.

Enjoy your trip, Lola. One million pounds in exchange for your life by the time we reach the final port. Your choice.

19

I HAVE THIS FIXATION WITH TURNING POINTS. THE fork in the path, the bad decisions. I can pinpoint the exact moment that Sam and I began to unravel: Colin's death. I want time to stand still so I can warn myself to stay alert. To rectify the errors I now can't undo.

I realize now that I used to blame Sam for everything. For luring me in, for corrupting me, for changing me. But—and this is something I find hard to admit—it was already in me, lying dormant. Waiting for someone like Sam to give me the impetus to do what I secretly really wanted to.

One thing that I do believe is true is that we both wanted to save *us*. But, by paying more attention to the future than the present, we corroded from the inside out. At this point we weren't quite yet shipwrecked, but we were sinking fast. We spent instead of saving, lost instead of gaining.

Neither one of us knew how to deal with the fact that Sam was responsible for another man's death, so we buried our heads in the sand; we never talked about it. He had got away with it—it was recorded as an accident—which meant we could pretend it never happened. But a secret like that, it changes everything. If I spoke up, if I did the right thing, I'd go down with Sam too. Fear and indecision silenced me. I convinced myself that it really had been an accident.

He'd hide his phone whenever we were together. Disappear at odd hours. Whenever we had cabins with single beds, we slept separately. Loneliness and fear made me indecisive, but I knew, deep down, that the only thing to do was to leave.

I just couldn't decide when.

The timing had to be right. Plus, I was scared. Sam had never threatened me with exposure, but the threat was there nonetheless. I didn't put it past him to use me to save himself.

One time, we'd visited a carnival in Jamaica, joining in with the street parties that were so full of color, costumes, music, and, most important, life and soul, the very ingredients missing for Sam and me. He had secured us a villa overlooking the festivities where we could look down onto the streets as they swarmed with happiness. I could hear the rhythm of the drums, see the decorative flames lighting the streets, the flamboyancy of the multicolored costumes as the dancing crowds snaked through the streets. In the villa, there were many books on the shelves and I read a lot that long weekend while Sam disappeared. I didn't question him; I knew it was best if I didn't. That way, I could keep up my pretense of relative innocence. I knew that I hadn't done anything truly wrong, not really, because of our selection process. When it came to Sam, however, was I snaring myself in a net of guilt by association?

"I've thought of something to cheer you up," said Sam when he returned from one of his outings. "We're going shopping!"

"Won't the shops be closed?"

"Not that kind of shopping!" He grinned.

We negotiated the crowded streets, half walking, half dancing, part of the masquerade. We stepped into the lobby of a
luxury hotel, but my heart dipped. All hotels were beginning
to look the same. I assumed we were going to have a meal or
act like guests to use the pool and spa facilities, or have a game
of tennis, maybe, our usual methods of entertainment. But,
no, Sam led me along a corridor to a jewelry shop at the end.

He knocked on the glass door despite the Closed sign.
Within moments, we were welcomed in.

"Choose whatever you like," Sam whispered in my ear.
"It's all taken care of."

"How?" I whispered back.

"Just choose."

The lights came on, flooding the glass counters. I looked
and I looked, but strangely, there was nothing that I desired.
A headache formed. The shop owner looked at me, his expression inscrutable.

"Anything catch your eye?" asked Sam.

There was such hope and childish enthusiasm in his tone
that I felt pressure. Or was it desperation? Could he sense the
change in me, and this was his way of reminding me: *This is
what we could have.*

The three of us drank tea as I tried on piece after piece. I
looked at myself in the mirror, batting away compliments from
Sam. Try as I might, I just couldn't make a choice. I saw the
owner look at his watch. I didn't blame him.

"What about a watch?" said Sam.

"Sure," I said, pointing at one, the face encrusted with diamonds, just to end the whole charade.

Back in the villa, against the distant sound of drums and
singing, Sam and I worked opposite each other at the dining
table. Sam had found a way to access guest details ahead of

their trips, so our research was easier, as it could be done on-line. Also, less fun.

I glanced around the marble-floored villa, at the leather sofas, the giant TV screen, too many ornaments, the cheer-ful, vibrant art. All I could think was how large this place was to clean. I didn't want to have to spend at least an hour hid-ing evidence. The anticipation, fear and thrill of being caught had worn off.

After that, we flew to Bridgetown, with two days to spare before our next work contract. A cruise with a four-week itin-erary around paradise. It would be the same guests, the same places, the same cabin, the same us.

We stayed with JJ, drinking rum, bellies full each night after a barbecue, watching the flames die down. JJ was single again. Sam had been right about that after all.

Sam went out one evening because he had someone to see. I could tell by the look of pity in JJ's eyes that it was time for me to make proper decisions.

In JJ's spare room, I searched Sam's belongings for clues that would justify my feelings. There wasn't much. He always car-ried his backpack with him, but I did find something.

A receipt.

Sam had bought me the watch; he hadn't stolen it.

I wasn't sure how that made me feel.

As if Sam sensed my feelings, he had the back of the watch engraved soon afterward, as if that would make it more spe-cial, some small mark of permanence. *To the woman I love, xxx.* It didn't change anything. Nothing could.

20

NOW

Day One
Staff Itinerary: Orientation and preparation.
Guest Itinerary: Out-at-sea day.

Eleven days to Barbados…

THE FAMILIAR TILTING AND ROCKING OUT AT SEA IS usually soothing, but not this time. Dread punches me in the gut the moment consciousness hits. I open my eyes. Lucy's bed is empty. I check the time: 8:00 a.m. I delay facing the outside world by gazing out the porthole. Blue sky: tick. Aquamarine water: tick. Brilliant sun: tick. Another day in paradise: no. Anonymous blackmailer left behind in England: no.

The reason the threats stopped isn't because I left them behind. It was wishful thinking. The person who has a grudge against me and Sam has boarded this yacht and is right with me now. Or has paid someone to be here. Somebody rich like Alexandra could do that because she thinks I betrayed her. Unless Sam has used my money to pay someone? Perhaps it was Sam who wanted to get rid of me all along. He's already stolen my money, now he wants to silence me.

Shit. I've barely slept and I can't mull over any more grim possibilities right now because of my meeting with Thomas.

I take the quickest shower possible, pull on some shorts and a T-shirt, and leave the cabin.

Opening the door to the conference room, I see Thomas sitting at the oval table, files out in front of him. His pen is poised.

"Take a seat," he says, gesturing toward a chair.

I do as I am told.

Thomas hands me a list of names and places. He confesses that he loves lists. To be fair, I do too. I scan the islands, and familiar names leap out: *Turks and Caicos*, *Saint Lucia*... But the one that really catches my eye is the penultimate one.

Bridgetown.

"Be aware that this can all be subject to change. The itinerary can be altered if any of the guests wish it. Do you have any initial questions?"

"How many people are there on board in total?"

"Aside from the three of us staff—you, me and Lucy—there are ten guests. Josephine and Harrison and their parents, and Gina, Norma, Mariella and Garth. There are also five villa staff who will disembark in Bridgetown, plus twenty-two yacht crew. This includes the captain, medical staff, catering, Daniel, who is in charge of security, and so forth."

He hands me another list, typed on a sheet of paper. The color scheme for the engagement celebration is gold and sapphire. It includes various decorations—ribbons, gift bags, linen tablecloths.

He stands up, opens some cupboard doors and points.

"How do we get extra supplies of anything if we need them?" I ask.

"I'll introduce you to the relevant yacht crew and they'll be able to assist with any requests. We also have use of a helicopter if something is particularly urgent or crucial. The one main rule is that we never say no. Everything can be done, no matter how big or small. It's your job to say yes. Any problems are to be kept hidden from guests, at all costs. You speak to me and I'll deal with any issues if you don't feel able to."

"Even if I have to wake you up in the middle of the night?"

"Try not to, naturally, but—yes. Now, moving on… Our bride-to-be loves costumes, so we're having a themed evening and all the outfits are stored in a single cabin. You need to plan ahead and get permission to access the room because it is occupied by a woman named Annie. She won't be disembarking until we reach Barbados, as she works as a nanny for Mariella. Her husband is bringing their four children to the villa."

"Does Annie not mind sharing her cabin with a load of costumes?"

"There's nowhere else to store them," he says. "Unless you're offering to have them in your cabin?"

"No, thanks. What about the Wi-Fi?"

"Good and bad, depending on where we will be. Just don't put off anything urgent. That's my best advice. Next thing— everyone in the party is keen to explore, but not in a typical guided-tour format. I would like to use your knowledge to help create bespoke itineraries, to show them places that are more authentic."

"I can do that, no problem." I pause and then ask the question I've been burning to ask him. "Something I'm curious about is why you chose me over the other two candidates you mentioned."

Thomas looks at me as though he is mulling over something vital and top secret.

"Honestly?"

"Honestly."

"I didn't want someone to accept the position just because they thought they were getting a free holiday," he says. "People can get very starry-eyed. It takes a certain type of person who can hold their own among this lot. Plus—" he smiles at last "—I liked you. You were the right person for the job."

"Really? You kept that well hidden."

"I've made the mistake before of getting too friendly with staff. It doesn't work. You are here to help ease my workload. I don't want to have to listen to any boyfriend woes or home-sickness traumas."

"There won't be any of those."

"Good. Although, covering my ass, there is a duty of care to ensure that you are okay, so don't suffer in silence if anything does crop up. It's just that I would prefer that you phone a friend back home or suchlike rather than bring it to work. We are in the business of professional fun and fantasy."

"I'll bear that all in mind."

He must hear something in the tone of my voice. "I'm not trying to teach you to suck eggs," he adds, "but things will be different from how you've worked in the past. On cruise ships, I imagine there are some limitations depending on indi-vidual company rules. On board here, there are *no* limitations and rules. This type of demanding work is not for everyone."

At least he is being honest. I prefer it to some of the wishy-washy people I encounter who insist that they "really don't mind" about certain details, when, really, they do. Some cli-ents think that they are employing a mind reader.

"I hear you," I say. Loud and clear.

"Right. Next on the agenda is hobbies and interests, so you can get a feel for the kind of expectations everyone has when it comes to excursions. They provided these details themselves."

I skim-read to get a flavor.

Josephine: Thrill seeker, prefers being on the move rather than stuck on a sun lounger.

Harrison: Jet-skiing, fishing, scuba diving. Never happier than when by the sea.

Mariella: No traipsing around in the midday sun. Likes horse riding, tennis and martinis at sunset.

Gina: Just a kid at heart! Waterslides, action and jet-skiing.

Garth: A "go with the flow" kind of guy. Hates being stuck in groups.

Norma: Happy with pottering around local markets and lunching in the shade.

Alicia and Charles: History, museums, art and nature.

Sebastian and Arabella: Botanical gardens.

"A varied bunch," I say.

Any one of these names could be Whoever It Is.

"I'm sure you'll figure it all out. Right, next thing…" He opens a drawer and slides out ten navy oblong boxes. Then he reaches down again and removes two rolls of gold wrapping paper and Scotch tape.

"Please, can you wrap these up before we break for lunch?" he says. "Welcome gifts."

"Sure." I don't relish the thought, yet I imagine that it affords Thomas a great deal of satisfaction to have someone like me to hand over the more menial tasks to.

"I'll leave you to it," he says. "I've plenty to be getting on with myself, so I will see you back here after lunch." He gathers up his files, pen and tablet, then pauses. "Just one other thing. I appreciate that you have signed a confidentiality agreement. However, on top of that, there is a very strict no-photographing-the-guests rule. And no personal social media giving away locations. It's up to the individual guests what they choose to disclose about themselves."

Fine by me. The fewer images floating around online, the better.

"I get it," I reply. "What about CCTV?"

"It may or may not be used," he says. "It's up to the guests' discretion. But if I were you, I would assume that you are being watched all the time."

"Sounds ominous," I say with a smile.

He throws me a look that I can't quite interpret.

"Just remember, we are not their friends. Josephine, especially, likes to keep her distance," he says before leaving me alone, surrounded by lists and the gifts.

Once he's gone, I can't resist. I open one of the boxes. Inside are platinum bracelets, made into daisy chains. Simple, but stunning. In some of the others are silver pens. I take out one of the bracelets and do up the clasp around my right wrist, holding up my arm to admire it. It suits me.

The door opens. Josephine.

I move my arm down to my side.

"Oh. I'm looking for Thomas."

"He's just left."

"Thank you."

She shuts the door. I place the bracelet back in its box. Outside the door, I hear the crackle of a walkie-talkie. I wait a few seconds before opening the door, but there is no one in sight.

I shut it again and start wrapping, but I feel watched. Paranoia hits. What if this is a test? But I reassure myself—I can pass any test. I've proved that.

It's not as though I'm a thief.

21

THE LAST TIME I EVER SAW ALEXANDRA WAS THE evening before I was stopped by customs in Barbados. The first time, however, was on our way to Jamaica.

Surprisingly, she wasn't in the best suite—that had been booked by a prince and princess I had never heard of—but she was in the second best. It was decorated in royal blues and golds and had a living area with a sofa that faced the ocean, and its own aquarium.

I was one of her designated butlers, another new role for me.

On the very first evening, she asked me to play poker with her after I had unpacked her belongings. It took me two hours to hang up and fold away all her clothes, to neatly arrange all her toiletries in the bathroom. The best job, however, was unpacking her jewelry. Her pieces were from all around the world—images of India, China, Japan, Nigeria, Oman, Sweden, Morocco, Turkey and Greece adorned the rectangular boxes with matching lids. How I wanted a collection such as that, particularly the emerald necklace, its dainty oval stones surrounded by diamonds.

I sat opposite her on a gold-backed chair and found it hard to take my eyes off her pearls. It brought real meaning to the phrase *eye-catching*.

I asked her about her travels. Her stories made mine pale in comparison. She had been married three times—all of them a disaster.

"Don't do it," she said. "Don't tie yourself down."

"Too late," I said, smiling, as if I was joking.

"Maybe you'll be one of the lucky ones."

She asked me questions about Sam and it was hard to answer because he and I hadn't yet agreed on what story we were going to spin. We hadn't even agreed yet that it would actually be her. She may not have been right, there may have been someone better. According to our latest online research, there were several potential options. I kept the details vague.

"My first husband was rich," she said, in return. "I made the age-old mistake of thinking that money would buy us happiness." She gazed at me steadily. "I didn't marry him *because* he was wealthy. I was dazzled. Too young to listen to my parents, who said they gave it two years, max." She smiled. "We lasted for three, but I think that was stubbornness on my part that we made it past their two-year prediction."

I laughed. "Sounds like the sort of thing I would do."

"Husband number two was my favorite," she said. "We lasted ten years and we had a son whom we both adored. He gave me two grandsons."

I didn't want to share with her my lack of desire for children, so I focused on my cards: ace, king, queen. When I looked up, the pearls around her neck caught my eye again. She had a similar set in one of her many jewelry boxes.

"You're such a magpie, Lola," she said, looking over her glasses at me. "I noticed you studying my jewelry boxes."

"Only one person calls me that," I replied, both embarrassed and annoyed at myself for making my admiration so obvious.

It's a myth, I had read, that magpies steal. I didn't share that fact out loud with Alexandra.

"You remind me of someone," she said.

I didn't bite.

"Myself," she said eventually, under her breath.

That night, Sam didn't come back to the cabin until past 4:00 a.m. I was still awake, dying to tell him about the mysterious woman.

"It doesn't sound as if our usual stories will fit," he said. "We're going to have to flower it up a little. Think of a real sob story."

"Actually," I said, only realizing the truth as I said the words out loud, "I don't think she's right for us. I like her. She's nice. Funny. Interesting."

"I think she sounds perfect," Sam said. "There's no point in wasting time for less return. If she's asked you to play cards with her, she clearly likes your company or is lonely. Either way, it's good for us."

"No. I don't want to target her. There's another woman," I said. "Her husband recently died of a heart attack." He'd worked way too hard, apparently. She's fulfilling their dreams by traveling without him. But it was the way she talked about his employees...how they had complained when she had to get rid of them.

"It wasn't my fault that Brian died," she'd said. "Not my fault that he hadn't made provision for everyone. I needed the money more than them. No one understood that. They wanted to reason with me and buy time, but I got the lawyers in. Soon, they did understand."

"She reminds me of Colin," I said now, to tempt him.

"No," he said. "I think Alexandra sounds better."

Unease unfurled in my stomach, and I regretted letting the cat out of the bag. Alexandra was nice, gentle and wise. The sort of person I always imagined I would be if I was lucky enough to grow old. Having lost both my parents, it cemented the idea that none of us were guaranteed old age. It explained some of my impatience, my desire to have it all now. We are all just one slip, one car, train or plane accident, one diagnosis, one potentially horrible thing away from serious injury or death.

"No," I said. "Not her."

I thought that was the end of it.

Alexandra shared more stories. She'd lost husband number three in a souk in Marrakech.

"Everyone laughs when I tell that story," she said, "but it's true. He always got lost, he had no sense of direction whatsoever and, inconsequential as it may appear to others, it really was the final straw. He couldn't do anything right. I filed for divorce the moment we returned from Morocco. I'm much happier on my own. I meet so many interesting people—hear so many stories. I'm looking forward to hearing more of yours, Charlotte."

And so I told her. I told her the good things about Sam, how we had met, how I had felt so spellbound, how vibrant he was, how alive, how full of energy.

"But, Charlotte, and this is the important thing...are you happy?"

I batted the question away with a smile and a joke.

"He's perfect for husband number one."

Naturally, when I first flew out to meet Sam, all loved up

and naive, I would never have anticipated that some of the happiest and most content moments of my life would end up being these sessions with Alexandra. I had friends, but distance and mutually busy, conflicting work patterns meant that mostly I was alone. Sam had temporarily filled that gap, but now there was a definite void. Our schemes meant that real connections and conversations couldn't exist. I had to compartmentalize, just like I'd had to with Megs in Alaska. With Alexandra, I felt a dormant urge to open up, to have real conversations rather than second-guessing what I should be saying and when.

"And what would husband number two ideally be like?" she asked.

"The opposite of Sam."

The words flew out of my mouth. I waited for guilt or regret to take over at my impulsive urge to tell the truth for once, but it didn't happen.

"Sam aside, I'm curious as to why you are working on this ship," she said, before quickly adding, "Don't get me wrong, you're a good butler. You'd be surprised how many aren't. It's an underestimated skill to be in the right place, at the right time, when a guest needs something, yet discreetly disappear when they want to be left alone. What did you do before?"

"Sam is pretty much the only reason I'm working here. It's practically impossible to get work as a couple," I say. "Let alone be on the same ship, at the same time, and, on top of that, to get any decent length of time off together. So, if I want to be with Sam, then I take the jobs I can. I was a travel agent before."

"And is it worth it? How long do you plan to continue this lifestyle, if you don't mind my asking?"

"I don't know for how much longer," I said truthfully. "Did you work?"

"Mostly volunteer work, fundraising, hospitals, helping out at the children's school when they were younger."

"I volunteered at some local dog kennels for a short while. I loved it."

So true. And, in that moment, I wondered if I hadn't met Sam, if I hadn't developed my expensive tastes, would I perhaps have settled down and been content with the ordinary things in life? Yet, still, despite the self-awareness, I knew that there was no going back. The ship to a more simple life had most definitely sailed.

But suddenly, my pleasant evenings with Alexandra came to an abrupt end. There had been no advance warning that she was tiring of me.

"I'm going to the theater," she told me one evening. "Then the casino."

The following day she was busy, and the day after that. Sam and I had yet to agree on a target, and time was slipping by.

We docked in Falmouth. I had been given extra work duties because another butler had sprained his ankle. Sam didn't seem concerned.

"I'm taking Alexandra for lunch," he said, naming a restaurant with stunning views of the ocean.

Double betrayal hit. Sam *and* Alexandra. I felt sick, right down deep inside my stomach.

"I said no," I told him. "She's not right."

Sam ignored me. I followed him out onto the deserted deck toward the bow. Most of the passengers had already disembarked.

"I said no!"

I felt fiercely protective of her.

Sam pushed me away and I slapped him in the face, not caring that we were out on deck, not caring if anyone saw. He pushed me against the railings, deliberately and slowly, so as not to make it obvious what he was doing. He then held my head down so that I was staring into the sea. I thought of Colin as I focused on the waves lapping against the sides of the ship so far below. I wondered what my final thoughts would be if Sam ever decided to get rid of me in a way that made it look like an accident.

"Without me," he said in my ear, "you're nothing. Don't forget that. You don't get to change the rules. You don't get to decide. I don't want to partner with someone who isn't fun anymore. Someone who's lost her edge."

My ears stung as he tugged the earrings out of them. Rubies. He put them in his pocket.

"I've been too generous," he said. "You demand too much. You're sucking the life out of me."

As I watched him walk away, I knew I couldn't pretend anymore. My stomach was permanently in knots. Sleep wouldn't come easily; food lodged in my throat.

But how could I tell him I wanted to leave while we were trapped on board together? And when? I had been in denial for too long. It was time to come up with some plans of my own. So I began preparing for the end.

22

NOW

I HAVE UNDER TWO WEEKS TO FIND OUT WHO THINKS I deserve to die unless I come up with a fortune as we travel from island to island, port to port. Sam might be waiting for me in Barbados—at JJ's house—having hidden away on his friend's superyacht to make it there. If I can hold on until then, I believe I will find answers.

Meanwhile, I am stuck on board this yacht wrapping gifts on behalf of Thomas when what I really need to be doing is finding out who is behind the threats. And why. Every time fresh fear rises, every time I look out at the vast horizon, the same questions go around in my head. Why is someone so certain that I have a secret million pounds stashed away?

I wrap the presents as quickly as I can. Once I finish tying ribbon around the gifts, I break for lunch.

Out on the pool deck, Lucy is sitting on a purple yoga mat in the shade.

Garth is lifting free weights. His biceps bulge. He places them down, waves hello and takes a long sip of water, tipping his head back.

At the bar, Arabella and Sebastian are sipping cocktails. I take a seat at one of the smaller tables, shaded from the sun.

"Water? Cocktail? Fruit platter? Chicken or seafood salad?" asks a smiley crew member. Her blond hair is pulled up into a neat ponytail. She is barefoot, her toes painted crimson.

This normal day-in-paradise scene feels surreal, given my situation.

"Water, please. And I'll take a chicken salad."

Lucy rolls up her yoga mat and comes over to join me.

"How was your first morning working with Thomas?"

"Interesting," I say. "How was yours?"

"Fairly quiet. Josephine and Alicia came in for a mother-and-daughter pampering session, but they only wanted manicures."

My chicken salad and water is placed on the table in front of us by the same smiley crew member.

"What can I get for you?" she asks Lucy, listing all the options.

While Lucy mulls over her reply, I take the opportunity to ask, "How long have you worked on this yacht?"

I intend to speak to everyone on this vessel and get the measure of them.

"It's my second season. I love it. Some days I have to pinch myself that this is what I'm being paid to do."

"Sounds amazing. Do you know all the crew you're working with?"

"Some better than others." She smiles. "I've worked with the captain before. And my boyfriend is one of the chefs."

Another doomed away-at-sea romance, I think, unkindly. After Sam, it's hard to believe in love anymore.

Lucy selects the same salad as me. As soon as we're alone again, I turn to her.

"Can I talk to you about something, please?"

"Sure."

"I'm being stalked. I think they might be watching me now."

"Really? Oh my God, how horrible. They would have to be a pretty determined stalker," she says. "We're in the middle of the Caribbean Sea. How do you know?"

"They are determined. Last night there was a note on my pillow."

"Someone was in our cabin? Jesus. Do you think it's Harrison?"

"No."

"It's a terrifying thought. We should report it to Daniel or the captain."

Before I can reply, Thomas approaches us. "Nice to see you're hard at work."

"It's my lunch break," I say.

"We're discussing something personal," says Lucy. "Charlotte's ex is missing, and she's concerned that—"

I shoot Lucy a warning look.

She mouths *What?* at me.

He sighs. "Well, I imagine I have a duty of care legally to ask if you're all right and tell you that I'm here if you need me, but really, I hope this isn't going to interfere with your work?"

"No. Anyway, it would be a police matter," says Lucy.

Thomas looks concerned.

"Sounds serious. Now you're going to have to tell me," he says. "If there's anything dodgy going on, I need to know about it."

"He's off the scene. There's nothing much to tell."

"That's good to hear," he says. He looks at his watch. "Don't

forget that you're expected back at work as soon as you've finished lunch."

"Please don't say anything," I say to Lucy, as Thomas walks
away.

"Sure, I understand. My lips are sealed. But I'm always here
if you need me."

I order an iced coffee before I head back to the conference room.

Thomas is already tapping away on his laptop as I push open
the door. The air-conditioning feels too cold after being out
on deck. He says a brief hello before he continues typing away.

I sit opposite him and open up an email from Mariella, listing
all the quiz questions and requirements for Gina and Garth's
joint bachelor-and-bachelorette quiz.

What did Gina want to pursue as a career when she was ten?
How did she and Garth meet?

Garth has equally dull questions. I add in some questions of
my own to liven things up before handwriting them all onto
small sheets of paper, rolling them up into mini scrolls and
tying them with red ribbon, as requested. Anyone could do this.

I open my laptop and get my teeth into some real work.
There is a polite knock on the door before it opens. A crew
member requests that Thomas meet Josephine out on the pool
deck. He straightens up from his chair without hesitation.

"Back in five," he says to me. "No shirking."

He leaves his laptop open. I stand up, ostensibly to stretch
my legs, but I just can't resist. Rows of spreadsheet figures. I
click, tap and scroll. *Expenses.* The cost of the extra flowers
for the engagement party on the penultimate night alone is
illuminating. I should have charged double my fee.

Recruitment. And there I am. He wrote notes after our initial
meeting: *Well-presented, professional, experienced, enthusiastic, no*

luxury yachting experience, eager—too eager?! Check references. Unfamiliar names, presumably other candidates' details, are listed.

I click on his laptop history.

"What the hell are you doing?"

Thomas strides into the room and closes his laptop.

Shit.

"I was just looking to see if you had updated the itinerary. I overheard Josephine say that she was keen to add Aruba to the list of ports if it was possible." True. "Sorry, I had no right to look without permission. It won't happen again."

"Do you know how many people would die for a job like this?"

"I said I'm sorry."

My apology doesn't appear to placate Thomas.

I sense him watching me as I do everything he asks: I book tickets for botanical gardens, email horse-riding stables, check out cable-car timetables and match up the dress sizes to the guests for the available costumes. I unwrap new leather handbags from their packaging. Yet no matter what task I'm doing, I can't fully concentrate. I keep glancing up. Outside the porthole is nothing but blue sea and blue sky.

We finish midafternoon. Lucy is taking a siesta; our cabin is dark. I change into my bikini and pull on a dress. On the pool deck, three women are sunbathing. One is Alicia, the other two are villa staff. I select a lounger as far away from anyone as possible, slide my bag beneath it, remove my glasses and ease myself into the water. It's more of a plunge pool, not large enough to complete many lengths, but it feels nice to wash off the day after being stuck in a freezing office with Thomas. I lean against the edge and put my arms out to catch some rays. I close my eyes.

I am aware of chatter, discussions about how to dress for dinner. I hear them leave, their voices disappearing inside. By the time I emerge from the water, I am alone. I dry myself before reaching down for my bag. Panic hits. It's not there. I can't see properly. I feel around. Nothing. That bag contains *everything*. I walk over to the bar area, where I can see someone polishing wineglasses.

"Excuse me." I hesitate. How best to word it? "Do you know if anyone has tidied away my bag? I left it under the sun lounger over there." I point.

"I'll come and help you look for it," he says. "I've only just got here. You are the only person I have seen so far."

He walks back with me to the loungers and starts looking beneath them.

"Is this it?" he says, holding up my bag.

Relief.

"Yes, thank you."

"You must have put it beneath a different bed. It's easy enough to do."

I put on my glasses and sink down onto a lounger to check the contents of my bag. All there. Thing is, I know where I put it. And then it dawns. Someone wants to mess with my mind.

The man who found my bag returns with a kind smile and a glass of water that he obviously thinks I need, but I don't see friendliness and good service. Instead, I see a stranger or an old contact of Sam's. I see someone who could have rummaged through my bag and then lied about it.

Yet, if I keep calm and think straight, it could also be an opportunity.

"I used to work on cruise ships, and I'm wondering, have you worked on yachts for long?" I ask him.

"Seven years."

"Wow," I say. "You must enjoy it."

I used to hate it when people said things like that to me when I worked on ships.

"Sure beats working for a living."

"I can imagine. Have you always worked on smaller yachts or did you ever work on cruise ships?"

He laughs. "I wouldn't call this yacht small," he says. "Usually I work on smaller ones. But to answer your question—no, I've never worked on bigger liners. Too big. Too impersonal."

"What about the other crew on here?" I ask. "Do they have cruise-ship backgrounds?"

"No idea. You'll have to ask them. I think one of the chefs may have at some point, but again, maybe not. I meet so many people…" He shrugs.

"Any chance you could show me around? I'm curious."

"Sure," he says. "I'll have to check with the captain first. Wait here."

He returns after a minute or two.

"Follow me," he says. "I'm Jon, by the way."

"Charlotte."

Although I'm familiar with the guest layout: the gym, the cinema room, the sauna and the lounges, we pass through doors I hadn't spotted before, including one that states: Crew Access Only. I like walking through it. It feels forbidden and it also makes me feel more at home, more at ease with my role. We walk along a narrow corridor that opens out into a dining area. Five people, four of whom I recognize, sit at a table. Two are wearing crisp white uniform shorts, sipping from mugs, and the others are in casual clothes.

They hide their surprise, make an effort to say cheery hellos, but I appreciate that they must feel a little put out that Jon has invaded their sanctuary with a visitor. I wouldn't have liked it.

"Hi," I say with a smile. "Sorry for the interruption. I won't stay long."

Jon indicates that I should sit down near the end of the table. The cramped conditions are in complete contrast to the space on the other side of the door. On the wall is a large map and various rules, safety regulations and reminders.

"Charlotte used to work on cruise ships," Jon says.

They look utterly disinterested.

"I'm working on this trip," I say, stating the obvious, as some of them have already had to deal with my various requests for scissors, sticky tack, needle and thread, black marker, spare buttons, additions to costumes, and other miscellaneous bits and pieces. "Sometimes it feels a bit strange, like I'm neither one thing nor the other. I was curious when chatting with Jon about whether I would have worked with any of you in the past or if we had mutual friends. Small world and all that." I pause. "Sorry. That's an annoying question."

I sense a collective thawing toward me.

"Actually," one of the guys says, "I did do a season, but it was years ago and I don't remember anyone in particular. Did you have someone in mind?"

"Sam. Sam Young. A croupier." As I say his name, I study all their faces for even a flicker of recognition. There is none. "It's a huge, massive long shot," I say.

Everyone shakes their heads politely.

"No, doesn't ring any bells."

"Didn't really come across any of the casino staff."

"Are you all permanent crew on this yacht?" I ask.

"Pretty much," says one man. "People come and go, depending on seasons and requirements, but on the whole, we're a team."

"Who is the owner?" I ask.

I haven't been able to find that out.

"He's rarely on board," says Jon. "Although, his wife often is. Most yacht owners, even the wealthiest, charter out their boats. It costs a daily fortune to keep one running and they barely use it. It's like a new toy at first, they invite all their friends and family, sometimes separately, if you know what I mean. Some of the things I've seen on board are pretty unbelievable and shocking. Not on this yacht, though," he quickly adds, "but then the excitement appears to wear off and the time between their visits gets longer. Once, we all sailed to the South of France, but then the owner changed his mind, he wanted to go to the US Virgin Islands instead, so we sailed back again. This isn't even the only yacht he owns."

One of the women throws him a look as if to warn him against speaking out against their employers, past, present or future. She shifts uncomfortably in her seat.

Jon takes the hint and stands up.

"I'll introduce you to the captain before we head back. He's given permission for me to take you onto the bridge."

"Sure," I say.

There are mumbles of "thanks" and "goodbye" before we walk out, past a galley, where one of the chefs—Jack, apparently—says a curt hello.

"Actually," I say, once we are out of earshot, "before the bridge, would you be able to show me around the rest while it's quiet and most people are working? I'm curious how it compares to cruise-ship living."

"It's not that exciting," he warns, "but okay."

We walk through another door: Keep Closed at Sea.

We pass the laundry room, which is narrow with a wall of spinning washers and dryers. A random memory: they were always one of the more populated places on cruise ships, especially toward the end of the trip. There were never enough machines. There were always queues, and passengers would get irate if others didn't unload their washing or drying the moment the cycle stopped. Two erect ironing boards lean against the opposite wall and neat piles of folded white-and-navy towels and sheets line the shelves.

Two small offices contain wooden desks, large computer screens, maps and files. A food storage room is hidden beneath a trapdoor in the larder.

"So we won't starve if the engines and locator beacons fail and we drift hundreds of miles into the middle of nowhere. We can live off tinned stuff for weeks, if not months."

Jon opens the door to a mini gym containing a treadmill and a few free weights and another room containing a sofa, an armchair and a table that is littered with yachting magazines, local newspapers, and empty mugs and glasses.

"It's not usually this much of a mess," says Jon, apologetically. "I'll show you my cabin," he says, as we walk down a narrow, short corridor, "but I can't invade anyone else's privacy. Some of the night-shift workers have only just got up."

"Of course," I say as I stare into a tiny space with bunk beds.

One bed is neatly made up, the other is a crumpled mess.

It reminds me how fortunate I am. Jon shares with another guy (whose name is actually Guy, as it turns out). On a tiny shelf, crammed with deodorant, a phone charger and a book, is a photograph of a woman standing in front of the Sydney Opera House.

"Girlfriend?"

"Yes."

I like that he doesn't say "Yes, but…" then come out with the "but not when I'm away working" usual line. It makes me warm to him even more, but it also means that he's off-limits, which is a shame. It had half crossed my mind that a dalliance (to use Sam's word) would be a welcome distraction.

I take note of the way back as we head for the bridge, through a No Access door.

Although I met the captain—"please, call me Tim"—and the crew briefly on the day we boarded, they were just a sea of names and faces. I go through the motions of asking if they know Sam, but there are more blank faces. Only the captain seems vaguely familiar, but not enough for me to pinpoint why.

I return to my cabin. The beds have already been made, the bathroom is smudge- and drip-free. I pack a small bag to take up to my "office." It's only as I'm ready to leave that I notice that beside the towel swan on my bed is an orchid stem. As I pick it up and drop it in the trash can by the desk, I notice that Lucy's bed is white and pristine, not an orchid in sight.

I look down at the purples and pinks. I don't see beauty, I see something sinister or a message from Sam. It gives me the chills.

23

I NEVER FOUND OUT WHAT HAPPENED AT LUNCH BEtween Alexandra and Sam, but he no longer mentioned her as a possibility. All Sam would say was that she was interesting but that I had been right: she wasn't suitable. Which most likely meant that she had not fallen for his patter. It made her one of a few, I reckoned. I was pleased. Sam wasn't just losing his magic in my eyes; his ugly behavior and increasingly violent tendencies were affecting everything. And all Alexandra would say of Sam was that he was charming. *Charming* is an adjective that now makes me wary.

The card games with Alexandra picked up where they had left off, and we added chess and canasta into our nightly routine once she had returned from dinner. I guessed she'd seen through Sam and wanted to put it behind her. I was glad that she hadn't fallen for his charms. She valued our friendship more than his smarm.

Sam managed to wangle it that we got some time off together in port: Pigeon Island, Saint Vincent, Grenada, the perfect amount of paradise. Alexandra didn't want me to book the cruise excursions; she wanted to be free to explore alone. I would see her disappear off into a taxi or waiting for a car at the exit to most ports.

Things started to pick up. This always happened—the ebb and flow between Sam and myself. Every time, it would bring a wave of fresh doubt. The night before we docked in Saint Vincent, we met the perfect couple—Marcus and Tanya. So perfect that I'm sure that Sam and I would have made friends with them naturally if we hadn't been so out for ourselves.

Even now, I reflect on the price I continue to pay: fewer genuine friendships, fewer proper connections.

Marcus was a charmer. He was totally transparent about it and Tanya played along with his flirting by smiling in an indulgent fashion. They were wealthy, fun, dead against having children and out for maximum enjoyment. Our conversations revolved around holidays and about grabbing life with both hands.

I didn't plan to seduce Marcus. Not consciously, anyway. Perhaps, though, deep down, I knew it would force me to wake up to what it was I needed to do: get away from Sam. I feared he would never let me leave, not with all the secrets we shared.

Tanya had gone on an island tour of Saint Vincent and Sam had disappeared. I genuinely thought that he was with her—why wouldn't I, given his past record? I was pissed off, hurt and humiliated. Before that, I had been focusing on Devon, our joint dream. I wanted to believe Sam's reassurances that the other women "didn't mean anything," but nonetheless, I had let him get away with it. And worse, I had done it because I valued our lifestyle more than my own self-respect. I fed my green-eyed monster great big chunks of steak until it had completely taken over my rationale.

Marcus and I had lunch at a hotel, and when he suggested that he book a room to finish off our second bottle of expensive wine in private, I said yes. Because the thing is, I did want to. I was attracted to Marcus; I enjoyed his attention. Although I didn't realize it at the time, I think I knew this would be the end of me and Sam.

While Marcus was in the shower afterward, I couldn't resist picking up his watch and studying it. Cartier. I put it back down on the bedside table when I heard the shower turn off.

I was wrong. About many things. Firstly, it transpired that Tanya really had gone on an island tour—alone. Not with Sam. She raved about it afterward, torturing me with pictures of turtles and unspoiled, white, powdery beaches. I felt wretched. It also turned out that Sam had been looking for me. My phone had died after I had given up tracking him down earlier. When I charged it and switched it back on, there were seventeen missed calls.

Sam seemed to sense what had happened. I denied it. But deny, deny, deny was something that Sam had always impressed upon me.

"If you're ever questioned, stay silent. Deny everything, even if they say they have proof. If there's doubt, there's a chance. If you confess, there is no chance."

So, deny I did. But, of course, he had taught me never to admit to anything, anyway, so naturally, he didn't believe me. He lost it.

"You've ruined everything!" he yelled. "Everything we ever worked for, everything we ever had between us."

"No! You did that."

"I thought you loved me," he said. "I thought you trusted me."

"I did! But you've let me down and lied and cheated time

and time again. I'm sick of covering for you, sick of living like this."

"That's rich," he said, his face contorted in rage. "Considering you were the one who wanted more and more! You were the one with the taste for jewels and luxury fucking goods!"

He smashed up our cabin and my right calf was sliced by a flying glass before it shattered against the desk. I hit my head against the door in my haste to get away. His violence had escalated on the night of Colin's death—at some point, he had lost it enough to shove Colin down the stairs. These were the thoughts that ran through my head as he pulled me back—that and the terrifying knowledge that he was capable of killing me.

Unless I killed him first.

Security were called by one of our neighboring cabins, no doubt because of all the violent noise and shouting. But, of course, Sam smoothed things over with them while I hid in the bathroom. I was shaking with rage and fear, and I didn't trust myself not to tell the truth about what Sam had just done. Yet I also knew that if I opened my mouth to one of our colleagues, Sam would find a way to make them believe him and not me. I had to be one step ahead of him, plan things carefully and calmly.

I reasoned with myself that this was the lowest and the ugliest we would sink. It wasn't.

24

AS WE APPROACH THE SHORELINE OF TURKS AND
Caicos, I experience brief relief to see land, even if it is just
the cruise-ship terminal flanked by rocky beaches and rows
of crammed beach umbrellas blocking the view of the silky
sand. I told myself in bed last night that anytime I feel truly
uncomfortable or threatened, I can jump ship and board a
flight. Deep down, I know that this is not true. Sam's and
my chickens are coming home to roost and I will have to face
whoever or whatever it is alone. It is darkly reassuring, in a
twisted way. Living with the subconscious fear of a tap on the
shoulder has taken its toll. Even before Sam's betrayal, I had
a nagging, intuitive feeling I would only ever truly get away
with things if I worked alone. I must narrow it down, find
any links to Sam or Alexandra. Keep an open mind but trust
no one. To not just survive, but to thrive, I must rewrite history. I am innocent; Sam is not. I must believe that.

Josephine is clearly the person I need to impress, so the first
excursion planned, without much assistance from Thomas, is

a horseback tour, followed by snorkeling and swimming with stingrays. The bad news is that she wants Thomas and me to accompany them on the ride, to bring water and snacks, spare sunscreen, "that kind of thing."

It is blisteringly hot as I guide everyone into three separate Jeeps. Ten guests, plus Thomas and me. I envy Lucy today; she is staying on board. I do not feel like clambering up onto a horse, as much as I love them.

We're all given riding hats. The guests have new ones, while Thomas's and mine look they've been used plenty of times before.

Next comes the horse allocation. I make it very clear that I am a *beginner*, although the large black horse I am given to ride—Jaguar—does not look as if he has ever had a novice ride him.

"Don't worry, he's an angel," I'm told.

People mount horses and then get back off them again. I have to dismount to go back to the Jeep to pick up Alicia's sunglasses, which she's forgotten. The guests swap, compare and discuss. It feels never-ending until, finally, all twelve of us are on horseback. Alicia, Charles, Sebastian, Arabella and Norma lead the way, along with one of the guides. Directly behind them are Josephine and Harrison, followed by Gina, Garth and Mariella. Thomas and I are at the back with another instructor.

"Enjoying yourself?" asks Thomas.

"No."

"Me neither," he laughs. "Come on, Charlotte. You look miserable. Haven't you ever heard of faking it until you make it?"

My horse picks up speed. I do not feel in control. I sink into the saddle. My spine jars with each step.

"Sit straighter, like this," demonstrates our guide.

It makes no difference. I curse the enthusiastic, wanting-to-impress-Josephine me of yesterday.

"Can you make my horse slow down, please!"

"Just relax," Thomas calls out.

I try to. If I were on foot, I would be impressed. The ocean is the clearest I have ever seen on any of my island travels. We bypass mangroves. Coconut palm fronds sway in the gentle breeze. I do not want a gentle breeze. I want clouds, rain and a decent wind. I fall into some kind of rhythm, thank God. We pass cheerful-looking houses, a church and sailboats with imaginative names.

We meander pleasantly along a coastal path, with Jaguar stopping every now and then to paw at the ground slightly. The area widens out as we approach the open, white sandy beach. Clear blue waves brush the shoreline. Our guides lead us to the water's edge as our horses obediently—even mine—step through the sea.

We all stop. Jaguar appears good at copying his stablemates as he does the same. The lead guide dismounts to snap some pictures of us all before we continue.

Harrison falls back until he is riding alongside me.

"I'm sorry again about the other day, it really was clumsy. It was the shock of seeing you again. I didn't mean to be abrupt."

"It's fine."

It is. He's apologized, it's over. I'm not holding any grudges.

I concentrate on holding the reins as tightly as Jaguar will allow as we slow trot. Up down, up down.

"I had convinced myself that something bad had happened to you, you see."

I don't see.

"When you were gone from the chalet," he continues, "I

felt terrible. I hated myself. I know I should have treated you better."

I don't fill the silence. I want to hear what he has to say.

"There was the body of a skier found near the village, not long after you had gone. A woman had frozen to death. I was terrified that it was you. It wasn't, of course, because here you are trotting merrily alongside me—" he grins "—but I have never forgotten the fear I felt, and the guilt."

A few yards in front of us, Thomas slows down. Is he trying to listen in?

"Where was Josephine at the time?" I ask.

"Skiing in Colorado," he says. "We weren't in contact, but we reunited at Easter."

I realize that I don't actually care, not really.

"Apology accepted. I'm fine, as you can see."

"Excellent stuff."

Jaguar speeds up and we overtake Thomas, Arabella and Gina.

Just as I'm beginning to think that maybe it's not too bad after all, I hear the sound of the crack of a whip behind me. Jaguar seems to sense that he has one chance to bolt for freedom, one great opportunity to get rid of me, and he takes it.

His trot becomes a canter, then I'm pretty certain a gallop, although I can't tell the bloody difference, as we pass the entire group and head for the horizon. Sand stings my face as my saddle loosens and starts to slide over to the right. I grip the reins tightly as I try to straighten myself and pull the saddle upright, but I can feel myself slipping farther. I focus on Jaguar's hooves churning up the sand. I can feel the vibrations of his steps through my entire body.

Unable to hold on any longer, I let go, but as I fall to the ground, my right foot gets stuck in the stirrups and I am dragged for a good few yards, pain shooting through my knees and elbows as I'm scraped along stones until I fall loose. Jaguar careers off before stopping and looking behind as if he has no idea what he has just done.

I can feel the thundering of more hooves and I put my hands over my head to brace myself, but an assortment of brown, black and gray horse legs come to a halt before I hear a cacophony of voices asking me if I am all right.

My head hurts, my back aches and my ankle feels slightly off.

"Let's see if you can stand up," says Garth, who for some reason has taken charge. "I had to do a first-aid course last year for work."

Between him and the lead guide, I am up on my feet. Thank God, no broken bones. Another instructor, who is clearly some kind of horse whisperer, has taken hold of Jaguar, who looks as if he is the most gentle, innocent horse.

I see the two guides examining the saddle and the girth.

I am helped up onto an instructor's horse and led back, with Jaguar walking alongside us. Back at the stables, there is much confusion and denial. The girth was frayed but it looked like a straight cut, which could have caused the saddle to slide.

"This is unheard of," says the owner. "We are a top-class stable."

I leave Thomas to deal with the paperwork and insurance formalities while I insist everyone gets back in the awaiting Jeeps.

"I'm fine," I insist.

But I am not. My legs feel weak and all I want to do is get back on the yacht and take a cool shower. I think back. There was so much confusion at the stables about who was riding which horse, so much bloody indecision that I cannot recall anyone being close to Jaguar. Someone was, though. Someone got close enough at the stables to cut my girth—just enough that I didn't fall straightaway—and that someone knows about horses, which doesn't narrow it down at all because every single one of them is an experienced rider, apart from me.

We drive from the stables to a hotel. I shower in the hotel dayrooms and change before lunch. It feels good to take off my pants and socks, replacing them with a dress and sandals. I examine my ankle. My right arm feels bruised, yet there is no evidence of anything blossoming across my skin.

At lunch, I am seated next to Arabella, Harrison's stepmother.

"Are you sure you're okay?" she asks. "You don't have to put on a brave face. I would be terrified, absolutely terrified. My neighbor was trampled by his horse after it was spooked. He is still in a wheelchair, poor thing. No one would mind if you went back to the boat. We're all adults, I'm sure we can find our own way to the beach this afternoon."

"It was a bit of a shock, but honestly, I'm okay now," I say. True. "My horse had attitude."

Everyone at the table laughs, which lightens the intensity of what just happened.

"Which islands have you visited before?" I ask, trying to change the subject.

"We have spent the odd Christmas in Barbados," she says. "But Sebastian has had a rough time of it of late. Several niggling health issues, then he was mugged. Harrison suggested that some sunshine would do him the world of good."

"Sorry to hear that."

I am.

"People think they can just steal whatever they please whenever they feel like it. He blames himself. He was out jogging at night on a deserted route." She takes a large sip of wine. "Still, it could have been much worse," she suddenly adds, as though she regrets confiding in me. "Much worse."

Yes, it could've been.

I'm unsure how to reply so I opt for: "The world can be a dangerous place at times. I'm glad he's all right now."

Thomas settles the bill after lunch. As we wait on the jetty for the small boat, I look around. Harrison has his arm around Josephine's shoulders. Alicia and Charles are shooting videos. Garth is sitting on the edge of the jetty, paddling his feet. Gina and Mariella are chatting. Arabella sees me watching her and smiles. Paranoia weaves through my mind. Did she tell me that Sebastian had been robbed for a reason?

On the beach I spot a trio of teenage girls taking photos of the *Cleobella* in the distance. They are smiling and laughing and happy in their posing. A couple are swimming. The man is the same height as Sam, with a similar hair color. Normal people leading normal lives. I used to pity them. I used to think that Sam and I were the ones on the one and only path to happiness.

The boat driver indicates that we should board. Salty air brushes my face during the mere minutes it takes to get to the next beach. We disembark and gather round on the sand while everyone listens to the stingray expert. Josephine's toenails are painted crimson to match her bikini. Gina's toenails are dark blue in contrast to the fine white sand. Mariella is wearing an emerald one-piece, with pale pink toes and a silver anklet, not dissimilar to mine but with a seashell instead of a mermaid. Garth fiddles with his large watch, a Tag Heuer sports version, if I'm not mistaken. He also wears multiple multicolored bracelets around his wrist. Harrison puts his arm around Josephine and pulls her close, kissing her neck. None of them look like they would deliberately cause me harm.

Lucy appears in a Jeep and rushes down to join us.

"I've never seen stingrays before, can you believe it?" She steps out of her dress and drops it carelessly to the ground. She is tanned, wearing a white bikini. "Thomas said it was fine to join in as long as I keep myself to myself. I was having just the best time on board. Honestly, it was sheer bloody bliss not having to worry about being summoned to work, but if I regret one thing about my working history, it's that I didn't make the most of every opportunity. I was too busy falling in love with the wrong men and wasting my time holed up with them in crappy, dark cabins."

"Weren't we all?" I laugh, as I decline a snorkel being offered to me.

I learned to free dive on one of Sam's and my honeymoons (we had a few) in Jamaica. There is something so uplifting and freeing about holding my breath for as long as I can. Sam and I used to compete. I would always win. He hated it.

I swim farther out, to get away. I turn around, take a deep breath, dive down and swim just above the seabed. While the silence below the surface has always creeped me out a little, it is magical and almost surreal, like being in a slow-motion, color movie. It's a different pace of life beneath the sea. The stingrays glide past elegantly, skimming the seabed.

When I stop to take a rest, my feet are surrounded by tropical fish; I wish I could name them all. Seaweed sways gently in the water.

As I approach the shore, I sense someone alongside me as I break the surface. Harrison. He touches my arm as he points to a stingray circling our feet.

"Look! Isn't this out of this world?"

I look up. The rest of the group are all distracted by the stingrays, their backs to us. Apart from Josephine. She is staring straight at us.

I smile, but she does not return the gesture. She whispers something to Gina, who turns to look at me too. Harrison, oblivious, keeps pointing at our feet. I walk out of the sea and begin to towel dry. Beneath a parasol I spy Daniel, silently watching everything.

Back on board the *Cleobella*, I aim for the hot tub to soothe my back and ankle, both aching after the accident. By the time I return to our cabin, it is in darkness. Lucy is having a siesta.

I crack open the curtain to let in a little light. I glimpse something on my bed. The towel art today is shaped like an oyster and in the center, instead of a pearl, is one of the gifts I wrapped up. I recognize the gold wrapping paper.

On Lucy's bedside table I spot that she has received a gift too and has unwrapped it: one of the pens.

I open mine, feeling a twinge of excitement. I love gifts. One of the things I miss about Sam is his generosity. I pull open the lid of the navy box. Only, mine is not a pen, nor a daisy bracelet.

It is the very last item Sam ever acquired for me: a watch. It must be the same one because on the back it's engraved: *To the woman I love, xxx*. He took it back on our last-ever day together, he said I didn't deserve his generosity after our vicious argument.

I never thought I would see this again. I never wanted it in the first place and now it's as if Sam is trying to taunt me or remind me of what he called my ingratitude.

I look out of the porthole; we're on the move. Sam isn't here, he's out there somewhere. But someone connected to our pasts *is*. If I find out exactly what happened to Sam, then

I can ensure my own safety. I am being poked with an invisible stick. And I still don't yet know who by or exactly why.

It's then that I spot a note tucked inside the box:

Tick, tock. Counting down the days until the end. Unless, of course, you are careless enough to have another accident. One million pounds. Watch out, Lola.

25

SAM WANTED ME TO CONTINUE AS IF OUR MASSIVE fight had never happened, while he targeted Tanya.

"Enough," I said. "We've done enough. It is not a game anymore. These are real people."

Sam ignored me. He was going to do as he pleased anyway. I needed to warn Marcus. I had to seize any opportunity. I'd made arrangements with Alexandra for after dinner so I sent word from the reception desk to let her know that I would be late for our evening get-together. Instead, I spent my time loitering near the main dining area. When I spied Marcus excusing himself from the dinner table, I followed him.

"Sam knows," I said. "And he has a temper."

Marcus looked stunned. Sam came across as so placid, no one could image him with a temper.

"Thank you for telling me," he said.

He returned to the dining area. But as the desserts were served, then the coffee, I could see the intensity and concern in Marcus's expression as he appeared to only half listen to whatever the person to his right was saying.

Marcus and Tanya went to the casino, as they did every night. Sam worked his charm on Tanya, expertly excluding Marcus from the games and the conversation. Marcus was no longer the charmer. He had encountered someone who was brighter, bolder, unafraid of the consequences.

The following night they didn't appear at their table for dinner. My mind conjured up various worst-case scenarios. Had Marcus confessed to what we'd done? Had Sam told Tanya?

Another couple told us that they had disembarked in Martinique. "Family emergency."

Relief.

Sam had smiled at me, put his arm around my waist, then squeezed so hard that he left a bruise.

I knew that when we reached the end of the trip, we would divorce. I made a vow that I would use our money to do good, make a positive difference to people's lives. It was becoming increasingly hard to justify my actions.

Sam didn't come back to our cabin that night. I went out on deck and paced. Flashes of various arguments came and went. I was never alone: the omnipresent CCTV loomed.

I shuddered as I passed beneath the endless cameras facing all directions with the creepy, beady eyes of unknown staff hiding unseen behind the lenses. It was what I imagined prison to be like: no privacy. Other tortured night owls roamed the deck. I stood near a railing and looked down into the jet black of the water, the swirl of the foaming white tips of the waves lit by the boat's lights. I wondered what it would feel like to give in to the siren pull of oblivion below. Strangely, I used to think that it would be better to be in a sinking ship than an about-to-crash plane, but thinking about it properly, neither option is better than the other.

"Paradise not what you thought?" Alexandra's voice startled me. "Fancy a cognac?"

I did.

We shared more stories that night. I opened up about Sam (not everything, obviously).

"It seemed like such a romantic idea to give up everything and run away to sea. Just like in the old movies."

"A lot of them are tragic, too," she said with a smile.

"True. I thought that Sam and I were different."

"Everybody thinks that. I dated a man in between husbands whom I fell for deeply. Yet he only wanted me for my money. My friends warned me, but I wouldn't listen." She smiled. "I got my revenge, though."

"How?"

"Among other things, I arranged a large birthday party for him at one of the most expensive restaurants, then left him to pick up the bill."

We both laughed.

She complimented me on my excellent taste in jewelry. I invented an aunt I had inherited them from, not that I think Alexandra would've asked me how I came to own such incredible pieces. I just always felt safer if I wrapped a lie around the ownership of my vintage possessions.

She showed me a brooch—a stunning, delicate butterfly. It had been given to her grandmother who had been engaged but had fallen in love with a forbidden man who had lived in France. Alexandra had spun such a rich story of secrets, lies, intrigue and ultimately heartbreak, that the brooch felt alive with history.

"My grandmother would like the thought of me sharing her story," she said. "She had dementia and would call my mother every night, begging to be freed from her private hell. When I saw the impact it had on my mother, it made me feel helpless. I think that is why money is important to me. I want choices."

We discussed the importance of living our lives to the full.

"I would like you to have it," Alexandra said, handing me the brooch.

"I couldn't," I said. I didn't deserve it.

She insisted. Afterward, she told me how her daughter had died in a bus accident, aged fifteen.

"You remind me of her," she said.

I couldn't refuse the brooch after that. I came clean about Sam's temper. I admitted I was scared. She told me about a place I could visit at our next port of call where I could get my jewelry repurposed.

"They also make excellent copies, if that helps. Start saving, keep a diary. Leave him sooner rather than later."

I took her advice. I had my mermaid pendant turned into an anklet, for a start. I could no longer bear to wear it in its original form; it was too stark a reminder of my shattered dreams, yet I didn't want to throw it away. I wanted to keep it as a permanent reminder not to make the same mistakes twice.

With Alexandra's encouragement, I grew stronger. But Sam seemed to sense the change in me because he asked if I was planning on leaving him.

"No," I lied. "But this isn't the life I signed up for."

"I won't let you leave me," he said. "We're bound together. If you go, I won't be able to trust you. I won't be able to relax, wondering if you have the urge to confess all to a new man."

"I won't say anything, ever."

"You're right, you won't."

Alexandra and I plotted. I would book both Sam and myself flights to London on the day we were due to disembark on the final stage of the cruise. I would persuade him that we should go to Devon, talk it through.

"In reality, just get a lawyer and cut all ties," she advised. "Sam will drag you down and then he will leave you in the gutter. Forgive me for saying this, but you should never have trusted him. People like him, they don't do it for you. They do it for themselves. They are dangerous. If I were you, I would get the hell out now."

The night before, Sam and I had found a quiet spot out on deck.

"It's the stress of these long trips that gets to us," he said. "We'll do shorter ones, make different plans."

I agreed with everything he said. That was a mistake. It alerted him to the fact that I was planning something different. Sam knew that, these days, I would never just agree to everything he wanted without a fight.

He brought up Marcus again and I brought up all the others. I shivered out in the night temperatures. The drama of the last few weeks, the lack of sleep, the adrenaline, it was all catching up until the sun rose on another beautiful day.

Approaching Bridgetown, despite my sorrow and tiredness, I was aware enough to sense that something was wrong. As the engines slowed down, we slipped into port, and I spotted a coast guard boat. It wasn't that unusual but fear formed deep in my gut and I couldn't shake off the sense of something ominous. I imagined armed police swooping, helicopters hovering.

I packed the last few things into my bags, pleased to be leaving the cabin and the ship behind. While Sam showered, I sat on the bed, staring at the wall. I almost didn't notice it because I had long given up hoping to search the contents as it never left his side: Sam's backpack. It was too good an opportunity to miss. I couldn't resist, although I wasn't sure what I was looking for. I rummaged. Horror hit. Alexandra's emerald necklace, surrounded with diamonds—my favorite—was nestled in his secret compartment. In his phone (he thought I didn't know the code) were her details, the types of things he could sell. I felt sick. She would think that I was part of his betrayal. I had told her too much.

I closed the backpack, put it back where it had sat on the bed.

A few moments later, Sam emerged from the shower, still wet, towel wrapped around his waist.

"I'll be back in a minute," I said.

I tried to phone Alexandra, but even though she was in the "emergency-use only" camp of phone ownership, she didn't reply. The lines for the main exits were already heaving, the corridors were rammed. There was no point in trying to get to her suite, it was too far away. The elevators and stairs would be busy; it was disembarkation time.

I returned to the cabin; Sam said that we needed to go.

I allowed myself to be rushed because I wanted to get away, to track down Alexandra and explain that the theft didn't have anything to do with me.

I shouldn't have panicked. I should have remained calm.

The pier at Bridgetown was long. It was hot and the relief when we reached the cruise terminal was immense. Until I saw the lines.

"That's unusual," I said to Sam. "I wonder what's going on."

He shrugged.

I was hot and bothered, so it was a clue I didn't pick up on. For someone who had been in such a rush to leave our cabin, I should've picked up on his nonchalance as something to be wary of.

"Shit! My watch!" he said, holding up his left arm to show me. "I'll have to go back and get it."

"It will take ages," I said. "Report it to lost property. Ask one of your friends to mail it."

He had many watches and the one he'd left was not particularly special to him. The second clue I missed.

"I'll catch one of the shuttle carts," he said. "I'll be quick. Make sure you stay in the line. We don't want to lose our place."

I know now that Sam must have realized I was planning something and that's why he left me alone in the customs queue. To remind me that he would escape and that I wouldn't. I couldn't outsmart him. He left me to deal with the consequences, knowing that if I incriminated him, too, he would already be long gone. I believe he was somehow behind my sudden release, too, as if he wanted to show me that no matter where he was, he would be in control.

Alexandra would think I had betrayed her friendship and confidences. I hated Sam in that moment, more than I've ever hated anyone. I vowed to track him down, to force him to fix whatever he'd done. But he emptied our bank accounts and hid in Mexico, as I later found out when he got in contact again, when something or someone had drawn him out of hiding.

And that is why I am in this situation. Searching for an unknown ax before it can fall.

26

NOW

Day Two Evening
Itinerary: Bachelor-and-bachelorette quiz,
informal dinner, 8:00 p.m. All to attend.

I STARE AT THE WATCH.

"Game on," I whisper under my breath.

I want this over with. I want to move on without fear of exposure or consequences. I can't change what I did, so this is the only way forward.

There are ten days until we reach Bridgetown, Barbados. Ten days to smoke out Sam's accomplice or some link to Alexandra to discover exactly who or what I am up against. Just over a week until I can turn my back on the past.

I stride to Thomas's cabin and rap loudly on his door. He opens it, looking disheveled.

"Did you give me this gift?" I say, holding up the box.

"Yes. You look pissed off. Sorry, is this like discovering that Santa isn't real? There were two spare pens because Alicia said that she and Charles had enough pens and trinkets to last them several lifetimes."

"When did you put it in my cabin?"

"I didn't. I gave it to Lucy when we got back," he says.

"You weren't around. Feel free to thank me for my generosity anytime."

"Thank you."

"A pleasure."

I head back along the corridor as he shuts the door behind me. I'm back in our cabin. "Lucy! Lucy? Wake up!"

"What?" she says, lifting up her eye mask. "Is there a fire drill?"

"No. When did you put the gift Thomas gave you on my bed?"

"I don't know. When he gave it to me, I left it on your pillow. Why?"

She sits up and takes greedy sips from a plastic bottle of water.

"On my pillow? Are you sure?"

"Yes. What's wrong? Oh, sorry, hun, did you think it was a secret gift from Harrison? Shit. Sorry, I didn't think. I didn't mean to raise your hopes."

"No, of course Harrison wouldn't give me a gift. There's nothing going on," I say impatiently. "Did anyone else come into the cabin?"

"Only if they crept in while I was dozing, which isn't a nice thought."

"Are you absolutely sure?"

"Yes. You're scaring me. What's the matter?"

"Someone tampered with my gift," I say. "I didn't get a pen or a bracelet, I got a watch."

"I'd call that a result," she says, looking less concerned. "It shows you must be doing a good job if Thomas values you that much. Shit! Is that the time? I have to make Gina and her mom look beautiful before tonight."

She rushes into the bathroom and shuts the door. I hear the cascade of the shower.

I make a decision. I'm not going to run, only to be tracked down again. I'm going to act as if I have done nothing wrong, have nothing to hide.

As I prepare for the evening ahead, I take care with my makeup and outfit. I will play a role, like Sam and I used to. We had no proper ending to our relationship, our ties were never cut. It feels like a step forward to now have an end in sight, a line in the sand, however frightening… Since Sam and I split up, I have drifted, aimless and fearful. Once I find out who my tormentor is from the cast of Agatha Christie–like suspects, I will convince them of my innocence. I will send them Sam's way. I smile at myself in the mirror. Game very definitely on. I clasp the watch onto my left wrist.

The thing that stands out to me about fear is that it isn't all-encompassing, it's like background noise, it ebbs and flows.

I take the stairs, despite my heels. The bookshelves in the reading room are well stocked. There are plenty of books on sailing and yachting. Most tastes have been catered for and it appears to have been added to by previous guests, leaving behind their holiday reads. I like this idea.

I place the scrolls of paper with the bachelor-and-bachelorette-night quiz questions neatly on the sofas and chairs. The questions I handwrote got progressively worse and more cringey as I went down Mariella's list.

What is your partner's favorite animal / item of clothing / part of their body / embarrassing moment?

I stare out of the window. The sun has almost set and an inky blue stains the sky.

"Charlotte?"

I swing round. Harrison. He comes and stands beside me. The sun dips beneath the horizon. There is nothing but dark outside the window. He smells different now from how I remember from our evenings together in Val d'Isère. I'd top up his friend's whiskeys, brandies and Baileys after dinner. We would wait until everyone else was asleep or had passed out, drunk, then we would switch off all the lights and lie in front of the dying fire.

I loved the stillness, the snow and serenity. Being at sea is similar, but with an underlying sense of danger, however calm the surface.

The door opens. A crew member enters and begins setting up a bar in the corner.

"Drink?" Harrison says. "Do you still love mulled wine?"

I laugh, pleased that he has remembered.

"Yes, but I'll have a white wine for now."

"Sure," he says, asking for one and getting a brandy for himself.

"Cheers," we say simultaneously.

"I've been wondering, how well do you know everyone?" I ask, taking a sip of wine.

"Fairly well."

"What about Garth, then?"

"Nice guy. This isn't his scene, not really. He's a land lover at heart."

"What about Gina?"

He looks at me, waiting for an explanation.

"I'm trying my best to make everyone happy, but information is thin on the ground. Thomas likes to 'maintain professional distance.'" I mime air quotes. "I'm hoping to get more jobs like this in the future, so I want to make a really good impression. I would appreciate your help."

He relaxes. "Gina is well-intentioned. She's into causes, always getting Josephine to sign up to support something or other. Mainly animals, but human rights too. Garth likes an easy life—golf, holidays. He's happy for Gina to be the primary earner."

"What are they like as a couple?"

"Fiery. Whenever they are around at ours, it only takes a few drinks before the digs start. Personally, I couldn't take the drama, but everyone is different. Neither one has called off the wedding yet, so I guess all's good."

"And you and Josephine? What are your future plans?"

He looks at me, as though trying to figure out whether to trust me or not.

"I won't say anything," I say.

He reaches for my wrist and glances at my watch.

Goose bumps prickle my arms. Is it a coincidence that he's looking at the watch?

"The others will be here soon," he says. "We should arrange to meet somewhere more private where we can talk properly."

"I'm not sure that's a good idea."

"Maybe. Maybe not." Harrison leaves my side as Gina steps in, stunning in a midnight blue dress and silver high-heeled sandals. She looks radiant and happy, just like I once was.

"Nice dress," I say. "Gucci?"

I don't think it is, but compliments should be as close to the truth as possible.

"Thank you. No, I had it made."

"Well, whoever they are, they have talent. It's gorgeous."

I stand near the back as the others trickle in.

Mariella makes a speech about "tradition" and bachelorette parties "all being a bit of fun, not to be taken seriously."

I watch. I watch them all. I watch Mariella as she drinks her champagne quickly and holds it out gratefully for a refill. I watch Josephine as she not-so-secretly keeps glancing down at her phone and replying to messages.

Restlessness takes hold. I don't like this feeling of being out of control, of waiting for something bad or unknown to happen. I decide to poke the bear. Any one of them could easily have a secret second SIM or phone. I get out my phone and type a reply to the last threat I received.

Where are you?

Four people look down or take out their phones within a minute. Josephine. Harrison. Gina. Arabella.

The quiz starts.

"What's Gina's ideal honeymoon destination?" Mariella asks the room.

Josephine is tapping away at her phone while people call out: "The Seychelles!" "Bermuda!" "The Maldives!"

I see Garth look over at Gina when a particularly risqué question arises. He makes a face and she smiles.

Norma snaps photos on her phone.

I hold my breath, but nothing happens.

Thomas opens the door, takes a look around and mimes a thumbs-up sign at me. I nod and mouth *All's good.* He gives me another thumbs-up. A waiter walks past him carrying a tray of drinks. There is a loud crash as the tray falls from his hands, hits a small glass table and smashes onto the ground, spraying Alicia and Charles with Lord knows what.

My phone vibrates. An unrecognized number.

I'm watching you...

I look up. Every single person in the room is preoccupied with helping to clear up the smashed glasses.

Everyone, except Harrison.

27

Day Three
Itinerary: At-sea day. Free time permitted. Evening
1920s-themed party. Staff attendance required.

Nine days to Barbados...

I AM AN ACTOR IN A SILENT MOVIE DRESSED IN A black-fringed flapper dress, wearing a dark bobbed wig. I am surrounded by gangsters and Gatsbys. Jazz blares. We are in the main lounge area on board the yacht.

"You've done an amazing job with the hair and makeup," I say to Lucy, who is sipping a grasshopper cocktail. "I barely recognize anyone."

"It was fun. Maybe you and Thomas can make every night a themed one," she says. "Everyone got into the swing of it. Well, nearly everyone. Not Josephine. She's hard to get to know. I don't expect everyone to spill the beans about every area of their private life..."

"But it's fun when they do," I interrupt.

She laughs. "My lips are sealed. But seriously, the woman doesn't say anything. She thanks me, is polite, but the time with her drags."

"I'm sure you'll win her round," I say. "From what I remember, you were always good at drawing out information from guests."

"Yes, I was good at that, wasn't I?"

"You were."

"What about you and Harrison?" she says. "I saw you together yesterday, out in the sea."

"It was nothing," I say. "Josephine saw us too. Gave me a look."

"Yeah, I noticed." She pauses. "Do you ever think about meeting someone else? Moving on from Sam?"

"The thing with me and Sam was that we burned so brightly together, nothing else compares. Sometimes, I fear it never will."

I take a sip of a highball. It's too strong.

"Yet you knew he was unfaithful?"

"Yes and no. He lied a lot, yet he was always credible. It's hard to explain, but he had this way about him that made me trust him."

"What will you do if he is alive?"

I like the fact that she is willing to consider the possibility, rather than totally writing it off.

"Kill him," I say.

We both laugh.

"Seriously, though, where do you think he would be if he was hiding? And why would he want to disappear?"

Is she trying to suggest that I am clinging on to false hope?

"Sam had friends *everywhere*," I say. "One owned a superyacht, not as nice as this one, but still, a *superyacht*. He had friends in Liverpool, Manchester, Sweden, Italy—all around the Caribbean." I don't mention JJ. "He always knew most of the crew on every ship. He was worried about something just before he went missing," I say.

"You were still in contact?"

"I wanted a divorce," I say.

I wanted the money he conned me out of.

Mariella comes over to compliment Lucy on her skills.

"Amazing job!" she says.

Mariella's dress is covered in shimmery ruby sequins.

"I had it specially made for tonight," she admits when I compliment her.

"Oh?" I say. "Did you know in advance that there would be theme nights?"

She gives me a strange look.

"Of course. It was my idea. Gina loves costume parties."

"I thought Thomas only worked for Josephine?"

"Yes, he does, but Josephine and I are good friends. We go way back. She's a social butterfly, kind and generous, but she's not an instigator. An intimate trip such as this was just the absolute best idea I could think of to get the three of us friends to spend time together. It also being Alicia's birthday was a bonus for Josephine. It's hard to think of original gift ideas all the time." She lowers her voice. "Between us, Garth doesn't like Gina going away on her own. He thinks she will get into all sorts of trouble, that we are a bad influence. But she loves him, so we must love Garth too. That's how it all works, don't you think?"

"I guess so."

I look over her shoulder and spot what looks like Harrison and Josephine having a disagreement. Harrison puts his arm out as if to calm her down or reassure her. I move away and sit down at a table among the older members of The Party. In a mirror, I can see Josephine put her drink down on the bar and walk off. Harrison follows.

"How are the cocktails?" asks Norma.

"My highball's too strong, but Lucy is enjoying her grasshopper. Would you like me to order you one?"

"Yes, please."

I approach one of the bar staff with my request.

Norma is delighted with her grasshopper.

"Excellent taste, my dear. Minty, but nice. Not overly sweet."

"I'm glad you like it. What do you think of the trip so far?" I ask.

"It's wonderful. The main thing is that Gina is happy."

We both look over to where Garth and Gina are dancing. They have barely left each other's side all evening. I consider what Mariella hinted at—that Garth is the possessive type. He's probably the person I've spoken to least.

"Of course," I say. "I will do my best to make sure that Gina has the most wonderful time."

"Although, having rich friends helps," she says. "The fact that Mariella owns this yacht and has arranged all this is just the ticket."

"Mariella owns the *Cleobella*?"

"Yes, and not just this one either. You wouldn't know it, though, would you? Such a lovely lady, so down-to-earth."

Very much so.

"And how about you, my dear? Are you enjoying yourself? Such a fantastic opportunity. I would love to have done something like you're doing. Although—" she takes a sip of her cocktail "—I'm sure it's hard work keeping so many people happy."

Norma is nice, despite exuding an air of wanting to be liked and recognized for her past. I have dug into her background (as I've done with them all, naturally), and she ran a very successful stationery business. Dormant me wants to coax her to open up. I smother the desire. I swore I wouldn't let the thrill of the chase take hold again.

"I am enjoying myself, thank you," I reply. "It's not as if I'm on my own, and Thomas is very efficient. And that reminds me—I must mingle," I say. He won't like it if he sees me chatting for too long.

But in truth, once an event is underway, I am not needed. The crew are amazingly attentive, better than I ever was even at my best and most hardworking. No request appears too small or too big.

I take off my shoes, and holding them in my hand, I go outside onto the pool deck. Light highlights the blueness of the water. I sit on a lounger and take out my phone. I message JJ.

Working on a cruise. Will be in Barbados in just over a week. Would love to visit!

I feel a twinge of guilt as I press Send. It's not just a social visit. He has something that belongs to me. Before I returned to England, I took a detour via his house.

I sit by the edge of the pool and dip my feet into the water. My phone pings a reply.

Will be good to see you! JJ

I hear muffled voices on the deck above. They get louder as I see the captain, Tim, and Mariella walk down the stairs. They don't see me as they stop and lean against the railing. The lights of other yachts are visible in the distance, little dots of white. I see Mariella put her hand on his back before she turns to walk inside, in the direction of the party. She stops when she sees me.

"Oh, hello, Charlotte."

Tim swings round.

"I was just telling Mariella that there is a spot of bad weather heading our way tomorrow, a small storm," he says. "But please feel reassured that it's nothing to worry about."

"Thanks for the warning. I'll pass the message on."

It's their acting normal that makes it come to me why the captain seems familiar. He's the man Mariella was with at the racecourse. I wonder… Maybe Mariella didn't instigate the organization of this trip out of the kindness of her heart and desire to spend time with friends. She did it to come away with her mystery lover.

I look at her with fresh eyes and I can tell that she knows that I know. It would be useful to have her on my side. She knows all sorts of things that she can now share with me. Starting with what Harrison and the others are really like.

28

NOW

Day Four
Itinerary: At-sea day. Free time. Onboard entertainment provided
by yacht crew–games, movie, yoga, mini golf. Meals, smart
casual. Staff, free time at lunch. Attendance required for dinner.

Eight days to Barbados...

THE STORM IS ANNOUNCED MIDMORNING. THROUGH the portholes, I can see the crew tidying away loose items and covering up the deck furniture. The wind is already picking up. I am grateful to be cozily inside the conference room with Thomas, handwriting place names for tonight's dinner and rearranging the seating plan. Thomas is a big believer in table rotation, it turns out.

"There's nothing more dull than for people to sit next to the same person night after night on holiday, especially if you are married to them," he says. "Variety is definitely the spice of life. Some of them, particularly Sebastian, don't like it and may complain, but just politely ignore him. Personally, I think Arabella loves it."

I think so too. I smile as I place myself between Harrison and Mariella.

The boat starts to rock. Gently at first, but I can sense what's coming. The sea splashes up against the window. Thomas glances at me for reassurance and this small role reversal is pleasing.

"Is this normal? The captain made it sound like a small bout of bad weather, nothing to be worried about."

"It's his job to say that." I feel bad at the look of horror that passes over Thomas's face.

I don't add that I imagine it is going to get much worse. I love storms. There's something exhilarating about the roar of the waves and the anger of wind, among the sheets of cleansing rain. I love the smell of freshness afterward.

I am right about it worsening. Within half an hour, Thomas has taken to his cabin. The Wi-Fi is intermittent, which is concerning because it makes me anxious to feel out of phone contact with the outside world in case Whoever It Is strikes when I'm alone.

I go for a walk, determined not to give in to the nausea. It feels so much worse on a boat this size and I have experienced some bad storms in my time. I stand near the doors leading out to the pool deck, watching the rain fall and the drops merge and run down the panes. It's soothing.

"Beautiful, isn't it?" says a voice, as someone comes to stand beside me. It's Harrison. I didn't hear him creep up on me.

"I love it," I admit. "Where's Josephine?"

"Lying down."

"I think most people are, although I think it's better to keep upright, myself. Are you stalking me, by the way?"

"No. I just…like being with you."

"You'll get me fired."

"For what?" he says in a challenging tone.

"I have an idea," I say, ignoring his question.

It's not a good idea, it really isn't. I'm in enough trouble as it is, but there's something so irresistible about the forbidden. There just is.

"Fancy a movie?" I ask.

"Sure," he says, a smile creeping over his face.

If he's the mystery tormentor and is going to harm me, where better than in the dark? Forewarned feels safer than an unexpected stealth attack.

Half an hour later, the rocking and the swaying feel worse, but I am cocooned in the darkness, sitting beside Harrison watching a James Bond movie.

"Did you know that you can stay in the villa where Ian Fleming wrote about James Bond in Jamaica?" he says. "I looked it up. It has its own private beach and you have your own dedicated butler and resident staff, a bit like on here, but even more exclusive. It sounds like pure heaven. The pictures of the building and grounds are like a film set. It's a dream of mine to stay there one day, but I would have to be a lot richer than I am now."

"Really?"

"Really."

"Do you wish you were wealthier?"

"I will have to marry a rich woman," he laughs.

"That rules me out, then."

He looks as if he has something to stay, but then refocuses on the screen, his face lit up by the flickering images. He looks so harmless.

We are plunged into light as the closing credits roll.

"Charlotte?" Thomas's voice calls out. "A word, please? I've been looking everywhere for you."

"I'll catch you another time," I say to Harrison.

I step out into the corridor, blinking from the light.

"What are you doing?"

"He wanted to watch a movie," I said. "I was the last person standing. Everyone else had taken to their beds. What was I supposed to do?"

"Just be careful," he says. "Harrison doesn't think sometimes."

"What does that mean?"

"Just keep your distance. Like you've been asked."

"Yes, sir," I say.

Annoyed at his attitude, I wait until he walks upstairs before I go down to knock on Mariella's door under the pretext that I am checking on everyone to see if they are all right.

She opens the door and doesn't seem surprised to see me.

"Do you need any seasickness pills?"

"No, thank you. I'm fine. The yacht crew have already given me some."

"Excellent. May I come in?"

"Sure."

She stands back to let me walk past her. I sit down and look around her suite. She is untidy; clothes are strewn everywhere.

"Tea? Coffee? Champagne?" she asks.

I notice that there is already a half-empty bottle of champagne on the side, along with a glass.

"Go on, I'll join you."

"I know it's a mess," she says. "But it's my first time away from the children—properly away. They had school and are flying to the villa in Barbados with my husband, so it's not long until I see them. My husband and I..." She trails off.

"I'm not going to say anything," I say. "I'm not going to say that I saw you with the captain."

"Thank you. I appreciate your discretion. It's very complicated, truly it is. Tim could lose his job if our relationship became common knowledge. Plus, there's all sorts of problems it would cause for my family if my husband found out."

"It's honestly none of my business," I say. True. "But if I've figured it out, what about the rest of the crew?"

"Tim and I are discreet," she says.

Not that discreet, I want to say.

"I'm hardly without my secrets myself," I say. "Harrison and I had a fling years ago, but he's asked me to keep it quiet."

"Oh. Right."

I see her taking it in, mulling over what type of position it puts her in, friendship-with-Josephine-wise. I believe it puts us on a more level playing field, which makes what I'm about to do next much easier.

"Yes, water under the bridge. Thing is," I say, taking a sip of too-warm champagne, "I'm in a bit of a difficult situation."

"Yes?" She sounds guarded, afraid of what I'm going to ask.

"I would love to know a little more about Thomas. And, of course, it goes without saying, it goes no further..."

She hesitates.

"I'm not asking for deep, dark secrets," I say. "Nothing untoward. I just wondered how long he has been working for Josephine."

"Oh, gosh, I don't know. Years. Why do you ask?"

"I'm wondering how much influence he has over her, to be honest. The reason being is because I'm hoping to get more work from Thomas in the future, and I really can't figure out what makes him tick. He seems a little intense at times."

"Let's see..." Mariella says. "He seems very loyal. He's good at being around when you need him, then disappearing when you don't."

"What have the other people who have worked with him been like?"

"Oh, they vary a great deal," she says. "Not everyone lasts long. He has another assistant who normally accompanies him, but she was unavailable for this trip."

"He's a hard taskmaster," I say.

I'm about to start probing some more, seeing if I can get her to open up a bit more about Harrison, Josephine and some of the others, but we are interrupted by Annie, one of the villa staff, bringing in an iPad for Mariella "to say hello to the children."

Annie exchanges pleasantries with the children's other nanny at home before blowing kisses at the screen and handing the tablet over to Mariella.

I stand up to leave, my legs feeling slightly wobbly despite the storm having blown over. As I walk toward the door, I see a photo in a frame. It's Mariella, with a man and four children, all grinning, on board the very same superyacht in Monaco that Sam and I visited. I frown to myself and look closer. The man, Mariella's husband, is Sam's friend Owen.

He is my biggest link to Sam yet, my strongest clue that Sam is alive and somehow behind all of this. Not only were they friends, they went back a long way. Owen is wealthy enough to hire whomever he wants, especially if Sam persuaded him. It means that any one of the crew could be watching me. I feel more vulnerable and watched than ever.

Mariella waves me goodbye, clearly eager for me to leave.

I smile back, shutting the door behind me, my mind almost blown.

It is blown even more when, in my room, the towel art is not a cute animal or sea creature. At first, it's hard to figure it out, but as I study it in detail, I realize that it is two towels shaped in the distinct outline of a skull. It has two dark seashells for the eyes and several smaller ones to make up its grinning black teeth.

29

PRIDE DICTATES THAT I DO MY JOB WELL. THOMAS asks if I can help him out, come up with something fresh and original. I have booked a day on an Island of Fun with its own water theme park. There are fresh and seawater pools, lagoons and waterfalls set among lush gardens for the guests who are looking for something more sedate, and thrillingly steep slides for those who are looking for something more.

This checks off practically everything on the collective wish list. Even Thomas is impressed.

"I've never even heard of this place. How did you find out about it?"

"Contacts," I say, secretively.

Mariella, aided by Tim, in truth.

The wooden railings on the private jetty are decorated with orchids and ribbons. I rip several petals off at random when no one is watching and scatter them into the sea. Beneath coconut palms, we are offered ice-cold towels from silver trays and

coconuts with straws for the water. I cradle mine and enjoy
the feeling of being away from the yacht. It juts out of the
sea, like a rock. Impressive as it is, it can't compare to a cruise
ship, where it really is possible to hide away.

The lagoons are heaven. Cool water sprays off the waterfalls as we are shown to our personal cabanas for the day. I
booked individual ones for the entire party, including Lucy,
Thomas and the villa staff. I sold it to Thomas as a "bonding
and thank-you" day, which he in turn sold to Josephine, no
doubt, encouraged by Mariella. Either way, it doesn't matter
because it's win-win. Everyone is happy.

I order coffee and fruit and share maps of the layout of the
slides and island. The villa staff immediately head off for one
of the most thrilling slides, one of which has a vertical drop
and another transparent one that shoots through a shark tank.

Once the guests are settled, I walk around on my own and
explore. Immediately beyond the sanctuary of the lagoon, it is
already busy. Two cruise ships have docked on the other side
of the island and the place is heaving with children and teenagers. Only to be expected, but the shrieks and piped music
is peace shattering.

Upon my return, everyone, apart from Charles, Alicia and
Sebastian, who are lying on loungers and reading newspapers,
has gone exploring. I pull the curtains around my cabana and
sit back, enjoying being offstage, with no one watching, no
one needing attention, and get to work.

I sift through messages and emails on my tablet. There is
one from George, Sam's father. I click on it with trepidation.
George *doesn't believe that Sam would simply disappear and put
us through this*. He wants to arrange a memorial. I don't reply.
A memorial would add fuel to the idea that Sam is dead, and
until I know otherwise, I choose to believe that he is alive,

that he has a plan and knows exactly what he is doing. There is no other viable option at the moment but to wait this all out.

Feeling less inhibited than I do on board with my online searches because there are so many other guests on the island that I don't think my searches will stand out, I check out what everyone has written and updated online. Garth: nothing. Gina: pictures of sunsets and sunrises. Harrison and Josephine: aerial pictures from their helicopter ride. Mariella is *longing to see her children*. Norma: pictures from the beach in Grand Turk; ditto most of the others.

I search for pictures of Mariella's husband, who, according to her, is with the children and heading for the villa in Barbados. So, Owen is not with Sam, then. There is no mention of her husband's shady past, only of his multiple charitable donations and fundraising efforts for environmentally friendly companies. The man I met with Sam made no mention of a family. There were no photographs on board his yacht, only silent employees who excelled at fading into the background. I think back to conversations between him and Sam, trying to figure out if we went there for a reason other than a holiday. Nothing stands out, other than their shared history, which could be loyalty enough if Sam was desperate for his help.

Eventually, I emerge from behind the curtains, determined to find the most deserted pool possible for a decent swim. But the first person I see is Daniel. I fall into step alongside him. It's time to have a chat, perhaps get a feel for if he would be able to help me.

"How's it going?"

"Fine." He smiles.

"I didn't realize that Mariella and her husband own the *Cleobella*. Have you worked for him before?"

"Why do you want to know?"

"I met him once, on a different yacht. I'm curious as to how many yachts one person needs."

Daniel laughs. "It's not about need."

"I get that."

"How's it going for you?"

"Fine, except…" I hesitate.

Daniel doesn't bite. We stop by the slide with a vertical drop and watch as the horrified and delighted swimmers emerge from the pool, only to rush off to line up and do it all again.

"I had kind of a stalker before I left home," I say.

"A *kind of* a stalker?"

"Someone threatened me. Someone who has issues with my ex. Honestly, I think they may have followed me here."

"Here?" He glances around.

"On the yacht. Or someone is being paid or encouraged by them to feed back information about me."

"What evidence do you have?"

"Messages. The last one said they were watching me."

"It doesn't mean that they are, although it's always best to take threats seriously. Did you speak to the police or anyone about it back home?"

"No," I say. "It's hard to talk about it because my ex was… complicated, and I wasn't sure if the threats were real at first. Now it's just a feeling that I'm being watched."

"I'll keep an eye out," he says. "Keep all the messages. They may be able to be traced. You can come and get me anytime if you're concerned. Likely as not, they'll get fed up and move on if it really is your ex, rather than you, they have a beef with. Although, I must say, it's not really my area of expertise. Mine is more terrorism."

"That's reassuring," I say with a smile, wondering if I've given away too much.

It feels nice to unburden my worries, just a little. Until I reach Barbados and see JJ, I have to keep my fear bottled up.

"Fancy a go?" he says, pointing to the slide.

"No."

"Go on," he says. "I'll go if you do."

I look up to see Lucy. She clambers out of the pool. It's strange to see her with wet hair and no makeup. I'm so used to seeing her looking immaculate.

"Going to give it a go?" Lucy says. "Or what about the shark one? I'm going to do that next."

"I don't like the thought of it," I say.

"Feel the fear," says Daniel. "It's part of the fun."

The three of us walk around to the shark slide, which has the biggest queue. Ahead of us is Thomas, one of the villa chefs and Annie. Farther ahead are Josephine, Harrison, Gina and Garth. There is no sign of Mariella. I wonder if she has sneaked back to the yacht under some pretext to see Tim while the boat is quieter than usual.

As we get to the top of the line, I hear the screams. I want to change my mind but I force myself to keep going. There are ten people in front, then eight, then seven.

"I don't want to do it," I say. "I'm walking back down. I'll take pictures of both of you."

Six people, five, four.

"No," says Daniel. "You'll regret it. You go first. We'll all be right behind you."

It is my turn, and before I have time to talk myself out of it any further, I sit down and I feel a hand on my back before the world drops and I am falling. Specks of dark flash by before I plunge into the pool and feel the sting of water up my nose. I want to get out. Although I know there are no sharks in the landing pool, that they are safely away behind glass, it's messing with my brain. As I'm about to surface, blinding pain hits as someone crashes into my back, winding me. I struggle to catch my breath.

I focus on the surface and half walk, half swim to the edge. I pull myself out and sit, feeling dazed.

"Are you okay?"

I see a blur of concerned faces.

"Someone crashed into me," I say.

"Probably a kid," says Thomas. "It happened to me earlier. Do you want a glass of water?"

"No," I say. "It's nearly lunchtime. I'll head back to the lagoon and arrange lunch."

"Are you sure?" says Lucy. "I'll come with you."

I walk with her to the locker area while she gets her towel and her bag. She hands me a spare towel and I wrap it around myself. I have the beginnings of a headache.

The day is a huge success. But not for me because nothing feels like an accident anymore. The smallest thing has meaning. And what if I'm wrong about everything? What if someone doesn't just want blood money—what if this isn't about Sam? What if it's about me?

I am grateful to get back on board the *Cleobella*. In the bathroom, I lock the door but I still can't relax. I watch the handle, expecting it to suddenly move downward like a scene in a horror movie. My headache eases after my shower and I sit on my bed, a towel wrapped around me.

"Do you think," I say to Lucy, "that it's really necessary to have our beds turned down every night? And cleaned every day? It seems too many people to have in and out of our cabin. I'd rather relax and leave stuff lying about."

"What is wrong with you?" she says. "You have someone to clean and tidy up after you, someone to replenish the fruit bowl, give you fresh towels, make sure that you don't have to put up with slimy, disintegrating pieces of soap all over the basin, and you want to opt out? No way! It's not as if anyone is going to steal anything! Unless you are hiding the crown jewels or something?"

"It just makes me feel uneasy, all the lack of privacy."

"But you must be used to it, surely? And it's so much better than on the ships?"

"I guess."

"I think we need to make the most of every moment. I'm bored with my clothes. Can I borrow something of yours? You can borrow something of mine, too, if you like. Look." She pulls a sunshine-yellow dress off a hanger. "This would suit you. I could do your makeup."

"Sure, why not? Help yourself, but not the sapphire dress. I'm saving that for the engagement party."

"I've had my eye on the red one, anyway," she says. "The shimmery one."

I sit down on the dressing-table stool, facing away from the mirror, and close my eyes as Lucy brushes my lids with eye shadow and my cheeks with blusher.

"Right, mascara next," she says. "Keep still."

As she starts on my left eye, she pauses. "I've a confession."

"What?" I open my eyes. So, this is what this free makeup session is all about: her guilty conscience.

"I don't think it will matter, she promised not to say anything. I swore that there was nothing going on between you and Harrison."

"There isn't."

"Well, exactly. So there is nothing to worry about. Right. I'm going to do your other eye… Keep your eyes closed."

"Lucy! What did you say and to whom?"

"When I was doing her hair last night, I let it slip to Gina that you and Harrison had known each other in the past. She seemed a bit shocked, to be honest. I backtracked, said maybe I had got it wrong. She agreed that she wouldn't say anything to Josephine, but..."

"But what?"

"She said that it put her in a difficult position. I thought that maybe you should have a chat with Harrison, suggest that it might be a good idea if he said something first..."

"Maybe. But, really, there's nothing to hide. Not on my account, anyway."

At least, not when it comes to Harrison.

The message alert on my phone makes me jump.

"What's wrong?" asks Lucy. "It's not...?"

Relief floods because it's Lewis, nothing ominous.

"It's nothing bad," I say.

Strangely, sometimes silence feels worse than a threat. It leaves me with a horrible sense of an invisible net closing in.

30

Day Six
Itinerary: Morning guest excursion in port. Staff attendees
Thomas, Lucy, Charlotte. Two yacht crew.
Afternoon free time. Optional jet-skiing, kitesurfing, onboard
waterslides.

Six days to Barbados...

SAN JUAN IS A NEW PORT TO ME. I NEVER HAD THE
opportunity to visit, seeing as, in the end, my cruising career wasn't as long as I'd anticipated. I have brought along an
old *Guide to the Caribbean* for nostalgic reasons. Inside, Sam
wrote: *With all my love, forever. Sam x.* Flicking through it, I
noticed that I have highlighted in luminous yellow the El
Yunque National Forest describing *lush waterfalls and bamboo
groves.* Now I am here.

My backpack is heavy because Thomas, Lucy and I are carrying the group snacks and spare water. The trails are steep,
and the humidity, despite the shade from the trees, is almost
overwhelming. Even Lucy, usually immaculate, looks hot and
bothered. Her bright red top is sticking to her back and her
hair is tied back. My sneakers don't have as much grip as I'd
assumed. My breath is heavy as we navigate slippery, uneven

paths. I intermittently duck to avoid overhanging branches. Rain forest sounds of croaking frogs and chirping birds dominate. A light mist hovers above the trees.

We gather for a break at a fork in the paths. After studying the signs, the group opts for the more difficult route. We begin our descent; it is hard to balance in places due to the mud. Lucy and I cling to each other. A light rain begins to fall without warning. I put my hand out to steady myself as I almost slip on a rock. My hand touches something sticky, like sap. I stop to wash my hands but my right one is turning red, as if stung by a nettle. I pull the small first-aid kit from out of my bag and apply lotion until the stinging subsides. The rain stops as abruptly as it started.

I look up. Lucy has continued ahead. The collective footsteps and voices disappear until I am briefly alone. It is a rare moment of bliss. I snap some photos and videos of my surroundings: snails clinging to the bark of a tree, and a bird—shimmering blue-and-green peacock colors. I take a large gulp of water before reluctantly following the trail down to catch up with the others.

We are rewarded with breathtaking views of a waterfall, a rushing cascade, its rainbow colors hovering above the mist. Coolness brushes my face as I inhale lush freshness. Below, a rock pool, the perfect swimming hole.

I find a space behind a rock and strip down to my bathing suit. It's a welcome feeling to shed my clothes and feel cooler. We aren't alone as a group; several other tourists are swimming and taking pictures beneath the rushing spray of water. They are mostly couples, looking carefree. I feel a pang of regret. I would love to have come here with Sam during the early days of our relationship, sneaking off to find a private, secluded spot in this tropical paradise. Beautiful as the scenery is, it's lonely being here in my present situation.

Everyone is taking photos, so I ignore the no-photos rule. Lewis loves commenting on the pictures I send him. He hasn't traveled much, and I want to encourage him. My phone camera captures the blue of the water, the white spray, moss-covered rocks and the rich greenery. Members of The Party naturally creep into the images, including one of Harrison and Josephine, their arms around each other, taking couple selfies. They look very much in love. Who knows, maybe they are. Josephine looks over at me and smiles. I smile back. Thomas glares at me as if to warn me against something, but everyone is taking photos, including himself. It's impossible not to. Gina and Garth pair up with Harrison and Josephine, and Mariella takes a picture of the four of them with the waterfall in the background.

I step into the water and swim toward the falls. As I stand in front of the cascade, I'm soaked by the refreshing spray. It's the best moment of the entire trip so far as I feel the tension briefly lift from my neck and shoulders.

"Gorgeous, isn't it?" says Lucy, standing next to me. "Shame we're the food and water carriers and not here on holiday with some gorgeous men!" She points to a spot on the rocks above us. "Imagine having a tree house just there and enjoying a vista like this every day! Do you fancy a climb up the rocks?"

"It looks slippery."

"We'll be careful. Come on! Think of the pictures we'll have to show off with!"

I follow Lucy up after grabbing my backpack, navigating between the rocks, avoiding the moss-covered ones as we climb. I look behind. Gina and Garth are copying us. We reach a section where the rocks flatten out. I place down my bag and we both sit on the edge of the rock face, feet dangling. Spray brushes my face. The sounds of the jungle are drowned out by the rush of water, which appears louder up here.

"Excuse me," says Gina's voice. "Any chance one of you two could take a photo of us?"

"Sure," says Lucy, easing herself up.

It bugs me that they clearly want to stand in the position where I am sitting, and I obviously have no choice but to move out of the way with good grace.

Garth and Gina put their arms around each other and smile. They kiss and then they make funny faces as they pose while Lucy snaps with their expensive and professional-looking camera.

"How about taking a picture of you two?" Garth says afterward.

"I'm fine, thanks," I respond automatically.

"Yes, please," says Lucy. "Go on, Charlotte. It'll be fun to have a memento."

We swap places with Gina and Garth. I remove my sunglasses from the top of my head and put them on properly before smiling as if I, too, am happy and carefree.

"Carefully step back a bit," instructs Garth.

I look behind me. Although it didn't feel as if we'd climbed too high up, looking down it appears much higher than I first realized. Lucy steps back.

"Careful," I say to her, taking a small, tentative step back myself.

We both grin for the camera, and Lucy grips my arm. Then, as we both step forward, my feet slide on the rock. I hold on to Lucy to regain my balance until we're safely away from the edge.

Two women appear behind Gina and Garth.

"Excuse me," says one of them. "Weren't you in that reality show a while back?"

Gina looks embarrassed but agrees to pose for a photo. The two women beam for the camera as Garth snaps the picture, before they head back down the way they climbed up.

"What reality show?" Lucy asks.

"Oh, it was a long time ago," Gina says.

Lucy looks disappointed.

Gina and Garth head away from us, along a barely perceptible path hidden beneath the rich green ferns. As we watch them walk away, I see Harrison and Josephine making their way up toward us.

As they approach, I see that my backpack has fallen to a ledge below.

"Shit!" I say. "My bag. It's got everything in it. I'll have to climb down and get it."

Still barefoot, I ease my way down the side of the slope, holding on to overhanging ferns and placing my hands on the driest rocks to steady myself. As I reach down to grip my backpack, I slip, screaming. The sound of rushing water fills my ears as I thump down onto the precipice. I see faces looking up at me surrounded by white bubbles of the stirring water.

Above, I hear Lucy's voice, then Harrison's and Josephine's.

"God, Charlotte, are you all right?" they chorus.

My knees sting like they haven't done since I was a child. Inelegantly, I push myself up into a crawling position, then sit up. I feel shaky. I push myself away from the ledge using my palms and gather my breath. My knees are grazed.

Harrison appears at my side.

"Are you okay? Can you stand up?" he says.

"Yes, I think so. I dropped my bag," I add, unnecessarily.

He helps me stand and follows me as I climb back up, handing me my bag when we reach the top.

"Thank you," I say, reassuring the trio that "I'm fine. Just hurt pride."

"You gave me a fright," says Lucy.

As Harrison and Josephine take pictures, I can't be sure, but it sounds like she says the words *attention seeker* to him.

I am the opposite of that, but it stings, nonetheless.

At the bottom, I take a short dip to wash my knees.

"Everyone's ready to head back," says Thomas as I emerge.

I dry myself behind a rock and change back into my sweaty pants and T-shirt before sitting down and tying up my shoes. By the time I emerge, it appears that I am alone.

"Hello?" I call above the rush of the falling water.

No replies.

I head back to the path we climbed down. Still no sign of anyone.

"Hello?" I call out again. "Lucy? Thomas? Anyone?"

The silence beyond the waterfall is eerie and sinister, no longer beautiful and serene. As I begin to climb, I hear a noise and a rustling behind me. I see Arabella, standing a few feet away, beside a tree. She is staring at me.

"Arabella?"

She looks back down at her camera. Harrison appears behind her.

"I didn't capture it," I hear her say.

"Where is everyone else?" I ask.

"They've headed up that path over there." Harrison points in the opposite direction. "We said we would wait for you. Arabella saw this stunning bird. You should have seen the colors."

"I missed it," she says, sounding gutted. But then she smiles.

"But I did capture this lizard or chameleon-type creature. Look."

She lifts her camera screen to show me a perfectly shot image of greens, browns and yellows.

"Incredible," I say.

My heart is still thumping with thoughts of being lost deep in the jungle, hiding from my tormentor with only snakes, spiders and who knows what else for company. We catch up with the others at the top of the slope. There's more photo taking and wildlife spotting before we head to a picnic spot. I hand out mangoes, slices of pineapple and papaya neatly packed into Tupperware, coconut macaroons, chips and water. By the time we board the 4x4s to return to the harbor, my feet are blistered, my knees are aching and the skin is peeling where I was stung on my hand.

Back on board the *Cleobella*, I decide to ease the aches in the Jacuzzi. As I approach the hot tub, I'm disappointed to see that someone has beaten me to it. Josephine is sitting with her back to me. My need is greater than hers, employee or not. Her earlier words—*attention seeker*—still irk.

I hesitate. I should come back later when it is vacant. But I don't want to. On the side, I spot her watch. I approach her from behind. She doesn't appear to be able to hear me above the rush of water. I can't steal it, it would be way too obvious that it is me, but I can give her a sign that I don't like the way she watches me, hawklike, as if I'm just dying to steal Harrison from her. No doubt Gina has added a dollop of fuel to the fire, but if Josephine has issues or concerns, she should discuss them with the man in question, not me. I might be many things, but I am not a boyfriend thief.

As I approach, my shadow falls. I hesitate. I feel as if I am stalking her, like a cat after a bird. Nothing. Her eyes are closed, without a care in the world, which maybe she hasn't because she isn't stuck on board a yacht with someone who has threatened her life. I slide her watch into the water and see it drop into the cauldron of white bubbles. I do feel bad that the crew may have the not-fun job of draining the Jacuzzi, but it was too irresistible. Petty, I know.

I unwrap my towel from around myself and step in opposite her. She doesn't open her eyes as I slide in. I put on my sunglasses and tilt my own head back as though I, too, am soaking away the cares of the world. I have to hold the pose for several minutes, but it's worth it to observe her expression when she opens her eyes. As she climbs out, I smile.

She wraps a towel around herself, looks on the side for her watch, then climbs back into the Jacuzzi, feeling around. She looks at me.

I remove my sunglasses. "How did you enjoy the morning?"

"It was fine." She glances around. "I've lost my watch."

"You probably left it in your room. I'm always doing that. It's so annoying."

"No. I had it here. I remember looking at the time."

"I'll help you look."

I feel around with my foot, trying to avoid the jets. There's something about the nozzles that gives me the creeps. At first, nothing, then I poke it with my toe. I bend down and reach it.

"I think I can feel something. Is this it?"

"Yes, thank you." She looks at it after drying it down with her towel. "It's okay, thankfully."

"That's a relief."

"Waterproof," she adds.

"Excellent," I say, holding up my left arm. "Mine too."

Josephine gives me a strange look before saying, "Actually,

Charlotte, it's probably good that we have this time together. It gives us a chance to have a little chat."

Here we go.

"Yes?"

"Has Thomas informed you yet of what the plans are for Antigua?"

Easy.

"A rain forest visit, zip-lining and shopping."

"Sounds good. We won't need you to accompany us," she says. "I understand from Thomas that there is plenty to be getting on with on board."

"Of course."

"And another thing, Charlotte…"

I remain silent. This is all thanks to Lucy's indiscretion with Gina, who has clearly voiced concerns about me and Harrison.

"Please let me or Thomas know if you run out of things to keep you occupied. I like to be a relaxed employer, but equally, I expect hard work, trust and absolute loyalty. I'm sure you understand?"

I try to tune out her words; I do know how to play the role of an obedient employee. Although the words stick, I don't want to give her any indication that she has, in any way, got to me.

"I completely understand. And I do appreciate being recommended for the role, so thank you."

Josephine frowns slightly. "We rarely take on people unless they come highly recommended," she says. "Especially not for our holidays. Time is so precious. We can't risk any drama on board."

"I agree," I say.

Having had the last word, I get out and do a brief towel

dry of my legs and arms. The hum of Jet Skis starts up. I look over the railings and see Gina, Garth and Harrison twisting, snaking and crisscrossing trails through the sea.

Josephine settles down on one of the loungers and starts applying sunscreen. I have the urge to get under her skin even more by lying on the sunbed beside her, but, of course, I don't.

I head for the sauna, away from all the sounds and people. I ladle some water from the sauna bucket onto the rocks and watch them steam, before I make myself a little bed with a towel and lie down on the warming wooden slats. It eases my aching muscles as warmth seeps through my bones.

I hear someone walk past. Crap. I want to be alone. The footsteps disappear, thank God. I plug in my earphones and listen to Aerosmith. Sweat forms on my forehead and trickles down my face. I feel drowsy. I sit up, remove my earphones and stretch. I try to push open the door, but it won't budge. I try again. Nothing.

"Hello?" I call out.

Nothing again. I look around for something to help ease the door open. I feel dizzy from heat and rising fear. I take a sip of water and try the lock again. Still jammed.

"Hello?"

Silence.

I pick up my phone and send exactly the same message to Lucy and Thomas.

I'm in the sauna. The door is jammed. Help please!

No reply. Sweat snakes down my back as I look around the small room and then I spot the alarm cord. I pull it. No one comes but I try the door again and it unlocks. Thank God. I step out, breathing in fresh air. I walk back to the pool. Josephine has gone. The Jet Skis have quieted. It is eerily silent, as if I am alone on the yacht.

I love the smell of a fire. On the barbecue grill, steaks and burgers sizzle. The yacht crew have turned the beach into a true tropical paradise. Mini lanterns (not dissimilar to the shape of my favorite Narnia lamp) dot the area. Luxurious cream-colored daybeds are lined up beneath them. The summer beach-party music plays discreetly in the background, not loud enough to drown out the sound of the waves lapping against the shore. Seashells and rainbows of roses decorate the tables, seafood kebabs on beds of ice with fresh salads and exotic fruit platters sit on white linen tablecloths that flap gently in the breeze.

I look around at the assortment of people as we all sing "Happy Birthday" when the candles on Alicia's cake are lit. Not that it would be obvious, but no one looks as if they have hate in their eyes. None of them looks capable of being malicious. But then again, I don't either.

"No, thanks," I say to the offer of a slice of lemon cake—Alicia's favorite, according to Thomas.

I stand up and stretch. Dusk is imminent and mosquitoes are likely not far off. I take some repellent out of my bag and spray before I head for the shoreline.

"Back soon," I say to Thomas before he can say anything.

I stroll barefoot. Sand sticks to my ankles. I watch as my footprints are washed away by the sea. I look back. The crew are clearing up. I see the first group of guests gathering at the water's edge, waiting to board the tender. I look out at the *Cleobella*. It easily eclipses the other boats. If I were a tourist, I would look out at the view and wish that I was able to go on board, imagining the type of people who could afford to own or charter such a yacht.

Back on board, Lucy and I invite two of the villa staff to make up a small room party. It's like being on a proper holiday. I drink, not caring about tomorrow. I barely remember getting into bed, the room is spinning.

I wake up. It's still dark. I can hear Lucy's breathing as she lets out the odd drunken snore. There's an almost intangible sense of someone else in our room, watching us—or just me. My eyes feel heavy and awareness dissipates, dreamlike.

Come daylight, all is as calm as the turquoise ocean beyond the porthole.

It was just a dream, yet I still can't get Sam out of my mind. I type him a message, but it doesn't send. I scroll through my phone, rereading all his old messages, looking for any clues I missed. There are none. I go through his folders and documents again and stare at old photos and video clips of us in happier times. I keep scrolling until one in particular catches my eye. It's of me, standing on the upper deck of one of our last-ever cruises. I am wearing work pants and a white shirt. Beside me is Sam, his arm around my shoulders. Who took this photo? It doesn't look as if either of us knew we were being photographed. And then suddenly it comes to me that there's something obvious I haven't yet done: the CCTV footage from the hidden cameras on board this yacht will be able to tell me everything I need to know about the person who is threatening me with harm.

31

IT IS RAINING WHEN WE ANCHOR IN THE HARBOR IN
Antigua. Thomas messages me to ask what the backup plan
is. Crap.

I don't want to admit that there isn't one. It was my job to
(a) check the weather, and (b) to have backup plans. I shut my
trusted Caribbean guidebook and I hastily go online. Thomas
had planned for zip-lining through the rain forest and some
shopping (Arabella, Alicia and Norma are keen to buy souvenirs as part of their holiday traditions). All of which can still
go ahead, as the rain isn't heavy. I send Thomas a link to the
Museum of Antigua and Barbuda, just in case.

There's a rap on my cabin door. Thomas.

"I hate links," he says. "Don't ever send me any unless they
are vital. It's lazy. I can look things up myself. You are not
employed to merely send links."

I can't argue. He's right.

I put in more effort by booking a luxury vehicle and a driver
for the day to ferry them around in style.

I smile and wave as everyone leaves. I love smiling and waving; I feel like royalty. I wait until the tender is out of sight before I ask one of the women working out on the deck if I can speak to the captain.

She radios him.

"He's having breakfast," she says, "but you can go through."

I enter through the Crew Access Only door and find Tim eating a large bowl of cereal topped with pineapple, watermelon and papaya.

"Morning," I say. "Is it possible to take a look at the CCTV from the day before yesterday, please?"

"Not very easily. Is there a security reason why you need to check?"

I stick as close to the truth as I can.

"Yes and no. I got stuck in the sauna and I thought I heard someone outside while I was calling for help, but no one came."

"I see." He looks at me as if unsure how to respond. "How did you get out?"

"The door eventually unlocked."

It sounds ridiculous as I say it.

"I'll have one of the maintenance guys look at it. But I can't have unauthorized people looking through any recordings."

I take a deep breath.

"Actually, it's a bit embarrassing. It's not just the sauna… I think someone has been in my room. I don't want to make a fuss in case I'm wrong."

"You think it's one of the yacht staff? Has something been stolen?"

"No. But I would feel happier if I could just review the CCTV from the day before yesterday to put my mind at rest."

"I'll have a word with Daniel," he says.

"I already have."

"I'd like to speak to him myself to see what can be done to make you feel more at ease."

Damn.

"Thank you."

It's hard to hide my disappointment. I am nowhere nearer to an answer. I need to search where I haven't yet done so. The rooms are cleaned and tidied while everyone is on shore. All entries are logged by individual key fobs, so it is tricky to gain access to others' rooms.

"There's one more thing… I need to pick up something important from Josephine and Harrison's room. She's gone ashore without it. Any chance you could let me in their suite?"

He looks at me.

"Mariella didn't think you'd mind," I add. "She said to ask you."

I smiled slightly as I said "Mariella" so that he knows that I know about the two of them. I can only imagine what's going on in his brain. I don't feel proud of myself, far from it, but he has put himself in the position by having a secret. That's the problem with secrets—they weaken your situation and morals in more ways than one. I can sympathize with him. Hopefully what he and Mariella have is worth it.

He doesn't look impressed. He stands up abruptly.

"If you're quick," says Tim. "But I'll come with you."

"Sure."

Opulent is the word that springs to mind as Tim pushes open the door. So much space. They are both tidy. Books are neatly stacked on their bedside tables. Windows surround the whole room, and a separate seating area with sofas, large cushions and a glass coffee table fills one side of the cabin. Fresh envy gnaws. Sam and I were supposed to live like this.

"Are you all right, Charlotte?"

"Yes, yes, I'm fine, thank you. I'm thinking…"

I'm dying to check the bedside drawers and beneath their pillows, or open the wardrobe. Someone who used to work as a housekeeper in large hotels told me that—and I have no idea if this is true or not—those were the main places where people hid things.

I go to the desk and make a show of pulling open the drawers.

"Now, where did she say she'd put it?" I say out loud.

"Will you be much longer?"

"Hopefully not."

I scan the contents, looking for something I can take that won't be missed. Something catches my eye. It is a printed sheet with all my personal details on it: date of birth, Louise's home address, my passport number, my fake bio. A surge of anger. Josephine has been checking up on me. Is it because of Harrison or a more sinister reason? I have a thing about people who are careless with others' personal information. Details such as these are worth a small fortune to the wrong people. I take it. She will assume she's misplaced it.

"I need to get back," Tim says. "I'm going to have to ask you to leave now if you can't find what you're looking for."

"This is it," I say, holding up the printed sheet. "Thank you."

But Tim is not the type of man to be manipulated without some pushback.

"I'll arrange for the boat to take you to shore," he says. "So that you can deliver the paperwork to Josephine."

"It's fine, thank you," I reply with my biggest smile. "I'll just snap a picture and send it to her."

"I would feel happier if I knew you were going to deliver it personally," he says, smiling too.

"Sure," I say, giving in.

He speaks in his walkie-talkie, calling for Daniel and also requesting that he and I be taken ashore. I go through the charade of boarding the boat.

"What's up?" asks Daniel.

"The CCTV," I say. "I need to see it. It will help ease my mind that my stalker isn't on board."

"Why do you think they are?"

"Too many things have happened for it to be a coincidence. I'm scared."

"Thing is," he says, "there's no CCTV in the guest areas. We had specific instructions that the guests were not to be filmed. They're on holiday. Josephine, I understand, is very camera shy."

"Why didn't Tim just tell me that?"

"He probably didn't feel at liberty to say. You aren't his employer. But seeing as you're so concerned, we can get the local police involved," he says. "It could shake your stalker up a bit if he is around."

"No," I say. "Thank you."

I am alone in this, once again.

I disembark, Daniel returns on the tender and I go for a walk. It's not an entirely pointless exercise, though. I see something I wouldn't have otherwise—Garth and Arabella, having a coffee together in a café, oblivious to me walking past.

The intricacies of relationships at sea—friends, colleagues, lovers, acquaintances—have always fascinated me. Crew and friends become each other's family. Cut off from reality, work routines and social time creating the only real structure, intermingled with glimpses of paradise, we existed in a separate world. There was always an unsettling sense, something not feeling quite right, at the beginning of each new season or voyage as new teams were formed, loyalties created and hostilities arose.

Upon my return to the yacht, there is no sign of Tim. At dusk, the boat lights illuminate the water and it's the first time that it strikes me as odd that the others aren't back yet. Half an hour later, I message Thomas.

Where are you?

Still out. We're going to a restaurant for dinner.

I message Lucy. She doesn't reply. I stroll up and down the decks and through the empty rooms, turning on lights as I do so.

I order a pizza and a beer, and one of the chefs comes out personally to place it in the pizza oven for me. I order another beer, then another. I feel bad, as I can't do the pizza justice. Living on anxious anticipation has robbed me of my appetite recently. Food sticks in my throat.

"It's quiet tonight," I say to the chef.

"Yeah, it gives us a bit of a rest. Some of the crew have gone ashore. Although, rumor has it that the owner may come on later."

"The owner? I thought he was meeting everyone in Barbados, at the villa?"

"I have no idea," he says. "That's just what I heard. People change their minds all the time."

I wonder if someone has tipped him off about Mariella and Tim. I hope not. I kind of want them to get away with it. I take out my iPad and have what feels like a millionth go at working my way through Sam's files and documents. I sift through more photos of his school years and his travels around the globe. There are many of different women. It shouldn't hurt by now, yet it does. I still cannot figure out the password to access his encrypted files. It's freshly frustrating.

I stand at the railings and look down into the lights reflected on the water.

Goose bumps prickle my arms as I look around. I am alone on deck. Not even the chef is here. I step back into the shadows.

I stand, unsure of the best thing to do. I peer over the rail for any sign of the others returning. The harbor feels unusually silent. A boat approaches, but it passes by, aiming for a different yacht.

The sound of another boat's engine fills me with relief. I look over the edge as it approaches. It is not the usual tender, but a dinghy. A man, with his back to me, steps out. He is tall, as tall as Sam.

I rush down the stairs and through the Crew Access Only door so that I am not alone. There are no crew members in the general area. Just as I'm about to walk past the galley and up the stairs to the bridge, the power goes off. Pitch-black. There are no emergency lights. I trip over what feels like a cardboard box and land on my hands and knees. The noise of my fall, followed by silence, is terrifying. I am alone.

"Hello?" I call out.

I sit still on the floor, not sure whether to use my phone flashlight or not as my eyes try to adjust to the darkness. I think back to my tour of the boat with Jon and reorient myself. I hear footsteps coming from the bridge. I'm about to call out again when something stops me. I feel my way along the corridor, past the laundry room, which I can recognize by the smell of fresh linen. I inch my palms along the wall, counting down the doors—one, two, three—until I come to what I hope is Jon's room.

I open it. I can hear two sets of footsteps now, in the dining area to the left. I shut the door behind me but there is no lock and nowhere to hide. I feel around, climb onto the top bunk and slide myself beneath the duvet to flatten myself against the wall. My heart is thudding so loudly. If anyone enters the room, they will surely hear it.

The door opens and I have to bite back the urge to scream. I see a flashlight through the duvet. I shut my eyes like I haven't done since I was a small child to ward off monsters. I hear breathing. At first, I think it's my own, but then I realize it's someone else's. *Blood money, blood money.* I hold my breath. Something clatters to the ground.

"Shit."

I recognize the voice. It's Jon, but I am frozen with fear. What if it's Jon who is after me?

"Bloody hell," he says.

I can hear him fumbling around for whatever it was that he dropped.

The door shuts. Silence.

The lights come on and I hear the sound of the engines again. I sit up. I climb down, my legs cramped and aching. I open the door and listen. I hear several voices. Thank God. Feeling a bit ridiculous at my overreaction, I walk down the corridor, hoping to leave without being seen, but as I turn the corner, several faces stare at me. The crew.

"What are you doing here?" asks Tim.

"It went dark. Someone was following me."

He looks as though he doesn't believe me.

"There's no one on board who shouldn't be," Tim says.

"We've been on the case. I'm afraid that you have no right to be down here."

"Do you know what happened?" I ask. "There were no emergency lights, nothing. Is this thing safe?"

No one replies, and I suddenly understand. The power was switched off. Deliberately.

Back in my cabin, there is a plain white note card in the jaws of a towel-art crocodile:

Time is running out, Lola.

32

Day Ten
Itinerary: Diving in Saint Lucia.

Forty-eight hours to Barbados... So excruciatingly close... So excruciatingly far...

I SEARCH FOR FLIGHTS TO BARBADOS FROM SAINT Lucia. I want off this yacht ASAP, but there are no seats immediately available to book.

I am stuck until we hit Barbados. Then I can escape. I flick through my guidebook again as we approach Saint Lucia in case Thomas expects me to come up with any more plan Bs. The Diamond Botanical Gardens are listed as a recommended place to explore—a tropical paradise with hummingbirds, underground springs and waterfalls. Unfortunately, I won't be visiting. Thomas wants me to go shopping to source some particular types of flowers that Gina likes.

He sends me a list: ginger lily, lobster claw, there's even one called a bird-of-paradise. I'm also to buy souvenirs for the guests to take home because they're going diving today and won't have time.

Before we dock, he comes to my cabin and hands me a credit card.

"This is the one I use for all business expenditure," he says. "You can use this today for all the purchases so that you don't have to submit endless receipts. It'll save us both time and effort."

He watches as I place it in my purse.

"Anything else?" I ask.

"I understand that you had a word with the captain the day before yesterday? Is there anything you want to tell me?"

"No."

"I wish you'd come to me first. I would help, you know."

"I'm fine," I say.

I am. It's not long until I see JJ. He should be able to shed some light on what's been going on with Sam and where he could be.

"Right, well, anyway, I've asked Lucy to go with you."

We take advantage of the freedom by taking a cab to the largest shopping area. I feel a spree coming on. Temptation beckons in so many places. I can feel the pull of the old me. The thought of the credit card Thomas gave me—free money—is just too much. Lucy and I split up for an hour.

I ignore the shopping list and instead try on clothes, bangles, necklaces, rings. I buy a penknife as a memento and a long lilac skirt with my own money. I don't give in, although I discover that the card lets me withdraw cash, which I could somehow explain away as expenses. I hesitate. I don't take out the maximum amount; it would be too obvious. I opt for two hundred dollars, an amount I don't consider greedy.

I meet up with Lucy for lunch in an outdoor restaurant, both of us ordering crab salads and glasses of white wine. I write a postcard to Lewis. On the front, there's a picture of Saint Lucia's famous landmark, the Pitons, two mountainous volcanic plugs, in front of which is cobalt blue sea and the lush, rich greens of land.

Wish you were here. Charlotte. X

I message JJ.

Not sure of an exact ETA but see you soon!

"This is the life," says Lucy, settling back into her chair and taking a large sip of wine.

Her cheeks are slightly flushed.

"Kind of," I say. "It would be better to be here with someone."

"I'm sorry about Sam," she says. "I wish you could meet someone nice. He was a fun guy."

"Sometimes."

"What was his dark side? Drugs or gambling?"

"Well, he was a croupier," I say.

We both laugh.

"Seriously, though, you need a bit of good luck. What about James Bond?"

"Married."

She orders another glass of wine.

"I was with a married man for a while," she says. "It didn't end well."

"Does it ever?"

"I know this sounds naive, but I really did think he was different."

For a moment, I think she's being serious, but then we both start laughing again.

We're in the process of ordering a third glass of wine each when I get a message from Thomas.

Please add local spices to your list. You can buy them at the market.

He also lists the brand name of a hot sauce for Alicia.

We finish our wines and decide it's too hot for a coffee. I offer to pay the bill, feeling slightly guilty when Lucy thanks me. She doesn't know that it's Josephine who really paid for our meal.

I google the market. It is another short taxi ride away.

The market is shaded beneath umbrellas and a thatched roof. Low tables are crammed with local fruits and vegetables. Beneath the shade are clothes and a variety of souvenirs: baskets, bags, hats, T-shirts. In the fruit-and-veggie part of the market, I look around for the flowers. I ask for the ones on Thomas's list, but they don't have them. I buy what looks like ginger lilies, then bulk up the rest with roses. It is hot. My bags are heavy. I shouldn't have drunk wine, I should've stuck to water. The scent of flowers and fruit, at first so appealing, is now cloying and oppressive.

I scan the area, looking for the rest of the items on my list. I ask a stall owner and am pointed in the direction of the spices and bottles of hot sauce. When I go to pay for them, my purse is gone. I check and check again. I can't find it. Apologizing, leaving my parcel at the stall, I look around but I can't see Lucy or any sign of her long yellow skirt.

Panic sets in. I check my bag again thoroughly. It's definitely gone.

I wander around, disoriented. It's getting more crowded. I wasn't concentrating on the direction when we walked in. I let Lucy take the lead. When I used to go on shore with some of the other cruise-ship crew, there was this general feeling of safety at being in a group. I would switch off, go with the flow of the crowd.

Calm down, I tell myself. I see the edge of the market and I make my way toward the space. Someone jostles me, but when I swing round, there's no one there. I keep an eye out for Lucy but there is no sign of her. I message her. No reply.

But then I hear her voice: "Charlotte!"

I swing round and see her clutching a bunch of orchids.

"What's wrong?" she says.

"My purse. It's been stolen."

"What? Just now?"

We retrace our steps, but of course we don't find it.

Back on board, Thomas is not impressed.

"I'll have to cancel the card and bother Josephine to sort out a new one," he says.

"I'm sorry," I say. "But it was obviously an accident. I'll have to do the same with my cards, not to mention the cash I was carrying."

Not entirely true. I only took the card Thomas gave me, luckily.

"I thought you were an experienced traveler?" he says.

Lucy obviously feels sorry for me because she tries to change the subject.

"How was the dive?"

"Apparently, it was amazing," he says. "They saw barracuda, eels, trumpet fish…"

"No sharks?" I can't help asking, childishly.

Apparently, none.

Mariella comes to my cabin later that evening with some herbal anxiety pills.

"Lucy says you had your purse stolen today. Try these," she says. "You'll sleep like a baby."

"Thank you," I say. "I will."

Untrue. I'm unable to rule anyone out as a suspect. Mariella's husband is Sam's friend, her lover is the captain of this yacht, plus she helped organize this trip. There is no bloody way I'm going to swallow any of her pills. I've stayed alive and unharmed this long; I'm not going to blow it at the eleventh hour.

33

NOW

Day Twelve
Itinerary: Barbados, two-day stay. Guests to villa, free time.

I WANT TO CRY WITH RELIEF WHEN THE CAPTAIN AN-
nounces that we are approaching Barbados. I am about to escape my luxury prison. Even the guests have had enough. I
heard Alicia and Charles snapping at each other. Garth and
Gina no longer come down together to have breakfast à deux.

I go out onto the deck and watch as the shoreline gets closer.
It feels unbearably slow, as if the freedom of land is beckon-
ing me, it's so tantalizingly close. As we pull in to the harbor,
I want to shout out loud at the crew to hurry up.

The villa staff disembark first, Mariella accompanying them.
Thomas has arranged for most of The Party to take a short
historic walk around Bridgetown to "get a good leg stretch"
and then have lunch at a popular restaurant.

And as for me… I have left a few personal belongings on
board so as not to flag up my imminent departure by cram-
ming my necessities into a backpack. I explained to Thomas
that I need the day off for personal reasons.

"It isn't good, you taking time off at short notice," he says.

"There are mountains of things to get ready for the grand-finale engagement party. My lists are never-ending."

"I won't let you down," I lie. "I'll be back later."

I smile, trying to reassure him, but he folds his arms and doesn't say anything else.

I stand at the end of the jetty and take a moment. It's strange, being back in Bridgetown. Surrounded by the other super-yachts and luxury boats, along with passengers and crew going about their daily business, everything feels normal. There is a breeze. The sails of a small sailboat flap gently. Waves lap against the shore. Tourists lounge on their villa balconies or on the nearby silky white beach. Restaurant tables are covered in pristine white tablecloths with wineglasses and navy napkins, ready for the lunchtime crowd. I can almost convince myself that life is back to how it was "before." I close my eyes, enjoying the warmth of the sun on my face, and almost believe that when I open them, a younger, happier version of me will reappear. As will Sam.

I feel bad about not saying a proper goodbye to Lucy, but I'll message her when I can and I know she will understand. I walk over to a taxi and give JJ's address. I want my arrival time to be a surprise. If Sam is somehow there, I want to catch him out. We pull away. I take a trip down memory lane. The palm trees lining the street are as tall as I remember. Beyond, I see surfers catching the waves. We pass a rum distillery before weaving through residential areas, green lawns bursting with floral color. The other drivers are friendly, letting one another in and out of the traffic. Shoppers walk by carrying bags of fruit, others holding umbrellas to shade themselves from the sun. I listen to the local radio. A presenter discusses the weather before playing a song I have never heard before.

The driver drops me right outside JJ's house. His cottage is nicely familiar with its white walls and sky blue window shutters.

"Would you like me to wait?"

"No, thanks," I say as I get out. "I'll be fine."

But who knows?

I unlatch the gate and walk up the short drive. Sweat slides down my back. I am scared. My earlier bravery and optimism are fading. I cup my hand around my eyes and peer through the front window of the house. Nothing. No car in the drive and no sign of JJ's motorbike either. I go to the door and knock. Still, nothing. He's a chef at a local beach restaurant; he never used to start work early.

"JJ?" I call out.

Silence. Perhaps I *should've* called ahead and been more precise about my arrival time. I don't know what I expected. To see JJ and Sam sitting out on the porch, sipping a coffee, discussing the old days? Playing cards?

Regardless, self-consciously, I call out: "Sam!"

More silence. I walk around the back and peer through the kitchen window. There are no signs of life, other than an abandoned breakfast bowl and mug on the table. I knock on the back door. Nothing. I message JJ.

Hey! I'm at your place a little earlier than expected. Where are you?

I'm relieved to see that he reads it immediately.

I didn't realize it was today. No matter, back in fifteen/ twenty!

I send a thumbs-up emoji.

There is an outdoor room to the side of his house, a shed,

really. I push open the uneven door. It scrapes along the ground. There is nothing interesting and certainly no Sam. Wooden shelves, jars of nails, *stuff*. There is some garden paraphernalia and a swimming pool net with a retractable metal pole.

I wander up to the plunge pool, which is surrounded by a stunning rock formation. In the center is a fountain that feeds into the pool. I love the sound of water trickling. I find it calming. I slip off my shoes and dip my feet. Five minutes pass, then ten. I hear the sound of JJ's bike in the distance, getting louder. I stand up, dry my feet with my ankle socks, shake them out and put my shoes back on. I watch JJ as he parks, cuts the engine and removes his helmet, his whole face lighting up in a smile.

"Hey, long time!"

"Good to see you again." True.

We hug. He looks chilled, not like someone who is hiding someone who doesn't want to be found. He unlocks his front door. I follow him in. It's quiet. I can hear my heart beating. In a rush of fear, I look out for Sam. The living room is dark and cool. I hear a scratching noise from the kitchen. I swing around as a cat pads out as if to greet us, then jumps up onto a sofa, watching me. I walk over and stroke it.

"Coffee? Tea? Lemonade? Something stronger?"

JJ puts down his helmet and gloves on a shelf.

"Lemonade, please."

He goes into the kitchen. I follow. He opens the fridge. It is crammed with vegetables, cheese, meat, milk and bottles of pickles. Way too much food for a person living on their own. Sam loved cheese of all kinds. He always said he could live on it.

He pours two glasses of fresh lemonade from a jug.

I accept the glass from him and he opens the back door. Outside are two chairs and a small round table decorated with mosaics. I place my backpack at my feet and take a sip of lemonade. It's beautifully tart.

"If it's not cold enough, I can grab us some ice," he says.

"It's good, thanks."

In the distance, a dog barks. A siren blares. There are no sounds from inside. Now that I'm here, I'm not sure how to word everything I wish to say.

JJ breaks our silence.

"I was sorry to hear about Sam," he says. "I've been meaning to get in touch with you."

His whole face looks sad.

"What did you hear?"

He looks at me in the same way a lot of people have been looking at me lately, that mixture of concern and confusion, as if they're making an assessment as to how far along the denial dial I am.

"That he is missing. That he fell off a cliff and was swept out to sea. That they found his clothes," he says gently.

"They found a jacket," I say. "That's all. No body."

"I see."

"Actually, JJ… I was half expecting him here. I had messages from him right up until he disappeared, and since then I've had some strange ones… I don't know if they're from him or someone else entirely. I'm confused. I don't know what to think anymore."

"He's definitely not here. I haven't heard from him for well over a year. I live with my girlfriend now, Alison. She's at work. There's just the two of us. And Cecily, our cat. Well, Alison's cat, but she's starting to warm to me now too."

I smile but my insides are knotting, thinking about Sam.

"I'm happy for you."

The thought of finding Sam has been keeping me going. I don't have a plan B. My thoughts scatter. JJ looks and sounds sincere, but then again, so have many other people in my past before I have discovered that they are lying. I take a breath, then another sip of lemonade before placing the glass down gently. To my horror, my throat tightens and the threat of tears feels real. I take another sip.

My recent fantasies have been shattered. I realize in a thunderbolt that I've been harboring unrealistic expectations. I'd imagined that he'd secretly set sail from the south of England all the way to Barbados, collapsing with exhausted relief as he finally made it to shore. I pictured him contacting one of his many friends—someone who would help with a phone, cards and an identity. Then he'd come to JJ's. Or he might have hidden in a small, conveniently abandoned beach hut, catching fish, picking fruit and collecting rainwater. I have also had images of him staring out to sea (with a pair of binoculars that have magically appeared), watching out for me so that he could steal what's rightfully mine. Distraction and misdirection were Sam's favorite weapons. Except I have been misdirecting myself. I don't know if this makes me feel worse, or better.

I must look really sad because JJ takes my hand.

"If he went into icy waters, then there's no way he could survive. Surely? Not even Sam. He used up all his nine lives, Charlotte. It happens. Sam was always drawn to the flame, we both know that. Maybe he got burned. I am sorry. I know you loved him. He loved you too. Probably as much as he was capable of loving anyone. Grief is normal. Rage too. You don't have closure."

"Thank you. I know you're trying to make me feel better. His body hasn't been found. It was dark, maybe that isn't what happened. Maybe his girlfriend lied or got confused about the time."

"I read stuff about her. She seemed pretty plausible. The police obviously think so too. Sam wasn't invincible, Charlotte. None of us are, however much we like to think it. Me, especially. Alison hates my motorbike, but it's about balance, I reckon."

"I feel alone," I say. "Like I'm the only one who thinks it's odd. It feels like it has been dismissed as an accident. He was scared. Someone was after him. They're after me now."

JJ takes a deep breath. "And I'm guessing you can't go to the police?"

"No," I say. "There's something else. I need the package I left here."

"You sure?"

"I'm sure."

"I'll be glad to have it out of the house. It gives me sleepless nights sometimes. If Alison found out, especially if she knew what Sam was like, she would kill me."

I feel bad. I told him it was a gift from Sam (kind of true), but JJ knew Sam and his ways only too well.

He stands up, goes into the shed and steps back out clutching a trowel. We walk through the garden, past the pool. He rolls a couple of small rocks bordering a flower bed to one side and starts digging. He lifts out a blue plastic bag and hands it to me.

"Thank you."

It's such a relief to get this back. After everything, it feels good to finally have this in my possession again. I push it down into my backpack.

"Be careful," JJ says.

"I will."

We both hesitate as if unsure what to do next.

"Do you want to stay here?" he asks.

"No, but thanks for the offer."

"You okay on the back of a bike? I have a spare helmet. I can drop you back at your boat?"

"No, thanks. I'm going to take some time alone."

"You can come to work with me, if you like. You can hang out on the beach. I'll make you some lunch?"

"Sounds good," I say.

He washes our glasses and locks up the house. Outside, he hands me a red helmet. It has been a long time since I've been on a motorbike. Drew had one and we would go pretty much everywhere on it. Louise made him sell it. Seems she is better than I when it comes to sticking up for what she wants in relationships. At first, I feel wary, out of control. But as JJ speeds up, I realize I'm enjoying it.

"Faster!" I shout in his ear.

He turns and takes a scenic route past the ocean before we park up outside a beach restaurant.

"This is where I work," he says. "I make the best fish sandwiches you will ever taste in your life. Guaranteed."

He organizes a table beneath the shade of a red-and-white-striped umbrella and orders me a beer. Most of the tables are already occupied. I sit and stare out at the beach. My backpack is safely at my feet, one strap wrapped around my ankle. A group of teenagers play volleyball. Several children are building a sandcastle, shrieking with delight. Already, the *Cleobella* and The Party feel far away. I search on my phone for hotel rooms to give me the headspace to organize what comes next.

One of JJ's colleagues brings me out another beer and a fish sandwich. JJ is right about how amazing it is. Wonderful as it has been to eat five-star food all day and every day, I have been dreaming of spaghetti Bolognese or a burger and fries.

This fish sandwich is the best thing I have tasted for days and I realize how nice it is to have an appetite. The more Whoever It Is has been preying on my mind, the harder it has become to eat much or sleep deeply. I am looking forward to my own room tonight, the chance to sleep in a double bed, free from immediate fear.

JJ comes out to have his break with me. We both sip iced coffees.

"There's one more thing I would like to say," he says.

"Go on."

"Sam was my friend, but we both know he was selfish and out for himself. I'm sorry, Charlotte, but I think he's dead. I really do. I think he messed with the wrong people at the wrong time, and whoever they are, you don't need them in your life either. Do yourself the hugest favor and move on. You and Sam split up for a reason."

He leaves me alone with my thoughts. It's kind of him, but of course no one knows the truth about me, the hollowness I used to experience in the aftermath of a successful job, the craving I'd immediately feel for another project. My greed grew into an addiction. I craved the feeling of the chase, the pull of a shiny new prize in sight. Maybe this is my punishment: to never be truly known. JJ likes me because he doesn't know me.

"Excuse me," says someone. "Is this seat taken?"

They point to a spare chair.

"No, take it."

I shift my own chair to remain in the shade. Hotel rooms are expensive, so I check out Airbnbs, then flights, but indecision clouds my mind. The world really could be my oyster and it feels important to make the right moves, to steer clear of danger. The limited funds in my bank account won't last long. I draft an email to Thomas inventing a dire family emergency, ready to send later today. He won't pay me my full fee, I know he won't, but I am not getting back on that yacht.

I was going to wait until I was completely alone, but I can't resist taking a peek. I unzip my backpack. I take out the blue plastic bag, and without removing the contents, I run my forefinger along the smooth emeralds and diamonds. Alexandra's necklace. I would never sell it unless I was absolutely desperate. I hide it again, gently shoving it back into my bag.

The sun starts creeping up my left leg and arm. I shift my chair again until I'm in the smallest patch of shade. I look around; there are no spare tables. Too hot to sit any longer, I go inside and give JJ a wave. He is busy. I mime giving him a call later.

I walk past the parking lot to the pavement. There are no taxis in sight. I stand beneath a tree and wait. Nothing. I look at the local map. There's a hotel resort a seven-minute walk away, pretty much in a straight line. There will be plenty of cabs there.

I ignore the offers to sell me things as I walk alongside the road. It is hot, way too hot. I keep an eye out for a passing taxi as I realize my mistake in walking. I hesitate, wondering whether to turn back.

"Would you like to buy a souvenir?" asks someone, stepping in front of me. "Necklaces, bracelets, watches?"

"No, thank you."

I push on. I get a sixth sense that I'm being followed. Uneasiness permeates. *You're imagining it*, I tell myself, but I don't really believe that I am. I stop, pretend to make a call. There is no one following me. As I put my phone away, a car speeds past, then another, narrowly missing me. I am too close to the roadside. I look around, relieved to see that to my left there is a path leading back to the safety of the crowded beach. I step onto it. I look behind me. I *am* being followed by a tall man wearing mirrored sunglasses. I move over to the side and he passes me by without a glance. I sigh with relief and wipe the sweat from behind my neck with the back of my T-shirt. I really need water.

I aim for the beach. I can see a café in the distance. I focus on that. But dreaded realization dawns that there *are* footsteps behind me and my fear switches from hope to unavoidable reality. Too quick. They get closer. I speed up, staring ahead. Mirage-like, sun glints off the waves, little flashes of gold. So close, I'm almost there, yet I can't keep up my pace. As I'm about to swing around, I feel a fierce tugging at my backpack and lose my balance. I put my hands out to break the fall but there is a roaring sound in my ears. I see red, then black, as I am hit; a vicious pain explodes through my head. I slam into the ground and my palms and knees scrape and sting. Tufts of grass poke out of the sandy path, pebbles, an abandoned ice-cream wrapper. I grip the straps of my backpack. I must not let go. I try to get up, but I feel weighted down. I must *not* let go. Then, nothing.

34

AWARENESS SEEPS INTO MY CONSCIOUSNESS. OH, God, it has happened. I'm in a prison cell. I'm certain of this, even though my eyes remain closed. I can feel it.

A hard bed beneath my back. A pillow, thin or nonexistent. My body aches. A tap drips.

I focus on the rhythmic pattern of the dripping water, but it doesn't soothe. The opposite. My head throbs. A door slams in the distance. Loud voices. Footsteps. Fear mounts deep in the pit of my stomach and doesn't subside until I am certain that no one is approaching me. I wait. The sounds dissipate.

Unmistakable tropical heat gently suffocates. Stale sweat permeates my nostrils. I lick my bottom lip—it tastes of the salt tang of blood. I hear the gentle whir of a ceiling fan. Movement. Stillness. Stillness. Movement. Hope ignites. Perhaps I am wrong. Comforts such as these do not indicate a jail cell. I take a reassuring breath before slowly opening my eyes.

White. Gray. Panic. I can't focus properly. Everything is blurry. Did I remove my contacts? I shut my eyes and breathe, drawing on every calming technique I have ever used. Pungent disinfectant dominates. I do a body scan. Toes, feet, legs and arms. All good, so far.

My gaze comes to rest on a Bible, beside me. Things are becoming clearer. A plastic jug and a glass of water sit on a wooden table. A basin, the white ceramic snaked with brown cracks. A hospital? A clinic? Not prison, after all. Good. I sit up and take a large gulp of tepid water from the glass on my bedside table.

I pull back the sheet and swing my legs over the side of the bed, grounding my feet on the floor. I glance down and see that I am wearing the clothes I put on this morning. Was it only this morning?

On a plastic chair rests my backpack. I scramble forward and tear open the zips. The plastic bag is gone. Oh, please God, no. Shit. I keep desperately checking and feeling around. I don't want to believe it. But it seems someone has stolen it, along with one of my copies of Sam's USB. The thought of this getting into the wrong hands makes me want to throw up. My phone, my credit cards, my laptop are there. Thank God for small mercies. Frantically, I check my messages.

Several missed calls from JJ and Thomas. Some from Lucy. Three calls from a number I don't recognize. Two anonymous ones.

Thomas starts off with *"Where are you?"* and ends with threats. *"Don't expect me to pay your full fee."* Finally, concern. *"I hope you're all right. Call me!"*

One anonymous text. **Got you!**

Shit, shit, shit. I'm going to be sick. There's an en suite bathroom. I lock the door behind me. I wash my face and stare at myself in the mirror. There is a faint bruise on my forehead and a small lump. I don't look like I've just spent over a week cruising the Caribbean. It's hard to gather my thoughts. I need to get out of here, but random thoughts haunt me. Will the police want to question me?

I open the bathroom door. First things first. I need to speak to someone who can get me out of here. A man walks into the room. Sam? My stomach flips. No. Shit. It's Thomas, followed by Lucy.

"Oh my God," she says. "Look at the state of you. I've been so worried. What were you doing?"

"Walking to a resort when someone attacked me," I say. "Where am I? How did you find me?"

"In the nearest hospital. Your friend JJ was worried. He assumed you were going to get a cab but then he saw you head off walking alone instead. He decided to leave work early to find you and give you a lift. You weren't answering your phone. He explained that he didn't get very far before he noticed activity by the side of the road. A crowd had gathered, then an ambulance and the police. He phoned again but you still didn't answer, and he couldn't see you anywhere. He then realized that it was you who was being attended to by the emergency staff, but you were unconscious. He contacted the marina, then spoke to the captain, who called us. He sounded pretty shaken up. Said he felt guilty."

Poor JJ, none of this is his fault.

"Did anybody see who attacked me?"

"No. From what we understand," says Lucy, "you were lucky. JJ wasn't far behind you, apparently, so you couldn't have been there long. Maybe your attacker was disturbed."

Thomas looks at me. "But the good news is I've spoken to the doctors and you're mostly fine. Bruised, but fine."

Hope flickers. "So I can leave?"

"Not quite yet. I don't think it's that simple," he says. "The police need to speak to you, and…" He looks at Lucy. "They need to make sure that you really are *all right* before you can be discharged into our care."

"Are you serious?"

"Unfortunately, yes. I'm disappointed at the lengths you have gone to just to get out of working." He smiles. "Don't think I won't hold this against you. Plus, I am most definitely not a babysitter."

Lucy looks aghast until I start laughing, even though it hurts my head and ribs. Then she starts laughing, and so does Thomas. We all laugh as though this is the funniest thing that has ever happened to us. It feels good. Until I remember how much trouble I am in.

"I don't need you to hang around," I say. "It could all take ages. My friend JJ will come and get me. You two go back to the *Cleobella* and I will see you later."

"Absolutely not," says Thomas. "I'm under strict orders to bring you back to the yacht in one piece."

"I thought they were all staying at the villa?"

"There has been a change of itinerary. Gina and Garth want to have the party and then sail earlier than planned. They'd like some extra time in Trinidad and Tobago after Lucy told Gina that they were among her favorite places to visit when she worked on the ships. They're heading back to the yacht now, along with Mariella's children and husband."

"I'm not coming," I say. "I'm staying here."

"I'm afraid not," says Thomas. "Josephine wants you checked out by the onboard medic too. Sorry to sound heartless about it all, but we don't want any lawsuits. We will look after you until everyone is sure that you are one hundred percent well."

"Please listen to him," says Lucy. "I want to keep an eye on you too. I would never forgive myself if I left you alone in a hospital in a foreign country."

If any cruise-ship crew were ill while working and had to be left in a foreign hospital, another crew member would always be allowed to stay with them until their family members were able to be at their bedside. It was simply unthinkable to leave anyone vulnerable and alone.

"I'll go and sort out the paperwork," says Thomas. "Lucy, stay here with her. Make sure she's okay."

As Thomas opens the door, a police officer enters the room. I am trapped, twice over.

I go through my story. Nothing was taken, it may even have been an accident. I was badly dehydrated—silly me, I should have known better. I was confused. It all happened really quickly. I am grateful to the medical staff and everyone who has helped me, but I am fine. Totally fine.

Physically, that's true. But I'm badly shaken. The message *Got you!* proves that it was *them*. Whoever It Is. Is it just luck that I'm still alive? I start to shiver. And what also isn't fine is that it has brought all these people to my bedside. I was trying to get away.

Finally, I'm discharged. Thomas and Lucy hover as I sign paperwork. Then they escort me out, one on each side as if I am too fragile to manage on my own, and we get into a cab. Lucy sits in the back with me and insists on holding my hand. It's suffocating. Thomas gives the driver the name of the marina.

I phone JJ but he doesn't answer. I open the window to let in some air.

"I'm not getting back on board," I say. "I've messaged my friend JJ and he will come and pick me up from the harbor," I lie.

Thomas turns around and looks at me.

"We've had this conversation. It's my job to make sure

you're all right. Don't put me in an awkward position. Sleep on it. The boat isn't sailing until later. If you're not up to working, fine. But everyone wants to make sure you're in one piece. Bizarrely, they've grown fond of you."

I smile, despite everything.

We climb out of the cab.

"Your backpack is big to lug about, isn't it?" says Thomas.

I shrug. I don't want to get back on board the *Cleobella*. It does not look like paradise on water. The portholes are like prison-cell windows. I no longer see grace and splendor, I see it for what it is: a trap.

I walk along the jetty and it wobbles underfoot, like I'm walking the plank. I say hello to one of the yacht crew. Hugh, I think his name is. It suddenly bugs me that I can't remember.

"Are you all right?" Hugh asks. "Can I help you with your bag?"

"No, thanks. I'm fine."

I clutch my bag a little tighter as I step on board the *Cleobella*.

He speaks into a walkie-talkie. I hear a crackle, then: "She's on her way."

They're all waiting, I realize.

I turn to step back off the yacht. This is all a mistake, a big mistake. Every part of me knows I should get off, run away. Lucy and Thomas are right behind me, and coming down the stairs in front is Tim.

I'm trapped.

"What's going on?" I take out my phone, panic rising.

"Let's go and sit down somewhere," says Tim. "You've had a big shock."

"I'm fine," I repeat. How many times have I said this? "I just need to lie down."

Thomas, Lucy and Tim exchange more glances.

"Let's go somewhere private," says Lucy, linking her arm with mine and forcibly guiding me toward one of the lounges.

"I wish someone would just tell me what's going on," I say. "It's worrying me."

"No one wants to worry you," says Thomas. "Sit down." He points at a leather sofa.

I sit, keeping one eye on the exit. Lucy hands me a drink.

"A brandy," she says. "Take a sip."

"I've had loads of painkillers."

"A sip won't hurt."

I take a small one, but it burns like acid and makes me feel even queasier.

"I'm really sorry," Tim is saying as Lucy takes hold of my hand again and gives it a squeeze. "We received some difficult news from your friend Lewis. He didn't want to tell you over the phone. He thought it was best if you were told in person, so that we can support you."

I think I know what he's going to say, but my mind fills with too much horror and confusion to process any thoughts rationally.

Tim carries on speaking. "The police have been trying to get a hold of you too."

I remember the missed calls on my phone.

I know now what he's going to say. But it's still hard to take in the words.

"Early yesterday, your husband's partial remains were re-covered. He was not found in the area where he was pre-sumed to have gone missing. He was farther along the coast, in a more rural area."

"I'm so sorry," says Lucy. "I just can't believe it."

I can't either.

Sam has been dead all along. Which means I was definitely

lured here by someone else. Someone like Alexandra. It could be anyone. There never was a plan made up by Sam to escape. There was only ever a plan to harm me.

I find a quiet spot out on deck and call Lewis. He answers within one ring. He doesn't know any more than I've already been told.

"I'm so sorry," he says. "I know how much you didn't want to accept that Sam's death was a possibility."

I thank him, reassure him that I'll be fine, and then I call the police.

Foul play is not suspected. Which means that Sam's killer is off the hook. I am now their sole target. All the warnings were just the warm-up act.

35

NOW

LUCY IS SITTING ON HER BED, WATCHING ME. IT IS creepy rather than comforting. It's dark beyond the porthole, and stars are glistening. Another night in paradise. The memory of what happened earlier comes flooding back. The plastic bag, my USB. Fresh waves of dread hit me. Hard.

"Why are you watching me?" I ask.

Lucy looks offended. "I want to make sure you're all right. Medic's orders."

"How long have I been asleep?"

"About three hours."

"I can't believe I slept."

"Well, you did have a bump to the head and loads of drugs, mixed with shock. I can't imagine how awful you must be feeling."

"Pretty shit."

An understatement. It's not just a pounding headache and feeling woozy, it's icy fear. Did someone stage a mugging to kill me or did they want Sam's USB? If they were to break Sam's encryption, might there be something on there to in-

criminate me? I feel sick at the thought. But Alexandra's emerald necklace has gone too. Was that a nice bonus for the
thief or was it intentional?

I sit up and reply to messages from Lewis, from Sam's father, from my sister. Everyone wants to know if I'm all right.
Short answer, no. I reply to everyone stating that I'll be fine.

"Lucy, I'm not feeling good. I would feel better spending
the night on shore. I need to get off."

"You've only just woken up. You've got a bit more color
in your cheeks. Besides, you can't get off," she says. "We're
docked way out in the harbor. Thomas has gone ashore in
the tender to pick up some last-minute things for Gina and
Garth's engagement party. They were delivered to the villa
in error, along with one of the cakes. The head chef is making another. It sounds like it will be magnificent. It's in the
shape of a diamond engagement ring!"

She waits for me to react but, honestly, I couldn't care less.

"Go and have a shower," she says. "The party starts in an
hour. Josephine wants to thank you, Thomas and me, and
all the other staff. I've heard that she's got a speech planned."

I still don't care.

"I can't go to a party tonight as if nothing has happened."

"Just keep busy," she says. "That's what I would do. Don't
let Sam fuck this up for you too. I'm sorry if that sounds harsh,
but it's true. See this through and then go home. Plan his funeral. Say goodbye. Do whatever you have to." She pauses.
"But remember—you don't owe him your loyalty." She pauses.
"Do you want to talk about Sam?"

"No."

Yes.

"It was to be expected," I say. "It's just that..." I swallow,
finally understanding the truth. "I liked to think of him as

someone who would always land on his feet, no matter what. Because, the thing is, if Sam can die, then…anyone can."

Even me. Especially me.

Lucy comes and sits beside me.

"I would feel better knowing that I'm close by to keep an eye on you. Plus, I knew Sam too. You can talk to me about him as much as you like later." She pauses. "I've finished doing everyone's hair and makeup. They all look stunning, even if I do say so myself. Do you want me to do yours?"

When I don't respond, she says, "Let's get you dressed," gathering herself and patting me on the hand. "You were saving the long sapphire dress for the party, right?"

I nod. I loved that dress the moment I saw it. I fell for the always-successful sales method of seeing the dress on one of the shop mannequins in a boutique window before I left for Miami. I pictured myself wearing it, imagining that I would exude the same type of haughty elegance if I were to wear it. I couldn't afford it but I tried it on, regardless. I had to have it. I bought it on my credit card, then reported it as fraud. The boutique manager was nice. I didn't want her to be out of pocket. I figured it was better for the card company to swallow up the bill, rather than a small-business owner.

After my shower, I give in and put it on. I'm glad that I decided to acquire it. It feels good, like fresh armor as I head into battle in unfamiliar territory. I look in the mirror. I look almost normal for a person who is in fear for her life.

"Looking good, hon," says Lucy. "Give us a twirl."

I do so. The fabric swirls around me.

"Gorgeous!" says Lucy as she picks up her makeup case. "Right, let's go to the salon and flower ourselves up."

A micro expression of fear crosses her face. She looks at me and quickly smiles, all traces of what I saw erased. A chill comes over me. I've never heard Lucy use this phrase before. It was one of Sam's favorite expressions.

I follow her up the stairs, my dress swishing around my ankles. Lucy adjusts the lighting in the salon and orders me into her chair. She opens a bottle of champagne and pours two glasses, bubbles spilling down the side of one.

"Cheers!"

We clink glasses. I sip, trying to unravel exactly what it is about Lucy's words that have unsettled me so.

"Look at us," she says. "Who would have thought we would end up here?"

Indeed.

My phone vibrates. A message from Lewis, even though it is almost midnight back home. I click it open.

> **I've been looking at your photos and there's one of a woman in a red top standing near a waterfall. She was my mystery date!!! The one who ghosted me. Different hair color but it's her, I'm sure, unless she has a twin. Why is she with you???!! Weird.**

I turn my phone around to hide the screen from Lucy's sight. My hands feel shaky. Lucy smiles at me in the mirror.

I smile back. I watch her, heart thudding, oblivious to my inner turmoil as my mind scans, lighthouse-like, for all the little clues I missed. I don't need to scroll through my photos to know that Lucy was wearing a red top the day we visited the waterfall.

She blow-dries my hair; the heat of the dryer burns my neck. Afterward, she insists that I need more makeup than usual.

"Not being rude, Charlotte, but you should make more of an effort."

Her phone beeps at the same time as one of her eye pencils snaps.

"Bugger! Do me a favor and grab a sharpener out of my bag, would you?" she says, taking a gulp of champagne before picking up her phone.

I unzip her bag. I fumble around. Lip gloss. Foundation. Prescription sleeping pills. Seems Lucy needs more than her eyeshades and earplugs to sleep. I can't see a sharpener. But there is something that catches my eye. A lipstick with the lid half-off, which isn't actually a lipstick at all but a memory stick, disguised. Like the type Sam used. I glance up. She is still furiously typing on her phone, then stopping every few seconds to take a gulp of champagne. I push the lid onto the USB and slide it into my own clutch bag. I look up and almost jump. Lucy is looking at me.

"Found one?" she says.

I rummage around in her bag some more.

"Yes. I'll sharpen it," I say.

I lean over the wastepaper basket, twisting the pencil. My hands feel weak and shaky, as if I've done something wrong. Which I most certainly haven't. I brush off residual shavings from the sharpener, return it to her bag and hand Lucy the eye pencil.

I hold my breath as she leans in close.

"Close your eyes."

Her breath smells of toothpaste and champagne. I wonder if she can hear my heartbeat. Lucy and Sam. Sam and Lucy. Why did Lucy pretend to be interested in Lewis? Because she wanted information about me. She could easily have worn a wig. She presses the eyeliner near the corner of my eyes, which weep a little. I hear her ease a tissue from out of the box in front of the mirror, then she gently dabs. Then I feel strokes of a brush as she applies eye shadow.

"Open your eyes again," she says. "Right, now for blush. Suck in your cheeks for a moment."

I do as she asks.

"Ta-da, what do you think?"

I don't look like me. I look like the best version of myself. Greens and browns are expertly shaded above my eyes. I have long eyelashes. It's impossible to tell that I've had a rough day.

"You've done an amazing job, thank you."

My voice sounds normal.

"Excellent. Top up our champagne," she says. "I'll just finish up my hair and makeup and then it's off to the ball we go."

I smile and look down at my dress. It gives me fresh confidence. My anklet slips down my ankle slightly as I stand up. In my ears are pearls. Real, but pearls are simple enough that they don't scream for attention. They are timeless. Elegant. Classy. Alexandra taught me that. That and not to trust anyone. A lesson I should've learned a lot younger.

"Ready?" says Lucy.

"Ready," I say.

We walk side by side to the outside deck. I spot Mariella's husband, Owen, who has joined us. He nods a curt hello to me but shows no real sign of recognition. Two of their older children are sitting with tablets near the bar. Apparently, the younger two are back at the villa with their nanny.

I accept a bright yellow cocktail from a passing crew member as Harrison approaches.

"I'm sorry," he says. "I heard the news."

"Thank you."

I am touched at the look of concern in his expression.

I don't have time to waste with small talk. I need to get off this boat before we set sail for Trinidad and Tobago.

"Are you returning to the villa tonight?" I ask Mariella.

She looks surprised at such a direct question.

"Yes. Daniel is going to come over on the boat with us. We won't be carrying on for the last part of the celebrations. We just came to celebrate Gina's special evening."

I must board that boat with them.

I start to slip away to the cabin to pack my bag. I'm only halfway down the stairs when Lucy's voice calls out from behind me.

"Where are you going?"

"I'll be back in five," I say, twisting around with a smile.

"Don't be too long. You'll miss the best part of the evening."

In our cabin, I check that my laptop, chargers, spare USBs, credit cards and all my other important belongings are packed. I stuff my clothes into my bag, not bothering to fold them properly. I keep an eye on the door; I don't trust Lucy not to come in under the pretense that she's making sure I'm all right. Laptop under my arm, I open the cabin door, hurry down the corridor and step into the cinema room. If I hide from immediate view, it will buy me some time to dig. I plug in her memory stick.

It was too much to hope for that it wouldn't be password protected, but I have a hunch. I type in the joint password Sam and I used. I am right, first time. Sam gave this to her. My screen fills up with pictures of him and her. Lucy and Sam. Very much a couple. Seeing him so alive, so happy, is a fresh punch to the gut. I click on the dates. Photos of Lucy and Sam date way back to before he and I married. Oh. My. God. Lucy most definitely was one of his other women.

But why has she pretended to be my friend, back then and

now? I search some more, my fingers typing so fast that I keep making mistakes and hitting the wrong keys. There are lists: Lewis's home address, photos of me taken by Sam, my client list. How the bloody hell did she get that?

I message Lewis.

Did you ever leave this mystery woman alone when she came back to your place?

I wait. He's read it. Thank God he's not asleep yet. *Typing…* The door to the cinema room opens. I crouch down by a seat and gently close my laptop lid.

"Charlotte?" Lucy's voice calls out. I can hear my own breathing.

"She must be somewhere," I hear her say to someone as the door closes again.

A message from Lewis.

Yes. She wanted a take-out curry from a place that didn't deliver, so I went out to get it. Have you asked her about me?

Not yet, but I will. She's deceived me too. More ASAP.

I open up my laptop and restart my search.

I go cold. There are lists of people Sam and I befriended. Colin is in there, too, plus a copy of his obituary. I feel sick. Does she know what Sam did? Is this what all this is about? I keep searching. Under *Jake and Megs* are Jake's bank account details. They aren't the only bank details: there are lists of up to twenty others. Alexandra Armstrong. Even poor Basil and Madelaine didn't escape his greed, despite their generosity.

Looking at all this information, I still can't quite piece it all together. Was Lucy involved with Sam's identity theft? Why, then, is it only me who is being threatened?

I am blinded by a bright light. I drop my laptop, and it clatters to the ground.

"There you are," says Thomas. "What on earth are you doing here in the dark? Lucy's worried sick. She's scared you've had a relapse or something."

I check my laptop screen. Not broken, thank God. I pull out the USB and place it in my bag.

"I wanted time alone," I say. "To grieve. In peace."

"Sorry," he says. "Are you feeling up to returning to the deck? Josephine wants to thank you."

He stands and watches over me while I return my laptop to my cabin, then follow him back to the party.

Lucy comes scuttling over to my side the moment I step out on deck. She takes hold of my hand and squeezes it. I stiffen.

"Thank God you're okay." I want to demand answers from her, but Josephine rises to give a speech, which she reads out from a handwritten piece of paper.

"Thank you all for coming," she says, as if we have all popped over to our local pizzeria and forked out for a bowl of pasta and a bottle of house red. "It means a lot that you all took the time out of your life schedules so that we could be together. Thank you, also, to Mariella and Owen for their hospitality. The *Cleobella* is, without a doubt, absolutely the best yacht I have ever been on."

Polite smiles and sips of champagne all around the table.

Josephine raises her glass.

"Cheers to us all. And a very heartfelt thank-you, too, to each and every one of the staff."

Everyone smiles. *Hear! Hear!* rings out. Mariella smiles over at Alicia, as does Charles. Garth takes a large glug of champagne. His glass is topped up and he takes another gulp. Harrison looks at me. I smile, not caring who is watching. Thomas looks at me with concern on his face. He has told me not to push myself tonight. Work-wise, I won't. Arabella is looking at her phone. Sebastian is gazing out to sea. Gina smiles but her eyes dart toward Garth and his multiple empty champagne flutes. Norma is also keeping a watchful eye on Garth.

I feel detached. A combination of tiredness, painkillers, champagne, shock, disbelief and anxiety because I'm not sure what, exactly, to be afraid of. Lucy is laughing at something Harrison has said and she looks so benign, so innocent, as if she really doesn't have anything dark or deceitful on her mind at all. Then again, I never used to, either, when I was befriending guests. Ditto with Sam.

I wait and watch. Thomas shares the video clip of Josephine's speech on the group chat, which means that everyone—apart from Sebastian—is looking at their phones.

"I'm sharing it with my sister in Australia," exclaims Gina, "so she can experience the moment!"

She looks thrilled.

"Right, everyone," says Josephine, "listen, please. It's time for the important speech of the evening."

Garth takes his cue and stands. He fumbles around in his pockets for his speech. He mentions all the usual: love, patience, acceptance. He tells a funny anecdote about when he and Gina first met. At the end, he does a mock "official" proposal and presents Gina with a ring. He opens a blue box, oyster-like, and she acts all surprised, pretending she hasn't actually seen the ring before.

Everyone smiles at her joke and deliberate bad acting. I smile too. As I do so, it strikes me how surreal it is to be this outwardly dispassionate when my whole world has been up-ended.

Garth places it on her finger, and she displays her left hand to everyone. The phones all come out again as everyone clicks away.

"Let's go and dance," says Norma. "In the bar area."

I watch them all filter inside. I hold back. I have to shake Lucy off, get my bag and catch the small boat headed for the shore with Mariella and Owen.

Harrison comes back out and picks up his phone from the table. "Aren't you coming in?"

"I'm going to give the dancing a miss," I say.

"All too much?" he says. "Totally understandable. Obviously, I didn't know the guy, but…"

"Thanks."

We stand in silence. We are alone on deck. Inside, the bar is lit up like a cinema screen. Everyone is happy, or giving a good impression of being so. Garth and Gina are slow dancing. Josephine and Mariella are laughing. Lucy is looking out the window in our direction.

"I'm going back in," he says.

I lean against the railing and take a deep breath. While doing so, I get this strange compulsion to jump. I have a sudden, violent desire to experience what it must have felt like for Sam before he fell. Slowly, I take off my heels and pad barefoot down the steps to the lower deck. I need to get away sooner than planned. I don't want to risk hanging around waiting for Mariella and family. Hugh is standing near the tender, cleaning the deck with a mop. I tell him that I need to go to shore in five minutes.

"It's an emergency. I just need to run back to my cabin to get my bag."

Hugh doesn't question me.

"Sure."

I run upstairs. I check through the window. Everyone is still at the party, including Lucy, who is talking to Garth.

Back in my cabin, I grab my bag, then head outside to the small boat. There is no sign of Hugh. Instead, Jon stands there.

"What are you doing here?" I ask.

"Are you all right, Charlotte?"

"I'm in a hurry," I say. "Hugh said he would take me to shore."

"Bit late in the evening, isn't it? Hot date?"

"Ha ha. Something like that."

"Hugh just went upstairs. I'm sure he'll be back in a minute."

"I'll go and find him," I say, walking back up the stairs.

Where the hell is he?

As I walk along the outer deck, my phone rings. JJ. I stop to answer it. But before I can do so, I feel a push, then another hard shove, that lifts me up, then over, and my stomach drops. I am falling. There is a sting as I smack the surface before I feel myself getting pulled under. Seawater goes up my nose. My dress sticks to me, making it almost impossible to swim as I get heavier. I aim for the surface and look up at the lights, before I choke and go back under. I hear a splash, as if someone else has jumped in too. A life ring. I cling on to it. When I look up, it's hard to focus, but I see four faces looking down at me: Harrison's, Jon's, Lucy's and Thomas's.

I slip back beneath the water.

36

NOW

I AM WRAPPED IN A BLANKET AND BEING OFFERED brandy in the main lounge. Everyone, it seems, is gathered around, watching me.

I take a large sip of Sebastian's favorite cognac. It's warming. I take another welcome sip. It soothes my aching throat. Lord knows how much seawater I swallowed. My eyes are stinging and I can't stop shivering.

"I need to get back on shore," I say. "It's an emergency. Where's my phone? Where's my bag?"

"It's fine, don't worry, I have them," says Lucy.

"Can you give them to me?"

"Sure, in a minute." She smiles. "When you're properly dry and have stopped shivering."

"Mariella," I say urgently. "I need to get back on shore. I need to come with you."

"Of course," she says. "But we'll need to wait for the boat to return."

I look over to my right. The tender is gone. Clutching at straws, I say, "What about the helicopter? Where is the pilot?

Rather than hanging around for the boat, we could fly to shore."

Everyone looks at me and I hear low voices.

Ex-husband dead, fell into the sea, head injury, was in hospital, saw her standing by the railings, shock, grief…

I shout loudly just to make them all stop.

"It wasn't an accident. Someone pushed me! Where were you, Lucy?"

"Me? At the party. Why would I push you, Charlotte? We're friends."

"Yet you made it out on deck pretty quickly. I saw you peering down at me." I look around. "Did anyone see what happened?"

"Everyone said not," says Tim.

"Well, someone knows something, because I did not jump."

Before anyone else can respond, I hear the sound of a motor approaching. It's the boat, thank God.

"That'll be the doctor," Harrison says. "Not long now." He tops up my cognac. "Best thing for shock. And it's the first and no doubt the last time my father will ever share this with anyone."

I smile to show that I get the joke, that I'm perfectly all right, given the circumstances.

"I blame myself," says Thomas. "I thought this evening would be a good distraction for her, but I fear it was too much, too soon."

"Don't blame yourself," I hear Josephine say. "None of us realized how much she was suffering. She put on a very brave face."

Someone steps off the boat carrying a medical bag. The onboard medic rushes up to have a word and takes out a first-aid kit.

"I really wish everyone would stop talking about me as if I can't hear. I don't need a doctor," I say. "I need someone to listen to me."

"She's in shock," says Thomas. "She's not making sense. She was attacked yesterday and then she received some bad news."

A light is shone in my eyes. I try to push the doctor away and stand up, but my bones feel weak. I am shivering and feel nauseated.

"I'm fine," I say.

My standard response of late.

"Let's get her back to our cabin," says Lucy. "For a start, she should change out of those wet things."

I must get off the yacht. And away from Lucy and her fake concern. Yet I feel very tired and numb. All the faces around me start to slightly fade and blur. I know I mustn't, but all I want to do is close my eyes.

I am in bed, in my cabin. I look around. My dress is lying on the floor, crumpled and useless. There is no sign of my bag, my phone or anything of use. My plan to escape after the party was a true counting-chickens mistake. Seems I've made a lot of those. I look down at myself and realize I am wearing a pair of Lucy's pajamas.

Outside the porthole, all I can see is sea. We are on the move. I am truly trapped.

In front of the door, sitting in an armchair, is Lucy, holding her favorite, very sharp, pair of scissors.

"You're awake, finally," she says. "The doctor and crew wanted to send you back to hospital, Charlotte, but I persuaded them not to. I told them how scary it would be for you to wake up all alone, in a foreign country, with no one around. I promised everyone that I would keep an eye on you. I told them you'd been drinking a fair amount. So, really, it would be nice if you thanked me, hon. There are a lot of people who are going to have to go without facials and massages today because of you."

I feel like I might throw up. I take small sips of water until I feel better.

"You drugged my brandy," I say.

Lucy doesn't deny it but we are interrupted by someone knocking on the cabin door.

I leap off the bed and rush toward the door.

"Help me!"

"Sadly, she's still not herself," Lucy says through the gap in the door. "Come back later. Or no, actually, don't. I'll let you know when she's up for visitors."

Lucy clutches her scissors and raises her hand as though she has a knife.

I step back. She looks as if she wouldn't hesitate to use them.

"Lucy, what on earth is all this about? You're acting part nurse, part jailer."

"You know what you did. What you both did."

A pang of guilt swiftly replaced by fear. I don't know what she's referring to, specifically.

"What did *I* do? I know all about you and Sam. Surely it's me who should be waving scissors in *your* face? He was my husband."

"You used people," she says. "You both used me. Then, totally out of the blue one day, he told me it was over between us."

"I really don't know what all this is about," I say.

"You do," she says. "Go and sit on your bed."

I do as she demands. For now.

"JJ is expecting me. He'll be wondering what has gone on. He'll be worried about me."

"Well, he hasn't called you or messaged since last night, so he can't be too worried." She looks pleased with herself. "In fact, your phone has been quiet."

"Can I have it back?"

"No."

I can't sit on the bed and do nothing. "I need to freshen up and get dressed," I say. "I need my bag. All my clothes are in it, along with my toothbrush."

She doesn't react.

In a calm voice, I point out, "You have my phone and there is no way of escaping from the bathroom."

"Five minutes," she says, standing up. "There's a spare toothbrush in there. Use that. Don't lock the door."

I ignore her, locking the door quietly behind me, and look around for something—anything—that might be of use as a weapon, but the bathroom has been cleared. Apart from the spare toothbrush and some travel-size toothpaste, all that's left is a clear plastic shower cap and a half-empty bottle of body-wash lying on the shower floor. I brush my teeth, staring at myself in the mirror as I do so. I look dreadful. Dark rings circle my eyes and I'm deathly pale.

I jump as the door handle rattles.

"I told you not to lock it!" yells Lucy.

I psych myself up and open the door, full of fresh determination and strength to confront her.

"You can't keep me locked in our cabin."

"I won't have to," says Lucy. "I'll explain how I found my scissors—which you stole from me—under your pillow and that you're a threat to yourself and others. To use Sam's phraseology, I'll flower it up. I imagine you will be whisked away. And who will everyone believe, do you think?"

"What do you want?"

"The money you stole. It's not yours. It belongs to someone else."

"What are you talking about? And who do you think it belongs to?"

"Just transfer the money over to me, like you've been asked to nicely many times, and I'll take it from there."

"I can't pay any *blood money* because, for one, I haven't done anything wrong, and two, Sam emptied our joint bank account when we split up. I certainly don't have a million pounds. Why on earth would I be working as an assistant to Thomas if I had money? You haven't thought this through, Lucy. And you still haven't explained who I am supposed to pay this mythical money I haven't stolen to. Or why you seem so convinced that I had anything to do with said fictional theft."

"I don't believe you. Sam said…"

"Sam said a lot of things. He lived by different rules from us lesser mortals."

"Nice try," says Lucy. She opens a bottle of white wine and pours herself a glass. "I haven't slept, so it still feels like night to me. Cheers!" she says as she raises her glass.

I ignore her.

She places the scissors down on the desk next to the bottle of wine. The wine and the scissors reflect in the mirror.

Outside it is a beautiful, sunny, perfect Caribbean day.

I think it all through. When Lucy found out about Sam and his sidelines, maybe she blackmailed him? Perhaps, when that didn't work, she then decided to focus her attention on me as some sort of twisted compensation for Sam's treatment of her.

Retributive justice. Having been on the receiving end of Sam's cruelty, I can almost—only almost—sympathize with Lucy.

"Sam owes me," Lucy says. "Owed. I guess I can use the past tense now."

"What exactly does he owe you?"

"I met him before I met you. He didn't tell me that he was married. In fact, funnily enough, he didn't mention you at all. I was stupid enough to believe that all the secrecy was because we were work colleagues. When I found out about you, he asked me to be patient. Patience didn't get me anywhere."

"Sam's the person you're angry with," I say. "He lied to me too."

"I believe you knew about me all along but you just didn't care as long as you got what you wanted in the end. You're a heartless bitch who uses people. You and Sam worked together. You dragged me into your games. You squeezed information out of me when I thought we were merely having friendly chats, and you used that information to harm guests like Jake and Megs, to name some of your victims."

"No, that's not how it was. And why are you bringing up Jake and Megs? You barely knew them."

"I got to know them well enough because they were such a lovely couple. And you're lying! How I've just explained it is exactly how it was."

She holds out the USB stolen from my backpack.

"I took a look at this. Trouble is, I couldn't access anything useful or anything I hadn't already found out. I know Sam kept his account details hidden on various memory sticks, like the one you had in your possession. But the good news now is that I have you to help me out."

"They're encrypted. I don't have Sam's passwords. I wish I did."

"Sit down," Lucy says to me, pointing at the desk chair in front of the mirror.

"*You* attacked me," I said. "You stole my USB. Where's my necklace?"

"*Your* necklace. That's a joke. Sit. Down." She picks up her scissors again and points at the chair.

I do so. She places a laptop next to the wine bottle.

"Get me into Sam's bank accounts, either on his laptop or via the information hidden on his USB. Or transfer the money from yours. I'm prepared to be very flexible, as long as I get my money." She takes a sip of wine before she continues. "Everyone saw your destructive behavior last night. I confided in Josephine and the others—reluctantly, of course— that you were having suicidal thoughts because of Sam. Everyone knows how much I've tried to support you."

"Is this *Sam's* laptop?" I ask.

"Yes. He gave it to me but without the password to get in. But I want you to search it. As you rightly say, Sam said a lot of things."

I hesitate. I genuinely don't know where to start. I have spent hours going through Sam's files and documents to no avail.

I open the laptop lid. First, I attempt our wedding date, but of course that's not right. I try the names of the various ships we worked on, the first hotel we ever stayed in. I am locked out after too many attempts.

Lucy slams the laptop lid down so hard that it stings my knuckles.

"You're not trying hard enough."

"I can't make myself know what I don't know." True. "Lucy," I say, "Sam was a master manipulator. I get it. If he persuaded you to do things you didn't want to, don't blame yourself. But…don't be like him. He's gone. We can both move on. I don't understand why this has to be so complicated."

A lot still doesn't make sense to me.

"How did you know I would be on this yacht?" I ask her.

And then, as I slowly piece it all together, it does make sense.

"You're working with Thomas? You had him hire me. You used a bona fide client name from the list you stole from Lewis's to make me believe that I had genuinely been recommended. What's in it for him?"

"It's him you owe the money to," she says. "Do you honestly expect me to believe after all that you and Sam stole that you can't access any of the cash? Call yourself a master criminal?"

"And Thomas?" I prompt. "Why the hell would I owe him money?"

Lucy still ignores me, typing something on her phone. Minutes later, there's a knock on the door. She gets up and in walks Thomas himself.

"Are you going to make Lucy see sense?" I say. "Or at least explain to me, please, what's going on?"

Thomas stands beside Lucy.

"I recruited Lucy for Josephine's last few work trips abroad on the recommendation of my father and stepmother," he says. "We got chatting, as you do, when we were in Lake Como, and a very interesting story emerged."

"Which is?"

"That you and Sam were responsible for the death of my father."

I am not responsible for the death of anyone. Although… please don't let all this be about Colin. I have learned to bury the guilt of my inaction, hard as it was. I don't want it all raked up again.

"You've lost me, really lost me. Am I supposed to know who your father is?"

Thomas looks at me as if assessing whether or not to impart this piece of information or whether I am bluffing.

"Do you remember that lovely couple I mentioned earlier? Jake and Megs?" says Lucy.

I do. But I stay silent.

So, not Colin. Thank God. Still, my heart keeps thudding because although my aiding and abetting was mostly unintentional when it came to them, I feel renewed rage at Sam for having taken things too far.

"You came to the spa and read their medical history before you took them on a hike in Alaska to siphon even more information out of them."

Still, I don't say anything. But I remember the walk we went on and I remember Megs's sorrow at not becoming a mother and I remember that Jake had a child, the product of an affair. I remember other random things, too, like the smell of freshness in the air, the coolness of the forest, the view from near the top of the mountain.

"Jake was my father," says Thomas.

I marry up the picture I have of Jake in my head and study Thomas with fresh eyes, looking for the resemblance, all the while wishing that Sam were here to face his own bloody music.

"Oh, please, Charlotte," says Lucy. "There's no point in remaining silent. This is all going to come out. I knew Sam was up to something. I found thousands of dollars, euros, pounds, all sorts of currencies hidden in his cabin. I found lots of different account details too. I kept a close eye on him."

She pauses for breath.

"I confronted him and he told me that it was all because of you. That you were so greedy, needy and demanding and that he wanted to divorce you, but you wouldn't let him go."

She pours another glass of wine and offers Thomas and me one as if we are in a bar. Thomas accepts.

I shake my head.

"And you believed him?"

"No, of course not. Not at first. But then you kept popping into the spa, asking for information, and you wore expensive-looking jewelry that you tried to hide beneath your tops and long sleeves, but I was watching how you were with people."

"And how was I, exactly?"

"You thought you were charming and witty, but you were obsequious and clearly envious of the wealthy guests."

Ouch.

Lucy continues. "Seeing as we are getting everything out in the open, I let Sam buy me off. Five thousand dollars. It was given as a gift, of course, but I knew it was to shut me up. And I took it because I needed it and I also believed that I deserved something after all he had put me through. And it all worked out well because Megs recommended me to Thomas. I told her how unhappy I was with my life. How I needed a new direction. The lovely Thomas gave me the kind of jobs I used to dream of. I no longer had to work backbreaking hours."

"What happened to your father?" I ask Thomas, although I have a feeling that I don't want to know.

"He died," Thomas says, "because of your and Sam's greed. Jake's identity was stolen, his bank accounts raided, and he lost nearly everything he had worked for. It took over a year to sort out the mess. The money had been stolen so expertly that he felt helpless. Megs tried to help him. My own mother tried to help. Megs contacted everyone they had traveled with and spoke to anyone she could, but in vain. The money was gone, and no one could help."

"I'm sorry to hear that, genuinely I am."

I feel like shit.

Sam always swore that he never took more than anyone could afford. He promised me that. I never agreed to him selling details of people. I never obtained information for that purpose. But I do remember Megs mailing me. *I would hate the same kind of thing to happen to such a nice person as you.* I also remember sending her sorrow-filled words to Junk. For that, I am ashamed.

Memories come flooding back because I also remember Sam and George burning papers in his garden. That's where the information must have gone, to George. I have been a part of something bigger and more insidious than I ever dared to admit or was too blind to see.

"What do you mean you're genuinely sorry? It's exactly what you set out to do!" says Thomas. He drains his glass of wine. "Here's the worst part. My father was driving to the pharmacy to pick up his latest prescription for his anxiety and depression. He was distressed. He received a call that morning that meant that he and Megs were going to lose their house as a result of all the thefts—a direct result of what you and Sam did—because they could no longer afford the payments. He took a bend too fast. And now he's not here and Megs and her entire family are broken and utterly devastated."

I feel sick.

"It's awful," I say, "truly dreadful. But there's no proof that Sam was involved. Sadly, it's such a common thing to happen."

I can't implicate Sam, despite his death, because the links to me are too strong.

"I am sorry," I continue. "It is tragic. But why all this?" I wave my hand around the cabin. "What does Josephine have to do with it?"

"Josephine didn't have anything to do with it. She trusts me. Lucy and I just had to be patient and pick the right time," says Thomas. "You were easy enough to find. You went back to your hometown, tail between your legs. We waited until the right trip came up to offer you the opportunity. We were going to invite you to Mustique initially, but that trip fell through. I must admit, I was keen to meet you in person after all Lucy had told me about you. She told me that she perceived you and Sam as this golden couple, the kind that have millions of followers or have their own reality shows. Only, you two weren't famous. In the end, it turns out you were both nothing."

I don't react to his goading.

"This still doesn't make any sense," I say. "Sam and I had split up. If he did something to your father after we were planning to divorce, that has nothing to do with me."

"Of course you'd say that. Do you expect me to believe you? Sam told me that you were clever. Let's see if he was right." Lucy looks at her watch. "Time's up."

"Yes, let's try again," says Thomas. "We want the money back for Megs, plus compensation."

I try again with the laptop but it's no use. My head feels woolly and achy.

"I need my own laptop to try the USB," I say.

"You can use my spare one," says Thomas. "But remember, I'm watching over your shoulder the whole time. I will see everything you do. Just like when you couldn't resist taking a peek when I left you alone in the conference room."

I plug in the USB but the files and documents blur on the

screen. I've been through all of this so many times. His financial details are not accessible, or they are just not there. "This is madness," I say. "You are trying to hold me accountable for something I didn't do."

Lucy shoots me a look of pure hatred. It's odd, seeing her without her friendly, amenable air of happy-go-lucky friendliness. I catch her eye in the mirror and it is the wrong thing to do because she picks up her scissors and hacks off a chunk of my hair. She drops it onto the keyboard.

"That's enough!" I grab the scissors from her and feel the sharp scratch as the blades slice through my right palm. Thomas pushes me back down.

"We. Want. The. Money."

"Every time you get it wrong, you lose another piece," Lucy says.

"You have a choice, Charlotte," says Thomas. "Either you gain access, or Lucy and I have to decide what exactly to do with all the incriminating information we have on you. Lucy says that another man, named Colin, died, too, after spending time with you and Sam. It doesn't sound like a coincidence to me. Perhaps the local police would like to hear what we've got to add to the histories of the last people to see him alive?"

At the thought of Colin, a new wave of fear rushes through me.

I type the name of our house in Devon: *SeaLaVie*.

Access not authorized.

Lucy opens the blades and snips again, deliberately slicing the top of my ear. The burning pain is swiftly numbed by fear. Lucy's anger is escalating; she is losing control.

37

I LOOK DOWN AT MY CHUNKS OF HAIR AND TOUCH the side of my cheek to feel the blood running down it. I reach for a tissue. Yet, in a strange way, the fear is somehow calming. This was never about Alexandra or any link to her. It was all about my own guilty conscience. I experience a curious mixture of relief, shame, anger and fear.

Lucy's expression is resolute but her eyes are glazed. She holds up yet another strand of my hair and slices. She deliberately lets the blades graze my neck and collarbone.

I type in Sam's birthday, his hometown, the names of all the ships we worked on. I've tried all of these before to gain access to his encrypted files, but I try again, using different combinations of capital letters and numbers.

Nothing.

As Lucy tugs at my hair again, I cry out in pain.

"For God's sake, I'm trying! The more you threaten me, the more my brain freezes."

Lucy just stares at me in the mirror. We lock eyes. Thomas puts both of his hands on my shoulders and speaks in such a

calm, measured way that it is almost more frightening than
if he were shouting.

"Try harder, Charlotte."

Lucy nods her agreement.

Thomas continues. "Did you ever think about your victims, Charlotte? The shattered dreams, illness, shame, fear.
The list goes on and on."

Thomas is wrong. I was careful. I chose targets wisely. Sam
is the villain here, not me.

"There are no *victims*. And I look forward to proving you
both wrong."

I see Lucy and Thomas exchange a look in the mirror. Were
they starting to doubt themselves?

I type in the date Sam and I first met. Bequia. The island
where we first met, the names of the people we befriended,
the date we split up.

Access still denied. Thomas slams down the lid, just like
Lucy did, and Lucy picks up her scissors.

I lock eyes again with Lucy's reflection.

"How did you get the watch that you left on my bed?"

She ignores the question but not before I have caught sight
of a slight smirk.

I am tired. I really have exhausted all options when it comes
to guessing Sam's passwords. My neck aches. My eyes are
scratchy. My mind is utterly shattered.

An idea comes to me.

"I need my bag," I say to Lucy. "I really do. I've something
that could help."

"Like what?"

"Like another memory stick that Sam gave me," I lie. "It
may not work, so don't get scissor-happy, but anything is
worth a shot."

Thomas and Lucy exchange a look.

"I'll go and get it," says Thomas.

Lucy pulls the armchair away from the door and Thomas leaves.

My plan to get away from them may just work.

For now, it's just her and me.

"Anything else you want to tell me?" I say. "You and Thomas have been trying to frighten me since I stepped foot on board. You deceived my roommate, Lewis, who is a lovely, kind man. He has never harmed anyone."

"I didn't mean to upset Lewis. Thomas and I figured that if you were frightened enough while on board here, if you were isolated enough, that you would open up to me, pour your heart out. But no. We figured that you would be too scared of getting caught to spend the money you stole too soon. We guessed that you would lie low by working for a few years, then—poof—disappear like magic. I had to get to you before that happened. Thomas scared you at the horse ride."

"What else did you do?" I demand. "I could have died."

"You're not dead right now and we need you to do what's right. When you mentioned a stalker, we thought you were going to open up. Yet again, no. We were forced into stronger action. Thomas didn't *want* to follow you, then mug you, but you were planning on jumping ship. Everything that happened, you brought it upon yourself. I had to kick your bag onto the rocks below at the waterfall. In fact, I had to work really hard because you stupidly and stubbornly refused to pay the money. You forced us to be a lot more inventive when all we wanted was for you to make amends with a decent and fair amount of compensation."

I keep her talking.

"Who was looking for me that night when there was the power cut on the boat?"

"Thomas came back early in a water taxi. It was his idea to cut the power. He said you had been messaging him, asking when they would all be back. He said you were already jittery."

"Did Sam ever buy you orchids?" I ask.

Suddenly, I need to know.

"Yes."

"Oh, Lucy," I say. "He bought them for me every single time he had to apologize for the latest shitty thing he did. When I saw the orchid on my pillow, it was those types of details that reinforced my belief that he was still alive. It was cruel of you. Was it Thomas who took the orchid to my sister's?"

"Oh, *Lola*," she says in a nasty voice. "Does it matter?"

"It matters because I thought we were friends, Lucy. You fell for Sam, just like I did. That's the only crime. There is nothing that you couldn't have come and spoken to me about." Untrue. Nonetheless, it is mildly satisfying to scrape back some of the moral high ground.

"However much you pretend otherwise, Charlotte, I see you. I know who and what you are. And by the way, your stolen purse had nothing to do with me. That was pure karma."

The door opens and Thomas carries in my bag. As he hands it to me, Lucy snatches it from him.

"Where is the other USB?"

"In the zip compartment," I lie.

She searches and, of course, doesn't find anything.

"Give it to me," I say. "It will be quicker."

She relents.

I pretend to rummage for a second or two.

Passport: check. Phone: check.

I make a dash for the bathroom and lock the door, dialing JJ's number. It rings. The door handle rattles and shakes. Ring, ring. Ring, ring. Voice mail.

Hands still shaking, I manage to send a message to the group chat.

Lucy and Thomas are holding me against my will in our cabin. Please. Get me out.

The door rattles a few more times, then stops. I hear voices, thank God. It goes quiet. The bathroom door opens. Thomas and Lucy are standing there with Bill, the medic, and one of the yacht crew, clutching a master key.

"Thank goodness you're all right, Charlotte," Lucy says, flinging her arms around me while simultaneously pinching the back of my arm.

"Let's take a look at you," says Bill, ushering me toward my bed.

"Charlotte's not herself. She tried to kill me with my own scissors, didn't she, Thomas?" Lucy is a good actor; she sounds genuinely frightened.

Thomas backs her up.

"Yes, she's out of control. We're scared she might harm herself."

I look over at the desk. The scissors, wine and laptop have been removed.

"Bill," I say. "I just need to get out of here. Can we talk in private?"

"So you can jump overboard again?" says Lucy. "Not on my watch. We're here to look after you." To Bill she says, "I made a mistake by not letting her go to the hospital. Please, can you calm her down? I'll never forgive myself if she does anything to harm herself."

"This is ridiculous," I say as Bill offers me a pill from his medical bag. "I'm not going to harm myself. I am perfectly fine."

There is another knock at the door.

Thank God, help is here.

A voice. It's Harrison. "Everything all right in there? Charlotte sent a strange message on the group chat."

"Help me!" I shout.

"Everything is fine," Lucy calls out. "Bill's here. Charlotte is a little upset."

"Don't leave me here with them," I say to Bill. "Please. Just let me explain everything to you. I am not going to harm myself."

Bill's phone rings. He answers it.

"Excuse me," he says. "Hello?" A pause. "Yes, I see."

He disconnects.

"That was Josephine. I understand you're upset," he says, "but everyone believes it's best that you rest. I do too. As soon as we reach the next island, we can get you properly checked over once more, and then you'll be free to go as you please."

Behind Bill's back, Lucy mouths *Colin*. Thomas folds his arms and stares at me.

"I'll be fine," I say.

"Are you sure you don't want anything to help you sleep?" Bill asks.

"Sure."

"Well, I'm only a call away if you change your mind, or Lucy can come and get me."

Bill says something quietly to Lucy on his way out.

"Thanks, Bill," Lucy says, showing him to the door and shutting it behind him.

"I'm not very impressed at all," she says. "Are you, Thomas?"

"No," he says. "I don't think Charlotte is taking us seriously enough. In fact, I'm extremely pissed off."

Gone is the prim and proper Thomas. He has my phone in his hand. He grabs me by the wrist and forces my index finger down on my phone to unlock it.

"I'll just type a message on the group chat apologizing for your outburst and explain that you feel fine," he says.

Lucy opens the desk drawer and I assume that the scissors are going to put in a reappearance. But no, she takes out a syringe and a vial. I see her push the needle in and withdraw the plunger. Thomas pins down my arms as she approaches. "No!" I shout, twisting and kicking. "Don't do this, Lucy!" I shout.

And in the moments before she does exactly that, I have a moment of horrible clarity. Lucy killed Sam.

38

NOW

OH, GOD. I AM STILL ON THE YACHT. BUT I'M NOT IN my cabin. I am lying on a double bed in Mariella's vacated suite. It's dark but the moon is full; silver light spreads across the room, outlining Thomas sitting on the sofa. He is staring over at me as if he can tell that I have opened my eyes. I remain rigid and shut my eyes again while I assess and think. My mouth and throat feel dry. I listen. There is no sign that Lucy is here. I hear the clink of ice cubes against a glass and I smell whiskey.

"Thomas," I say, sitting up. "I need water."

I switch on the bedside lamp.

He looks alarmed. I must look a right sight, but he gets up and pulls out a plastic bottle from the minibar, walks over and hands it to me.

"Who brought me here?"

"We both did. We thought you could do with lots of fresh air."

He walks over and slides open the doors. The guardrails have never looked so flimsy and insignificant. I sit, observing and thinking.

Dawn is still a way off. A welcome cool breeze brushes my face. I get off the bed and put my feet on the floor, ready to make a run for the door, but my legs are too weak.

Thomas seems to sense what I'm planning because he comes over and sits beside me. His face is flushed, his eyes look blood-shot and haunted.

"There's nowhere to go, Charlotte. Nowhere to hide. It's time to stop and face up to what you did. You have blood on your hands." He pauses. "Spending time with you, retelling the story now, it brings it all back. It makes it clearer in my mind that you need to pay for what you did."

"Not me. Lucy's the murderer, Thomas. She killed Sam. You don't want any part of this, you really don't. She will drag you down. I am sorry for what Sam may or may not have done to Jake. But really—this isn't a good thing to do. You're an intelligent person. Don't go along with her schemes."

"You're trying to shift the blame onto Lucy now? I don't believe you. I'm not listening to your excuses and stories, Charlotte. Give us what you owe."

I persevere.

"Where did she get his laptop from? And the engraved watch she left on my bed? It was mine, but then Sam took it away from me when he was angry and hurt."

Doubt flickers in his eyes.

"Where *is* Lucy?" I ask.

He picks up his phone, and minutes later, Lucy reappears. Sam's laptop is under her arm and she is carrying a large makeup bag.

"Ready to try again?" she says.

Thomas takes out his laptop and places it on the desk. I ignore it.

"What happened to Sam?" I say.

She looks momentarily taken aback.

"He had an accident."

Thomas's eyes widen. I like watching him digest the unpleasant news that, after all his subterfuge, he is siding with a potential murderer.

"What happened?" I say. "I think I have a right to know how my husband died."

"We want the money first, don't we, Thomas?"

"Yes," he says.

But there is less conviction in his voice.

Lucy swings around and points the scissors in his face.

"Charlotte is bluffing about not knowing how to gain access to the money. How careless would she have to be to let Sam take it all? She's playing stupid, acting like she's penniless. They were married, it should be a fifty-fifty split, at least. We can make her pay us. We've gone to all this trouble, set up special accounts. I need this money. Megs needs the money. We agreed that it was the right thing to do. It belongs to you, Tom."

She opens the laptop lid.

"Come *on*, Charlotte."

I try again.

As I do so, Lucy takes out *my* emerald necklace from her bag and drapes it around her neck, admiring herself in the mirror.

"I can see what you find so appealing about jewels, Charlotte," she says. "Is this the one you stole from the poor old lady? The one that made an entire cruise ship get searched? It must be worth a fortune."

I don't like her referring to Alexandra as the "poor old lady" and I also don't like seeing the necklace on her. It's mine.

Desperate as I am to put an end to this, I can't know what I don't know.

"How about we go to a bank in port?" I say. "I'll take ID, of course. Explain that I'm Sam's wife. That he has tragically passed away and I will ask them to access his accounts—transfer whatever I can."

"A bank?" says Lucy. "For God's sake. What era do you live in?"

She and Thomas exchange a look.

"We've had enough," she says. "You're messing us around. Clearly you need some help to jog your memory."

She opens her large makeup bag and removes another syringe and a vial.

"I made sure I took enough from Bill's bag when he came to our cabin to deal with you, but the story will be that *you* stole it during the big fuss you created earlier."

Oh, God.

"Only, this time you won't wake up. Then—" she points to the balcony railings "—it will be goodbye, Charlotte. This time you won't pop back up. You'll be weighted down with a personal anchor. I reckon a couple of bottles of champagne in your backpack on your back should do it. What do you reckon, Thomas?"

"No, it would take more than that."

As if to prove a point, he opens the fridge and starts removing bottles of wine and champagne.

Now I know why they risked dragging me—unconscious—to this suite instead.

Lucy slides three bottles of champagne into my backpack. She lifts it up with one arm.

"No, not heavy enough."

She doesn't seem to realize that there isn't room for another.

"You want to murder me?" I say. "Like you murdered Sam?"

Lucy's expression is pure hate.

"You've got another twenty minutes," she says.

I don't doubt that she means it. Her breath reeks of wine and she hasn't slept for God knows how long.

"And then what?" I say. "I'm your only shot at trying to get what you want."

"I'll find someone who can break the codes eventually," she says. "You're not useful at all. In fact, you're becoming a liability. It's very disappointing, after all our efforts."

I give it another shot.

"Stop staring at the screen," I say. "It's distracting me."

I scan, desperately. A file name catches my eye. *Vacations*. Sam would have used *Holidays*.

I click.

Encrypted.

Of course.

I type our *shit hit the fan* code: *BonVoyage*.

I am in.

Thank God.

Details of trips Sam and I took together are listed benignly, but the fact that he used *our* code gives me the motivation to think harder. The dates! The dates of our trips are all incorrect.

"I need a pen and paper," I say.

They both look at me.

Lucy seems to pick up on the relief in my voice because she opens her own bag and hands me a notepad decorated with cats and dogs, along with a pen.

I start writing down numbers and letters, replacing the incorrect ones with the right dates.

Lucy and Thomas both look over my shoulder as I access an account in the name of Sam's father. Several hundred thousand pounds appear beneath his name. And this is only in the one account.

"There you go," I say, turning the laptop screen around to show her. "You can change the password yourself. It's all yours to do what you like with. We can end this now."

Lucy pushes me out of the way and taps so fast her nails scratch the keyboard. Thomas steps in to help. The figure falls to zero.

I wait, barely breathing, but she doesn't ask me to access anything further. She doesn't seem disappointed that it's less than a million. In fact, they both look as if they can't quite believe it has happened. Lucy appears less frenzied. Her breathing is calmer.

"Now, tell me what happened to Sam," I say.

"I want that memory stick first," she says.

I yank it out. Lucy tries to take it from me. I pick up a paperweight and hit her with it, hard, on the side of her face, before turning toward the railings and throwing the USB into the sea. There is nothing left in her possession that connects me to Sam.

My actions trigger fresh rage in Lucy.

"Hold her, Thomas!"

He grabs me from behind and holds my arms behind my back, then pushes me to the floor. I am winded. My cheek stings where my face hit the carpet. I struggle, but Thomas is stronger. I can see Lucy preparing the syringe. Oh, God, not again. I mustn't end up like Sam.

I kick Thomas but he grabs me tighter.

"You don't want to do this, Thomas. Let me go!"

As I feel Lucy tug my arm, I scream, and she jabs me in the shoulder with the syringe.

Yet…nothing else happens. The world does not go black. Lucy says, "Fuck. I didn't do it properly."

I look up to see a wine bottle flying toward my face. I shut my eyes and raise my arms to cover my head. She misses; it only grazes the side of my head, but I keep my eyes closed and pretend to go limp. The pain in my shoulder is excruciating.

"Drag her to the railings," I hear Lucy say. "I've got ribbon in my bag. We can use it to tie her up."

It takes both of them to hold me down, but despite my struggling and kicking, they succeed in tying my hands behind my back and attaching the ribbon to the metal rails. My wrists sting as I tug. I am exhausted.

I open my eyes. Lucy is sitting on a chair beside me. I shut my eyes again as if drowsy.

"Tell me about Sam," I say. "You owe me that."

Silence. At first, I think she isn't going to say anything, but then she starts speaking softly.

"He made me so many promises," she says, looking down at me on the floor. "And I believed him. Every. Single. Time."

"Sam loved the thrill of the chase," I say.

"I kept a close eye on Sam, which wasn't easy. He lied, even on his social media, about where he was and what he was doing. But then he met Perfect Penny after you, and she loved posting things about them online, so it was easier to follow him. I couldn't believe it when she posted that she was going to Devon. That was our special place. I didn't love him with quite the same level of intensity anymore, but I also didn't see why he should get away with everything."

"I own that house," I say.

She looks shocked but doesn't say anything.

"When were you there?" I ask.

"The first time was once when you were in between tenants. He told me that you and he had split up. I met him in Mexico, twice, too. I thought it was just me and him, now that you were gone."

"There were probably at least a couple more women before Penny," I say, unable to resist.

She speaks in a monotone, as if distancing herself from her words.

"His death was an accident, it really was. I called him and told him that I needed to see him. He was in the house and I went there, but he said that I couldn't stay, that we were over. He didn't want me in the house because I was his dirty secret. We weren't anywhere near the place where the reports said he fell. We were a few miles farther along." Lucy takes a deep breath, then speeds up as if she is trying to get the next part over with. "We were walking and he was lying and denying. He even pretended he couldn't remember Jake, he said that I was delusional, and even though I knew what he was like, I was angry because I knew that he was just saying what he thought he should say, not what was real, and then we fought and he…fell. He was gone. He genuinely, honestly, just fell."

I open my eyes properly and stare at her.

"You pushed him," I say.

"No, he fell."

The three of us sit in silence. Dawn is imminent. Flecks of pale yellow and gold begin to stripe the horizon. The ribbon is slippery, easing around my wrists. I daren't look directly at Thomas. I don't want to make any sudden movements. Every now and then he gives a little cough or I hear the clink of ice in his glass. My head hurts. I can feel blood, sticky, in my cropped hair.

"Why, then, didn't you call the police? The coast guard? Anyone? No one looked for him until Penny raised the alarm."

"What would have been the point? He fell over the edge of a cliff. Why would I want to make things worse for myself? What do you think Sam would have done if the roles were reversed?"

"It doesn't make it right."

"It doesn't make it wrong."

"He was afraid, just before he died. He said that someone had been threatening him."

"I wanted him to admit to what he had done."

"You had his bag," I say. "He didn't fall with that. He carried his backpack everywhere. That's how you had his laptop."

"I discarded his jacket nearer the house," Lucy says, "so it would look like he had fallen there. I called you from Sam's phone, several times. You never picked up."

"What night was this?" I say.

She tells me. And it plunges me back into uncertainty. If that is the case, then it couldn't have been Sam who put the memory stick and the note in my bag.

It had to be someone else.

As I process this, I sense Lucy's mood change. She is watching me. I look ahead as I ease the ribbon off my wrists. Sunlight rises in the sky; shimmering gold reflects off the water.

"You're not leaving now," she says. "There's no way I can trust you."

"You got what you wanted," I say.

"Not quite," she says.

She stands up, a wine bottle clenched in her hand again. I see streaks of blood—my blood—on the white printed label. I will not end up like Sam. I free my hands and I see the shock in Lucy's expression as I leap up to grab her weapon. I miss, but grip hold of her forearm. Lucy pulls her arm free and raises it high. As she attempts to hit me with the bottle, she trips over a large decorative seashell. Her body slams against the balcony rail and she drops the bottle, which thuds onto the carpet. I grab at the emerald necklace from behind and tug, hard, as Lucy reaches up to her neck. Once, twice, a third time before it breaks off and is released into my hands.

From behind me, Thomas grabs my shoulders and pulls me away from Lucy. She bends down to pick up the bottle. As she turns to hit me again with it, I twist my head to the side and the bottle smashes down onto the railings. Thomas releases his grip on me as he ducks out of the way of the flying glass. Lucy raises her arm again; the jagged edges of dark green are ugly against the streaks of reds and oranges in the sky beyond. I do what I have to. I push. With all my force. Lucy falls backward onto the ground. I reach down to prize the smashed bottle from her, and as I do so, Thomas pushes me out of the way. I fall, too, knees first, the pain only briefly registering as I leap up to stop Thomas from hurting me again. We collide, facing each other as he then slams me against the railings. The metal judders as I catch my breath. I look at him and I can see the hatred in his eyes. He comes at me again. I smell whiskey. I step to the right. His body crashes into the railings, which shudder and vibrate once again but they do nothing to stop him. Thomas's height was an advantage only when he was overpowering me. As he tumbles into the ocean, all I can hear are Lucy's screams.

"You've killed him!"

"No, he fell!"

We both look down into the water. There is no sign of Thomas. I turn and face the aft of the yacht. In the wake I can see Thomas bobbing; already the distance between him and us is growing.

"We have to alert the crew," I say. "He isn't trying to swim or wave for help. He must've hit his head on the way down."

As I turn away, it's the sudden movement in the corner of my eye that alerts me to Lucy's intention. She grabs my arm.

"You're not going anywhere," she says. "You go in and save him."

I do what I have to do once again. I shove her. Hard.

The shock on Lucy's face as she falls backward and over the railing is terrifying. But…it's too late. I had no choice but to save myself.

It's what Sam *should* have done.

39

THEN AND NOW

I RUN FOR HELP. THE ALARM IS SOUNDED, LOUD AND urgent, as the crew leap into action. It seems as if every single one of them is out on the deck as the yacht turns around to locate Lucy and Thomas. I am simultaneously afraid of them being found and of them not being found.

But even in the midst of my panic, twisted hope forms. Dark secrets are self-silencing. By coupling up with Lucy, Thomas has become a criminal, limited his options, now and in the future. He has become someone more like me.

Lucy is found first. She has swallowed a lot of water. Under the captain's orders, the *Cleobella* is returning to Barbados to get Lucy proper medical attention. Thomas is a different story. He has not been found. The thundering of approaching rescue boats and helicopters in our immediate vicinity is deeply unsettling.

At Bridgetown, the crew are given permission to dock immediately.

"How on *earth* did it happen?" Josephine asks me as we wait for the police.

Everyone is so shocked, so preoccupied, that no one comments on my new short haircut.

"We were drinking a lot, taking photos," I say. "It seemed that Thomas didn't consider his surroundings properly. He sat on the guardrails, then slipped backward. It was terrible."

It was.

Josephine looks aghast.

I look at Lucy, still wrapped in a blanket, and she looks at me. Honor among thieves, however twisted and misplaced. Neither of us can turn the other in without incriminating ourselves.

"And Lucy jumped in to save Thomas," I add. "Such a hero."

She glares at me and I just know she's biding her time, waiting for the best moment to contradict my story and drop me in it, despite her own crimes. The police are going to interview her separately, at the hospital to which she is about to be whisked away in a private car by Josephine and Harrison.

Once we've all relayed our own stories and answered the police questions, we are then left, anchorless, awaiting news of Thomas.

Around me, I hear "a tragic accident" repeated over and over.

The stilted goodbyes and thank-yous, the assurances from the yacht crew to keep everyone updated with the search—they are all a blur.

"Cars have been arranged to transport everyone to the villa," Gina says.

"I don't need to go there," I say.

"I'm sorry, Charlotte, but I really must insist on behalf of Josephine. Ultimately, she feels it's her responsibility until it has been confirmed by a doctor that you are fit to fly home."

I sit in the back of the car with Gina and Garth; Daniel sits in the front. I stare out the window as we pass a beach, crammed full of carefree-looking tourists, a complete contrast to Gina and Garth's dissections of Thomas and his most likely fate.

We pass through the gates and enter the drive leading up to the villa, palms swaying in the gentle breeze. From the outside, it certainly looks even more luxurious than anything Sam or I ever stayed in.

We're dropped off. Mariella and Owen come to the front door to greet us, their faces pale.

"We couldn't believe it when we heard. We've been praying for a positive outcome."

The villa staff have prepared all our rooms. Daniel doesn't leave until Mariella and Owen have sworn to keep a close eye on me. From the window in one of the upstairs guest bedrooms, I watch the cars drive away.

Now that I know how to, I figure out Sam's bank codes, one by one, by deciphering the incorrect holiday dates. By the time I have finished, I have gained access to five different accounts. It is deeply satisfying to discover that Sam, in the end, did the right thing by warning me to watch my back and by finally giving me access to his riches. What Lucy got her hands on is a mere drop in a large ocean. I exhale loudly and give a little shout out loud.

"Yes!"

I am free.

It is late afternoon when we hear the news that, unlike Sam, who wasn't discovered immediately, Thomas, tragically, has been.

I feel numb. I hate what he did to me yet I understood his desire for revenge.

I ask one of the villa staff to arrange a car to take me to the hospital. One thing is clear: Lucy needs silencing. I predict that she is hoping to slip away and lead a quiet life, to put all this behind her. Good luck to her. I won't let it happen.

At the desk, I pretend to be Lucy's distraught sister. Turns out there was no need; she has already discharged herself.

Let Lucy think she has given me the slip. I know all the ways to tap into her newfound greed, to hook her, to lure her in online, snippet by snippet, temptation by temptation, a trail of golden crumbs, and I'll be waiting at the end... Secrets weakened Sam and they weakened me. She won't be an exception. She will not live her life off the fruits of my labor.

I message Lewis.

The woman's name is Lucy. You had a lucky escape.

I message JJ to let him know that I am all right, and then, finally, Lucy.

I won't forget what you did.

It will stop her from getting too comfortable. The message does not send, however. Her phone number has been changed or I have been blocked. No matter, she can't disappear completely, she can't hide from me. I have her notebook, the one covered in cats and dogs, which she handed to me when she was so desperate to get into Sam's bank account. It's full of fascinating personal tidbits, like how she is planning to fly to Goa with *my* money.

It's peaceful at the villa. It's the kind of peace that feels as though nothing bad can ever happen. I sit on the porch area and stare out to sea, sipping tea. I do this every morning.

Everyone except Mariella and family have flown home to deal with the aftermath in private.

Mariella comes out onto the porch and joins me.

"We're leaving in a few days," she says. "But the owner says you can stay on for as long as you like."

"Thank you," I say, then ask her quietly, "What about Tim?"

"He is taking some time off, then he has some work in the Med, come spring. I don't know when I will see him again. I know it must look bad…"

"It's not up to me to judge," I say.

While staying with Mariella, Owen and their children, I have adopted Daniel's policy of seeing no evil, hearing no evil, speaking no evil when it comes to thinking about Mariella and Tim.

"Owen and I have an arrangement. We lead fairly separate lives, but Tim, being an employee of his… Well, it crossed a line. Tim isn't going to accept any work from Owen again, so it will work itself out, somehow."

"I hope it does work out well for you." True.

We sit in silence.

"It was you, wasn't it, who put the package in my bag at the races? You were there. You had a connection to Sam. It's the only thing that makes sense."

Sam must've had me followed when I didn't respond to his calls.

"Yes. Owen asked me to do him a favor. He and Sam, they went back a long way. I didn't know anything about you or Sam. I trusted Owen when he said it wasn't anything illegal. He said it was important, that it was something that might save your life. Sam had begged him to do it, apparently, told Owen that he knew where you could be found. I felt guilty about Tim, so I agreed to do it, as I felt that I owed Owen for what I was doing behind his back. I told him I would go to the races with a friend." She pauses. "I watched you disembark from the boat. You looked exactly like your photograph. I was horrified when you smiled at me and then again when you recognized me just before we boarded the yacht, but Owen assured me it was nothing to concern myself with. He reassured me again that I hadn't done anything wrong."

"Secrets make liars of us all," I say.

I haven't told Mariella the full story, just that Lucy wasn't quite the friend she had made herself out to be and had been seeing Sam behind my back, plus playing horrible tricks on me to make me think that I was losing my mind. Lucy deserves to be badly thought of.

"The owner is coming over here for evening drinks," she says. "They want to meet you. You can have a discussion then about length of stay, dates and what have you, once they have deemed you suitable. I imagine that is what the visit is all about."

I've got an inkling that it is much more than that. The story doesn't feel over yet.

A silver car with blacked-out windows appears in the drive at 6:00 p.m. The driver steps out and opens the back door. My stomach drops. It is not who I expected. Because, even now, I still half suspect that Sam will show up, bursting with stories and lies. It will take time for me to feel truly free from his legacy, to accept that he is gone. *She* emerges, wearing a shimmering long dress in peacock blues and greens. She hasn't aged. If anything, she looks even better. My heart thuds. I know there'll be a reason she's here.

"Hello, Charlotte."

"Hello, Alexandra."

It feels good to see her again, despite my trepidation.

We sit on the porch, surrounded by the noises of the cicadas, and sip rum cocktails with pineapple juice. Owen only stays for the one. After that, he has calls to make. Mariella wants to put the younger children to bed. Alexandra and I find ourselves alone.

"Why are you here?" I ask. "I've tried to get in touch with you."

"I heard what happened to Sam."

"I still can't believe it. The funeral is in a fortnight and I can't decide whether to fly back just for that or not. I did love him."

The luxury of money is the options it affords. Stay here, go there. I can do whatever I please.

"I'm only here now because Sam's gone," Alexandra says. "There was no way I could trust you before. He had his claws into you too deep."

"I didn't take your necklace. Or anything else. It's important to me that you know that. Sam planted it there. I feared you thought I had betrayed you. I didn't. I tried to find you, but you had already vacated your cabin."

"I think we've got our wires crossed. Let's start from the beginning. The moment I realized I had been conned, I felt such a fool. I was so angry. It shouldn't have happened to someone like me. I wasn't going to let you and Sam get away with it. I thought if I reported the theft to the ship's security, you would both get caught and it would teach you a much-needed lesson."

"Sam was tipped off by one of his mates," I say. "He knew in advance that we were going to be searched."

"When I realized he had got away with it, I had him followed," Alexandra says. "There was no way I was letting him off the hook after what he had done."

"I thought at first that you and he had double-crossed me," I say. "But you saved me. They gave the necklace back to me. Thank you. How did you know that Sam had set me up?"

"I suspected, but wasn't one hundred percent sure. I wanted to see you *both* punished. Because you had been left to face the music on your own, I said that I'd made an error. That I had gifted you the necklace and forgotten all about it. I explained that I was very embarrassed at the fuss I had caused, and so on. I wasn't going to let you take all the blame while he disappeared off into the sunset. I used to listen when you were telling me stories about your marriage, wondering if you were ever going to come clean about what you two were really up to. I gradually realized how much he had sucked you into his schemes."

"I doubt I would've even been stopped if it hadn't been for Sam. When he was pulled over by customs, he must've made a point to suggest it was me they were after."

"He was a right slippery eel, that man," she said. "He gave the private detective the slip in Mexico even though I had more than one person following him. I had to shut down several of my bank accounts because of the details he had stolen. I had no doubt that he would follow through with his thefts."

"I tried to contact you many times. You're not so unslippery yourself."

"Timing is everything. It really is," she says. "I needed to be sure that you wouldn't reunite with Sam."

"I thought you wanted revenge. Either you or Sam."

"I can see why."

We sip our cocktails in reflective silence.

"Do you want your necklace back?"

"Yes."

"It needs mending. The clasp broke. Sorry."

I open my bag and hand it to her. She takes it, looks at it, then hands it back to me.

"On second thought, you can keep it. It was never mine in the first place."

"Oh? What do you mean?"

"I have a proposition," she says.

"I'm listening…"

"I started out just like you, only in the South of France. I progressed from there. I told myself that I would stop one day, but it snowballed, business was good. I wasn't like Sam—or you—because I genuinely believed in wealth redistribution. I wasn't an angel, of course not, but I worked hard. I donated to hospices, caretakers and the elderly. I wanted—and still do—to give the voiceless their voice back."

Well, I never.

"Oh my God. It takes one to know one," I say. "You had me and Sam sussed right from the beginning. I did try to talk him out of it, you know. I told him you weren't suitable. But he took you out to lunch, showered you with attention and you canceled your plans with me."

"I know. But I wanted to see what Sam was like in action. I wanted to get the measure of you. Were you good? Were you bad? Were you just like him or highly influenced? I did feel betrayed and stupid that he had targeted me. I, of all people, should've known better. Initially I trusted you. I didn't trust many people—still don't—and I thought, at first, when Sam started smarming around, that you were encouraging it."

"No," I say. "Quite the opposite. What is the proposition you mentioned?"

"Society may call me a criminal, but real criminals walk among us, Charlotte, and they are the people who make de-

cisions to worsen lives, not improve them. And they don't
care. So many decisions, it seems, are made by people with
wealth and power, who can't, or won't, understand what life
is like for those without. We will not be real criminals, Charlotte. You and me, we could give something back to people
who really need it by redistributing the wealth of people who
don't deserve it."

"Where do I fit in?"

"I think we would make a good team," she says. "I have a
new home in Monaco. You could be my daughter who has
come to visit, if you like. Or my niece or my goddaughter.
We could mix the stories up for variety."

It sounds ideal. I don't even have to think about it.

"There is someone I'd want to invite," I say.

"Oh?"

I tell her about Lucy.

"I want to entice her to a job or a lifestyle in a similar way
that she lured me."

"It sounds as if it will be simple enough," she says. "Her
ill-gotten gains won't last for long now that she's developed a
greed for easy money."

"A once-in-a-lifetime opportunity," I say. "For an experienced, dedicated beauty therapist who is free to travel at
short notice. Competitive rates, lots of time off, that kind of
thing. Obviously, for it to properly work, I will flower it up
to make it irresistible."

It will make the hunt more interesting and varied, make
it feel even sweeter when I have tracked her down and when
she realizes that she messed with the wrong person.

"And what will you do if she bites?"

"Make her pay," I say. "I haven't decided exactly how yet,
but I'll think of a way."

Since I found out that Sam is no longer alive, I've been dreaming about him more than ever. On occasion, I experience with him the cold shock as he hits the water. Hypothermia takes hold, or the worst one, the eerie sensation of being alone at sea. In my dreams, fishing boats or ships pass by him. So near, yet so far. As Sam's hand reaches out, the lights fade into the distance, swallowed up by clouds.

Alexandra stands up.

"Which way is the bathroom?" she asks.

"You don't really own this villa, do you?"

"No," she laughs. "But I have spoken to the real owner and paid for you to stay here for another week. I may join you too. We can take some time to figure things out, mull over the details."

I like the sound of that.

Alone, I bend down and take off my anklet. I walk the few steps down to the garden, stepping on the lush, green grass and along to the end of the lawn. I cross the road and throw the anklet as far as I can into the sea.

"Goodbye, Sam."

A great weight lifts.

Alexandra is back on the veranda when I return.

The butler comes out and asks if we would like our cocktails topped up.

"Champagne," we both say.

This is a celebration, after all. I know exactly who I am now and in what direction my life is headed.

Lucy won't bite immediately, I appreciate that, but Sam taught me patience and Alexandra taught me to trust myself.

Sam paid for what he did to Colin. Lucy must pay for what she did to Sam, one way or another. Sam would approve.

As Alexandra and I sit opposite each other, in matching

wicker chairs, it feels like old times. I take a deep breath of the rose-scented balmy air and a large sip of icy champagne as I survey my new, flowered-up version of paradise.

★ ★ ★ ★ ★

ACKNOWLEDGMENTS

The past year has been challenging for everyone, so it was a very welcome distraction to be able to island-hop around the Caribbean, immersed in Charlotte's world.

A huge amount of teamwork is involved in publishing a book. I'd like to thank my wonderful agent, Sophie Lambert, for all her amazing work, kind support, encouragement and wisdom. Also, huge thanks to my brilliant editors, Jack Butler, Brittany Lavery and Kate Stephenson. I'm very grateful for your patience and expertise. Thank you to the fantastic team at C&W, including Emma Finn, Katie Greenstreet, Luke Speed, Jake Smith Bosanquet, Kate Burton, Alexander Cochran, Matilda Ayris and Hillary Jacobson at ICM. Also to the rest of the incredible Wildfire team, Alex Clarke, Ella Gordon and Serena Arthur; everyone else at Headline, Rosie Margesson, Jo Liddiard, Rebecca Bader and Lisa Brewster; and the wonderful teams at Graydon House and HarperCollins Canada, including Susan Swinwood, Margaret O'Neill Marbury, Randy Chan, Sean Kapitain, Heather Connor, Leo MacDonald, Karen Ma, Cory Beatty and Kaitlyn Vincent. I appreciate all your hard work and talent. A big thank-you, too, to eagle-eyed copy editors Karen Ball, Vanessa Christensen, Jill Cole, and proofreader Rachel Malig.

Massive thanks to the incredibly supportive and generous writing community: booksellers, librarians, bloggers, readers, reviewers and authors. Thank you for your wonderful work and for spreading the word.

Thanks to everyone who kindly shared their knowledge of the cruise-ship industry and private flying: Lisa, Lucy, Geraldine, Maria, Phil, Susan, Linda and Sarah. Thanks to Graham Bartlett, crime and policing adviser, for his advice. Any mistakes are my own. I sincerely hope I haven't left anyone out!

My generous and tolerant early readers deserve huge thanks, too: Geraldine, Roy and my mother, Rona.

Another big thank-you to all my brilliant writing friends for their support, kindness, insight and humor. It means the world.

Special mention and thanks to my parents and sister for all their encouragement, as well as my parents-in-law, extended family and amazing friends and neighbors for all their support. My husband keeps things going while I lock myself away to immerse myself in a different world and listens when I need someone to bounce ideas off. My sons make me laugh and keep my spirits up. I wrote the following sentence in the acknowledgments for my last book and I'm writing it again now because I can't think of a better way of putting it. Their love and pride in what I do means everything.